I0780998

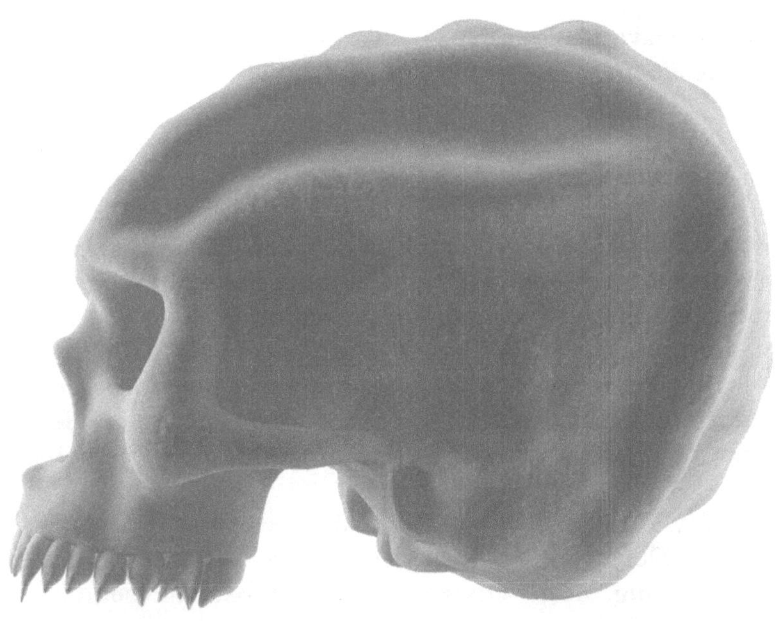

BITE: A VAMPIRIC ANTHOLOGY

Published by Graveside Press 2024
graveside-press.com

Editing: Kelley York and Hannah Rebekah Graves
Cover Design: Sleepy Fox Studio – sleepyfoxstudio.net
Interior Formatting: Sleepy Fox Studio – sleepyfoxstudio.net

eBook 978-1-964952-53-6
Print (KDP Paperback) 978-1-964952-84-0
Print (Paperback) 978-1-964952-51-2
Print (Hardcover) 978-1-964952-52-9

No part of this book has been created using Generative AI.

BITE

A VAMPIRIC ANTHOLOGY

For a list of potential trigger warnings,
please turn to page 326 or visit our website:
graveside-press.com/cw/bite

THE SEPTIMUS CURE

Michael A. Reed

Lupe dusted me off and placed me on the curtained table. A pair of wide-eyed twin boys gawked at my bodiless head, their mouths curled, wet, and ready to hook. They had never seen a skull with fangs because vampires weren't supposed to exist. Even a dead one like me. When they didn't stop staring, their mother shooed them away, and I was left wondering which one had a softer neck.

"If you think you can trick me, I'll teach you otherwise," the mother said to Lupe. She set a wad of cash on the table beside me. A believer in the Septimus cure. I figured it wouldn't be long before I was in her bedroom. Perhaps on her nightstand paired with a warm glass of Sangiovese. Whose blood would she feed me? Hers, I hoped.

Silent, Lupe drew the cash into her long sleeve and pointed at me. She smiled under the cloak of her dress, as she often did. I was her carnival show, after all. Her mystery in the box. Of course, she knew what would happen to the mother and her children when I was traded away, but that never stopped her from taking the money.

Hyper-focused on me, the mother didn't blink. Her eyes were bloodshot. A victim of sleepless nights. There must've been a nightmare in her life she just couldn't shake, and that made this exchange all the more entertaining.

For nothing but a good show, the old lady lit a candle. She babbled a sentence in Romanian, the only words she knew in that language, and basked me in what she claimed was unclean, ancient light.

The mother memorized Lupe's movements. Every imaginary ritual. The way she bent her fingers back, as if some spirit had overtaken her body. Over the years, her pretend possession had become almost convincing. Someone in their right state of mind would be able to sense the deceit and move on, their petty Yelp review already forming in their minds, but the mother was no such person.

Nobody who came to Madam Lupe's shop had any sense at all. Exactly as we liked it. Still, I had to admire the mother for her contempt; she hated that her life had been reduced to a psychic's trickery. She could hardly hide the venom brewing on her tongue. It must have taken so much willpower to keep that profane whip tame behind her lips.

"Tell me what to do," the mother ordered.

"You must squeeze the blood onto the skull," Lupe said.

She sprinkled a few droplets of water on me. It felt cold on my dry bones, and I loved the way it evaporated into the grains of my jawline, yet it wasn't what I craved. I preferred something a little more red.

"That will cure him?" the mother asked.

Lupe nodded. "His name is Septimus. Say his name when you do it, otherwise your blood is wasted."

Calmly, the old woman picked me up from the table and held me out to the mother. I could sense the mother's hesitation. Once a customer believed in the idea that my bones could heal their loved ones, they always committed to the ritual.

With hands limp and damp as dead fish, the mother grabbed me. She didn't know how to hold me, a supposed vampire skull, so she cradled me like a child in the crook of her arm. Pressed against her side, I heard her steady heartbeat, the *thump, thump, thump* of a woman willing to do anything, and I smelled the palatable aroma of blood pumping through her veins.

"Get in the car," the mother said to her boys. The twins scurried inside a shabby station wagon, laughing and pinching each other. The mother set me in the passenger seat and tested the point of my fangs with her finger, no doubt wondering if I was real or some well-crafted theater prop. She had enough faith to pay for my services, enough desperate longing to put me in the car with her garden-fresh children.

Before starting the car to drive home, the mother placed a thin blanket over me as if that could keep me from seeing them. There would be plenty of time for hiding later.

I looked forward to it.

The front yard was marred with dead grass and crab weed crisps that had been fried under the summer sun. Plastic fountain drink lids and fast-food bags were caught in the bush branches. Nobody bothered to pick up the neighborhood dog crap, and the short chain-link fence that guarded the home sagged under the weight of maggot infested trash bags.

Inside the house wasn't any better. The dishes were caked with week-old spaghetti sauce and strewn across the countertops. Useless items labeled "For Sale" were piled by the front door, the dregs of unsuccessful yard sales. An ever-growing layer of gray dust coated the windowsills and the bookshelves.

I'd been a guest in homes like this before. These people hadn't always been poor, but whoever needed the Septimus cure had been sucking the family dry. From the stack of bills on the couch, it seemed even the house itself wouldn't belong to them much longer. In a way, I might be doing the family a kindness. I could exchange a lifetime of misery for a few nights of suffering. I'd call that a fair trade.

By examining the endless card applications pinned to the fridge, I learned the mother's name before she even made it up the stairs. Athena. Such an elegant, regal name for a woman imprisoned in a garbage pit like this. It wore her out, too. Her predicament didn't befit her standing.

Perhaps that is why she called on me. It might not be about saving the person she loved; she only wanted to escape her dungeon and go back to high-brow reading, neatly arranged charcuterie boards, afternoons at the wine bar with her girlfriends, and a shopping spree at Nordstrom's where she intentionally avoided the clearance rack.

"I'm home, Henry," Athena said as she placed me on the nightstand beside a man that I assumed to be her husband.

Henry didn't respond. Couldn't respond. He wasn't dead, but it wouldn't be long before he faded away with all his blood confined to his flesh. I felt his life hanging in the humid air and nestling in the festering mold that clung to the floorboards beneath his bed. Coma, I presumed. He had probably been sent home from the hospital to spend time with his family before he died. If his illness didn't kill him soon, his wife's abysmal hospice care would. Or, more likely, I would.

He was the sickness Athena wanted to cure. The root of all her problems. Whoever Henry had been before was long gone now. That much was obvious, yet she must have convinced herself that he could return to the man he had been with the right medicine. Me. He would go back to work. He would clean the kitchen, the yard, the garage. These were all things Athena could do herself, but it didn't suit her, and that made me like her even more. Her blood, sharp and aged like an expensive cheese, might curdle in my mouth. A rare cuisine my ethereal tongue burned to taste.

Athena sat beside Henry for a short time, gently rubbing his head. Labored breathing was his only response. Tired of waiting for a miracle, Athena left Henry's side and locked the door. The boys were yelling at each other downstairs. It was a perfect guise for whatever she planned to do next.

She took a letter opener from their dresser. It wasn't the sharpest tool for starting a ritual summoning, but it wasn't my skin she had to slice. The letter opener pressed to her palm, she quivered, all her ideas of self-preservation delaying the inevitable. When she finally cut herself, she winced but did not close her eyes. Determined, she squeezed her blood onto me.

"Septimus," she said, mindful of Lupe's instructions.

Athena's blood trickled down the crown of my skull and splashed into my gaping eye sockets. She was delicious. As mean as she looked to be, her blood was nothing short of savory. Pomegranate seeds. Grape leaves. Sea salt. A hint of dark chocolate. She would make for a fine dessert to cleanse my palate after a night out on the town.

It wasn't much blood since she hadn't cut herself too deeply, but it would be enough. For as parched as I had become, even a sprinkle could rouse me.

Tonight, when the family slept, I would return in the shadows as a temporary ghost of myself—a very hungry ghost. I would start with Henry, since he had been so lovingly served on a platter beside me. Then I would taste-test the boys. Only a sip. If I wasn't careful to curb my appetite, I wouldn't have any leftovers for the nights to come.

When the sun had set and the moon was high in the dark sky, once everyone was asleep and Athena's blood had soaked into my fangs, I awoke. Athena didn't sleep in the same room as Henry. At first, that disappointed me, but it would make it easier to eat my dinner in peace. I didn't want my sweet tooth to spoil a proper three-course meal.

I formed my body in the corner of the bedroom. My wings emerged from the hanging shadows, and I drifted down from my eternal resting place, the thin layer between life and death, a layer as superficial as the space between skin and muscle. Silent and undetectable, I crawled along the wall and onto the carpet. I slinked to the bed and found Henry beneath the sheets. His chest rose and fell. Any breath could be his last, so I didn't delay.

Goosebumps peppered his skin as I licked his bare neck, my fangs grazing his jugular. The moment I found my favorite spot, the point just above the collarbone, I bit down. I was not harsh. My fangs slipped into him with the ease of a euthanasia needle. Like the mouth of a mosquito, Henry wouldn't know I had ever been there. Only the two incision marks would betray my presence, and nobody would notice until the morning.

Beef stew. Boiled carrots. Soft onions. Skinned potatoes and simple seasoning. Pepper. Sodium. Henry was a hearty meal. Rustic and urban, his blood filled my empty stomach. But I wanted more than that. I desired my body to reshape, my shadow to have bones and my soul to have contours. So, I kept drinking when I shouldn't have. I thirsted for permeation and my few hours of night dissipated as quickly as I had arrived.

My skull needed more blood to remain. Angry with myself, I receded into the air and vanished in the penumbra of dear Henry's room, his aftertaste inciting the fibers of my spirit. His wife and his children would have to wait for another summoning. Another turn of the moon.

In the morning, Athena found the bite marks on Henry's neck. She touched them, unsure if they were what she imagined them to be. Paler than the day before, Henry lay in his bed, his breathing slower and his pupils, trapped behind his eyelids, roaming the depths of his unending nightmares. He showed no sign of improvement.

Athena marched to me, her fists balled, and her jaw locked. I didn't deliver on the guarantee she had purchased. Madame Lupe should've said that a few nights were required for my work to take effect. At the least, such statements would have delayed Athena's frustration.

Fuming, she disappeared from the room and returned with a kitchen knife. This time, she wouldn't take any chances with the ritual. She held me in her hands, teasing me with the still-warm, bandaged palm. She unwrapped her wound, took a deep breath, and sliced.

Blood poured over me. I could taste Athena's rage this morning. Gone were the scents and flavors of sweetened flesh. She had been replaced with a boiling blood, a revenge on herself and me and Henry and the life she hadn't finished yet. Uncooked venison. Raw mushroom caps plucked from the forest ground. Sour rhubarb stalks. Balsamic glaze drizzled over burnt tomatoes and an overbaked French loaf that crumbled at the touch. A cacophony of hatred seeped from her pulsing cut, and I, mouth open wide, lavished in her unbound temper as it cascaded over my remnants.

"Septimus," Athena growled. "You better work this time."

But it wasn't a threat. No, it was a growing desperation. A primal plea for help. Athena was a doe stuck in the bramble, and she could sense the hunters moving in. The mountain lion's teeth. The bear's jaw. The man's gun. If someone didn't free her soon, she believed her life would come to a sudden, ugly end.

That night when I emerged from my hiding place, Henry was not alone. Athena sat in a chair next to the bed, my skull on her lap. Her piercing green eyes measured my immensity as I became my true self. She wasn't afraid of my bat head, my pointed ears, my clawed fingers, my chattering mouth. Tonight, I wouldn't sneak my meal under the table; I was an invited guest at the dinner party.

Standing next to her, I realized Athena understood my purpose. In the old woman's shop, I had treated her like everyone else. Like a pathetic woman who needed to be saved from her circumstance. Her only weakness was that she couldn't do it herself. The blood on her hands would be her own, dripping onto me.

She watched me nestle into Henry's neck, my fangs gripping his cartilage. Athena had given me so much of her blood that I could feast until morning. As I ate, she stroked the shadow of my back, and I purred. Nobody had touched my actual form in centuries. It made me ravenous. I ate faster and faster, the home-cooked warmth of Henry's blood spilling out of my mouth. I couldn't contain my hunger.

I lifted Henry's body off the bed and slurped the life from him. His spine bent towards my mouth from the force of my suction, but I didn't stop there. I gnawed his wrists, his ankles, his sides, his calves. Anywhere I could find a drop of his blood, I razed, unconcerned with pacing myself.

All the while, Athena whispered into my ear:

"Save me, Septimus."

"Cure me."

"Take him away."

"Make me whole again."

When I had finished with Henry's body, he was nothing more than a pile of bones wrapped in a bag of skin. He was most certainly dead, as Athena had wanted.

Lovingly, she wiped Henry's blood from my phantom lips, her fingers drifting in and out of my shadow. I could eat her right now, but my stomach bulged with Henry's insides. Whatever blood I could take from her, I wouldn't enjoy. Except she smelled delectable, and I could manage a snack.

Athena could feel my anticipation. She tilted her head toward me to expose her neck. Her long, dark hair fell from her ears, and the heat of her body rose toward my nostrils. She, the wicked thing that bought my services, was pure ecstasy. Alive or dead, shadow or bone, creature or man, none could resist the gift of temptation.

Carefully, so as not to ruin the moment, I sank my teeth into her neck. She shivered and gasped, but she didn't recoil. Free of Henry's shackle, his illness, his ward, Athena's blood had transformed once again. She was a rotten joy. All confectioners' sugar and maple syrup and melted butter and the grease that lines the pan after a well-grilled meat. It could make a vampire sick, yet I loved it. Loved her.

I let her go after a few minutes of bliss. Athena caressed the shape of my face as my hours waned.

"You can stay with me," she said. "We have many things to do together." The color of her face returned just as the sun rose and light drifted through the window blinds.

Her evil spirit matched my own. Whatever we did next, whatever nights we spent together, we would do it ankle-deep in a sea of blood. Summoned back to the darkness, my skull gripped in Athena's hands, I learned something new about myself for the first time in many years. That empty pit in my stomach didn't ache because I was hungry; it ached because I craved satisfaction.

THE HALLOWEEN GIRL OF COLD SPRINGS

J. Tonzelli

COLDSPRINGS, Oʜɪᴏ—Hᴇʀ ɴɪᴄᴋɴᴀᴍᴇ was first made popular in October of 1979. Many townspeople claim credit for the genesis of the moniker, but it didn't gain notoriety until most people read the headline in that month's local newspaper:

"HALLOWEEN GIRL" VISITS COLDSPRINGS FOR SECOND YEAR; SIGHTINGS ABOUND

From what townspeople have pieced together, it's widely accepted that "Halloween Girl" is actually Judy Johnstone, a former and seemingly perpetual nine-year-old citizen of Coldsprings, Ohio, who perished quite tragically in a house fire in 1978—also the year in which sightings of her were first reported.

These sightings have occurred on an annual basis in the week leading up to every Halloween, with this being the 35th anniversary of her death and subsequent first post-death appearance. What puzzles most people—allowing that most would find the idea of a routine ghost-girl sighting in and of itself puzzling—is that Judy Johnstone did not pass away on Halloween, but rather in the middle of May.

More on that later.

It was a mysterious house fire that claimed young Judy's life, the cause of which was never determined. Judy's parents, Gary and Debora Johnstone, were not home at the time the fire broke out, and upon returning, found that their house had burned nearly to the ground. A funeral was held for Judy later that week, her coffin filled with keepsakes and photographs, as her remains were never fully recovered.

Debora Johnstone is now in her late 50s and continues to reside in Coldsprings. She and her husband, Gary, who died of a heart attack in 1999, decided against having any more children following Judy's passing. Though Judy's death happened more than three decades ago, Mrs. Johnstone still thinks of her daily and offers up her own theory as to why her daughter chooses the last week of every October to appear.

"She loved Halloween. It was her favorite day of the year. I think she misses it. And I think she misses being a kid."

And though she says this with sadness, she often seems grateful to feel her daughter's presence every year. She continues: "She used to love putting on masks and costumes. She used to love pretending to be something unique or otherworldly. I remember one year I asked her, 'Judy, if you could only be one thing for Halloween, what would it be?' and she kinda looked at me funny, and said, 'I would be the sun. I would be so powerful that I could control legions of people. And those people would love me so much they'd give me anything I asked for.'"

Mrs. Johnstone laughs at the memory. "Her dreams were always bigger than life."

"I saw her one year. She was dressed as a witch," says Benny Randolph, a neighbor of Mrs. Johnstone. "She was chasing a black cat down the street. I remember at the time thinking how strange it was that she seemed to be holding one of those large pruning shears, all spread open—you know, the kind for thinning out bushes? But I'm sure it was probably a witch's broom or something. She looked so cute, like she was having a ball. Plus, she caught that cat!"

But a witch is not the only costume she's been known to wear. According to witnesses, the Halloween Girl has been spotted wearing several personas, such as a vampire, a ghoul, and even the grim reaper, complete with pale white skin and sunken black eyes.

"She's always had such an imagination," Mrs. Johnstone confirms.

One of the Halloween Girl's costumes, however, does not have her mother's approval: that of the blood-spattered fairy princess. "I haven't seen that one for myself, but I've heard about it," Mrs. Johnstone says. "I don't care for that one. But it's not like I have any say over her costumes anymore. I suppose she's earned the right to wear whatever she wants. It's her day, after all."

Despite her periodic gory visage, the Halloween Girl has become an annual staple of Coldsprings, and many of the townspeople look at her as a positive presence to counteract the more disturbing events that seem to spike during the famed October holiday.

"We had us a rogue pack of wild dogs one year, I believe, on Halloween night," recalls Mayor Hawkins. "No one ever saw them or heard them, and there were no track marks or paw prints found, but many of the town's pets were discovered mutilated in backyards; blood everywhere, and huge, jagged bite marks covering the poor pets' bodies. But if wild dogs weren't the culprits, then what else could have done something so ferocious and animalistic, you know? That was such an unfortunate time for Coldsprings. But the Halloween Girl… She was our light during times like those when our morale was low. She just made us see…differently. Things we should have been alarmed by or concerned about—they just didn't seem as important anymore."

In a 1988 interview, another neighbor, Peter Barnes, had agreed: "The Halloween Girl, as weird as it sounds, makes me proud to be from Coldsprings. It makes me feel like our town is unique. It's such a nice place to live that people refuse to leave—even after death!"

Barnes was later found murdered in his kitchen on an early October morning, one of his hands jammed into the sink's garbage disposal, his face beaten into an unrecognizable pulp, and his body drained of nearly all its blood. The murder was never solved, but Constable McGeehan isn't that concerned.

"It's extremely unlikely that a Coldsprings citizen was responsible for the crime, so the likely scenario is that an assailant committed this murder at random while passing through," says McGeehan. "I'd like to think we'll solve the case one day and give some comfort to the Barnes family, but I know in my heart the Halloween Girl would rather we focus on the bright side. Look, the strong feed off the weak like parasites; unfortunately, that's life. Bad things will always happen to us, but we have to learn to move on and treasure those around us who bring us strength." McGeehan pauses to scratch at two dime-sized wounds on the side of his neck and winces slightly from the pain. He rubs his blood-smeared fingertips together and laughs nervously. "I can shoot holes through bottle caps from 50 yards, but I'm a klutz in the morning with a razor, it seems."

Before another Coldsprings citizen, Father Calloway, passed away under unexplained circumstances, he was one of the Halloween Girl's biggest fans. "She is the brightness in our lives," he said yearly at the pulpit for the special Halloween mass held in her honor. "I welcome her every year, as I know you all do." In one particular homily, Father Calloway shared with the congregation this story (which also appeared in that week's church bulletin. It has been reprinted verbatim below):

Much like Christians look to the Lord Jesus Christ in times of suffering, we, the Coldsprings community, look to the Halloween Girl in similar times of woe.

And much like Christ, the Halloween Girl, too, died untimely, but also gave us reasons to hope and life for which to be thankful.

It was only one year ago, after having lost a nephew with whom I was very close to anemia, that my faith in the Lord was shaken. I was having terrible and reoccurring nightmares of a monstrous thing feeding from my nephew's body and infecting him with the sickness that caused the disease that claimed his life.

Night after night, when I had this awful dream, I struggled to see the face of the thing that was preying on him. I felt that if I could see the monster and confront it, I could stop the nightmares. And one night…I came close enough to see its terrible eyes and gaping grin for myself. Its teeth were so large that they forced the thing to bear a constant and devious grin, as if it were unable to tuck them inside its horrid mouth.

I awoke in a panic and found the Halloween Girl sitting on my bed. She looked at me curiously, and as I was about to speak, she touched her hand to my cheek, which was flushed from the dream. Her hand was cooling, almost ice cold, and I felt an immediate sense of calm. She smiled and bent to kiss my neck. It was quick and perfectly innocent, and just like that, she was gone. I slept soundlessly, and the next morning I awoke to a few drops of dried blood on my pillowcase. I knew at that moment this was the blood of Christ, and the Halloween Girl was not just a phantom or a spirit, but an angel sent from Heaven.

I thank her for that visit, which reinvigorated my soul. I feel as if I have been marked by her and will now always be protected.

Father Calloway died later that week at his home, and five days passed—one of those being the following Sunday, when he was due to preside over the town's weekly mass—before a member of his parish discovered his remains.

"Seeing his body was like a nightmare," says Sister Roberts. "It was torn to shreds, as if a wild animal twice his size had gotten into his room. Blood was…everywhere. But if there's one thing I can safely say, it's that he would want us to look to the Halloween Girl at times like this. She's our shining light. She's so bright… She glows so brilliantly, doesn't she?"

One fall in the late 1980s was especially hard on the town when a bus full of Coldsprings Elementary School students was found driven off the road—curiously, nearly half a mile into Warren Woods, after having cleared a path through thick trees and somehow negotiating fallen tree trunks, large rocks, and even Jamestown Creek. The bodies of the children had been decimated to the point that some of them could not be identified. The cause of the bus accident and the subsequent deaths of the children were never solved, but the town quickly forgot about the events. Trick-or-treating went on as scheduled the next day, as it was decided the children's funerals would be postponed until after Halloween. Along with the rest of the town citizens who were eager for their annual sighting of the Halloween Girl, the parents of the deceased students could also be found gladly opening their doors to hand out candy to all the trick-or-treaters.

"If you're lucky, she'll come to visit you personally," says one of those parents, Rhonda German, whose seven-year-old daughter, Jessica, had been severed nearly in two from her left hip to her right shoulder in the aforementioned bus accident. "The Halloween Girl is like contained magic. The things she can show you… They're just beyond description. I miss my Jessica every day, but the Halloween Girl is a good substitute!"

If you ask local Tanya Cardone about the Halloween Girl's latest visit, she will flood you with details about that year's costume and the glimmering of the girl's large, perfect teeth. "I don't think there's a single person in this town that doesn't look forward to seeing her every year," Ms. Cardone says, and lightly fingers a square bandage covering most of a purple bruise on the side of her neck, just over her jugular vein.

"The town gives Judy all kinds of treats when they see her," says Mr. Randolph. "They leave them outside on their front porch, or sometimes they hand them directly to her if they see her in the street. One year, I gave her some ginger pumpkin cookies that I'd baked. I guess I left them in the oven for a bit too long, because the edges were a little burned. Boy, she didn't like that! So, instead, I figured I would just feed them to my dog Jeb, but sadly, he went missing that same day."

"Oh, and don't give her peppermints, whatever you do," Mrs. Johnstone adds as she smiles nervously and lightly rubs at the bald stub where her right hand used to be. "She hates those."

"We look forward to seeing the Halloween Girl every year," concludes Constable McGeehan. "In the same way that kids will always go trick-or-treating on Halloween, she, too, will always come to visit Coldsprings that last October week. She knows we'll be here waiting for her. And we'll give her anything she wants. Just like we always have."

—

James Sprenger was a Staff Writer for the Coldsprings Ledger, Coldsprings, OH, at the time this article was written. James had worked tirelessly for the Coldsprings Ledger for 17 years before his recent passing. The publisher and staff offer their condolences to James' friends and family.

A FINAL REQUEST

Ryan Benson

FUNNY HOW A few sentences on a four-by-three card can change a person's life.

Xavier Glover unfolded the thick, textured paper embossed with his name and read the Garamond font aloud. "Your presence is requested at Moore Manor. Please arrive at nine p.m." Any communique for Xavier was unexpected, and one from a long-lost childhood friend proved especially surprising. Luther Moore wasn't simply his friend—they were blood-brothers thanks to a sharp soda can and Xavier's inability to say no to Luther. Although this dramatic act bound them for life, it had nearly cost Luther his.

Xavier reread Luther's name and chuckled as he recalled his friend showing off his blood-brother wound at school. Though Xavier's mother had cleaned and bandaged his hand, Luther's cut remained wild and untamed, like the boy himself. Eventually, Luther's palm grew fiery red. Suggestions of visiting the school nurse brought a smirk and thumbs down from Luther. How could his parents not notice? Luther had to carry tissues to dab the oozing discharge, but it was worth it for him. The grosser it got, the more attention he received from classmates, until it finally triggered a weeklong hospital stay and near amputation. Vintage Luther.

Luther never acknowledged his mortality or the frailty of his human body. Xavier supposed he'd spent his own youth the same way before that day in his twenties, when the curse took hold. Everything changed for Xavier in an instant. Had time molded a wiser Luther?

The years had certainly brought Luther fortune, if not insight. Xavier admired the monstrous front door of "Moore Manor." It reached almost twice his height.

He ran his fingers through his curly brown hair and exhaled. It was almost nine o'clock. Should he knock? Tiny cyclones of leaves danced around his feet. Maybe he should have brought Jeanette with him. She seemed to like spooky stuff these days. He'd told her to stay home because he'd wanted to see Luther alone. He had no idea why Luther had sent for him—assuming Luther had sent the correspondence in the first place. God knew Xavier had more than enough enemies willing to trap him in a ruse.

Xavier noted the twin lanterns flanking the door. The flickering flames would have glowed in Jeannette's hazel eyes. He preferred the flames to the sickly pallor of the blue-white LED lights that'd overtaken the city. A fire's light had an edge and threw fantastic shadows. Flames respected the dark, and so did Xavier. In fact, Luther had been lucky in scheduling the nighttime conference. Xavier only took meetings after sunset.

The lanterns illuminated the knocker, an iron ring in the mouth of a snarling lion face, equal parts enraged and depressed. Xavier knocked three times in quick succession and stepped back. Craning his neck, he examined the size and detail of the entire gothic dwelling—a row of cypresses and the overcast night had hidden the façade from the street. Somewhere within the house, a clock struck nine, and the door creaked open as if pushed by a light wind. Garbed in black, a lanky bald man of an indeterminate age lurked in the foyer. "Master Glover?"

"In the flesh, here at nine p.m. sharp, as requested." Though the figure towered a head taller than him, Xavier remained unshaken by the man's vaguely inhuman visage. He'd seen worse.

"Master Moore appreciates punctuality. You may call me James. Follow me." James's clawed nails danced at the end of his serpentine fingers as he beckoned Xavier inside.

James escorted Xavier down a twisting hall. The scarlet carpet's thickness ran uneven and tilted ever so slightly, throwing Xavier off balance. The runner curved with the hall, like a crimson river.

Xavier looked ahead to his guide. James glided over the floor with long strides and swinging pendulum arms but left no depressions on the plush runner. Xavier shrugged off the tall man's inexplicable weightlessness and swiveled his head side to side, allowing a self-guided tour of each passing room.

Luther still had the flair Xavier remembered, but with an upscale twist. Instead of a modern, minimal style of affluence, the house looked turn-of-the-last-century rich. As suggested by the exterior, the interior décor (oak furniture, floral wallpaper, tapestries) screamed gothic, resembling a set from Roger Corman's Poe movies, both opulent and somber. Luther had loved old horror films. Xavier never cared for pop-culture occult as a teen and cared less now after surviving unspeakable acts no director would dare put to film.

Xavier paused at the ballroom. He ran his fingers over the polished wooden door frame as the scents of mahogany and old leather danced in the air. Though resembling the rest of the house in its gothic aesthetic, large speakers and disco lights peppered the room, like the clubs he and Luther had snuck into decades ago. He could almost feel the deep hip-hop bass thumping in his bones. Luther must throw killer parties in a setup like this. The lack of an earlier invitation annoyed Xavier.

Did Luther have kids? Xavier failed to spot a toy, video game, or family portrait amongst the grandeur. If Luther had fathered any children, they were long gone. Xavier shook his head. Luther was never the domestic type—life as a latchkey kid could have that effect on a person—besides, there were a million and one reasons against procreation, some mundane and some, like in Xavier's case, extraordinary. Who was Xavier to judge? He remained petrified at the idea of discussing motherhood with Jeanette.

The tall man and Xavier entered a circular chamber distinguished by a double-high ceiling and a large wrap-around staircase. A small glass-encased orb perched atop an illuminated pedestal in the center of the room transfixed Xavier. He approached the pedestal, his hands and face close but not touching the glass, as if it burned with hellfire. Inside its enclosure rested a baseball bearing the signature, "Barry Bonds." The golden plaque confirmed Xavier's hopes—Luther owned Bonds' historic seven hundred and fifty-sixth home run ball.

"You did it, Luther," Xavier whispered to himself, grinning.

"Please sir, make haste." James ascended the stairs, gait unchanged, as if floating to the second floor.

"Wait, can I just—" Xavier needed a few more moments with the hallowed object. He surprised himself with his excitement over something as useless as a ball. Was this a dream come true, or was he asleep now?

James ignored Xavier and continued climbing. With a grunt, Xavier chased after him, effortlessly bounding up several steps at a time. They reached a set of double doors. Ornate golden doorknobs and intricate gargoyle relief carvings shouted this room's importance. James turned the knobs and threw open both doors, bowing as if taking direction from Corman himself.

Xavier's amusement at James's dramatics ceased upon entering the room. Built-in shelves of well-worn books lined two of the three walls, while heavy curtained floor to ceiling windows filled the third. However, the enormous canopy bed pushed against the fourth wall captured his attention. Inside lay a gaunt man propped up by pillows. Wires ran from the bedridden man's chest to a monitor producing rhythmic beeping more suited for a hospital than a mansion, while tubes snaked from ports in his arm to IV bags. His hairless skin pulled tight over his bones. Intense, smoldering black eyes remained the sole indicator of life in this husk—the unforgettable eyes of Luther Moore.

"I must be dreaming." Luther's voice proved surprisingly lively. It never wavered nor cracked. Clear and commanding as the last time the two men had spoken, like Xavier's old friend ventriloquized through this emaciated puppet.

With supernatural swiftness, Xavier stood at the bedside in a blurred instant. Normally, he hid his uncanny abilities, but this moment overwhelmed him. A clap echoed in the bedchamber as the two friends clasped hands as if arm wrestling. Once a juvenile test of might, their handshake now only contrasted their physical vitality. In their youth, they shared a similar size and strength, but as preternaturally strong as Xavier had grown, Luther had become that weak.

"You haven't changed." Luther squinted. "At all. No wrinkles?"

"You haven't—" Xavier paused. "Good to see you, too."

"Yes, yes." Luther wrapped his boney fingers around Xavier's hand.

Xavier felt the long thin scar on Luther's palm, the only defining characteristic of him past his voice and eyes. Despite life emotionally carving him up like a jigsaw puzzle, Xavier no longer formed physical scars.

"My, your flesh is warmer than I expected." Luther rubbed the back of Xavier's hand.

Xavier pulled away as if caught raiding the cookie jar. "I can't believe it's been twenty years. You've done well for yourself." Luther's startlingly poor health left Xavier's mind reeling in disbelief, and he hoped to steer the conversation away from their appearances. He put up his hands in a mock boxing stance before unloading a few soft, awkward jabs to Luther's shoulder. After years of fights, Xavier could throw a punch that would knock out a charging rhino. He cringed in embarrassment.

"You're not the only person I've surprised." Luther's white lips offered a sliver of a smile. "Remember all those asshole doubters from school? That number only grows as you age. Even friends and family turn on you if you don't throw scraps when you leave the neighborhood." Luther cleared his throat. "I'm glad you received my invitation—Xavier Glover isn't easy to locate. I've been searching since you disappeared."

"I've been traveling. Just got back from Thailand. Before that, I backpacked the Andes. Took a few years." Xavier forced out a laugh and playfully slapped Luther's arm. "We've both come a long way from Queens."

"Indeed, but your globetrotting tale is unnecessary. My PIs found you about a decade ago. Your lifestyle was quite…shocking, I admit." Luther waved to James, startling Xavier. The servant had remained as silent as a corpse, causing Xavier to forget about his presence. James handed his master a pile of photographs.

Luther straightened the eight-by-tens in his hands, fastidious as always. "But the most startling photos were the ones where you hadn't aged a day. Even now—ten years after the oldest photos and twenty years since we last met—you remain a teen."

"Oh, come on, man! You gotta at least give me twenty-five. Good genes and clean living." Xavier dug his fingernails into his palms. Why hadn't he tried to disguise himself? Was he cocky? No, much like revealing his superhuman speed, the excitement of seeing his friend blinded him to anything else. He acted like the young man he resembled and had dropped nearly every pretense he spent years building.

"Fine, I'll give you twenty-two." Luther furrowed his eyebrows. Deep lines cut across his forehead, despite his sickly lack of flesh. "That was your age when you fell off the earth, wasn't it?"

Xavier shifted his weight between his feet, feeling as if he were being led off a cliff.

"Luckily, my moral quandary regarding your 'habits' ended when you began robbing hospitals for your fix instead of violently taking it on the street." Luther wagged his finger at Xavier.

Xavier's plastic smile had almost disappeared. "You think I'm a druggy? We took D.A.R.E. together!" How much longer would he keep up this act?

"D.A.R.E. didn't cover your addiction. Although, I wonder if drugs would affect you in your current condition." Luther spread the photos over his lap and laid his steepled fingers across his chest. "How did you stop? Did the girl help you?"

Xavier almost asked, "Who?" but lacked the energy to lie. He gazed at the memories, now flattened and frozen in time on the glossy paper. An attractive brunette graced more than one picture. *Jeanette.* One pic captured them in an embrace Xavier would never forget. That hug was the first time he acknowledged to himself that he loved her. It was only months ago. Who took all these? From the age of some photos, they'd tailed him for years.

Luther smiled at Xavier's silent acknowledgement of the pictures' authenticity. "You two were the same age early on, and then we have some gap years where we lost you, but from the latest I've seen of her, she *has* aged. Still pretty, maybe even lovelier now, don't you think? I'm sure she'll make a fine older woman someday."

For Xavier, the willful denial of Jeanette's aging proved second nature. Wasted years had passed with him, too afraid of either hurting Jeanette or facing her rejection to admit his affection. Now, her impending death, though likely decades away, kept him savoring every second of their connection.

"I wanted to help—even though you would never ask—but I respected your decision to go underground." Luther paused a moment to catch his breath. With his involuntary reflexes slipping away, he forced his chest to expand and contract. After a few seconds, he spoke again. "Contact could've alerted the police, anyway."

At the mention of the authorities, Xavier scanned the room for James, only to find he'd vanished. It mattered little. Xavier guessed James was the photographer and knew his truth. The butler's entire demeanor established him as creepy and stealthy enough to stalk someone as elusive as Xavier. Even if he hadn't snapped the pics, James had to have known

Xavier's secret, considering how nonchalantly he'd handled the photos. If the manservant had wanted to involve the police or extort him, he would have already.

Xavier paced around the bed, stopping near the giant windows to open the curtains. Stars peaked through the clouds, calling him to join them in the sky, away from the beeping of the machines and his friend's biting questions. He had to come clean.

"I had no choice. I was like an animal. Every day I fiended for a fix. It clouded my mind for years—I did terrible things before my self-control reemerged." Xavier looked at his hands. "Sometimes, I still do terrible things. Jeanette saved me in more ways than one, but you'll never understand the self-discipline I required to reform."

"I can imagine."

Xavier shook his head. "I know for a fact that you can't. No one can."

"I'll take your word for it. I'm unsure if I could've 'reformed,' but I'm proud you did."

Xavier waved Luther off.

Luther ignored his dismissal, excitement dancing on his words. "You still kill, but it's limited to society's trash. You stopped one honest-to-goodness serial killer; you're the real Dark Knight!"

"Not funny." Xavier narrowed his eyes.

Luther collected the photographs and tossed them to the floor. "Down to business then." Corporate expediency replaced the joy in Luther's voice as he made his pitch. "Like you, my blood is polluted. I have leukemia and, obviously, not long to live." He pointed to the IV bags dangling like a condemned man dancing at the end of a rope. "I'm also in horrible pain, even with morphine at the highest level I can tolerate without it clouding my thinking. My imagination is all I have left, you know?"

"I'm sorry." A part of Xavier still failed to believe his bold friend, always up for an adventure, now lay confined to this room.

"Don't be, my friend. One way or another, I'll be free of it before long." Luther struggled to retrieve an enormous book from beneath the sheets. Xavier moved to help, but decided Luther would take any coddling as an insult.

"I have a final request." Luther pointed at the ornate tome. "This solves both our problems. My people tell me if you turn me with your bite, I'd be cured but exist as a rabid animal, since you're too far from 'patient' zero."

"They're right." Xavier glanced out the window. The clouds parted for the white, almost round moon. "At the beginning, I was lonely and turned others, but they were feral. It always ended like Old Yeller, with me putting them out of their misery."

Luther smiled, his thin lips pulling back over his teeth. "In this book is an incantation that can transfer your curse to me, thus effecting a cure for us both. The book appears blank to me, but I've paid top dollar for it and been assured someone with your condition will see the verses."

Xavier had encountered runes, bones, and manuscripts covered with writing only he and a select few could see. The exterior of Luther's book matched those other enchanted objects. Arcane designs beyond words made his long dead skin crawl and itch. Nausea bubbled up as his stomach churned with disgust worse than any hangover he'd experienced in his prior life. Plastered across the cover, three-dimensional shapes composed of impossibly infinite edges smoothed out before Xavier's touch. Their vertigo-inducing movement made him queasy, but something viscerally indescribable lurked below the surface, sickening him as much as witnessing someone's head cracked open to the white meat, or a sliced abdomen spilling guts onto the floor.

After swallowing his acrid, bile-tinged saliva, Xavier thumbed through the pages, confirming Luther's hopes. "It's Latin."

"Splendid!" shouted Luther.

Thousands of handwritten words snaked about the page, crashing and filling every inch of space. If Xavier focused on an individual word, they would freeze in place like scared animals but returned to skittering about once his eyes wandered. Somehow, the authors had fitted two diagrams onto the cluttered page. One contained scribbles of intertwined half-human subjects carrying out indecipherable acts of either love or perverse violence. The second diagram was a simple drawing of two men—one standing and one laying dying. "I have to think this over."

"Xavier the thinker!" Luther raised his hands over his head and deepened his voice, just like he did as a child when Xavier hesitated in agreeing with one of his schemes. "But don't forget, you wanted the family, the picket fence, the American Dream. I'm sure you still do. Soon Jeanette will be too old and confined to a bed like this, life slipping away."

Again pacing, Xavier wrung his hands. Had Luther waited until he'd committed to Jeanette before springing this proposal? Until they both had something to lose? No. He couldn't imagine his best friend, even after decades of absence, being so manipulative. It was kismet. Xavier glanced at the wires dangling off his friend's body—even Luther Moore couldn't control fate. "How about you? No heirs for your empire?"

"What good is a parent who is too busy for their children?" Luther's words took on a mocking tone. "Let's have kids!" He clapped his hands. "Then you have a child for your selfish validation or to check some box or fill a hole in your life." Disdain dripped from his tongue. "All I require for fulfillment is what I've provided for myself. I am my own legacy."

"My mother worked as much as your parents, and I never felt like a check mark to her."

"Another reason we must switch our circumstances. My plan will allow both our lives to align with our true selves!"

My true self, Xavier thought.

"After the book lifts your curse, you can resume aging, and maybe even catch up to Jeanette," said Luther. "Hell, you can subsist on burgers and fries again! Remember going to Charlie's Grille?"

Xavier rubbed his stomach. "If we had your current money as kids, I wouldn't have eaten anywhere else."

"I'll buy the restaurant for you. Rename it, 'X Marks the Spot.'"

Both men laughed the same way they had decades ago at Charlie's. Luther always had this effect on Xavier. Loud, hard guffaws filled the room until a coughing fit cut off Luther's laughter. Xavier advanced to offer useless aid, but Luther waved him away.

Something worked its way up and Luther spit it into a tissue. "Love is a funny thing." He took a weak breath and drummed his fingers on the cover of the book. "Human and inhuman authors compiled this knowledge over thousands of years. There must be a spell for everything." He leaned forward. "Once we transfer the curse to me, the book will allow me to read its words. I will forever be at your beck and call, like a billionaire genie without a bottle."

"It's not that simple."

"You could have a fulfilling life as a family man, Xavier." Luther twisted the monitor wires in his fingers. "I simply want to live."

Xavier stopped pacing. "Susan Ertz said, 'Millions long for immortality who do not know what to do with themselves on a rainy Sunday afternoon.'"

"Xavier, I *always* make plans for Sundays!"

"You'd be undead."

"Anything is better than dead-dead."

"I suppose—"

"Tonight is the full moon. The spell requires the extra magic generated by the end of the lunar cycle. You have until sunrise to decide, or we'll have to wait a month."

Xavier nodded, knowing Luther likely wouldn't last another month with the little meat left on his bones. But he had to think. *Tick. Tick. Tick.* Was this his chance to live a "normal" life? No doubt it was Luther's last chance to save his. Time slipped away, threatening to take their dreams with it. "Can you give me an hour to think it over? Maybe I'll take another look at the Bonds baseball."

"Of course. Take two!" Luther leaned back into his pillows. "But I'm not giving you that ball."

Xavier turned to the door.

"Before you go, can I watch you transform?" said Luther.

Xavier paused with his back to him.

"Blood-brothers?" asked Luther.

Xavier chuckled. Everyone wanted to see his transmogrification, but he always refused. "Blood-brothers."

Tingling sensations radiated through Xavier's body. With experience, the change came quick and easy now. Hair, skin, and sinew stripped away. No puff of smoke, just undead humanoid cells and tissue dissolving into the ether, changing, before reforming into the flying symbol of the night. He fluttered about the room and into the hall.

At the top of the stairs, Xavier reverted to his human form. The frail man in the bedroom had been his backbone—an impulsive firecracker complementing Xavier's pensive reserve. Luther had defended him in school and in the streets, although Xavier knew walking away would have been easier and smarter. He wanted to blame the curse for his loneliness, but Xavier had always had trouble connecting with others. Except for Jeanette, the only person he'd truly bonded with had been Luther. Now he had one night to make the most important choice of both their lives.

Xavier reached the bottom of the staircase and stood before the baseball pedestal. Years back, Luther had yearned for an autographed Barry Bonds ball in the window of the neighborhood collectibles store. Despite Bonds having put enough junk in his own blood, he remained the favorite player of both Luther and his father.

One day, Luther decided he needed the ball by any means. Xavier never discovered why his friend suddenly wanted the pricey item, but with Luther's father's birthday only a week away, a present for his old man seemed to fit. When the time came for Luther's teenage smash-and-grab, Xavier did what was necessary to protect his friend by tackling him to the ground. The two wrestled on the sidewalk until they attracted enough attention to discourage the youthful indiscretion.

A few days later, Luther thanked Xavier.

Meanwhile, instead of dreams of baseballs, Xavier had fantasized about settling down with the class "it girl" Nicole Jones. They could've shared a nice marriage in a pleasant house where his mother could visit and escape her own loneliness. With the curse transferred, he could make his dream a reality. Not with Nicole (he'd moved beyond childhood crushes), but with Jeanette.

Xavier loved Jeanette, and though he'd finally admitted those feelings to himself, his situation kept him from telling her. With this proposition, both he and Luther could live, so why did he hesitate?

Moments of meditation and contemplation stretched into hours as Xavier stared at the valuable piece of memorabilia. His mind drifted into a swirl of Luther and Jeanette, intertwining with his past, present, and future. Even from downstairs, Xavier could smell the decay of Luther's flesh, knowing he had the power to stop it.

The trials of Xavier's undead life had convinced him that the dead never decay, just their bodies. Souls move on to escape the decomposition, though his own existence proved the exception, death without decay and a soul too stubborn to leave. He had to stop Luther's painful rot, and transformation into the undead was the only cure left. But could he trust Luther? All Xavier knew was that he couldn't allow a person he loved to waste away.

Xavier placed his hands on each side of the case and squeezed until the plexiglass barrier shattered. Transparent shards littered the pedestal, but a quick inspection revealed none stuck into the ball. *Still mint!* After grabbing the treasure, he scanned the room to see if James had heard the display break, but the tall man remained in whatever shadow he'd crawled into. Xavier had no need for the butler anyway, now or in the future, and neither would Luther.

Xavier, resolute, ascended the staircase, this time taking each step one at a time. He ran his hands over the ball like a pitcher ready to throw the final strike of the game, taking care not to smudge the Bonds signature. After reaching Luther's bedroom doors, he rehearsed his future actions in his head. Earlier, their situation had masqueraded as two choices, but Xavier knew only one outcome had existed since Luther's invitation set all this in motion. With a sigh, he exhaled air he no longer needed to live and opened the doors.

"I'm glad you came. It's win-win." A fragile yet happy voice emanated from the bed. "Don't mind me. I sacrificed the morphine in case it interfered." The moon illuminated a wincing Luther. "Seems to wear off faster each time."

Xavier lingered in the doorway, tracing the baseball's stitching with his fingers, before tossing it to Luther. "For luck."

Even in his weakened state, Luther caught the ball and grinned. "Don't you know handling memorabilia decreases its value?" He squeezed it and rolled it in his hands, much like Xavier had done. "Thanks for stopping me from stealing that other ball back in the day. Last thing I needed was a prison record. You were my conscience."

Xavier nodded, taking the open book from the bed. "Let's do this." Could he correctly pronounce the words wriggling about the dense page? *Doesn't matter*, thought Xavier before shouting, "ME PAENITET FRATER!"

Both friends sat in silence. "Nothing," whispered Luther. "Try again."

With his heart breaking, Xavier humored him twice more, each time deflating Luther further and further. Words skittered about the parchment like cockroaches. Xavier didn't bother trying to read the text and focused on lying instead. "That's the spell. Just three words. There's nothing else on the page."

Defeated by pain or disappointment, Luther stared out the window at the moon while Xavier thanked God the body lying in the bed no longer resembled the friend he remembered. Both men teetered on the edge of tears.

Two words escaped Luther's dry, white lips. "I failed."

"You've accomplished so much in your lifetime. Just because it's ending before you want it to doesn't mean you failed."

"Death is the end. The *end*." Some fight returned to Luther's voice. "There are no new businesses, relationships, or even a new flavor of gum. There is nothing after the *end*. That's why they call it the *end*."

"You don't know that, Luther."

"Do you know something?" Luther perked up.

Xavier hung his head. "No."

"This grimoire offers a thousand ways to prolong life, but I refuse to be a ghost, or zombie, or some shadow facsimile of life." Powered by sheer willpower, Luther's imposing voice returned. "What you are is the closest to what I used to be when I was me, not this waste of a man. I built my companies from the ground up. I didn't have a father who loaned me a million dollars in seed money, or a CEO mom who got her friends to invest in my startup." Luther picked his head off the pillow. Tubes and wires swayed as he pointed to his chest with every word. "It was all built for me, by me, and it deserves to go on."

"Some things only matter because they *do* end, Luther." Xavier walked to the door and locked it. He turned and crept closer, canines elongating, preparing for the only true win-win situation. A tear rolled down Xavier's cheek. He couldn't hold the emotions in anymore. "You'd never overcome the bloodlust, Luther. You'd be a gun-wielding toddler, and I wouldn't be able to wrestle you to the ground this time. Who knows how many innocents I'd damn if I imparted this curse, but I know I'd damn you."

Luther returned his gaze to the moon, either unaware or indifferent. Xavier held Luther's shoulder with one hand and used the other to gently tilt his friend's head to the side. Blood vessels distinct as tiny blue rivers crossed Luther's tissue-paper-thin skin. Mercifully, hunger overpowered despair as Xavier's teeth entered his blood-brother's jugular—the fouled blood transformed into nourishment.

One final gift between friends.

Thirst quenched, Xavier pulled back and looked into the sick man's ebony eyes one last time. "You're right, my friend. Love is a funny thing." There was no evidence of something awaiting Luther after he left this earthly mess, but for Xavier, there was no doubt every ending led to another beginning. Luther's soul would be elsewhere, leaving Xavier alone to face his best friend's death, just as one day he would suffer a world without Jeanette.

"No more pain, Luther." Xavier allowed the sadness and anger to bubble up and consume him as he bit through his friend's boney throat. He thrashed back and forth like a hungry wolf, snapping Luther's neck. A continuous high-pitched tone replaced the monitor's rhythmic beeping as blood splattered onto the silk sheets, antique rug, and Barry Bonds' signature.

A DISEASE OF THE BLOOD

John Wolf

THERE WERE THREE. Two from behind and one in front. They encircled the old man like a pack of wolves, trapping him within the narrow alley of their hunting ground. They were young, excited, and grinned with crooked teeth at their prey cut from the rest of the civilized herd. Cruel eyes gleamed beneath tattered newsboy caps.

The boy in front was broad, well-built, and nearly blocked the entire alleyway. He pointed one banger-sized finger at the hatbox in the old man's hands. The black box was wrapped in plain paper with a single crimson ribbon tied around it.

"What ya got there, grandad?"

The old man looked up with weary, bloodshot eyes. His gray beard and papery skin glowed in the darkness. At the lead boy's approach, the old man swayed back and clutched the hatbox to his narrow chest. He looked ready to topple clean over just from the weight of his coat on his sticklike frame.

"Maybe he didn't hear you, Jack?" One of the two boys behind giggled.

The broad boy, Jack, took hold of the hatbox by the ribbon. He didn't yank the box away, just jiggled it like a worm on a fishing hook and smiled at the old man's moaning protests.

41

"Need a second hat there, do ya?"

"Yeah," the boys laughed, "forgot he's already got one there!"

The old man turned this way and that, attacked from all sides with nothing but the cruel, hungry faces about him in the darkness. One of the boys behind him knocked his top hat to the ground. More gray hair floated around his eggy head.

He swung out one hand in a feeble effort to catch his falling hat, but it fell to the ground before Jack kicked it away into a mud puddle.

Jack's vicious grin turned down into an outright predatory snarl. "Asked you a question, grandad. Give us what ya got." He could barely make out the old man's reply. He didn't lean in. All three boys had been raised in the city streets and alleys. They knew better than to get close to their prey. Even an old man like this could do some harm if he could take hold of a wrist, maybe rake their eyes.

Jack simply repeated his question louder. His guttural voice echoed up and down the damp brick before fading away into a city gone cold, dark, and silent as the grave.

The old man cleared his throat and said, "I am a doctor."

Jack looked around. "What do we care? Anyone sick here?"

The other boys proclaimed they were in excellent health.

When the doctor mumbled something else, Jack sneered and pushed him all the way over before he could finish.

The old man went down to the dirty cobblestones. A single crack erupted from his spindly right arm in impact. The hatbox tumbled into the shadows. Its crimson ribbon, a single splash of color among the dark proceedings, floated away on the cold breeze.

The boys closed in, but the doctor seemed to care little for his injured limb or the deadly circumstances surrounding him. All he seemed to notice was his hatbox lying on its side in a mud puddle, the lid ajar, water seeping in through the crack. He whimpered the same word over and over.

He crawled forward, reached out with his remaining good arm, and Jack promptly stepped onto his wrist. Jack pressed down a little further the more the man struggled. The doctor still squirmed ahead. He only stopped when a low, brittle snap emitted from his wrist, the sound like crackling kindling in a low fire. In the struggle, his shirt sleeve wound up his arm and exposed pale skin dotted with open puncture marks.

The doctor moaned. "Lucy…"

"Look here, boys!" Jack pointed at the scabby arm. "Doc's been in the medicine himself."

"Who cares?" One boy sniffed. "Just get his wallet and let's be off."

The third boy bent over and rifled through the doctor's coat pockets. He withdrew a gold watch, a billfold, and a fat coin purse. The doctor remained pinned beneath Jack's boot and kept crying out for someone who wasn't there. Jack followed the doctor's wild eyes to the hatbox on the alley floor.

"Carl," Jack called to the boy rifling through the doctor's pockets. He waved towards the hatbox. "Get me that."

Carl paused in his dastardly work. "The bloody hell I want with a hat?"

Jack produced a knife from his coat pocket, the edge shining silver and mean despite the starless night. "*Get it.*" His tone was sharp and deadly as his weapon.

Carl finished with the doctor's coat, huffing like a reprimanded schoolboy. "Hasn't got anything left in his pockets, anyway." He walked to the box, lifted it out of the puddle and gave it a vigorous shake. He smiled and rattled the contents again. "Christmas come early, lads."

Jack waved his knife. "Come on then. Let's have ourselves a look."

Carl did as commanded, prying open the lid and withdrawing a fine velvet hat. The fabric gleamed. Carl held it up and then popped it on his head.

"Let's see, am I fancy?" Carl's version of a woman's voice was high, tremulous, the sound more like a lunatic than the opposite sex. The other boys howled with laughter, the doctor at Jack's feet all but forgotten.

Satisfied with his performance, Carl looked back down into the hatbox for another source of entertainment.

He screamed.

No longer an act, but a high-pitched, animal shriek of terror. He bolted for the mouth of the alley, letting the hatbox drop to the ground as he did so. The other boy watched, dumbfounded, until Carl seized him by the collar and hauled him back into the well-lit city streets, leaving Jack alone.

Jack stayed right where he was, knife in hand, slack-jawed, stunned into silence. Icy terror gripped him about the waist.

Something had rolled out of the box.

Something round.

Jack moved for a better look. At least he tried to. His feet refused to move. He tried again, leaning, grunting, but his lower body felt made of pins and needles. More cold wound its way up from his groin. He stared down at a long vial stuck into his waist. The needle was nowhere to be seen, sunk to the hilt. Each ragged breath Jack drew sent the vial trembling. The *empty* vial.

The doctor's eyes were empty. His voice was no better. The words might well have been uttered by a corpse:

"Apologies."

The drug continued its work up Jack's torso and into his limbs. Just as he made to strike out with the knife, his fingers went numb, and the knife clattered to the stones. Whatever the doctor had stuck him with was an unseen assailant resistant to any brute means of defense Jack could muster. He collapsed to the ground and gasped for air.

The doctor crawled past, muttering the whole time.

"I am coming, I am coming…"

The world turned sideways. The dirty alley floor was now the wall, the cold, cloudy night the ground. From where Jack lay, the doctor slithered up the walls like a lizard to a pile of refuse and dug his malformed prize free. Unlike his hollow apology to Jack, he cooed and cried with pure love and desperation at the object held in front of him.

"Forgive me, my love. I would never have let them touch you. I would die before I let them!"

A venomous hiss filled the alleyway. Somewhere within the bestial sound, there might have been words, but Jack could not understand them. He didn't want to. He didn't want to be here for any of this. He just wanted to crawl away, to go to his shack on the edge of town, lock the door and light the lamps against the dark.

He could only moan.

The doctor rose on shaky feet, out of sight save for his dirty shoes. They shuffled into clearer view as he came closer. His words rolled down from above like a wrathful god.

"You scoundrels. Have you no decency? Laying hands on a lady!"

"Sod your decency, you crazy bastard!" That was what Jack wanted to say. All that came from his numb lips was a single croak.

The doctor's knees descended into view.

"I could never part from her, you see? The others, Quincy, Arthur..." The doctor's voice trailed away as some old memory seized his train of thought. Then he spat on the ground. "That damned Van Helsing, too. They all wanted her gone. She was no good for them anymore. They only wanted her as she was. But was she not still my Lucy?"

The doctor rolled Jack onto his back. Darkness swam in his eyes, endless as the night sky. His voice rasped with desire. Despite the rising madness in his words, he went about his tasks with the surety of a surgeon. The hatbox rested neatly on a laid-out handkerchief; the doctor withdrew a pair of spectacles and adjusted them on his nose before he began tapping Jack's throat with one hand.

"How could I ever stay away? Even from the grave, she called to me. Even from my marriage bed, I had to go. Love transcends death."

With a gloved hand, the doctor lifted a ghastly, charred head by its remaining red curls out of the hatbox. Below the crooked jaw was a withered stump of gristle for a neck. The skin, what remained of it, was the color of old snow. Where there was none: burnt bone. The lips were barely visible black slashes below the weathered nose. One cheek had collapsed in on itself, leaving the thin lips at a permanent, sly grin.

Jack's scream caught in his chest, burning like a brand, aching for release. He wanted to scream more than anything in his entire wretched life. The doctor, or whatever he was, was mad, absolutely goddamned mad.

When the doctor stroked the one intact cheek of the severed head, cooed into its missing ear, all Jack could do was piss himself. It ran down his legs and trickled into the rest of the gutter trash.

The doctor smiled. "Love can infect the mind, but it's what keeps us alive."

He continued tapping Jack's neck, with every strike whispering to his sickening companion, "Here, here. Here, here, love." Each tap of the fingers brought another placation.

The hissing came again and rose into a gleeful whistle. The bottomless, black eye sockets suddenly sparkled with light. Two cloudy blue orbs shone out of the darkness and focused on the prey lying frozen on the ground.

The thin lips parted and exposed two perfectly white fangs jutting out of the moldering gums. Jack finally managed something louder than an agonized groan from his paralyzed throat. It was really no help at all.

Seward worried it might take too long. Even in the dead of night, the city was never completely deserted. If someone came along now, they'd be finished. In his weakened state, he couldn't put up much of a fight. And this one was a big lad. Still, it'd been a long while since his love's last meal.

At least she worked quickly.

Lucy latched on and hadn't let go of the neck in over five minutes. Seward kept time on his pocket watch. The other boys had dropped it, along with his other valuables, when they fled. A small crack ran down the center of the glass, but the hands still went around in steady succession. Damaged, but still in good working order.

No one came back for the boy. The other two had run like rats, just as Seward had guessed when he'd originally picked up their trail on the east end of town. He rested his weary head against the nearby alley wall as Lucy continued feeding. The stump of bone beneath her head wiggled in his hands as she drank her fill. The boy had stopped making any noise or movement at all. That was good. Seward closed his eyes.

His love had already suffered enough. Both in life and death. Black bile rose in Seward's throat at the memories of his youthful days. He and the two men he thought of as lifelong friends: Arthur and Quincy. One dead to him, the other just dead. He thought of stakes and hammers in the dark, of shouted prayers in a desecrated crypt, of his poor Lucy wrought to pieces by those she loved and who no longer loved her in return. At first, Seward had been like the rest of them, blinded by rage and hungry for revenge.

But then their dreadful work had finished. Quincy in the ground, their vendetta against the Count served in full, the Harkers were gone, Van Helsing (damn him) back to his studies, and Arthur Holmwood… Another gout of rage bubbled up inside Seward at the memory of his two-faced friend. They had all moved on. They were all too happy to forget.

But to Doctor Seward, the melancholia and the darkness of memory were his life. That and other vices.

Seward grit his teeth. His arm itched like an entire colony of ants lived beneath his skin. Even after all this time, his other immoral need bit and clawed at him from the inside. He tightened his grip on Lucy's hair instead. He would not drop her again. She clamped down into the boy's neck with a muffled crunch. Suddenly, the boy's arms flew up, his eyes wide and white, fear and pain driving him into one last feeble attempt to save his life. He reached for Lucy; Seward just drove her further into the boy's neck. Blood gushed out the side of her mouth, spattering to the ground, and the boy went still.

Everyone had their needs. Seward had had his work, then his vendetta, and after that, the goal of picking up the remains of his life and forging a better one. He'd tried so desperately to forget her like the others. Surely a man of his station and value should've been able to carry on. Marriage to a woman of his class, the hopes of starting a family. But he could not forget those blue eyes staring up at him from the coffin, his Blue Lady.

Over time, a voice had beckoned to him from the darkness. He hid these desires from his wife and remaining friends. He hoped the morphine could drown the voice of his mysterious nighttime caller. Only when the dreams of his old love wormed their way into his waking moments did Seward finally understand what had to be done.

He'd taken so long to remember where Van Helsing buried her, it nearly drove him mad. Arthur was no help. When Seward came to call on him, the servant at the door turned him away.

"The Holmwoods are on holiday."

Happy.

Seward had been happy once. Did Lucy remember? Was there anything beyond feral, animal hunger left in those blue eyes which once captivated him? How could she not be grateful to him? He was saving her from an eternity of abyss! They could finally reunite! Him and his dear, sweet Lucy. After all this time. After all her other suitors had abandoned her to the shadows.

Another growl escaped Lucy's bloody mouth. Seward relaxed his grip and gently pulled her away from the boy. The growl only increased in pitch. He considered. Perhaps she was still upset at having been dropped so carelessly into the street. Perhaps she had just gone too long without feeding. She needed something more than just a single oafish boy. Seward's marked arm tingled again. Trading one needle for another, but he thought it a noble sacrifice. Anything to keep her.

Seward swallowed roughly and cleared his throat. He leaned in, but not so close, and whispered assurances to his single patient. Promised her there would be more to come, that they could start again. They could be together, forever.

Lucy hissed.

"There, there," Seward whispered as he laid her back into the hatbox and covered her with fine velvet. He always wept at this task. The hat had been a wedding present for her. Even after all this time, he wasn't sure who he wept for: himself, his dear Lucy, or that ugly thought lurking deep within his mind. Would she finally love him? Surely, she knew she loved him and how he had always loved her. The marks along his arm were proof enough. But would there soon be a night he would give her the last drop he had and lose her forever?

Whose voice had called out to him from the darkness while he slept? Hers? Or his?

Doctor Seward shook this heavy dread away and closed the lid. There was too much to do. His wrist would require some real attention, but he had a good room at the boarding house where they could be alone. Still, he winced sharply as he stood. He held the hatbox close against his chest. His heart beat against the thin exterior wall of the box. Lucy stirred at the sound and the box shook. To Seward it might have been hunger or perhaps rage. He clutched it tighter with his thin arm. He decided no matter the reason, it was a good sign she was so virile. She was coming back around. She would heal. She had to, so they could be together again. Seward and his Lucy.

The moon crawled out from behind the heavy black clouds and cast the city in silvery light. Seward took no notice. His heart, while beating healthily, hung heavy with the knowledge he could never give her up no matter what horrors might come. It *was* love in its own way, he told himself. A terrible disease of the blood, and like with Lucy's own horrific affliction, he knew there was no cure but one. The doctor shivered at the thought.

HUNTERS ANONYMOUS

AJ Martin

"Alright, everyone, let's take a seat," Ms. Patts crooned, her smile wrinkling the lines underneath her eyes.

Prince eyed the crowd; one girl twitched every time a chair scraped. Another grinned like his jaw would unhinge and collapse to the floor. Several of them clutched their Styrofoam cups of coffee and stared at the blue-tinted walls, barely there.

These weekly meetings were mandated by the Corporation, the conglomerate of five major hunting firms in the United States and Canada. Technically, *Prince* wasn't mandated— though he'd abandoned his post for four years without notice, he still wasn't considered a company fuck-up. That title was reserved for those who'd managed to take down entire cities going after one target.

Ms. Patts glided to the front of the room and sat herself in a thin wire chair, smiling brightly. "Now, then. Welcome to the first HA meeting of the fall!"

There was a weak, sad clap.

Ms. Patts smiled wider. "I know, I'm just as excited to be here as you are! I'd also like to thank Marianne for providing the delicious lemon bars and coffee. They're located in the back and up for grabs." She paused, tapping her clipboard. "But remember the rules! Only before and after meetings, never during. We don't want to take time away from each other, do we?"

Everyone nodded.

Ms. Patts eyed Prince before holding her clipboard to her chest. She leaned over and pulled a wooden stake from her bag. She held it out to the group. "Now. Who would like to share a story?"

The room remained silent, but Ms. Patts was determined. She made slow, deliberate eye contact with each of them. While the others were preoccupied with their shoelaces or the cracks in the walls, Prince looked directly at her.

Ms. Patts wiggled the stake. "Who wants the talking stake first?"

A small woman with thin blonde hair gently raised her hand.

Ms. Patts beamed and handed the stake over to her. "Thank you, dear! Please, speak up!"

The woman stood and smoothed her full-length skirt. She clasped the talking stake, shaking, and smiled timidly. "H–hi, my name is Anima."

"Hi Anima," the group chorused back to her.

She flinched a bit but gave a small smile. "Th–thank you. I was sent here just after my last tour with another hunting company. M-maybe you've heard of it: Bram Incorporated?" Prince watched Anima as she took a shaky breath and continued, "I–I, uh, I've been having nightmares lately. Really vivid ones."

"What kind of nightmares?" Ms. Patts asked.

"I…I did something horrible," Anima whispered. "Something I can't repent for, and n–now I dream of it every night."

Ms. Patts smiled sympathetically. "We would be honored if you'd share, but we understand if you don't wish to."

Anima shook her head. "No, I–I want to. I—"

She held herself, shoulders slumped. Staring at the wall.

"I was supposed to take out this creature who'd been killing people in a remote town in southern Indiana. I–I'm from there, originally. It was

a little girl who'd been bitten. She wasn't more than six years old. She…
she needed to be neutralized. Before the transition."

She stopped, but her mouth hung open. Her knuckles turned white
from clutching the talking stake.

"Go on, dear," Ms. Patts urged.

Anima gave a shaky nod. "I started asking questions, but…no one
said a word. It was weird because it's a hunting town. Everyone knows
about the Corporation, about my jobs…but no one wanted to help me
find the girl." She quickly wiped her tears.

Prince stared at Anima. A good hunter, he'd learned, had to be calm,
even cruel, when the families of people who turned got involved.

Didn't mean that everyone did it right. The Corporation was always
worried about the cracks where the truth would slip through, outing
hunters like Prince to the world. But the families of the turned were
often too terrified or skeptical to say too much. Anything worse that
risked the Corporation's exposure could be explained—disease, a gas
leak, faulty infrastructure, bad luck.

The death and anguish caused by loving families getting involved
during hunts could fill oceans.

"They begged me not to kill her. They knew what would happen,
but t–they claimed it was an accident, and…" Anima coughed. "That's
why I'm here. I… I–I didn't kill her before the transition. I contained her
instead, thinking that would hold her off until I could get help, but…"
The tears fell with rapid force, sliding down the woman's pale cheeks.
"She escaped, and we couldn't find her. They told me she meant no harm,
but she turned, and she was…eviscerating people, tearing them apart…
Leaving their corpses to rot—" She gagged, like she remembered the
smell.

"So, I…I managed to track her down. She was hiding out in the town
hall basement, but when I found her, the townspeople stood around her,
protecting her, so I set off a bomb in the basement. It was the only way,

and so many people died." Anima's knuckles were white from clutching the talking stake. "They died protecting her."

The room was silent, the nothingness of it suffocating and familiar.

Ms. Patts' smile cracked. "Uh, thank you, Anima."

Anima nodded, her eyes blank.

Wasting no time, Ms. Patts turned to a ginger haired man with a beer belly sitting in the chair across from Prince. "Sir, would you like to speak?"

"Sure," he stood and swiped the talking stake from Anima. "The name's Bear. I've been hunting for at least thirty years now."

"Hi, Bear," they sang, but Prince said nothing.

Bear fixed his gaze on Prince, and Prince glared back, baring his teeth.

The man's eyes skittered away before turning back to the group. "Like I was sayin', I'm Bear. I retired last year from the Harker Project. It was a hell of a time, shootin' monsters and gettin' the bad guys." As he spoke, his face fell. "But that last job, man. They make you work like hell to finish that last job."

He scanned the room and then grinned at Ms. Patts. "You've gotta understand. Back then, I was the best hunter. I did everythin', from the little bumps in the night to Satan himself."

The entire group snickered.

Bear sniffed and spread his legs, leaning forward as he spoke. "I was, uh, workin' a case down in Mississippi. It was the usual thing— kids wandering the swamp at night, still breathing but spaced out with marks on their necks and wrists. I figured it was standard, long-term feeding, y'know?" He paused, like he expected them to answer, but he didn't wait long. "When I showed up in Indianola, I got word that it was something else—apparently, there was an ancient artifact that could call on the devil…"

"Which devil?" A man with deep, blue-black skin from the far corner folded his hands together, disgust rolling from his body. "I can only do my work through *Lwa*, but you would call them the devil."

"I thought your gods weren't malicious?" Anima spoke up.

"You're right, they aren't. We invoke them to protect us from a world that is evil… From people like *you.*"

"Alright, that's quite enough." Ms. Patts' smile stretched past her ears. "Thank you, Fayard, for your contribution, but please wait for the talking stake." She turned to Bear to continue his story.

He nodded. "I'm not sure what the artifact was, but it was for the devil, Fayard. *The* devil."

"*Your* devil wears many masks," Fayard muttered. "Many of them are human."

"Sure, whatever. *Anyway,*" Bear forced the attention back to him, "I get this job. I go down to Mississippi, near the swamps. I'm told this artifact's at the bottom of Melton Lake near Indianola. The man runnin' the boat tells me this, and I'm thinkin' 'no fuckin' way am I goin' down in the swamp where goddamn alligators and cottonmouths live and gettin' it myself.' So, I convinced the guy that we needed to drag the swamp and find the artifact."

Bear coughed. He leaned against the seat, gripping the back of his chair. He dabbed his forehead with his red kerchief, his beady eyes blinking as the sweat dripped into them.

"I, uh, so I convince the guy to get someone from wildlife enforcement. Well, they weren't too happy with me, but I told them I'm from the Institute of Archeological Integrity, and I need to take a look." Bear chuckled. "I'm shocked they fell for that shit, but they always do, don't they? You gotta be from some high flyin' 'Institute' or 'Group' to clear out a swamp, but the local folks in charge are always too tired to check.

"So, before you know it, we struck gold. Turns out, a local woman was calling up the devil to turn those kids comatose. They'd come to her house every night, and she'd take a little blood here and a little blood there. She thought she wasn't hurtin' nobody, but she'd been using the blood to feed a whole colony of vamps shacking up right there."

Bear's eyes gleamed, so excited to share the story that he practically bounced from his seat. "God, I hadn't seen an explosion like that since my early days. I'd just gotten this tricked out bazooka with vaporized holy water, and it was a son of a bitch to carry around, but the wait was *worth it.*"

Fayard snorted. "And no one noticed a bazooka blowing up an entire swamp?"

Bear shrugged. "We told 'em it was protocol. Like I said, always too tired or stupid to check."

"Thank you, Bear, although I think you'll find that such methods are…frowned upon by the Corporation." Ms. Patts reviewed her clipboard, her hands shaking as she eyed the group once more. "Let's see… How about you? Jerome Prince?"

Thirteen pairs of eyes shifted towards him.

Prince cleared his throat and sat further back into his seat. "No, I'm just here to listen."

"I'll be damned," Bear grinned. He was clear across the room, but Prince could still see the tobacco stains on his teeth and gums. "Jerome Prince, the big bad hunter at Bram Incorporated, a kill rate of twelve hundred certified vamps, demons, and all the other creepy crawlies out there. What the hell did you do to piss off the Corporation?"

"Bear, leave it alone," Anima said. "He's choosing not to speak. We need to respect that."

"No, I wanna hear this." Bear turned to Jerome again and smiled. "What happened, Prince? On top of the goddamned world, but then you just up and disappear, and after four years you show up in Oregon, back on the job like nothin' happened."

Prince fought to keep still. He wanted to shut this guy up, to use his slaying kit to wipe that smirk off his trigger-happy, backwoods country face.

He folded his arms tighter, saying nothing.

Bear laughed. "See, if I'd disappeared from my job for that long, they would've given me the firing squad treatment. 'Cause you don't disappear for four whole years to go on picnics and sightsee, do you? You start working for the other side—those cute 'lil grassroots clubs run by tree-huggers, whinin' about how 'they mean no harm, they're just people who need help.' Is that what you did? Do you hunt for *them* now?"

"Bear," the notes of Ms. Patts' singsong voice had sharp edges. "I'll remind you that Corporation policy states accusations of that nature are forbidden during all HA proceedings. If you have a claim, you may take it up with the Corporation during annual review."

Bear just kept talking. "Then again, maybe there was a civilian who turned your eye? An' you just couldn't live without her—"

"What's your point, Bear?" Fayard asked, his voice tired.

"I'm just sayin' it ain't fair. You got special treatment, didn't you?" Bear's lip curled. "I *wonder* why."

The chair creaked as Prince leaned forward. Bear's self-satisfied grin slipped just enough for him to get some sense.

Prince didn't have to do much to make shitheads like Bear cower.

Before he thought better of it, Prince opened his mouth. "I've heard of you, too, you know. I know why you're here."

"Lookee, who said I wasn't the best?" Bear looked around like the others were an audience for his little show. "First meeting, and I get this asshole to talk. Go on, then. Tell me why I'm here."

Prince wished he hadn't said anything. He needed to watch, to wait, but he'd already dug this hole.

He might as well climb in.

"To be fair, I don't really know you, but I've met so many others like you."

Bear grinned. "Is that so?"

"Hunters like you like this job too much," Prince said.

Bear's self-satisfied smirk slipped from his face, and Prince took his chance. "You're wrong—I'm not feeding the monsters or hunting for them or whatever bullshit you've decided, but they've got some points. You jerk off to the idea of the next big explosion, the biggest kill, and you don't care who gets in the way."

Bear's nostrils flared. His eyes darted around the room, trying to scrape together allies against Prince. The others looked at the ground or at their hands. Some, like Fayard and Anima, just glanced between Bear and Prince, waiting for the next strike.

Bear sniffed. "What's your point?"

Prince knew this was too easy, that he needed to stay hidden and forgettable, but Bear pissed him off.

"My point is that you didn't choose to be retired. They kicked you out after that Mississippi job because you killed three vampires and twenty civilians, all of them children. You didn't bother to check before you blew up that safe house, did you?"

Bear's rage vibrated. Prince wouldn't have been surprised if the guy leaped out of his seat and charged him.

Ms. Patts eyed Prince with reprimand wrapped in concern. "Prince, I think we can put aside any personal differences. This is a space for closure and healing."

"Seriously?" Prince turned on her. "Listen, I'm not hunting anything except vamps, demons, creatures, you name it. I don't kill for them, and I certainly don't feed them, but…I've met enough of them to know that they're not hunting *us*. Sure, there are the ones that go all out and kill towns' worth of people, but…that woman Bear was so proud of killing? She was just trying to feed her grandkids who'd turned. She'd draw blood from the human kids and send them home." Prince was talking so fast he was spitting. "Most of the things we kill, they were people once, and they're not evil, they just…they need to eat. Like we all do."

The group was quiet. Ms. Patts' face was purple; she was struggling to maintain control. "Since you've decided to interrupt the group, why don't you share?"

Prince retreated as far back into the rickety chair as his large frame would allow. "I don't have anything worth talking about."

"Oh, don't be shy, Prince." Ms. Patts leaned forward, resting her drooping, sorrowful face on her knuckles. "We'd love the opportunity to hear your story."

"C'mon," Bear heckled, "what're you so afraid of?"

Prince gritted his teeth. "I'm *not* afraid."

"It's okay," Fayard said. "We've all got secrets."

Bear's arrogant smile returned. He tossed the stake towards Prince, who caught it on reflex.

"Go on," he taunted, sweat lining his lips. "Go on and tell us the story that broke *the* Jerome Prince."

"*Fine.*"

The other attendees jumped like they'd been bitten.

Sweat rolled down Prince's back. He was on the defensive. He was exposed, and he had nowhere to hide.

He eyed Bear with contempt.

"You want to know what I was doing for four years? I'll tell you."

It was my eight-hundredth job. I was only twenty-five, but I'd been working at Bram Incorporated for ten years. I was stranded in Shakopee, Washington. There was this little diner next to the motel, and I went in and ordered coffee.

I remember her, this beautiful woman with long dark hair and rich, brown skin, who came over and poured me a cup. She gave me a bright smile and said, "Coffee? At two a.m.?"

"It keeps me young."

She snorted. "You can't be more than twenty-one."

"Twenty-five, actually," I said. "Thanks for noticing."

She nodded. "What do you want?"

On cue, my stomach turned over. "I haven't had pancakes in a long time."

"I'll get you some pancakes." She smiled.

I went back to that diner for three meals a day for a week, and she was there. Her name was Brianna. She was twenty-three, attending Washington State part-time. She was studying to be a nurse, but she really wanted to be a doctor.

She had a little girl named Lulu.

"She's everything to me," Brianna whispered, holding the mug in her hands. It was my last night in town. I'd successfully completed the job, and I stopped in to say goodbye.

Brianna agreed to have breakfast with me.

"She sounds lovely," I said. I checked the clock. It was close to sunrise. I needed to leave.

Brianna turned to me, dark brown eyes piercing. For as long as I live, I will never forget those eyes.

We spent the morning and afternoon together. Once Lulu was done with school, we picked her up from the bus stop.

It was a perfect day.

Later that night, we ordered pizza and watched a movie. Nothing happened, and the longer I laid on that couch, Brianna in the crook of my arm, Lulu sitting in front of the TV, it dawned on me: I wasn't leaving. I would stay in this small town and live out the rest of my life with Brianna and Lulu.

That moment was the happiest I'd ever been.

For four years, I watched Lulu grow up. I sent her off to kindergarten and grade school. Brianna and I were expecting another kid in a few months.

We sat on our couch. Brianna reached for her Walkman and put the headphones over her large stomach.

"What are you doin'?" I asked as I rubbed her stomach.

"You're supposed to play Mozart and Beethoven, so that baby is smarter when it comes out."

I grinned. "So, our baby's gonna come out a cyborg, or what?"

She swatted me, and I laughed.

Lulu came running into the living room, holding out a bundle of construction paper in different shades of pink tied together with a white ribbon. "Mommy, Daddy, I wrote a story!"

"A story? Really, honey?" Brianna smiled.

"Yep! Look at it, look at it."

We laughed when she shoved the paper in my hands. I cleared my throat in that overdramatic way, and I read the title.

My Nighttime Friend.

"'I have a friend who only comes at night. His name is Barry,'" I read. "'He plays with me so long as I…I give him a snack. The first night, I gave him some of Mommy's chocolate, but he didn't like it. Then, I gave him some broccoli, but he didn't like that because no one does.'"

I made a face when I said it, and Lulu giggled.

"'I gave him all sorts of snacks, but Barry said he couldn't eat them. He told me he needed a special snack, and that…'"

My stomach churned. I scanned the next few lines.

It was a snack that only I could make and no one else.

He had to bite me to get it.

"Go on, honey," Brianna said. "Keep reading."

I ignored her. "Lulu, sweetie, do you remember getting hurt in the last few days?"

She shook her head vigorously. "No, Daddy."

Brianna gave me a strange look, but then she saw it first. "Lulu, honey, I think Dad's right… Come here." Lulu turned to the side and showed her wrist. I remember it with absolute clarity.

There were two faint pock marks on her wrist, perfectly shaped like the tips of fangs. They were still slightly red with purple rings around the wounds.

I threw the papers to the side and grabbed Lulu's wrist, examining the marks.

"Ow! Daddy, you're hurting me."

I smoothed over her wrist. "I'm sorry, sweetie. I got carried away."

"Jerome, what's wrong with you?" Brianna asked me.

I didn't answer her for a while. I kissed the mark on Lulu's wrist and said, "I think it's mostly healed up, but we'll watch it, okay? I need to talk to Mom now."

She pouted. "But you didn't finish my story."

"I know, but it's time for bed. We'll read it tomorrow?" her mom said.

I didn't want to raise suspicion. I'd managed in the last four years to keep my past life a secret from my family. They didn't need to know the depths of this world, the ways in which shit could go wrong at any minute.

So, I lied. I'd lied to my love and my child for four years.

I made a vow to check on Lulu later, to make sure that her room was protected. I'd warded the house with charms and salt before I moved in, but I'd relaxed too much. Had taken the relative safety of Shakopee for granted.

When Lulu left, I turned to Brianna. "I need to tell you something."

"What is it?"

I swallowed hard. "I think Lulu's been bitten by a vampire. A real one."

Brianna's brow knitted together but relaxed after a few moments. She started to laugh. "That's a good one, honey."

I shook my head. My eyes were stinging. "It's not a joke."

"Yes, it is," Brianna snorted. "Vampires aren't real."

I waited for a minute before saying, "Yes, they are."

Brianna just looked at me, the anger sparking in her soft brown eyes. "No, they are not."

I sighed. I got up from the couch and started to pace.

"There are things you don't know about me." I started.

"That's ridiculous," she said. "We're as good as married."

"You can marry people you don't know," I insisted.

"But I know you." She got up to stop me. She held my wrists, her deep eyes filled with worry. "Now, tell me what's wrong."

"I… I used to work for a company called Bram Incorporated…" I started slowly. "I was a hired gun for the company."

Her eyes grew wide. "You were an assassin?"

"Of monsters, yes," I sighed. "I'm… I'm a vampire hunter. I was in town on a job when we first met."

The room was silent, heavy like a semi-truck barreling down the road on a winter night. The moments before and after that truck loses control, there's this split second of stillness, the calm before the storm, that makes you level with yourself. Everything's in slow motion, and the truest parts of yourself become clear.

That was the moment before her face twisted into terror.

"You're sick," she said, holding her stomach as she hurried towards the stairs. "I let you into my home—"

"No, no, please—"

"I let you be my daughter's father." Her voice quaked. "I let you *touch* me and *fuck* me—"

I followed her, reaching for her. "I love you! I love this life. I would never hurt you—"

"I let you into my *heart.*" Then she started sobbing. I held her for a moment, a long moment, before she let me go and whispered, "You need to leave. I'll call you in the morning."

"No…no." I shook my head. I dropped to my knees, holding her waist. "Bri, please. Please don't make me leave."

"I have to, for my children—"

"*Our* children," I asserted. "They're *our* children."

She shook her head and peeled my arms away from her, sobbing as she went upstairs.

I did as she asked. I double-checked that the house was protected before I left. I couldn't leave them, especially because of Lulu. Brianna would have a new shit storm to deal with once Lulu wouldn't age, when she'd show signs of hunger.

Truth of the matter was, I had no idea if she was already starting to crave.

After a sleepless night, I came back the next morning.

I trudged up to the front door and knocked.

I waited. And waited. After ten minutes, I searched for my keys, calling first be damned.

Lulu screamed.

I slammed my full weight into the door. The wood splintered and blew open. Pain sliced through my now dislocated shoulder, but I kept moving.

I ran up the stairs and into our bedroom.

On the ground, my love, my partner, was bleeding out. Lulu leaned over her, her mouth stained red.

The blood was everywhere. It drenched the carpet, dripped off the walls… It spread over our pictures and our bed.

And Lulu sat there, her hands shaking. The blood on her mouth and cheeks mixed with her tears.

"D–daddy, I don't…I don't know w–why I d–d—" she sobbed.

I was having a heart attack. I was sure of it.

My breath was ragged when I said, "I know, I know you didn't mean it."

She kept sobbing, and while she was blinded by her tears, I pulled my gun from my waistband and pointed the barrel at her.

Prince cleared his throat.

"What happened?" Anima whispered.

He looked down. Clasped around the talking stake, his knuckles were pale. "I, uh… I killed my daughter."

Time stretched to fit the shape of the new trauma. No one said a word, not even Ms. Patts, the woman who thought a "talking stake" was a cute idea.

Finally, Ms. Patts cleared her throat. "Thank you, Jerome, for sharing."

He nodded and passed the talking stake onward.

After one or two more stories of horrific battles and lives lost, the meeting was declared over, and all attendees received a gold star for their troubles.

Prince got up and meandered around the snack table. He ignored Ms. Patts' pointed comment about "sharing the snacks" as he helped himself to enough food to feed an army and then some and proceeded to grab himself some coffee for the road.

"That's not why you were sent here, is it?" Anima's small voice said from beside him.

"I don't know what you're talkin' about," he muttered, reluctantly turning toward her.

She sniffed, holding her cup of coffee against her stomach. "You know, you technically never left Bram Incorporated. When I started, I'd heard of a string of murders made to look like vamps down the west coast and back up again. They happened to follow a particular pattern."

"Oh yeah?" he asked, bored. "And what's that?"

"They were all hunters." Her clear blue eyes narrowed. "You move around a lot, don't you?"

Prince towered over her. "Are you trying to make up for something, Anima? Is that why you're interrogating me?"

She breathed and broke eye contact. "No. I just wanted you to know that I understand telling a big lie to try to make things better."

Prince stopped short. He didn't say anything else, whipping his keys from his back pocket with a nod. Then he left.

In his car, he breathed a sigh of relief. He drove, the road too clear, too calm for this late at night.

Prince pulled into his driveway without incident. It was *their* house, the one he'd left years ago.

He parked in the garage, made a stop at the freezer and pulled out several blood bags.

As he opened the door, his little girl ran up to greet him.

"Daddy?" Lulu smiled, her fangs glinting in the dark. "Daddy, you're home!"

She threw her arms around Prince's legs. He had to stop himself from crying every time he looked at her.

She was meant to be fifteen now. She should have been going to school and discovering herself. She should have been doing all these wonderful, beautiful things.

Instead, she was chained to the house. He'd had too many accidents to just let her go. Her skin was completely gone, replaced by thick red scales covering her little body. Gremlin-like ears and blood-soaked wings beat as she greeted him.

He peeled her from his legs and handed her the blood bags.

He sat on the couch and turned on the TV. Lulu ripped open the bags and devoured them, blood spilling over the old stains. Lulu gorged on it, slurping sounds mixing with the dull thrum of the late-night news blaring on the TV.

"I'm sorry I couldn't get you something fresh, sweetheart," he whispered.

"That's okay." She leaped from the floor and curled up next to him, her scales grating on his skin.

"Are you still hungry?"

Her jaw opened—sharp fangs lining her gums since she had no lips—and made a slight chomp. She giggled and said, "Yes, but that's okay. I can wait until tomorrow."

A timid knock broke the silence.

Jerome shot up from the couch. He dragged Lulu by her chains and ran up the stairs, Lulu screeching and pulling with each move. He'd rigged her up to the bed frame when he heard the front door creak open.

"Prince? I—it's Anima, from group. The door was unlocked."

Prince held Lulu's demonic face in his hands. "We're going to play the quiet game. Can you do that?"

"What do I win?"

"I'll get you a nice dessert for tomorrow, someone sweet."

Lulu licked her sharpened teeth, her tongue slithering back into her maw. "I'll be quiet, Daddy."

Prince shut the door, which had been equipped with three chamber locks. He fastened all of them and then strode downstairs.

Anima stood in the middle of the room, the glare from the TV casting her in a blue shadow. The darkness shielded the blood, but a good hunter could smell it.

"Just give her up, Prince," Anima said.

"I don't know what you're talking about."

"Please, let me take her from you. Let someone else do this."

"Like I said, I don't know what you're talking about." Prince grabbed his stake gun from the waistband of his jeans and pointed it at Anima. "Now get out."

Anima just stared at him. She looked exactly like what Prince had taken her for at HA—she was timid, shy, and she couldn't handle the aftermath of her work.

But she was alone. She was confident that she could make him change his mind.

"Prince," she started, her voice soft and sad. "I know. I know what it's like, but you have to let me do this. I know about the other hunters. I know that you've been going to these HA meetings and finding hunters to kill. I know that you…that you've been bringing people back here. For her."

"If you knew, why would you come here?" he whispered.

"You were going to take someone with you tonight, weren't you? But you had to speak, and it blew your cover. You were watching them, but

I've been watching you. I have for a long time," Anima said. "Please let me help you."

Prince's hands shook, losing his aim. He let go of the stake gun, tears running down his face.

"Fine," he whispered. "Follow me."

Anima nodded, and Prince led her up the stairs. He unlocked the bedroom door and motioned for her to walk inside.

"This is my daughter, Lulu. Lulu, say hi to Anima."

Lulu's mouth cracked open like an alligator, teeth dripping with blood and bits of flesh from meals' past. "Hi, Anima!"

Anima didn't flinch. She waved. "It's nice to meet you, Lulu."

"Do you want to hear a story? I write stories," Lulu said.

Anima gave a small smile. "Some other time. Prince? Are you ready?"

"Okay," Prince whispered. "Okay, let me just…let me say goodbye."

Anima nodded and turned to prep her stake gun.

Prince knelt beside his daughter and kissed her on her fleshless cheek.

"I love you," he whispered.

"I love you too, Daddy," Lulu said softly.

Prince held her for a minute longer. Then he got up and walked toward the door.

"I'll be quick," Anima said. "I promise."

"Thank you," Prince said. He was standing at the threshold, one hand on the door, when Anima took a step forward.

Lulu growled.

Prince wasn't facing her when Anima spoke. "Why isn't she…? Prince, she's not in her chains—!"

Prince slammed the bedroom door shut and secured the locks. He pressed his body against the door while Anima banged on it from the inside.

"Listen to me, Prince, you don't have to do this, please don't— PRINCE!"

The door heaved, cracking just a little with the impact. Claws scraped the wood and Anima screamed a long, blood-curdling scream. She howled, and the door shook each time Lulu sunk her talons and teeth into the soft flesh.

Prince had heard the sound enough over the past ten years. Flesh torn from bone, Anima's cries turned to gurgles and, finally, nothing at all.

Silence. Long, twisted silence followed when a small voice called, "Daddy, I'm full!"

Prince shook. Tears flooded his eyes and fell down his cheeks, his hands trembling as he unlocked the door.

Blood everywhere. It was a memory and a nightmare, the past and present collapsing into one moment. He would never stop seeing this; their bedroom stained in red and viscera.

Anima's shoes and coat were submerged in the blood and the flesh staining the blue carpet. Chunks of pink, raw flesh spread from the bed to the door, and trails of blood splashed across the walls and ceiling.

Lulu crawled through the mess of Anima's remains, using her tipped wings to guide her. She wrapped her wiry, scaled arms around Prince's legs, looking up at him with solid black eyes.

"Can we watch a princess movie now?"

Prince swallowed, tears dripping onto Lulu's head as his lips touched her forehead. "Of course, whatever you want."

Lulu smiled and sailed down the stairwell. Prince followed, picking up evidence along the way. Now that the doors and windows were sealed, he was alright with Lulu exploring the house, testing her wings. They were clipped but didn't prevent her from jumping high into the vaulted ceiling.

She set herself on the couch, flipping through channels until she found a princess movie of some kind.

Dawn would break soon. Lulu would go to her room, deep in the basement of the house. He'd redone it so many years ago to make sure it had all her favorite things—Disney princesses, pink flowers, books and music. He'd even painted a mural to resemble the colors and pictures of a beautiful spring day, her favorite season. Each night, Prince bathed Lulu so the walls and the bed could stay exactly how she wanted them.

While she slept, Prince would clean the house from top to bottom. He'd take what was left of Anima's body, put it in her car, and send that car into a lake several hundred miles away.

When they inevitably asked at next week's meeting why Anima wasn't there, no one would have an answer. Hunters didn't have family waiting for them. They wouldn't be missed, and the Corporation would be glad that a potential liability was neutralized.

He'd have to decide if going back was the right choice, but he wasn't too worried. Jerome Prince was the best—he knew that they'd have to move on after tonight, maybe go up to Canada. There would always be another hunt, another place to settle.

But right now, Prince held Lulu in his blood-soaked shirt and watched a princess meet her true love on TV.

MEDUSA EVERMORE

P.R. O'Leary

I HAVE BEEN alive for thousands of years and still haven't learned how to read Russian. The letters are so bold and menacing. They march across the sign, black on pitted metal, indecipherable. But the surrounding symbology clearly translates the intent: a big X, exclamation points, everything printed in a solid red circle. It must say "Do Not Enter," or "Caution," or "Turn around and go home!"

The fence this particular sign is attached to is made of heavy-duty chain link, double-layered. Twice as tall as me and capped by thick, dense barbed wire heavy with icicles. The fence is long, the view in both directions lost in the falling snow. A dirt road had led me here, unused for years and, even though the storm just started, already covered in inches of downfall. The gate in front of me has probably not been used in years either. It could be swung wide to let in a truck. Instead, it's locked shut with heavy chains and a big fat padlock.

I kick my boots into the cold ground, making divots in the snow, trying to warm my toes. They should be much colder in this weather, but for me, a mild chill is about all I will ever feel. My hands I keep out of the wind in my pockets. The hood of my thick jacket I don't use. I have so much hair I don't need it. Long and black, it often gets me mistaken for a female. The hair, combined with my thin features and olive skin, had raised eyebrows this far into the Soviet Union (or Ukraine or Russia or whatever this area is called nowadays). I guess I'm *exotic* to them.

Little do they know.

Wind blows said hair around my head as cold winter air whips down the road between the pines. It being winter is one of the main reasons I came here now. The weather makes little difference to me, but the opposite is true for most people. They will spend most of the winter inside their safe. warm homes, especially this far north. Fewer people mean less interference. Not that I'm scared of an altercation. That wouldn't stop me. I just find it better to lie low and avoid any confrontations. I'm so tired of them.

Tired of everything.

The unpleasantness of humanity.

Waiting a few months to take this trip hadn't been an issue. I have nothing but time, anyway.

Looking at the sign again, and that language I don't comprehend, I'm reminded how rarely I see something I haven't yet learned about and how much I don't care anymore. After a while, even the act of learning something new gets old.

I grab the fence with my bare hands. After all these years, it's still a solid structure. A monument to Soviet engineering. Ironic, given what is on the other side. I pull myself over in one fluid motion, easily clearing the barbed wire and landing softly on the clean snow beyond. No one comes to investigate. This place is deserted.

The city of Chernobyl stretches out before me. Or what's left of it. I first heard about the disaster a few years ago, but I hadn't understood or cared to understand the ramifications of what had happened. I've lived through many a disaster in my time (might have even caused one or two), so another one somewhere in the world was inconsequential. But as news filtered in over the ensuing weeks and months, a clearer picture presented itself and an idea began to form in my mind.

Then, a key discovery was made which solidified everything: the Elephant's Foot.

That's what I needed to find. If there is something on this earth that could finally kill me—finally end this eternity of flavorless repetition—then that might be it. A new type of danger. Radiation. A strange physical energy that attacks the cells, altering them in microscopic ways, changing the codes that program the machine of the human body.

And the Elephant's Foot is the queen of all radiation. A mass of melted concrete, glass, and other wastes from the meltdown. In a closed chamber below the reactor, this molten mound of rock pulsates with heat, emitting that sweet, sweet radiation. Enough radiation, they say, that if a person ever got close enough to look at it, they would die instantly. It's a real-life Medusa, so imbued with strange atomic energy that years later it's still too hot to touch. So hot it's slowly melting into the ground even as I stand here.

Being this close sparks a long dormant fire of excitement in my chest. It's been a long time since I've felt anything like that. Anticipation. The anticipation of death.

Death would be the best thing that has ever happened to me. It's the only thing I've never done.

Besides learning Russian, that is.

I trudge through the overgrown grass of what used to be a street. A long-abandoned apartment block rises from the trees. Its edges are crumbling masonry like a dry sandcastle. Funny how the quality of architectural craftsmanship was so much better hundreds—even thousands—of years ago.

The pyramids are the most obvious example. Not sure I've ever seen anything like them since their heyday. Gleaming scions of the gods of Earth, meant to keep their memories immortal. Little did they know that one of the slaves who helped build them would outlive them all by millennia.

And no, back then I didn't let anyone know about my…condition. I never did. Well, I did once. Two thousand years ago. That didn't end well. People are still talking about it.

My mind wanders a lot these days. So many memories. Good ones. Bad ones. And millions upon millions of indifferent ones. My earliest memories are vague. Primal. I don't know how long I've been here or how I came into existence. I do know that in all my memories, I was then as I am now. My soul (if I have one) shackled to my body. My body shackled to the earth. Never to be removed. At least, never to be removed by any method I've yet to try.

And, oh, how I have tried. For as long as I can remember, I've had low moments. Moments where I felt the extreme claustrophobia of my interminable existence and needed to make it terminable. The first I can recall was jumping off a cliff. The landing hurt only for a second. My bones cracked, my organs were crushed. My skull burst like a ripe melon on the rocks, brain matter leaking onto the ground. I remember all of that because I never lost consciousness. My body may have momentarily shut down all of its functions, but I was still there. After the initial pain of the impact and the destruction of my mortal body, I felt nothing. I even briefly thought I had succeeded. That I was a spirit floating free to my final resting place.

But then, as if the damage was being rewound, everything started to heal. My bones shifted and snapped back into place. My organs expanded and filled with fluids. My skull reconstituted itself, and my brain throbbed and grew from my spine like an infernal sea creature. I was a marionette coming to life.

The pain returned. The pain of the fall but slowed down to a snail's pace. My body breaking in reverse. Oh, it didn't take long. But I felt it. I felt every second of that reassembly. Afterwards, walking away from where I'd landed on the rocky ground, leaving behind a man shaped hole and a puddle of humors, it was as though nothing had even happened to me. It'd been the same in the past with accidental injuries. Those would happen from time to time.

But somehow I'd thought this jump would be different. That the intention mattered. That the curse of immortality could be broken by a grand gesture showing that I had deemed it over. But deeming it did not make it so.

I tried again many times. More falls. A few crushings. Burning (the most painful). Drowning (the most uncomfortable). Slicings and bleedings were unsuccessful. My wounds close and I have an endless supply of blood. Starvation doesn't work. I don't really need food or water, although it does help my mood to partake.

Eventually, around the year 1100 or so, after a decade of trying on the regular, I gave up. A few centuries later, I had some renewed interest in the endeavor when gunpowder became all the rage. Although novel and quick, the effect was the same. No matter how modern and damaging the technology, it was always extreme pain, dissociation, a more painful reconstitution, and then the inevitable realization that I had failed.

But this… What had happened to this town, this was different. This was something new. Something atomic. Something…primordial. I needed to find the Elephant's Foot. Luckily, I was prepared. I'd done my research, figured out everything about where it was, and how to get to it.

Being around as long as I have, you learn certain skills. Or maybe it's that sense you cannot fail. That no matter what you do, there are no consequences, so breaking into buildings and stealing paperwork isn't that big a deal. What's the worst that can happen to me? I get put in jail? There aren't any prisons that can hold me.

This time, though, everything went smoothly, and maps and information were acquired. That is how I knew what road to follow to get here, and what streets to take now that I'm within the city limits.

Past the crumbling apartment block, the city looks ghostly. Houses and buildings are silent sentinels covered in snow. The streets are cracked and pitted. Trees and plants appear where they shouldn't be. Nature aggressively pushes through the concrete and the frost, grasping at life (ironic, given my goal, I know), unaffected by whatever fallout is thrumming through the area.

Can I feel it? Is that something unnamable under the ground? A soft vibration emanating from below. So soft that I don't know if it's there or I'm imagining it. Is it agitating the snow around my feet ever so slightly, individual flakes dancing to the unknown music, or is it the wind?

Eons of living have taught me that life is mostly disappointments. A set of lows punctuated by fleeting highs which grow more and more sporadic over time. I can't even remember when my last high was. At least a hundred years. This is my long, dismal way of saying that I am seeing the glass half-empty here. The sarcophagus half-closed. There is no vibration. This plan is probably not going to work.

I follow the maps I memorized and concentrate on that imagined thrumming. Pretending that it's getting louder and closer as I pass more abandoned buildings, wind my way through an amusement park full of ancient circus relics, weave between a school of abandoned cars in the middle of a road, and shimmy under a collapsing gate that leads me to the Chernobyl Nuclear Power Plant.

At this point, contrary to my pessimism, the vibrations are definitely real. But even so, the power that is causing them may not be exceedingly deadly to the likes of me. There is only one way to find out. I need to get to Reactor #4.

Aside from the lack of people, the reactor compound does not otherwise look abandoned. Through some fluke of climate, the structures aren't covered in mounds of snow like the others, and the grounds are not overgrown with vines and trees like the rest of the town.

The compound's central feature is a wide building, like a factory or a warehouse. Surrounding the central building are various attached structures. More buildings with pipes and ladders and metal struts as decoration. The reactors. Unremarkable in every way. The eye is instead drawn to the lone smoke tower in the middle of the concrete assemblage. But that's not what I'm here for. I head towards my destination, the structure all the way to my left, cutting across a small fenced-in area laid with brown and withering grass. I see a tiny sign, frosted over, and imagine it says "Do Not Walk on Grass" in aggressive Cyrillic font.

The reactor housing stands before me, a concrete offshoot of the main building, like all the others. I know this one is #4, and I know somewhere in its mechanical depths lies the goal of this expedition. There are no doors on the outside. The entrance is through the main building, but I do not need to hunt for it. I gently place my hand on the concrete. Barely noticeable, but it's not as cold as one would expect out here in the northern country. A small hope. I rub my hands across the smooth cement. I can feel its mass. Solid and many feet thick.

I stand back and kick out with all my strength. My boot hits the concrete like a sledgehammer, crumbling and splintering the section before me. Three more big kicks, the cracks ringing out through the cold air, and a section of the wall starts to fall. I eagerly push the hundreds of pounds of chunks aside to reveal the interior.

A force hits me from the opening. There is nothing there but more walls and pipes and machinery, the inner workings of the reactor, but I can feel something. It's a feeling like when your stomach twists in knots from bad food, but instead it's happening to all of your organs. And your skin. And your brain. It doesn't quite hurt, but it is very unpleasant. It's a feeling I want to run from. Want to escape. A healthy flight reaction of a healthy body.

This is good. This is what I need. The eagerness wells up within me. I twist the primal reaction to escape into a primal need to push forward. I rush into the structure. The electric sensation surrounds me, but I can feel the source. Something ahead of me and below.

With no heed for my personal safety (I haven't heeded that in a while), I charge forward, ripping machinery and pipes out of my way. Crashing through walls, drywall or concrete, it doesn't matter. Both fall before me. I pound down stairwells, run through corridors. It's dark but I don't care. I'm navigating by other means now. My fists and body get cut up from the charge. Slices and bruises. Blood coats my arms and face. But this time, the wounds aren't healing immediately. I let out an actual physical shriek of happiness, a wild call of a madman hurtling towards his doom and happy for the privilege to do it.

It's getting closer.

The Elephant's Foot.

Medusa.

I hear myself chanting, "Meeedduuuuusssasssaaa! Meeedduuusssaa!"

As I draw closer, the twisting sensation in my guts gets stronger, turning my innards into a sack of roiling snakes. My words are slurring. It's getting harder to move. Harder to make the muscles of my mouth speak clearly. Harder to get my body to go in the direction I want it to. I'm deep in the bowels of the machine. Medusa is so close. I turn to my right. She's there, only a few feet away. Too dark to see her, but I *feel* her. A rushing in my ears like a wave. My blood foaming in my veins. The skin around my hands ready to burst. My brain, a wet towel, filling my head.

I dive forward, hit an unmoving wall. The last obstacle to my destination. I take a step back, slam my shoulder into it. The wall subtly shifts but holds. Even in my frenzied state, I'm weaker than I usually am.

I take a step back—"Medusa!"—and hit it again. Something cracks. I'm not sure if it's me or the wall. But the wall is still standing.

Another step back.

"MEDUSA!"

I crash into the rock, hurtle through it, and fall to the ground. The pain, it's unspeakable now. My broken body. Organs grinding to a halt. The chemistry within me causing reactions that should never exist outside of a human body, let alone in.

But she's here. My goal. Just a little in front of me, out of my reach.

I crawl toward her. One leg doesn't work. One arm is fiery pain and bent at an unnatural angle. I drag myself. My skin sloughs off in wet ribbons as I slide towards her. *Medusa.* My hand hits her first, like touching a thousand needles. But I don't pull back. I rub my palm across her surface. Melted glass and stone. Ancient lava, still hot to the touch. Sizzling my skin. Scorching it. The heat reaches my bones, and it feels like they conduct electricity, like the pain travels through my broken skeleton, hitting every part of me from the inside.

Still, I drag myself on top of her. Lay down on her. Lay down on Medusa. I can feel my body melting. Organs turning to juice. I can't move anymore. Every nerve in my body being twisted into ropes and shredded down to their core. I'm no longer a man-shape. I'm a flat ball of pain. A giant amoeba of suffering. The hurt is becoming bigger than I am. Medusa is filling me up. Inflating me to bursting with agony.

My body is dying. I wait for the torment to end. It will soon. The moment will come. The moment when my spirit dissociates from the body, awaiting its inevitable reconstitution, or the moment when I just cease to exist. I lay there, agony-made-flesh, hoping for the latter. Hoping when this ends it's because my life has finally ended too.

But…the end never comes. No end to my life. No end to the torture. Somehow, I'm both alive and dead. My body clenched tight, holding my consciousness within. I'm not me anymore. I am torment.

And I'm still here.

And I can't get away.

I can't move. I have no legs, no arms. I am nothing but suffering and nothing is changing, and I cannot escape. I can't think and I can't speak, but the words run through my head now. A name. *Medusa! Medusa!* But this time, instead of a mantra of hope, it's a cry of anger.

An accusation.

A plea.

Medusa!

THE PIPER

Hannah Birss

From the Desk of "Father" Jester, Concerning the Events that Occurred in The Town of Hamelin, Lower Saxony, On the 26th of June in the Year of Our Lord 1284

We should have paid attention when the rats began to disappear.

I could be forgiven for my ignorance at the beginning. At the time, I lived alone, in a small, forgotten shack on the very outskirts of the town. My home was close to the Weser River, and I did my best to limit my exposure to the townsfolk of Hamelin and the casual cruelty they aimed at me.

They called me Jester—not because they thought I was possessed of a sense of humor or particular wit, but because I was hideous to look at and this amused the townsfolk. My appearance was not the result of a terrible accident, unless you count the accident of birth. I assume I came forth from my mother's womb with this affliction, as I was placed on the doorstep of the church as a newborn, my face sagging, my left side weak and barely able to move. Half of my face hangs numbly, without a semblance of strength or movement. My eye droops, and while I eventually managed to learn how to walk, it was with one foot dragging slightly behind me and my back hunched. I had focused on building up the muscle in my arm, and so have full use of it, though it sits at an awkward angle to my body.

I grew up as a foundling raised by the church in the attached monastery. There, I learned my letters through careful observation, and quickly became able to read and write. Though many of the monks looked upon me with disdain, the abbot took me under his wing and nurtured my love for God as well as for the written word. After he died, several unfortunate circumstances occurred in tandem around the monastery, and I made an appropriate scapegoat. The new head of the monastery tossed me out onto the streets at the tender age of twelve. There, I fashioned myself clothes from the cast-offs of the village, a pied outfit roughly sewn and cobbled together that only cemented the nickname I had carried with me since birth. Now, I cannot remember the name the abbot had originally given me. I'm sure that it was something appropriately pious. All that is left to me is Jester, and so Jester I am.

The disappearance and departure of the rats did not happen all at once. A few households remarked within my earshot on how the plague of rodents in their households had seemed reduced, as if the tide was finally beginning to turn in the constant war against the vermin. There were no bodies, no ominous signs, nothing to arouse suspicion. There were simply less of them.

I saw a strange exodus of them once. I had gone to the river to fill my old waterskin, and there stood a group of people at the muddy edge, broken apart into two sides like the red sea. Between them poured a horde of rats, running and writhing and falling all over each other in their rush to escape the town. They went into the water as they fled to the opposite bank of the Weser, swimming with their small arms flailing and their long bald tails swishing behind them like rudders. The noise—the panicked squeaks, the sounds of their claws scrabbling at the rocky ground—was overwhelming to my ears. I lingered further downstream, only creeping closer when I saw that the people were adequately distracted by the tide of vermin.

The townsfolk talked amongst themselves as they watched—the same things said over and over, a call and response that didn't contribute anything to the conversation. I tuned them out, observing the rats with a growing sense of dread. I could not put my finger on what made me so uneasy; it was different, and different was usually a sign of something bad, something to be aware of, a concept that had been ingrained into me long ago. The monks and townsfolk had seen to that.

To prove the point, a nearby villager elbowed his companion in the ribs, pointing in my direction. They turned toward me, sneers on their faces.

"Why don't you run into the river with them, Jester?" one of them mocked. "Do us all a favor?" His friend leaned down, snatching a dirty rock and whipping it at me.

I made a hasty retreat, slinking away as they continued to hurl their taunts and rocks, which stung against my hunched back. Their words themselves did not bother me; I had long ago developed both a literally and figuratively thick skin. To them, I was a hideous creature and therefore could not possibly be a man of reason or worthy of basic respect. However, injury was a very real worry of mine. With my own ailments and physical disabilities, combined with the solitary nature of my existence, any true injury or resulting infection could have disastrous, life-ending consequences.

I still should have told someone about that first odd night. I was wandering—searching for food or bits of clothing left abandoned in the streets or refuse piles, walking along the river's edge and down dim alleys. I preferred not to be visible during the day for obvious reasons, and the blanket of darkness afforded me comfort and safe passage. I was moving slowly, my eyes scanning back and forth, when I realized that I was not alone.

Another figure—tall, long and lean, a shadow lingering at the edges of human habitation— moved slowly through the streets, peering behind old clutter and moving aside piles of rubbish, frustration evident in every jagged, angry movement. In hindsight, I believe he was looking for the rats.

He moved to a window and made as if to open it. I called out sternly then, hoping to interrupt whatever nefarious plan he had in mind. It was then that he turned to me. No, not he—*it*, for it was not a man, not truly.

It was tall, much taller than I. His limbs were disproportionate to his body, and his long white fingers reminded me of spider legs wrapping around a windowsill. It was ghostly pale, mouth large, reminding me of a carp—a wide, grim slash in the middle of its face. His eyes caught my own, and they burned with a strange yellow fire.

The blood in my veins turned to ice. It must have been a *nachzehrer*, a revenant. Later, I would learn many other names that the creature went by—*strigoi, nosferatu, shtriga, vampire.*

I began to back away slowly. In a methodical manner, it stalked toward me. His eyes bored into mine. From his lips spilled a simple tune: three long notes hummed over and over again. I could make myself move no further. Within my head I heard a song, a complicated rising and falling, a melody that merged with the humming, overlapping one another until I found myself with no control over my body. I was trapped within the music, so wrapped up in his song that I couldn't even think to pray.

He took a few final steps, and a cold hand lifted to cradle my face. His burning eyes roamed over my twisted features, and it cocked its head. It moved me this way and that, the infernal song holding me tight in his grasp. In my strangeness, I was like a specimen to him—his clammy fingers fluttered over the numb half of my face. At one point, it stuck a finger in my mouth as if I was a horse, the pad of his finger prodding at my teeth and the inside of my cheeks. I followed his every move, examining him as it examined me. It was fascinating and terrifying to behold.

I did not mean to bite him—the rest of me was still as a statue, but when it poked at a part of my inner cheek it was pure reflex, and my teeth clamped down against his skin, drawing out a thick, viscous fluid that spurted onto my tongue and filled it with the taste of iron and of rot. His blood was cold. If I could have, I would have spat it out, but I was still an insect caught in the web of a spider and could not move under my own volition. With a hiss, it yanked my long brown hair until my neck was violently exposed. One of his long arms reached around to my lower back, holding me as if I was a lover. I saw a flash of long, sharp teeth before it buried them in my neck. It was excruciatingly painful, yet it was the closest thing to an embrace I had ever known at that point in my life.

When it was finished, it dropped me and turned and strode away. I lay there in the cold mud, blood seeping from the wounds on my neck. I drifted in and out of consciousness, that infernal song vibrating within my skull until the first rays of blessed sun shone their light over the horizon. At that, the sounds of the music faded away, and I found myself rousing. I dragged myself home, where I fell into a deep sleep that I did not awaken from until the late afternoon.

God forgive me, I did not know what to do at that time. I knew no one would believe me—that no one would believe without evidence that a *nachzehrer* had taken up residence in the town of Hamelin. In fact, they were far more likely to accuse me of misdeeds or consorting with the devil or some other thin claim and have me burned at the stake. And so, I continued to keep quiet.

Several disappearances were reported in the week that followed— drunken men and women of ill-repute going missing after dark and turning up several days later on the banks of the Weser. The rumor mill was not kind to them; they were all considered the lowest dredges of society, only a step above myself, and so their deaths were met with nothing but a shrug or a mean smirk. Certainly, no one attributed their deaths to a revenant. Only I knew, and years later I can still feel their blood on my hands as my period of inaction lengthened.

Why was I not killed? The question still vexes me. Was I over-full of blood? Was the creature not so hungry as to need to drain me? I slept poorly for those days, always waiting for the *nachzehrer* to knock on my door and finish his meal, or for the village to come for me as a scapegoat with their pitchforks and torches. Yet neither of them ever did—and as my anxiety grew, I stopped making my journeys into town altogether.

It had been two weeks since my attack, and days since the last drained body washed up. I suppose the *nachzehrer* grew hungry and impatient. It desired a feast—and so, it made for itself one.

One night, as I lay curled in my nest of rags, that same song crept in through the broken window of my squalid home. Unlike last time, I felt no draw to it. It was not meant for me. Gathering my courage, I opened my door a crack to see something approaching from the distance, heading toward the town. As it drew closer, I saw it was a child. Behind it were a few more, all of them occupants of homes in the outlying areas of Hamelin, all of them walking unsteadily on their feet, their eyes glazed and fixed on the horizon. The same three notes, repeated over and over again, echoing through the streets. The song itself came from the bell tower, amplified as the creature sang into the bell.

I slid through the crack in my door and reached out to grasp the shoulder of a young boy as he staggered past me. He shook me off, paid me no heed. I may as well not have been there for all the attention he gave me. The horror of the situation dawned on me. I ran down the road, weaving in and out of the parade of children. As soon as I reached the outskirts of Hamelin, I began to do my best to rouse the townsfolk.

I pounded on doors, not even stopping to see if the people inside had awakened before moving onto the next. People were slow to stir, but I shouted as I went. Parents awoke to find their young children's beds empty. The children marched, deaf to me and their parents, struggling and screaming as people began to pin them down or lift them up. Frantic parents ran through the streets, calling their young ones' names as they roughly turned children around, staring into blank faces.

The song had stopped—the *nachzehrer* presumably having descended from the belltower and moved to the front of the dark procession—but the children continued onwards, in their fugue-like state, listening to music only they and I could hear that led them to the edge of the forest. Someone began to ring the church bells in alarm, adding to the cacophony, as I continued to run through the town, doing my best to wake others. The children stepped purposefully into the dark shadows of the trees, and when their parents tried to follow, the little ones vanished as if ghosts.

After what seemed like hours, but only could have been no more than fifteen minutes, the town had turned from sleep into roaring chaos. The music in my head faded more and more until the children began violently erupting from their hypnotic states. They burst into tears and screamed for their parents, lashing out with their small fists and feet in their confusion.

When dawn broke, the final count was confirmed. Seventy-two children were gone, having followed the revenant into the woods. A great wail went up through the city. The church bells clanged endlessly, and the streets were filled with weeping parents and grieving families. In the town square, hundreds assembled to discuss what had happened and what would be done.

I stood off to the side in an alleyway, silently observing from the shadows so as not to draw attention to myself. After much debate, it was decided the lost children would be considered a sacrifice in the hope that the *nachzehrer* would be sated and move on.

I couldn't believe what I was hearing, how these parents were so quick to abandon their children. They took God's most precious gift and had decided it was worthy of sacrifice in the vague possibility the *nachzehrer* would leave them alone. Even the men of the church seemed willing to abandon them, regardless of how the souls of the children were at stake.

Instead of rescue, the town began to bustle with spiritual preparations for a potential return, protecting those who were left behind with no thoughts as to the ones that were taken.

I do not wish to speak more on the townsfolk. To this day, I keep a hard place in my heart for them that no amount of prayer or fasting has been able to soften. I had been abandoned as a child. I knew the pain of it, the heartbreak, but I had never been abandoned to a sure death, as these parents had done to their own flesh and blood. I resolved to find them myself and rescue them as I had never been.

It was late morning by the time I returned to my shack. During the previous long nights, I had fashioned myself a series of stakes, whittling endlessly. I collected my makeshift weapons and prayed over them. I went in my faith, kissing the weathered cross that hung on a scavenged bit of string around my neck. I was tired, but my body was strung tight like the strings of a lute, and I trembled with each step. I circled the town until I came to the tree line where the last of the children had vanished. I stood there for a moment, unsure, falling into a practiced silence. There were no footprints, and the first twinges of uncertainty begin to creep in, coloring my determination.

I closed my eyes, and that's when I heard it. A small thread of music. It wasn't so much a sound as it was a feeling. It was like a thread in my head, a vibration that when I focused on it, I could sense a small tug. I took a small step toward the origin of the music, and then another. With each step, the vibration grew, and I found myself humming along, following the trail left for me.

I don't know how far I walked—I was so focused on following the string of music by pulling myself along it that distance had no meaning. I sang to myself, and the connection between me and the revenant grew stronger. Deeper into the mountains I traveled, spotting more and more signs that a great many people had gone this way before me. Small bits of cloth and hair were caught on brambles, and the ground was stirred up by many feet.

By this point, the hum in my head had expanded to my entire body. Lightning ran through my veins, and many times I wanted to close my eyes and give into the music entirely. It was only by repeatedly pricking my fingers on one of the points of my stakes until I drew blood that I was able to maintain my sanity.

I came eventually to a cave cut into the mountainside. Roughly the size and shape of a man, the footprints led into it. I gathered the pieces and quickly assembled a torch, desperate to reach the children before the sun sank below the mountain range and the creature was again in its element. Once I had, I used my chipped flint to light it and went to enter the passageway. I turned sideways, squeezing into it, my shoulder and hump being scraped raw by the stone. The sting of it further shook me out of the music's trance, and by the time the passageway opened up into a large cave, I was almost free of its influence entirely.

I came out into a large and shadowy cavern. A large fire burned within the damp dark, around which the missing children huddled. Their eyes were dull and glazed as they huddled together like lambs, the smoke circling up and out through a natural hole in the ceiling. They did not so much as glance up as I entered.

Several of the children had already been drained, their bodies tossed aside against the cavern walls like so much refuse. My heart wept at the sight. Their small, still corpses stood as an accusation of my inaction, as well as a testament to their parents' abandonment. I will carry that image with me until I die.

And there he was—there *it* was. On the opposite bank of the fire, laying completely prone in ragged, stained clothes, its skin even paler than before. Its eyes were closed, its body completely still while the sun held sway. My head began to throb with the silent music again as I approached. I pulled out one of my stakes, and I hovered it above the creature's chest as I knelt next to him. It did not move, but three frantic notes reverberated through me. Three words, repeating over and over again.

Put. It. Down.

My hands trembled, and I found myself struggling to put the stake against its chest.

Put. It. Down.

I tried to stab the *nachzehrer*, but my arms locked at the last second and the stake glanced harmlessly off the creature's ribs.

Put. It. Down.

The music in my head swelled into a crescendo, and I fought with all my might the urge to drop the stake. Sweat beaded on my forehead, and my eyes darted nervously around the room. They fell upon the dead children, and my heart constricted. I found my lips moving as I began to repeat the lord's prayer. My faith gave me strength, and within myself welled the will to drive the stake into the chest of the unmoving revenant.

Blood sprayed across my face, the saltiness of it stinging where my lips were chapped and raw. Without thinking, I licked my lips. Again and again, I stabbed the beast, blood spattering my hands and my pied clothing. The music stopped. When there was nothing left but a bloody pile of flesh, I stood, crying and shaking, and dragged the remains over to the waiting flames, throwing them in. They sputtered for a moment, but quickly caught fire. As it began to burn, behind me the children began to cry and scream, asking terrified questions. I knew then that its hold over them had ended, and I turned to tend to them.

In the end, some of the children chose to return to Hamelin. As we said goodbye, the eldest carrying the bodies of the children who hadn't made it, I prayed that they arrived safely and were delivered into the loving arms of their parents. For those that had become victims, I prayed for their deliverance into the arms of God and for burial in the safety of consecrated ground.

But thirty or so refused to go back to their parents, citing difficult childhoods, rampant abuse, and the stinging betrayal of being abandoned to the vampire. Despite his "death," I found myself still able to hear whispers of the *nachzehrer's* music—and like a hound, I could follow those threads back to wherever it had come from. Because of this, I was able to find an abandoned mountain tunnel further back in the lair—a system of caves the creature must have traversed in his hunt for blood. We did not know where else to go, or what else to do, so we decided to follow it. We that remained gathered a number of torches and went back under the mountain.

After several days of wandering the caves and following that fading music, we found an exit, squinting into the bright light. Smoke wafted across a pale sky above the treetops, and when we followed it, we came to a quiet village where another, older monastery loomed over them. We made quite an entrance—a crippled man dressed in pied clothing leading thirty children through the town square. When people approached us with nervous anger, we told them where we had come from, what had happened, and what we had done. The relief on their faces had been plain, and they quickly explained their emotions to us. It seems that years ago, the *nachzehrer* had taken up residence in the moldering monastery above them, preying on the people of the town below. In desperation, they had made a clumsy nighttime attack on it. They described it as a literal bloodbath, as men and women had been frozen in place by its horrible tune, and it had slaughtered them mercilessly. But in the end, it was a bitter success, and they drove the *nachzehrer* into the mountains.

After conferring amongst themselves, they offered us the monster's lair out of gratitude and guilt. We moved into those drafty, leaking halls, and with the help of some of the townsfolk, I built my "orphanage" of sorts. There were, of course, some delays in integration, but now, several decades on, the place is repaired and many of the children have grown and gone into town to raise their own families. They visit me often, and the other abandoned or orphaned children that I have taken in.

For the most part, my life has been well-lived. I am comfortable and loved, respected by my children and the townsfolk, despite my twisted appearance. I never gave up my colorful clothing—though the scraps are of much better quality, and they are stitched together with love and brightly colored thread.

Some nights I still wake drenched in a cold sweat, the haunting music echoing through the halls we have spent so much time painstakingly turning into a home. Occasionally, there are accusations from the townsfolk below, but they are always quick to be silenced and their fears laid to rest.

So what if my children are quicker to respond than other children, more gentle and more pliable, if only when I sing three notes in quick succession?

So what if the sun brings more pain than it used to, and so what if I have aged very little in the decades that have passed since I tasted the *nachzehrer's* blood?

God works in mysterious ways.

HER OWN TERMS

B.K. Loomis

REGAN HAD KILLED people before. Plenty of people, over two hundred and fifty years. Some from hunger—fledgling accidents with lovers, mostly; accidents he'd learned from, after the tears—others in desperation or rage or fear.

But Frieda stayed with him. She, above all others.

The way she'd transitioned in a torturously slow few seconds, from the ecstasy and euphoria of being bitten to the faint gasps, pawing feebly at his chest as her life slipped away. It was too late by then, too much of her blood gone, her light snuffed out before her body had caught up. All he could do was take the last few swallows of her wine-flavored blood, usher her into death quickly.

She'd asked for a pleasurable end, after all.

Sometimes he thought she'd remembered something in those last moments of her existence. Maybe she'd been trying to gasp out final words, some instructions for what little family she had. He would've delivered them if she'd been coherent. Maybe it was the last vestiges of self-preservation kicking in, her body's instinctive attempt at a struggle, raised far too late.

In his more self-tortured hours, staring at the ceiling of his basement room while the world above played in the sun and he failed to sleep,

Regan wondered if she might've regretted it. Maybe she'd realized she didn't want to die under a man that was practically a stranger, that her desire to die happy and warm in someone's arms had meant something entirely different than she thought it had.

It didn't matter in the end, he told himself. What was done was done. He couldn't change anything and, though he often asked why she was there when she came to visit him, she never answered.

She would come tonight. It had been too long.

Regan rose from his bed when the light through the curtains over his basement window changed from gold to bloody orange. He was well fed after a visit with a lover, held in his sitting room (she'd wondered why he wanted her on the couch rather than his bed—he didn't have the words to tell her the truth), so there was no cause to go out tonight other than boredom; a constant companion in his centuries, too familiar to turn away.

He set himself to tidying up, a mostly pointless task. Made the bed, barely disturbed by his attempt at sleep. Straightened the pillows in his chair. Wiped the dust from his bookshelves and the little black urn with pink lilies on it, then vacuumed more dust from the floor. Fed the vacuum bag full of powder to the furnace, which ate it gladly and sent a puff of smoke into the air to be collected by the wind. Checked his freezer. Still humming softly in its corner, the emergency supply of pig blood inside as unappetizing as ever.

The breathing began as the light at the window turned to scarlet. Soft sounds easily attributable to shifting fabric or a mouse in another room. As the light shifted to bruised purple, the breaths became more definite, with hitches and soft gasps that couldn't be mistaken for a towel sliding off the guest bathroom counter.

He slowed in his cleaning, unable to focus. Picked up the unread books on his nightstand, deposited them on the correct shelves, picked up a couple of books that wouldn't require much thought to read (especially because he couldn't read while she was here, never could) and set them down where the others had been. Then he sat on the bed, watching the door.

Frieda appeared there after a few minutes. She hesitated in the doorway, leaning against the doorjamb as she let out a quiet sob, her hair hanging down over her face. A familiar chill of dread ran through him, looking through her nude, ice-pale body to the sitting room and stairs beyond.

He reminded himself that he was just as unnatural, just as frightening, a half-living corpse ruled by hunger and shallow survival.

The half-living corpse that'd killed her.

Regan pulled back the blankets he only seldom used, laying down on his side.

She stumbled across the room to join him, shivering and sniffling. He held out his arm to guide her to his chest, where she wrapped her skinny, mottled arms too tightly around him and began to cry. All he could do now was pull the blankets up around them both, rest his chin on the top of her head, and wait.

Regan met her in a nightclub where he'd been courting a former lover. He'd gone to the bathroom, leaving Regan to wait at the bar, trying not to look like an eternally youthful old man, sourly judging the music kids liked these days—as he was—when he spotted a plain, skinny, middle-aged woman watching him from the other end of the bar, fidgeting with the neckline of her faded floral maxi dress. She wore long skirts to cover the port on her leg, as she told him later. Most of her other veins had collapsed by that point.

If he breathed in deeply, he could smell she was ill. He wondered if the humans walking past could, too.

He turned his attention back to the whiskey he was pretending to drink, expecting to watch her staring out of the corner of his eye as he often caught humans doing when they saw—or sensed—what he was.

The next thing he knew, she was tapping him on the shoulder. Quietly asking, her voice quiet and eyes pale: "Are you... are you a vampire?"

She'd done her homework. Wore him down enough to admit his condition after a while because she had a proposition for him and hoped he was either kind enough or predatory enough to accept it. It was the latter.

All vampires were predators, after all; it was just a matter of how they showed their teeth. That was how they survived, and surviving was their only choice.

Dead Frieda shook, sobbing in his arms, her whole body tensing as she squeezed him until his ribs ached, pressing her face into the crook of his shoulder. He shushed her, staring at the wall as he stroked her cold hair, her frigid skin stealing the little warmth his body held. He didn't mind lending it.

The cancer had eaten through one of her kidneys, part of her liver, was making itself at home in her heart, lungs, and a million other places in her body. At some point, Regan's lover had texted him, telling him he wasn't feeling well and was taking a cab home, probably covering for jealousy at seeing him talking to some woman at the bar. Regan didn't look out for him as he left. They hadn't been together for the conversation. They'd barely been together at all.

"There's nothing left to do. I have a few weeks, a month at most. What I'm in now is called a 'last strength surge.'"

She was still toying with her dress, hiding her eyes as Regan kept his on her, looking for some sign of a scam or trap.

"If you want me to turn you, I won't."

"No, I don't. I really, really don't. I'm tired. I'm so fucking tired. I'm sick and I hurt and I've been through too much shit. I'm done. Really."

Regan shook his head, running his finger over his whiskey glass. "Then what do you want from me?"

He asked her that again now. She didn't answer, acted like she hadn't heard him. Probably hadn't. She'd never shown any sign of hearing him or being aware of him in any way other than burrowing into his arms, even when he'd been afraid, then angry, yelled at her, tried to hit her, tried to drag her from his bed to get her out of his home, out of his mind. No sense reasoning with whatever she was, but he tried.

He went quiet, closing his eyes, breathing in what remained of her rotting-organ smell.

"I have a few weeks, a month at most. I don't want to wait that long. I don't want to lose my mind or start shitting myself or—or anything else I watched my mom and granddad go through with this garbage." She looked up at him with sunken eyes. "I live alone. I'm broke. I've been in and out of psych wards and hospitals my whole fucking life. My family doesn't give enough of a shit to come take care of me, not even my dad. I have no one. I'm still a virgin, unless you count an orderly who took advantage, and I don't. I want to be with someone. I want one day of my life to be fun and warm and not trash, and I want to die happy. That's all I want, and I'll pay you with everything I have to help me do that."

Her voice started to tremble near the end of the last sentence. After a second of gritting her teeth, she unzipped her purse, pulling out a wrapped paper package.

"This is ten thousand. I sold almost everything I own," she said, her voice shaking as she held up the package and shook it, too. "I have ten thousand dollars left, and you're handsome and you're a vampire and you don't seem all crazy like young vampires, so I know you're probably good in bed after however long you've been alive, and I know you need sex and blood and probably money. I want—"

Tears ran down her face and she started to curl in on herself, coughing around them. Some drunk frat boys nearby stared, and Regan gave them a brief glare. They turned back to their own business as he rested his hand on her side, leaning in to shield her, acting the pale, sad-eyed gentleman. But really, he'd smelled the blood on her breath. Couldn't help it.

She met his gaze, her eyes so intense she looked almost angry.

"If you give me twenty-four hours of your time, you can have whatever part of this money doesn't go to cremating me. I want to spend a day feeling like someone gives a shit about me. I want you to treat me like your girlfriend for one full day, and take my virginity, and then... and then I want you to kill me."

There were details, but that was it. She wanted him to help her live, then help her die.

Regan needed the money. He needed the blood too, always. He thought that was all there was to it. It sounded simple enough. He'd killed people before. Plenty. He'd also loved people before. Plenty.

"Frieda," he whispered into the top of her head, where her hair had started to fall out before he'd killed her. "You remember when I took you out to the boardwalk for the night carnival?"

She kept crying. Tears flooded the front of his shirt. They would be gone as soon as she left, a few hours before morning.

"You remember how you got that ice cream, and we went and sat together at the end of the pier and just watched the moon?"

If she did, if there were any memories left in this shell of her, she didn't say. She just gasped, her breath catching in her throat, then released it with a groaning sob.

"That was nice," he said. After a moment's pause to rub at her arms, trying and failing to bring warmth to her, he continued. "I wish we could have done that again. I wish I could have shown you more. There's so much to see out there."

Frieda kept her face against his shoulder, seeing nothing.

She'd had a pseudo contract for him to sign, agreeing to what he'd already agreed to in words and an embrace. He didn't have to honor it, truthfully. He could've coaxed her outside of the club or into the bathrooms and just killed her there. But Regan liked to think he still had some honor in him, and besides, he didn't see the harm in waiting.

It was to start that Friday, when the places she wished to visit would be open. She'd never been to most of them—it seemed like she'd hardly been outside of her house, the hospital, and the local grocery store since she was a teenager. He agreed to help her get to where she wanted to go with his gentlemanly arm to lean on, take her virginity, kill her, and return her remains to her family. Simple enough.

When he met with her that Friday evening, just after sundown, he did so with all the seductive charm two and a half centuries of life had given him, purring sweet words and kissing her hand. That wasn't what she wanted. By the second hour of the first activity, walking through an amusement park, his arm was around her shoulders, and she'd convinced him to wear a glittery cat-ear headband she'd won, and a stuffed rabbit peeked out of his coat pocket. When they stopped to rest, which was often, he usually found himself laughing.

She'd started wheezing and had to sit for about an hour after the park closed. Then they got a cab. She kissed him for the first time in the back seat, and they rested their foreheads together, sharing breath for a long while until the cab stopped to let them out downtown.

Frieda couldn't dance or drink alcohol, but he carried her up the steep stairs to the second floor of the club to listen to the music, watch the dancers through the glass railings, and talk. Suddenly, he was reminiscing about the music that had been around when he was living, and how it had felt to watch as the sonograms he knew were replaced by vinyl, discs, and digital. She rested her head on his shoulder and listened.

When there came a lull in his speech, she asked him what the name of his favorite song had been when he was young. She looked it up online, managed to find a digitized old recording of the same song, taken over a century and a half after he died. They listened on her earbuds, one for each of them, heads together.

Regan started to hum that song now, the sound vibrating through his chest where her face pressed into it. He'd all but forgotten the tune until that night in the club. He went to the trouble of finding a record of it, as old as possible, and a record player old enough to play it. Spent a good chunk of the money she'd given him on it, money he'd intended to leave the city and start fresh with, just in case anyone with strong prejudices suspected what he was. Another part had gone to getting Frieda cremated and shipped home, as she'd asked.

The remaining three thousand hadn't seemed as important as it had when she'd entrusted him with it. He found a bake sale table for the family of a cancer patient, left out in front of their house and looking abandoned while out walking one night. He approached their front door, pushed the rest of the money through the mail slot, and walked away. He barely even saw the bald little girl in the picture taped to the front of the table. Didn't need to. He hoped the money did something for the pain.

He'd told her that story when she visited before, rambled on about it for hours sometimes, even though it was a two-minute story. She didn't seem moved.

After the club, she needed to rest. Regan took her home, but she wasn't ready to go all the way, so they just kissed for a while, then slept in his bed. Their sleep was light, patchy. She wasn't used to sleeping during the day, and he had things to think about. He held her and sorted through memories to pass the time, just as he did now, almost a year after her passing.

When she woke, they had but six hours left until her scheduled end. She wanted to go to the all-night carnival down on the boardwalk, so that was where he took her. They walked together for a long time. Played some games, won a prize that they gave to a young couple having some bad luck on the ring toss, shared some jokes and pleasantries. Got one scoop of cookies and cream in a sugar cone for her and sat on the bench at the end of the pier to watch the moon dance on the water.

She rested her head on his shoulder when she finished her ice cream. He wrapped his arm around her. She thanked him. Thanked him again. Thanked him a third time and started to cry. He held her hand, hushing her and telling her he was just glad he could help. For the first time in centuries, he didn't have to lie.

Then, Frieda looked up at him and told him that she'd only known him a couple of days, but that she thought she loved him. He told her the same. And for the second time in centuries, he didn't have to lie.

They kissed for a while. Her lips were sweet, tasted like ice cream but not enough for his body to reject it. He helped her crawl into his lap, straddling him in plain view of those back on the boardwalk, and she worked her fingers into his hair. When they broke apart, she took a breath, resting her forehead against his.

"Regan," she breathed, her eyes squeezed shut, her breaths shallow. "I think I'm ready."

He started to doze near the third hour of her visit, his humming breaking into fragments of a tune, then silence. She kept crying, her hands working in the back of his shirt. He'd been stroking her hair, but now his fingers were tangled through it, still, as he drifted in and out of a half-dream. He dreamed so seldom anymore that he thought the snatches of an ocean dancing and flashing in the moonlight below worn, salt-stained planks were real for a moment, that he was laying there on the bench with her and had imagined everything else. He could almost hear the faint music of the carnival behind them, smell the wafts of sweets and sweat and the rushing blood of the warm-bodied.

A clock chimed. He opened his eyes to a dark, musty basement room, and Frieda, cold, still crying into his chest.

He closed his eyes and chased the dream.

They walked down the street from the boardwalk to a convenience store. There, they bought what they'd need: lubricant, condoms, a bottle of wine for her—no sense protecting what remained of her liver now, though neither of them wanted to think of cleaning her down there afterward, hence the condoms. The cashier, after raising an eyebrow at the items, called them a cute couple as Regan paid, Frieda leaning against him with her eyes closed.

Frieda mumbled, "He's the cute half," cracking her eyes open to grin up at him.

The cashier said, "Long day, huh?"

Regan could only reply, "Long day," and give a fake smile, his voice tighter than he'd expected.

After the cab dropped them off at home, he brought her to his bedroom, lit candles he hadn't bothered with in years, and sat with her on the edge of the bed, watching as she took pain medication with a glass of wine. It would make his head spin when he drank from her. He'd be nauseous as his body processed her diseased blood for several days. But blood was blood. Fresh blood was vital for him. It was unheard of to have someone give all of their blood willingly. He should have felt thankful.

His shoulders were tense. He couldn't relax them. He made himself focus on Frieda, her telling him what she wanted, how she wanted him to hold her.

"I just... I just want you to touch me. Touch me like you love me," she said, staring at the empty wineglass in her hands. "And maybe bite me early on, so I don't start to hurt, because of the... the... you know, the chemical that releases when you bite people—"

"Yeah," he said softly. "Anything specific you want to try?"

She shook her head.

"I just want to feel good. Be kinda gentle with me so it doesn't hurt, and nothing kinky. Other than that...whatever you want, I guess."

"Got it," he said, swallowing hard, feeling like he was speaking to a death row prisoner. "Is there... anything else you want to say? Anyone you want to—to call?"

Frieda shook her head. "I already said everything. It's all in that letter I gave you for my dad."

She still didn't meet his eyes. He took the wineglass gently, cupped one of her hands in both of his, her skin so cold that it felt like he was warming her even with his body running at room temperature. He dipped his head to catch her gaze.

"Are you sure you want to do this? Maybe we should wai—"

"I'm sure." She said quickly, firmly. "If I wait, I might change my mind or get stuck on deciding or chicken out and die slowly. I don't want that. Please. I want this. I want it to be like this."

With that, Frieda pulled her hands free of his, drew his face to hers, and kissed him.

He woke to dead Frieda giving a particularly hard sob as her hands clutched at the back of his shirt. The clock across the room told him it'd been five hours since she arrived. She'd leave in an hour. Just a little more. Only a little more.

"It's okay, Frieda," he murmured into her hair. "It's almost over."

She didn't respond. Of course she didn't.

"You need to move on," he said, even if he was unsure if she was sentient or just a memory. Worth a try. "You need to go where your mother is."

Perhaps she was a hallucination. She waited until he was alone, after all. Waited until no one could see her having crawled into his arms, often pinning him on his back with her frail body that seemed so immeasurably heavy after her death. He'd heard of vampires losing their minds and hallucinating after starving for a while. Trouble was, he hadn't been without blood for more than a couple of weeks since the year he'd turned. Even then, it had only been a couple of months before he folded and took his first life.

Hallucination or not, she didn't speak. Just kept crying, tears and mucus soaking his chest.

He sighed, starting to stroke her hair again.

"Or you could stay. Waste both our time. You could be reincarnated by now, you know. Or in Heaven, or whatever's out there. Heaven sounds nice. Bet there's ice cream up there."

She keened, her voice broken. She sounded congested. He wondered if her throat hurt, if her jaw cramped up from her grimacing. He rubbed at it, got her saliva on his fingers, and grimaced himself. The muscles there didn't feel knotted up, at least. He didn't know how she did it.

"Oh, Frieda," he sighed. "Poor Frieda."

Her hands fisted in the back of his shirt.

When Regan made love to her, her hands grasped at his back, clawing when he let her feel his experience, and she kissed every bit of flesh she could reach. He felt almost like he was being eaten, devoured by someone so hungry they couldn't stop themselves. It felt strange to be the one consumed, but not unwelcome.

His instincts took over. His hesitation faded, replaced by reflexive, practiced movements, murmured praise, and fascination with soft flesh and the smell of blood. Her hands were warmer now.

He bit her in the first few minutes, on her left breast. She cried out when he did, clutching him closer. When he pulled back to kiss her after taking a few swallows of blood, her eyes were huge, dark, her cheeks flushed brighter than they'd been in months as the euphoria of the bite took over. Her fingers caught at his hair, pulling hard enough to sting, hard enough to pull him closer.

He gave her everything he'd learned over the course of two hundred and fifty years and countless lovers. Everything that wouldn't hurt.

He'd only bitten her three times and held her for an hour when he felt her begin to weaken, her cries of his name growing quieter. That was when he knew it was time to take more than a mouthful of blood.

The last bite was at her neck.

Bringing her to climax brought her blood rushing into his mouth. Helped keep her calm, too. He reached his own peak, partly brought on by the taste of wine and fresh blood on his tongue. Afterward, he kept his hands moving, kept her teetering on the edge. She didn't notice herself weakening, didn't notice how much blood he'd taken, her eyes closed to the spinning of the room, her shaking hands tucked between their chests. That was until she came down from her final climax.

Regan felt her hands grasping, pawing at his chest as she gasped, the life leaving her too fast for it to make a difference. He felt her jaw moving against his face, trying to form words, failing. He couldn't stop. It would only be cruel, letting her try to gasp out something he couldn't understand, to try to save her when far too much blood was gone from her, much less let her feel the pain of changing. Besides, she'd told him when she was in her right mind: This was what she wanted. She wanted this. He had to do what she wanted.

Her body went limp. He swallowed the very last of her a few minutes later, felt the wine and pain meds and sickness swirling through his own system, making his head spin and his stomach lurch as he sat back to look at her.

Her sunken eyes were still open, glassy now, her lips gray and skin blanched white from blood loss. She didn't look like Frieda. She looked like just another corpse. He'd seen enough to know, but he checked her pulse to be sure. Still.

He dressed, then he did the same things for her as he did for any other corpse he'd created: Closed her eyes, folded her hands over her chest and straightened her legs so she at least looked comfortable. Prayed to a god he didn't believe in over her. But for Frieda, he also took a soft cloth from the bathroom, wet a corner of it and held it so no water would touch his skin, wiped the semen from the corner of her mouth and trails of blood from everywhere he'd bitten her. Dressed her as well as he could without throwing her around like a ragdoll.

Smoothed her hair before covering her with a blanket.

Then he fetched his cell phone and phoned someone he wouldn't call a friend even with a gun to his head. It wasn't the first time he'd reached out to them, but he always hoped it would be the last.

The crematorium worker made sure Regan would have his usual "discretion fee" ready along with the price of cremation. Regan specified that he wanted them to wait until the following night to burn her and, for the first time, requested an urn. Two urns. A large one in plain blue to return to her family, and a small one with flowers on it.

It wasn't until Regan stood to unlock his back door that he realized his hand had been resting on her forehead as he made the call.

With half an hour left, she started to fade in his arms. He could see the blankets through her more clearly now, and her skin began to feel as though it were made of cobwebs. He hummed to her again when her crying, too, softened. Her hands loosened, and her head rested on his bicep. Her tears evaporated quickly from his chest, dissolving into nothing at the same rate she did. He watched the clock as he hummed, rubbing her back. The more she faded, though, the more he looked at her, and where her face hid beneath her hair.

Regan came to see her cremation in the evening of the next day. It wasn't a "service," and the man performing the cremation looked at him like he was insane, but it didn't feel right not to bear witness.

She was covered with his blanket still. It was surreal to see it swaddling a corpse.

He talked to his not-friend while they prepared the incinerator and her body. Told him a little bit about the person being burned for once. No details, just that she'd been ill and wanted to go out on her own terms. The worker at the furnace looked like he wouldn't care if Regan had laid her and killed her in front of him.

Regan weathered the heat silently by the side of the furnace as they put her in. As the tray she laid on rattled into the chamber, he felt the sudden urge to throw himself over the body, to scream and shake her in an attempt to wake her, or maybe bite and try to turn her. He didn't. He watched in silence as they closed the door and started the incinerators.

He'd had the same urge when he took too much from the first poor boy that'd loved him enough to bare his neck, and again when his first wife had died of old age. Yet again when his best friend followed her a year later.

It didn't work. Never did. He always felt just empty after, and his bites left only scars.

He was ushered unceremoniously from the room as she burned, went home to wait. Got her ashes at nine a.m. the next day. Skipping all that government paperwork really did cut down on time.

He drove to a different city to mail the box with her letter, belongings, and ashes to her father, with a forged death certificate for the insurance and a note explaining he was a "friend" who cared for her in her final days, and that she didn't want a funeral—just an ending to her story.

In the end, he supposed it was the truth.

And that was it. Their deal was completed.

She visited him for the first time a week later.

Regan looked up at the bookshelf across the room, at the little black vase-shaped plastic urn with pink lilies printed crookedly on it. Why had he decided to have them keep part of her back? He'd had a half-thought of scattering a pinch of her ashes in a few places—The Louvre, around the base of Big Ben, the California Redwoods—but he never had. He likely never would.

Thinking on it, that was probably why she haunted him. Her body being in two places at once like that, neither part returned to the earth nor the sea. He wouldn't have been restful, either.

Regan looked down at her. Almost gone now, a faint outline. She was silent, still. Her flesh had no substance, and he could move his hand through it. It swirled like mist where he did.

He cupped her chin as best he could with one hand. He wanted to know.

"Frieda?"

Miracle of miracles, she seemed to hear him. Her eyes drifted open, unfocused but directed toward him as the mist of her body continued to dissipate.

"Frieda, do you regret it?" he asked.

She was silent, gazing with unfocused eyes for a few seconds before they closed.

He sighed, resting his chin on the mist where the top of her head was supposed to be again, waiting for her to drift away.

She did, but not before she spoke for the first time since she'd died.

"No."

When the last of the mist in his arms dissipated, Regan got up. He stretched, walked to the window and looked out at the quiet, dark street, then checked the time. A few hours until sunrise. He had time.

He picked up the little urn with flowers on it.

At the night carnival on the boardwalk, winding down for the day, he threw a couple of rings before the booth closed. Bought one scoop of cookies and cream in a sugar cone, before the ice cream cart also closed. Took it down to the pier, where he sat on the bench at the end and watched the moon set, letting the ice cream he couldn't so much as taste slowly melt.

When the sky started to lighten and he had no more time, he stood, unscrewing the top from the urn. He paused, considering something more, something grander, a journey where he left a little bit of her at every beautiful sight.

She was tired. She was tired, and she'd told him she was done. In the end, that journey would only be for his peace, not hers.

The ocean could carry her anywhere she wanted to go, any distant shore she couldn't visit when she was alive. It could carry her up the Seine, the Thames, along the Redwood coast, into the clouds with the rain. Anywhere.

Before he could change his mind, Regan tipped the ashes into the sea. He held the urn for a minute, watching the ashes sink into the water, wondering if he'd regret it, then threw the urn in too. It was littering, and he'd never approved of that, but maybe a little crab could use it as a shell or something. He couldn't just throw it in the trash.

Finally, he took a lick at what remained of the ice cream, spat it out and wiped his tongue on his sleeve as his body rejected the not-blood and a wave of nausea hit him. He threw the ice cream cone into the water, too. She'd probably find that funny, probably laughed in the afterlife if she bothered to watch him. He laughed himself.

Regan stood at the end of the pier and watched the moon on the water. The sky behind him turned faintly pink.. His phone buzzed as one of his lovers called him to offer blood and sex before he slept. He let it ring.

He looked down at the ashes swallowed up by the water, then turned, walking back along the pier as the sun threatened the horizon.

When he got home, he turned off his cellphone, unplugged his landline, got into bed, and finally slept.

His bed stayed empty.

THE OTHER WOMAN

Rosalie Peng

THE OTHER WOMAN lived in a bland and sterile gray house at the end of the street. It was the type of house only someone without a soul could live in without losing her mind. It made sense that The Other Woman lived there; after all, she had to be soulless in order to seduce a happily married man. *Jane's* happily married man, to be precise.

Jane watched, crouched behind a neighbor's thick mulberry bushes, as The Other Woman unlocked her front door and stepped inside. Moments later, she appeared through the living room window. The afternoon sun was hot and scathing on the back of Jane's neck. Her wobbly legs ached for relief. She tried to ignore the stinging fullness of her bladder and the increasingly uncomfortable mud caked under her nails. She'd spent the afternoon ripping up the neighbor's lawn, fantasizing that her nails were tearing through The Other Woman's innards instead of grass. *How satisfying that would be!* It was only fair that The Other Woman felt the same heart-wrenching pain Jane had lived through since she discovered that Tom was, *once again*, having an affair.

It should've been the happiest time of her life; she and Tom were finally past The Rough Patch, and the Good Lord rewarded her faith and devotion with a blessing only He could give: two pink lines on a pregnancy test. *It was all worth it,* Jane had thought. All of it—even the stormy nights when she questioned her faith *and* her vows. Even the instance when Tom left Lily home alone, diaper full with oozing excrement, after his buddies convinced him to go on an impromptu bar crawl. Even after that last time, when Tom almost put his hands on Jane—

But things are going to change!

Jane had told Tom about the positive pregnancy test a fortnight ago, after she'd put Lily to bed. Tom had been ecstatic. He promised the affairs would stop. He swore he'd be a better husband and a better father to Lily. He had a growing family, and if that wasn't a reason to stop his philandering ways, nothing in this mortal world was.

That was until he met The Other Woman.

Jane wanted to tear Tom's heart out, too. *Tear it out, watch Tom's eyes widen, horrified as Jane pulls the organ out of his chest cavity, snapping arteries and vessels, and how fun would it be if she looped his intestines around his neck and hung him like that? Then, would he finally feel how she felt—strangled by her love for him?*

The urge to pee weighed heavily on her bladder. Jane realized suddenly the sun wasn't hot on her neck anymore. Time, too, had stepped out on her. During the hours she'd crouched behind the bush, spying on The Other Woman, the sun had tired of her antics and tucked itself behind the roofs of the surrounding cookie-cutter houses.

"Hello, Jane." The voice of a woman, The Other Woman, purred into the air.

Jane yelped, almost tipping over onto her bottom.

The Other Woman smiled as Jane stumbled to her feet. Jane flushed at her own clumsiness, scraping together the scraps of her dignity as she brushed the grass from her skirt and grabbed her purse. The Other Woman appeared to be some form of Asian, probably one of those green card-chasing home wreckers who didn't care about the good, Christian, all-American family she was destroying. The Other Woman stood tall and proud, shoulders back, chest puffed out, watching Jane with what looked like amusement dancing in her dark eyes. Jane hated The Other Woman's blasé nature; hated that while this woman pranced about in her tight little jeans and crisp white button-up, Jane's sundress was wrinkled and smeared with grass and mud stains.

Her hatred spiked through her like sudden road rage: white-hot fury crashed and burned down the highways of Jane's nerves, fanning flames and her temper to the boiling point. The Other Woman knew Jane's name. Did Tom tell her? She wanted to throw up at the thought of Tom and this harlot cuddled with him among her fancy pillows, laughing as Tom made fun of his *nagging, fat wife who just couldn't lose the baby weight when all his friends' wives did so easily, Jane, are you even trying—*

"Would you like to come in?" The Other Woman gestured toward her house. "You could probably watch me better from my couch. I'd wager it is much more comfortable than squatting out here."

Jane's face burned from being caught spying. '*What? Me, step into your lair? Never!*' is was what Jane desperately wanted to say. But her bladder had its own thoughts on the matter, so she meekly swallowed her pride and followed The Other woman across the street like a scolded child.-

The Other Woman unlocked her door. "Shoes off, if you don't mind. You can use these slippers." She gestured toward the shoe rack. Jane stared at the slippers. She hadn't seen a pair in a long time—not since she cleaned out her mother's house after her funeral. Tom didn't like having slippers in the house. Tom's mother called them un-American. Jane wanted to refuse out of spite, but habit overtook her, and she dutifully slipped them on and sprinted towards the bathroom.

She slammed the bathroom door shut behind her, nearly moaning as she hovered over the porcelain toilet. Then she flushed and carefully washed the mud off her hands, dreading the imminent confrontation with the person in the living room. Jane whispered a quick prayer as she stared at her clammy face in the mirror, gripping the silver cross at her neck. A vision flashed before her eyes: it was The Other Woman, gasping for air as Jane strangled her to death.

"*No, no.*" Jane shook her head, slapped her cheeks, and recited with fervor: "Be kind to one another, tender-hearted, forgiving of one another, as God in Christ forgave you." For a moment, she wasn't in The Other Woman's bathroom; she was in her pastor's office, sobbing as she relayed her marital woes. *Forgive them,* her pastor had beseeched her. Forgive The Other Woman and Tom. Jane's mind wandered to The Thing inside her purse.

"Lord, give me strength," she whispered and stepped out of the bathroom.

"Over here," The Other Woman's voice floated down the hallway.

Following that disembodied voice, Jane arrived in a sparsely furnished living room. The Other Woman sat on a loveseat, stroking her long dark hair absentmindedly as she watched the sunset through the living room window. She gestured for Jane to sit on the couch across from her. Jane sat, hands smoothing her dress beneath her thighs, her heart unexpectedly pounding. She felt the dying sunlight's warmth tickle her back and almost wanted to ask to switch seats: The Other Woman had the view outside the window, while Jane could only stare at her husband's mistress.

Separated by only a rickety coffee table, she finally took a good look at The Other Woman. Jealousy stitched patterns on her heart as she eyed The Other Woman's beautiful face, her striking brows just visible beneath thick bangs. A relaxed expression perched on The Other Woman's face. Her full lips wore that same saccharine smile from before, sticking Jane in place on the couch like an insect candied in a syrupy trap. Jane met her gaze, expecting to see shame, maybe even repentance.

Of course, there was none of that. Jane clutched her purse—and The Thing—closer.

Silence fell across the living room as the sun set, buzzing loudly like the dying songs of cicadas. Finally, unable to draw this out any longer, Jane broke from the molasses.

"You know why I'm here," she said.

The Other Woman nodded.

Jane took a deep breath. "This is hard for me."

Choose forgiveness, her pastor's words rang through her mind.

"But I needed to talk to you," she glared at The Other Woman, "you need to stay away from Tom. He has a family, a wife, and our daughter Lily, she just turned three. She doesn't deserve to grow up in a broken home."

"How's Lily's sprained arm?" The Other Woman asked in a surprisingly gentle tone.

Jane blinked. "H–How did you…" *Tom told her*, Jane's mind supplied, and her fury peaked. "You keep my daughter's name out of your whoring mouth!"

The Other Woman raised her hands in surrender. "Apologies, Jane. I'm asking from a place of concern. Lily's been getting hurt a lot lately, hasn't she?"

Jane's hands balled into fists, her nails digging in painfully. She wished she was still outside, where she could take her anger out on the grass.

"That's none of your concern," she snapped. "You need to stay away from Tom—"

"The injuries all seem to happen on Tom's watch, don't they?" The Other Woman mused, twirling a strand of hair around long, angular fingers.

"It was an accident!" Jane almost lurched to her feet, but her clutch on the pillows kept her somewhat tethered. A strange thought floated through her head. Why *am I getting so defensive? Isn't that the truth—?* She swallowed the rest of that thought as her scrambled mind warred against impulses she couldn't begin to decipher.

"My family," Jane gritted, "is none of your business. Please, leave us alone."

The Other Woman didn't seem to hear her. "Accident, huh," she laughed. "Jane, do you really believe that? Or did you force yourself to believe that after you found out you were pregnant?"

It was like the Almighty Himself held a bucket of ice water over Jane's head and emptied its contents without warning. The shock hit Jane with the force of a rolling boulder, landing heavily in her stomach. Her body buckled under this imaginary weight as surprise rippled over her face.

"H–How did you— Did Tom tell—"

"By the way, has Tom found out about your secret bank account?"

Jane stared at The Other Woman in bewilderment. "You," her words were slow and careful, "seem to know an awful lot about me."

The Other Woman grinned, her eyes curving into half-moons. "Why, of course, Jane! I've been waiting to meet you for a while. I did my homework."

Jane's right hand twitched, but she willed it to stay on the pillow lest it dive into her purse unassisted by sense, and she did something she could never come back from.

My God, this woman has been stalking me.

"What else do you know about me?" she asked, trying to keep her cool.

The Other Woman absently waved a hand, as though they were chatting about the most mundane gossip. "A lot more than you'd think," she said. "This was always about you, Jane. I wanted to get to you. The affair with Tom was miserable; I can't believe I put up with it for so long—what a temper that one has!" Something wicked gleamed in her eyes. "He'll be very mad when he finds out you've been squirreling away money that could've gone to his ponies."

"I haven't put more away!" Jane shouted. Breaths stuttered in her chest as trembles ricocheted through her body, sending waves of dread cascading through her veins. "I haven't touched that account, not since—"

"You found out about the pregnancy," The Other Woman finished. At Jane's stunned look, she reached over the coffee table and gave her a sympathetic pat on the hand. "It's common for victims of domestic violence to stay with their abusers. Especially when a baby's on the way."

"He never hit me," Jane whispered, "never!"

"Not all abuse is physical," The Other Woman said quietly.

"This is crazy." Jane shook her head, staggering to stand. Her knees felt like jelly, shaking beneath her as she swallowed a sob. "I'm not doing this! I'm not talking about this with my husband's Chinese whore."

"Chinese?" The Other Woman's voice sounded puzzled. "I'm Filipina."

"Whatever!" She forced herself to fully stand. She pointed a shaking finger down at The Other Woman. "Just stay away from me and my family!"

Her head spun as she stumbled towards the exit, holding her purse in a vice-like grip.

"Tell me," The Other Woman drawled, "where will the baby sleep? You live in a two-bedroom, right?"

Jane wobbled, her feet refusing to move, as though she'd stepped in something sticky. *Has she been inside my house?* "It will sleep in our room," she forced herself to stay calm, "until we move. We're looking at houses. We're moving far, *far* away from you."

"Hmm," The Other Woman's voice slithered into Jane's ears, licking at her lobes like a serpent's forked tongue. "Tom will be cranky about that, won't he? He's a big boy who needs his sleep. Remember when Lily kept crying and kept him awake?"

Jane did remember: it happened during The Rough Patch when she'd caught COVID and begged Tom to help their crying daughter. But when Lily's cries only grew shriller accompanied by Tom's screams, Jane had dragged herself from bed, almost passing out as she shuffled into her daughter's room.

What she saw that day still haunted her whenever she closed her eyes: *Tom, his hands around their daughter, and Lily—oh poor Lily, her head whipping back and forth like a wet rag. Jane's own scream joined the cacophony as she rushed to protect her child—*

"Sit back down, Jane," The Other Woman ordered.

Jane obeyed. A sort of hypnotic fog filled the living room, but rather unlike fog, it felt dense. *Sticky.* Jane felt like she was wading through thick mud as she returned to her spot on the couch. She wanted to scream, but when she tried opening her mouth, it would clamp shut as she felt something—bile, vomit, more *sticky mud*—erupt up her esophagus.

"You know Tom's not a good father," The Other Woman said gently. "That's why you were saving up money. You were going to take your daughter and leave."

"No!" The word stimulated all the wrong receptors on Jane's tongue, flooding her mouth with a sickening sweet and sour, bitter taste. "He's changed. We're looking at houses…"

"No, sweetie." The Other Woman chuckled. "*Tom* is looking at houses. Don't kid yourself! You don't have a say in where you move—or if you're moving at all. I doubt Tom is willing to leave me behind anytime soon. But this shouldn't surprise you; when's the last time you really decided anything? Or rather, when's the last time *Tom* let you decide anything?"

The Other Woman's words hung in the air like a cloud of mosquitos. Jane's thoughts swirled around her; of all the important decisions in her life, how many had she actually made? Tom was the head of the household, made all the big decisions. He even decided on the most trivial things in their lives, down to the brand of toilet paper they used. Jane had been happy to go along with his choices—until The Rough Patch.

Since then, deep in Jane's gut, the seas had been dark and stormy. Her small boat sailed cautiously on the waters of Tom's temperament. She constantly feared his mood would stir like violent tides, sending Jane and Lily to the bottom of the sea. Jane's boat had become waterlogged, and she broke her back scooping out bucketfuls to keep herself and Lily afloat, tossing overboard whatever sacrifices Tom demanded: her part-time job, her friends, her family…everything.

"Well," The Other Woman's voice cut through her thoughts, "I suppose you're choosing to be here right now. Just like you chose to skip your OB/GYN appointment to stalk me this afternoon." A quirked brow hid behind her bangs. "And you chose to bring *that* to our little meeting." She pointed at Jane's purse. Jane grabbed it and pressed it protectively against her abdomen.

The Other Woman laughed. "You asked what I know about you: I know that you haven't told anyone else about the pregnancy. Haven't even thought of names or put together a registry. Haven't been taking your prenatal vitamins. And," she smiled wide, her teeth gleaming in the darkening room, "I know that last night when you made up your mind to confront me, you had a little…"

To Jane's horror, The Other Woman raised a hand curled around an invisible bottle and mimed chugging noises.

"I know that you don't want this baby, Jane."

A tear rolled down Jane's cheek. Perhaps it was the exhaustion from squatting under the shrub in the hot sun all afternoon, or the fatigue that came with pregnancy. Or even the strange, sticky fog cushioning Jane's brain cells from forming coherent thoughts. She was tired—too tired to object. *But she had to object—to defend herself! Jane was a good mother, a good wife; she wanted more children, children with Tom!*

The Other Woman shook her head, as though she could read Jane's mind. "Remember when you were pregnant with Lily? Remember how you took the vitamins even before you conceived, how you attended each appointment like your life depended on it? The hours you spent poring over names and putting together a nursery? Well, that can't be expected of you now, can it? Things have changed: you're basically a single mother with how hands-off Tom is. You know Tom hurts Lily, you know it's not all accidents."

Tears slipped from Jane's other eye. "T–the baby," she croaked, "he promised h–he'll change for the baby."

"And yet," The Other Woman said as the sun's last ray extinguished, "he hasn't. The negging. The threats. The times he came close to hurting you. They haven't stopped."

The two women sat in silence as night fell. Cloaked in the darkness, Jane bowed her head, letting the tears flow. Tom couldn't see her right now. Her pastor couldn't see her. The Other Woman—well, Jane didn't care what the whore thought of her. The realization was quite freeing.

"I can't take care of two kids by myself." Jane hurried the words from her mouth, fearful that if she hesitated, they'd bottle up in her throat and implode. An exhilarating shock shivered through her as she uttered secrets she hadn't entrusted to her pastor or even God.

"I dropped out of college for Tom," she continued, wiping at her eyes. "I haven't held a real job in ages. Tom believes wives should stay home. I just…" she sobbed, "I wish someone else was this baby's father! God!"

The truth tore a harsh, bubbling laugh from her throat.

"I never thought I'd be in this situation. I did everything right! I waited for the 'right' man and even saved myself for marriage. I never drank or did drugs and I volunteered at church. So why is this happening to me?" She half-laughed, half-whispered in frustration, fat tears falling onto her lap. "I did everything right! I'm a good wife, a good mother, and a good Christian! I'm not a whore like you. Only whores get abor—"

Her mouth clamped shut almost reflexively, the word refusing to manifest.

The Other Woman stayed quiet, not disturbing the abyss that Jane had unloaded her grief into.

"It's too late, anyway. I'd have to go out of state to… to do *it*. I've got no family who can help me; Tom hated my parents, said it was them or him, and I chose him. I always chose him! My friends are all with the church. They wouldn't understand—they'd shun me! But… I can't have this baby," she admitted. "I can't be tied to Tom for another eighteen-plus years."

Jane sniffled and trained her eyes on the ground, too ashamed to lift her head as the foggy abyss dissipated. She stared at The Other Woman's slipper-clad feet, steadying her breath.

"It's dark," said The Other Woman, her voice a quiet thunder.

Jane buried her face in her hands. It *was* dark, which meant Tom would be home soon. He'd be angry to return to an empty house, no warm meal ready on the dinner table or a wife at his beck and call. It was strange, she thought, that she felt the safest and most relaxed she had in months, sitting here on The Other Woman's couch. *What if I stayed here forever?* It was a foolish thought: Lily was still at the sitter's, and Jane needed to pick her up before returning home to face Tom's wrath.

Her eyes closed, the heels of her palms pressed tightly upon them, blocking out the world. *It's peaceful,* Jane sighed, just as a strange noise filled the living room. A strange, wet squelching, like Lily grinding her wet rain boots on Jane's clean floors. Her nose wrinkled. A series of noises: *pop! pop! pop!* An iron-heavy stench percolated through the air. More squelching. Sounds and smells entirely alien to a living room's ecosystem.

Jane paid them no mind, engulfed in her misery as she was, preferring to remain blinded to the world around her. She heard what she assumed to be The Other Woman move around the room, passing behind where Jane sat on the couch toward the living room window. Fabric rustled as The Other Woman drew the curtains closed. A cool breeze wafted rhythmically against the back of Jane's neck. *Did she turn on a fan?* Elsewhere in the room, a tawny amber light flicked to life. Phosphenes danced behind Jane's closed eyelids, puncturing the peace she'd found in the darkness.

"Have you thought about divorce?" The Other Woman's disembodied voice came from somewhere in the room.

Jane was prone to allergies this time of the year, and the waterworks didn't help with unclogging her sinuses. She felt dizzy, and a dull ache inflated in her ears like balloons. It put pressure on her ear canals, muting her hearing. Perhaps that was why The Other Woman's voice suddenly gained a raspy hoarseness.

She snorted, eyes still closed. "You'd like that, wouldn't you? I'd be out of the way and you could marry Tom and get y–your f–fucking green card, right?" The expletive slipped out. Jane barely had time to reproach herself; it felt good, letting something so vulgar roll off her tongue. "I know how people like you think."

The Other Woman chuckled from behind her. The laughter rumbled and reverberated in Jane's chest, like a cat's deep purr. "I don't need a green card," said The Other Woman. "I have been in this country for a very, very long time."

"I don't believe in divorce," Jane tried again weakly.

"Lucky for you—" *It must be my sinuses*, Jane thought; The Other Woman sounded muffled, like her tongue and lips were moving out of sync, mushing sounds and syllables together. "—you don't need to believe in divorce to make it real. *Unlike your god.*"

Jane's eyes jolted open. The Other Woman's voice dropped several octaves with each syllable, sounding less and less human with each word. Her fuzzy gaze saw The Other Woman's slippers appear as she blinked the dancing dots out of her vision. Seconds passed. Then it hit her.

The Other Woman's slipper-covered feet were still there, daintily crossed under the coffee table across from Jane. Wafts of wind whooshed against her neck. A lamp glowed from behind the couch, casting a long shadow onto the living room floor. Someone—*something*—else was in the room.

Yet when The Other Woman laughed again, it came from behind her. A deep, rumbling guffaw. Slowly, Jane raised her head.

And screamed.

The Other Woman's legs remained on the loveseat, still wearing blue jeans, stiff and rigid, like those of a mannequin—except for the rush of blood that poured from where the torso had been torn off. Jane screamed and screamed, staring uncomprehendingly at the horror before her. It was like someone had taken an axe to The Other Woman's body, chopping off everything above the waist. She stared down into the pit of The Other Woman's pelvis, feeling her lunch bubble up her esophagus at the sight of the soup of blood and organs. Splintered white vertebrae peeked out like gory garnishes atop the cocktail of The Other Woman's innards.

"My God... My God!" Jane repeated, nearly falling off the couch. She froze when she heard the *flap-flap* of what sounded like a giant pair of wings. The long shadow shuddered as its wings fully unfolded. Jane reached for her purse, digging through it frantically until she felt the gun's cool metal barrel. She whipped around, screaming at the top of her lungs as she fired, hoping to hit something... anything!

Bam! Bam! Baa—clunk

The gun had jammed.

"No!"

Weaponless, Jane stared up at nothing short of abject horror.

The Other Woman's bisected torso was airborne, kept afloat by the flapping of skeletal black wings. Nothing of those beautiful features remained: the hairline had completely receded, the forehead bulged and elongated. The Other Woman's eye sockets sank back into the skull, the whites of her eyes filled with dark ink as fiery hot embers burned where the pupils should've been. The Other Woman smiled as Jane, petrified, wet herself. The corners of The Other Woman's mouth twitched violently, then ripped through her cheeks, revealing rows of serrated teeth.

What rattled Jane to her core was the gash where The Other Woman's torso detached from her legs; the heavier organs plunked to the carpet while entrails dangled from within the exposed ribs, a trailing bloody mess spread over the living room floor. Jane watched, hypnotized by the sight of the intestines unraveling, hanging from the flying torso. They were somehow fascinating; shiny, wet, squelching. The Other Woman's entrails dangled from that disembodied torso like thick, slimy streamers, twisting as though they had lives of their own, wriggling like slippery eels trying to escape her abdomen.

Jane turned away and promptly vomited. When her retches finally ceased, The Other Woman descended upon her, showering Jane's face with blood, thick with bits of skin and viscera.

"What are you?" Jane fought the lightheadedness that threatened her consciousness.

"In my country," The Other Woman rasped, "they call me *manananggal*. 'The one who separates.' Think of me as your Count Dracula—but gutsier."

"Are you going to kill me?" she whimpered, fresh tears flowing down her cheeks. "Drink my blood?"

The Other Woman snarled and wagged a long, clawed finger. "All this trouble I went through, just for blood? Ha, no!"

Jane scooted backward, her shoulder connecting painfully with the coffee table. The Other Woman pressed her face close to Jane's, and the light in the room disappeared beyond the veil of her black wings.

"My diet is different. I could barely control myself this entire time! You're carrying something delicious inside you."

The Other Woman stretched her mouth inhumanly wide. A long black tube—*her tongue!* Jane realized—unfurled, dripping saliva, and stretched to caress Jane's face, leaving a trail of sticky residue. Jane marveled at its sharp, tapered end. It was a straw-like appendage, not unlike the proboscis of a butterfly or perhaps a mosquito—ideal for entering small crevices and siphoning things out.

And just like that, Jane's terror evaporated, replaced by... understanding.

She was still scared—and the appendage was downright *disgusting*—but something else ignited inside her, brewing a morbid excitement. The seas had calmed. The sun slashed through the thick stormy clouds like the Archangel Michael himself had come to slay her demons. Her small boat bobbed on the waves. Ahead, she saw land.

Subconsciously, Jane's hand jumped to the cross at her neck. She squeezed her eyes closed as the tongue traveled to her clavicle and wound itself around her necklace and pulled. Jane's hand jerked, about to protest, then abruptly dropped to her lap. She gulped. The silver chain tightened, cutting into her skin, and then it was gone. Silver links melted into the pools of blood as Jane barely heard the cross hit the floor.

"It's against the law," Jane's final protest was a weak gurgle. "I know the law—I voted for it. A–and… Tom!" She sobbed her husband's name. "What would he think?"

'Screw what Tom thinks. This is your choice, Jane. Think of it this way; there's something I want. There's something you don't want. Lucky us, we can help each other out," The Other Woman rasped. "Women helping women."

The proboscis slid over Jane's collarbones, its sharp, tapered end toying with the neck of her sundress. Jane shuddered, her anticipation building. She held very still, somewhat like a child waiting for its mother to remove a splinter. The tongue paused, apparently waiting for consent.

Jane nodded.

The tongue gripped the dress's fabric and ripped it apart. The proboscis slid between Jane's exposed breasts, traveling the distance to the emerging bump on her abdomen. The Other Woman caressed the swell of her stomach, moaning, worshipping it like a starving beast yearning for scraps.

The Other Woman pressed the tongue's sharp tip into Jane's belly button—ready for extraction. Jane whimpered and closed her eyes.

In her mind's theater, her small boat washed ashore at a sandy beach.

She staggered onto land, crying in relief as warm sand covered her toes. Lily was there, laughing and clapping the merry way only a toddler could.

They were safe.

"Will it hurt?" Jane asked.

The Other Woman smiled, hunger and saliva dripping from each word.

'I'll be gentle."

PERFECT LITTLE STITCHES

Deborah Sheldon

ANGELO TOOK UP the scalpel and opened the cadaver's thigh, from hip to knee, with a single stroke. There was very little subcutaneous fat. Using firm, continuous passes of the blade, Angelo pared through the muscle within seconds and exposed the femur without scratching it.

"Very nice, as usual," Gary said. "Ah shit, you know what? I just went and notched mine at the hip-end."

"At the lesser trochanter?"

"I think so, yeah, the top bit that sticks out a little."

Angelo De Luca glared across the stainless-steel table at his new assistant, Gary Mathews, who was harvesting from the cadaver's other leg. Gary had started his working life as a butcher and still acted like one, even though the meat now was human, and therefore precious.

"If you would put your mind to the study of anatomy," Angelo said, "and learn about the attachments of soft tissue, you wouldn't keep making these basic errors. Haven't you read the books I loaned you?"

"Relax. Most of the bones we get are in shit condition, anyway."

"That's no reason to damage them further."

Gary sneered. "Even with this bloke? He's almost ninety. How good are his bones going to be? Swiss cheese. The poor bastard who gets these femurs will bust them in half on his first step from the hospital bed."

Angelo couldn't trust himself to speak.

Whistling, Gary returned his attention to the cadaver's thigh, slicing briskly towards the kneecap. Angelo heard the muted *snicking* sound as the scalpel contacted the femur, over and over. Oh, how Angelo despised Gary Mathews with his uncouth footy-beer-and-barbecue personality, his ginger hair sprouting thick as fur over pale forearms, his skin freckled and wrinkled as if he'd been pressed out of dough and left in the sun to crack; Gary Mathews, the jovial, under-educated idiot, the very antithesis of everything that a funeral director ought to be.

Angelo felt the familiar stab of regret.

This funeral parlour, "De Luca and Son", had been named after his father, Giovanni, and himself. It was supposed to be Angelo's legacy, but his own sons hadn't wished to continue the family trade. Once Papa Giovanni had died, money became tight. Staff members—those who aren't relatives—expected and received full pay and entitlements. Then there was the outstanding balance of Sofia's stupendous medical bills. Bankruptcy had loomed.

Until the arrival three months ago of Angelo's saviour: Heather.

Once Angelo had agreed to her unusual business offer, Gary Mathews was made the sole member of Angelo's staff, without consultation, by Heather the Body Wrangler. That's what she actually called herself, Heather the Body Wrangler. Angelo didn't know anything about her, apart from a mobile number.

Unlike organs such as the heart, certain tissues—including bones and skin—are still viable for transplant after death. Heather would pay up to four thousand dollars in cash for a complete set of usable parts, removed surreptitiously from a young and healthy corpse. Age and medical conditions lessened the remuneration on a fixed scale. At the very least, a diseased and elderly corpse meant a few hundred dollars.

The money had staved off the bank manager.

Yes, Angelo would go to jail if the police found out, but morally, it made irrefutable sense. Living patients either died or suffered permanent disability without these transplants. Voluntary donors were scarce. When cadavers would be wasted anyway, burned to ashes or buried to make worm-shit, what was the harm in first recycling their viable parts? No harm at all.

As long as the relatives never found out.

Because realising your loved one's remains had been pillaged, defiled, and dismantled must be the worst kind of unimaginable horror. Dear God, if such a fate had befallen Sofia… He could hardly bring himself to think of it. And so, occasionally, when Angelo couldn't sleep, he feared he'd made a pact with the Devil. A widower for nearly a year, he would turn to the empty side of his bed and weep to Sofia for forgiveness.

Now, Gary Mathews gazed at Angelo across the naked and muscle-splayed cadaver on the stainless-steel table, waggled the scalpel and said, "Mate, you couldn't cut butter with this bloody thing. Just let me go get my boning knife."

"No." Angelo's moustache quivered as he fought to maintain a neutral expression. "Our deceased clients are offering the living a wonderful gift. We will not desecrate them with implements intended for the carving up of animals."

Gary dropped the scalpel to the stainless-steel table and put his fists on his hips. "You know what's going on? What we're doing?"

Angelo flushed. "Yes, of course."

"Nobody has signed any release forms. Every document is forged. What we're doing, right here, is some seriously criminal shit."

"Please continue with the harvesting," Angelo said. "Once we've gathered the long bones, we'll move onto the saphenous veins, ligaments, and tendons. I'd like your help to sew the PVC pipes inside the limbs and to remove the skin and heart valves, if you wouldn't mind. After that, I'll take the corneas myself, thank you. Please take your break at that point. Embalming will begin promptly at three o'clock."

Gary stared back, nostrils flared. Angelo decided to continue with the removal of the femur. For a time, the only sounds were the flit of his scalpel, the steady drip-drip-drip of the tap into the scrub sink.

"Nobody is giving anybody a gift," Gary finally said. "We're stealing these body parts. We're stealing them for money. I'm a grave-robber and so are you."

Gary unfastened his blood-stained apron, flung it across a bench, and peeled away his latex gloves. He headed to the exit of the preparation room.

"Where are you going?" Angelo said, hoping that the *bastardo* intended to quit.

"To the boot of my car," Gary said, "for my knives."

Oh, she was beautiful.

She was the first cadaver of the day, this warm spring day that had followed a long, torturous night of rain and shrieking wind. Angelo slowly unzipped the body bag the rest of the way.

A child: such a beautiful young child.

Her jet-black hair lay in a halo of ringlets about her pale face. Angelo wanted to weep. The forensic pathologist must have been similarly affected. Following an autopsy at the Coroner's Court, the typical cadaver arrived at Angelo's funeral parlour in disarray, tacked together as roughly as a hessian sack, but not this child. The forensic pathologist had taken great care. The single incision from throat to pubis had been closed using small, neat sutures, as precise as any of Sofia's hand-sewn embroideries. Had there been an examination of the brain? Angelo couldn't see any sign. He smoothed back the ringlets framing the child's forehead. And, yes, hidden away within the hairline lay the tidy stitches circumnavigating the scalp.

According to the paperwork, the cause of her death was inconclusive. Teresa-Kate, eleven years of age, had died in hospital three days ago from an unidentified infection that had first paralysed her, and then triggered multiple and catastrophic organ failure. More than likely, she'd acquired the infection from the bite of an unknown animal, probably a dog. The included body diagram showed a large 'X' on the upper back. Angelo put down the paperwork.

Gently, he turned the child onto her side. Just above her right scapula, into the tissue of her trapezoid muscle, lay the bite mark. Could the paralysis have been symptomatic of some new strain of rabies? But Angelo was no microbiologist. If the experts at the Coroner's Court were unable to establish an exact cause of death, it was not for him to speculate. He zipped the bag closed and placed Teresa-Kate in the refrigerator unit. Then he washed his hands and retired to the lunchroom, where he washed his hands again.

As he ate his sandwich, Angelo perused his work diary. He'd spoken to Teresa-Kate's parents that morning. Anglicans, they wished to hold a home viewing before the funeral and burial, which necessitated an open casket. Teresa-Kate was already so perfectly preserved that Angelo's embalming and cosmetology skills would render her almost lifelike. After lunch, he would ring the family's priest to discuss and confirm details of the service. Satisfied, he'd just started on an apple when Gary Mathews shouldered through the lunchroom door.

Dropping the pizza box onto the table and sitting down, Gary said, "We'll get the whole four grand out of that kid."

A chunk of apple nearly stuck in Angelo's windpipe.

Gary folded a slice of pizza in half and crammed most of it into his mouth. A Hawaiian pizza, of course: a disgusting abomination that turned Angelo's stomach.

"She's perfect in every way," Gary said, talking as he chewed, "young and in good nick. This time, mate, we've hit the jackpot."

"No," Angelo said. "No, we haven't. You're wrong."

Gary stopped chewing, raised an eyebrow.

Angelo said, "Haven't you read the report? Seen the biohazard tape on the body bag? She died of a disease that sounds very similar to rabies. Her soft tissues could infect every single transplant recipient."

"I've already called the Body Wrangler," Gary said. "We're doing the kid."

Angelo felt blood mottle his cheeks. "If it has to be done, fine, I'll do it myself. You'll not go anywhere near her. You and your boning knives can burn in hell first."

Gary shrugged and kept eating his pizza.

Teresa-Kate lay naked on the stainless-steel table. Her arms and legs were thin, hairless and unblemished, pre-pubescent. What might she have done with her four-score and ten? That would be the question to torment her parents until the release of their own deaths. And, in a lesser way, that same question would also haunt Angelo. Since going into business with Heather, Angelo dreamed about many of his harvested clients, each one berating him and wailing for their missing body parts.

Enough.

He was a professional.

And according to protocol, he had to first take the leg bones.

He picked up the scalpel. The multiple bulbs of the overhead light beamed bright and white. The tap over the scrub sink dripped in a steady beat. It was almost 9 p.m. Hours ago, after sending Gary home, Angelo had arranged to meet Teresa-Kate's family priest tomorrow morning to discuss details of the funeral and burial.

The harvesting would be now or never.

As softly as the kiss of a downy feather, he touched the tip of the scalpel to Teresa-Kate's hip without breaking the skin. A moment passed. He held the blade over her anterior superior iliac spine—the outer crest of the pelvis—where, beneath the epidermis, dermis, and layer of subcutaneous fat, the attachments lay for the inguinal ligament and the sartorius muscle. One deep and decisive cut, following along the length of the femur, was the starting point.

Angelo couldn't do it.

Sofia came to mind, back when she first became seriously ill, confused, trying to cut rolled pastry on the kitchen bench with her hands as if her fingers had become knives. Leading her away, Angelo had shown her some of the framed embroidery she'd made over the years. Placated, Sofia allowed him to administer her medication. *Look at my nails,* she'd said. *Tesorio mio, watch me as I rend the world.*

These had been the last complete sentences she had ever spoken to him.

After forty-two years together, God, how he missed her.

Now, Angelo sniffed, scrubbed at his tears with the heels of both latex gloves. Then he pressed the scalpel into Teresa-Kate's left hip and dug in deep, slicing down towards the kneecap. He worked quickly, efficiently. After next stripping the tibia and fibula, he moved to the other leg, repeated the procedure. Then he deboned her right arm, her left arm. The meat of Teresa-Kate's flayed limbs lay shockingly red against the pallor of her torso. From the box of PVC pipes, he found the lengths that would fit. He spent the next hour neatly reconstructing Teresa-Kate's body, using sutures as translucent as fishing wire, making stitches so discreet that they brought Sofia's best handiwork to mind.

At close to 10:30 p.m., Angelo packed up his harvesting equipment. No matter what Heather the Body Wrangler demanded, he would not take this child's soft tissue. She had died from a rabies-like disease. How could Angelo claim to be helping the living if he deliberately offered up corneas and tendons that might carry infection?

It was time for the embalming procedure. He measured and mixed the chemicals. An incision near her collarbone exposed both the carotid artery and the jugular vein. One small incision in each, and he would insert the tubes: one to drain any remaining blood, the other to fill the circulatory system with embalming fluid. He pressed the tip of the scalpel into the carotid artery.

Teresa-Kate opened her eyes.

Angelo staggered back, dropped the scalpel.

The girl sat up, gazing at him, blinking dopily as if coming awake from a deep sleep. The sclera of both her eyes was black, as black as a fathomless pit.

"*Dio mio,*" he said, and tried to cross himself.

Teresa-Kate looked at the stitched wounds along her arms and legs, gaped at the line of sutures down the midline of her body, and gave a silent scream. The stretching of her mouth peeled back her lips, splitting the skin across her teeth. Her incisors, premolars, and molars were long, fanged: no longer human.

Teresa-Kate leapt from the table.

As she came at him, Angelo grabbed a stainless-steel instrument tray and struck her across the face. It slowed her momentarily. He hit her again, and again. When she staggered and dropped, he grabbed the bone-dust vacuum and brought it down onto the crown of her head, cracking her skull. She sprawled across the floor.

Angelo watched her for a long, long time.

When she still hadn't moved, his senses began to return. He put down the vacuum. The first thing he realised was that he had wet himself. The second thing was that, somehow, Teresa-Kate had been alive and now she was dead.

Angelo groped for a chair and sat down.

The dead coming back to life—he had read of such things occurring from time to time in faraway places like Zimbabwe, the Philippines, and Venezuela, where the deceased would wake up during their funeral. But no, this wasn't a misdiagnosis, a case of some poorly trained doctor confusing coma with death. At the Coroner's Court, Teresa-Kate's internal organs had been removed, inspected, weighed, sliced, and then tumbled together into a plastic bag, which was then sewn up inside her abdominal cavity. Good God, her brain had received the same treatment.

She still hadn't moved.

Incrementally, Angelo slid from the chair, approached. He used the tip of his shoe to turn her over. This time, she was definitely dead. One side of her face was smashed into a pulp of ruined skin and splintered bone.

Teresa-Kate had been alive.

And he had murdered her.

He vomited a little, wept. After a time, he regained control.

The child had already been issued a death certificate. Angelo would tell no one what had happened. Instead, he would spend the night using all his skills to repair and mask the damage he'd inflicted upon her. Tomorrow morning, he would give Teresa-Kate to her family so they could hold, in the lounge-room of their home, the girl's open-casket viewing.

Gary Mathews drove the hearse. Angelo's nerves weren't steady enough.

They delivered Teresa-Kate, dressed and perfect, in her casket. While shaking hands with her father, Angelo began to cry. Moved to tears herself, Teresa-Kate's mother attempted to embrace Angelo, for the love of everything holy, as if to *console* him after the evil he'd done to their daughter.

It was true; he had indeed made a pact with the Devil.

During the drive back to the funeral parlour, Gary harangued him about failing to strip the girl's corpse for the entire four thousand dollars. Angelo didn't have the strength to reply. Staring sightlessly at the passing scenery, he kept seeing Teresa-Kate's face, repaired to the absolute best of his abilities yet, on expert inspection, still carrying the marks of violence inflicted by his own hands.

He assigned Gary to meet with Teresa-Kate's priest.

Angelo got through the rest of the day on autopilot. In the evening, once Gary had left the funeral parlour, Angelo took from the locked drawer of his desk the business card of Heather the Body Wrangler and called the number.

"You beat me to it," she said. "I was just about to ring. Gary reckons you took the girl's bones and nothing else. Frankly, that's a wasted financial opportunity."

It struck Angelo that Heather didn't care about the living patients who needed transplants. This epiphany took his breath. It meant that he was, irredeemably, a sinner. Clearly now, he saw that his financial strife and the grief over Sofia's passing had muddied his judgement, allowed him to be led astray, led straight into the pits of hell.

"I'm sorry," Angelo whispered to the ether, to God Himself.

"I understand," Heather said. "A little girl; hey, things can get sentimental."

"No, I mean, I'm sorry, but I can't do this anymore."

"Can't do what?"

Angelo squeezed the handset. "I'm terminating our arrangement."

"Terminating our...? Okay, calm down. The arrangement stays."

"No. Things have happened. Thank you, and I wish you all the best."

Finally, she said, "For your sake, I hope you haven't snitched."

"Snitched? To the police?" Angelo gave a crazed laugh. "I haven't told anybody. Why would I? I'm as guilty as you. I don't want to go to jail either."

"Listen, hang tight, I'll be in touch. Don't do anything stupid."

Heather ended the call. Angelo stared at the handset. When he returned it to the cradle, he thought of Sofia, of Teresa-Kate, and then of Sofia again, until he wanted nothing more than to lose himself in alcohol.

At home, drunk, Angelo lolled across the couch. Later, his mobile rang. Stirring from his stupor, groggy, Angelo reached to the coffee table and took a gulp of warm sherry before grabbing the phone. He said, *"Pronto."*

"Excuse me?"

Angelo consulted his watch, swiped a hand over his numb face. Night lay heavy around the curtains. "Yes, this is De Luca and Son Funeral Directors."

"Mr. De Luca? Oh, thank the baby Lord Jesus."

Prescience needled Angelo fully awake. He said, "How may I help you?"

"I'm the mother of Teresa-Kate. You delivered her body this morning for the viewing. Something terrible has happened. She's gone."

Angelo sat up. "Gone?"

"I couldn't sleep. I went to check on her. The casket is empty."

"Empty? You mean your daughter's body has been stolen?" The shock rendered Angelo sober. "Did you call the police?"

"I've called everybody," the mother said. "Help me. Please, help me."

"I'll try my very best." Shaking in fear and anger, he hung up and called Heather the Body Wrangler. As soon as Heather answered, Angelo yelled, "Why did you do it? To blackmail me, is that it? A single X-ray will reveal the PVC pipes. Is that what you're planning? To hold that X-ray over my head?"

"Angelo?" Heather sighed. "You sound drunk. It's late. Let's talk tomorrow."

"Tell me what you did with Teresa-Kate."

"Who?"

"The little child: the girl with the raven hair."

"That kid you didn't complete?"

"Tell me where she is."

"I don't know what you're talking about." Heather paused. "Are you high? Having some kind of stroke? Look, I think maybe you should call an ambulance."

Unnerved, Angelo disconnected the call. If Heather hadn't stolen the child's body, where was it? He thought of Teresa-Kate leaping from the table, coming for him, and he shuddered. Perhaps Heather was right. Perhaps there was something wrong with him, like a mental breakdown. The strain of stealing from the dead must be unravelling his mind. Surely, he had hallucinated Teresa-Kate's resurrection. And those inhumanly long teeth? Why, gums always shrink after death.

Oh, deliver me. He put his face into his hands. *Deliver me, even though I don't deserve it.* The house shifted and creaked in the wind. Frightened, Angelo stared at the doorways leading to the kitchen and entrance hall. Nothing happened. Over the next few hours, he drank the sherry bottle dry. At around 4 a.m., he lurched toward bed. The mattress swam up and hit him. For the longest time, he didn't dream.

And then he dreamed of Teresa-Kate.

He woke up.

Or, at least, he thought he did.

Teresa-Kate wrapped her fish-cold arms about his neck and sunk her bite into the meat of his shoulder. The pain, the wet and sloppy sound of her fangs chewing into his flesh, made him shriek over and over.

As he drowsily came awake, the sound came to him slowly, soft and familiar and regular as a pulse, comforting him. Angelo tried, but he was unable to open his eyes. Confused, he attempted to sit up, failed. Cold steel lay beneath his naked body. And now he knew where he was: on the preparation table in his funeral parlour. That sound, that regular sound, was the dripping of the tap into the scrub sink.

Panic lurched through him.

Had he been drugged? Kidnapped by Heather and her body snatchers? The last thing Angelo remembered…drinking, passing out, the nightmare, that terrible nightmare about Teresa-Kate. How much time had passed since then?

What in God's name was going on?

More sensation returned to his body. He became aware of a strange emptiness within his chest, an abnormally heavy weight within his belly. Gradually, he understood what it meant. He had undergone an autopsy. His internal organs, including heart and lungs, were in a plastic bag sewn inside his abdomen. His death certificate would echo Teresa-Kate's: Angelo De Luca, fifty-nine, succumbed to an unidentified infection, administered by the bite of an unknown animal, probably a dog.

He wanted to scream. Was he dead? Undead? Had Teresa-Kate been conscious like this when he'd harvested her bones?

The door of the preparation room opened. Footsteps approached. Whistling started—it was Gary Mathews. Angelo strained to give a signal, but couldn't wiggle his fingers, his toes; in fact, couldn't even take a breath.

"Sorry, old mate," Gary said. "But you know how it is. Business is business."

The rip of Velcro, the one-two unfolding of heavy fabric. Angelo recognised those noises. Gary had opened the roll-bag of his butcher's knives. The subsequent *whisk-whisk-whisk* must be Gary honing a blade against the sharpening steel.

And that blade would be the boning knife.

THE BELLY OF THE BEAST

MA Hoyler

"Geez, Mailey, we're not gonna get into the party if you stop to gawk like a tourist every two steps." Tiffany pushed her friend forward, nearly knocking the taller woman off her shoes.

"I thought you said you had an in," Mailey replied, snapping out of her reverie and struggling to keep her balance. "I was just thinking—"

"And that's why you're never going to be a trophy wife!" Tiffany replied triumphantly, then hooked her arm through her roommate's. "Now, remember, you're June, right? Mailey-May, May-June, yeah? Easy to remember? And don't forget that I'm Ava."

"I don't see why we need aliases," Mailey muttered.

"You want one of these rich freaks to find you at home?" Tiffany asked.

"I thought that was the goal?"

"Yes, but the *right* rich freak, not just any rich freak." Tiffany patted her arm twice.

They walked up the drive, sticking to the side so the shiny black cars bringing guests could glide past them. Above them, the full moon glowed large and white. Within the next hour, the first shadow of the eclipse was due, but for now, it simply cast everything in shades of silver.

Just ahead of them, a group of guys in suits and ties were chatting a little too casually and laughing a little too freely. Mailey thought she recognized one of them as a coworker from the grocery store, but she didn't dare call out to him. The Mansion, as the townies called it, was famous for its exclusive monthly parties, and their high school years had been full of stories of people who tried to sneak in.

The group of men reached the stairs first and were intercepted at the door by a black-suited butler. Mailey and Tiffany stopped to wait.

"So how do you know this Mr. Thornhoe?" Mailey asked.

"It's Thornrake, not Thornhoe. We've been seeing each other for about three months."

Mailey snorted. "'Seeing each other'? What is he, old?"

Ahead of them, the butler gestured for the group of men to leave. Tiffany pulled Mailey toward the car that had just arrived.

"Remy!" she said, her voice higher and breathier than usual, a beaming smile on her face.

The man who stepped out smiled widely. "Hello, Ava. Is this your friend, then?"

"This is June," Tiffany replied, accepting his arm when he offered it.

Mailey smiled as she took his other arm. He was almost too handsome. His dark hair was perfectly coiffed, his skin airbrushed smooth and unblemished. The arm that held Mailey's was warm, even through his fine suit. They walked up the steps to the door, where Mr. Thornrake dropped Tiffany's arm to pull a shining invitation out of his suit pocket. The butler looked it over, then bowed and gestured them through.

The cooling night air melted into warmth inside. Mailey was escorted into a small crowd of guests in gowns and suits so beautiful they dazzled her eyes. Mr. Thornrake led them through the foyer and into the main room, which could easily have fit the entire parking lot of Mailey and Tiffany's apartment building.

Curved staircases on either side led upstairs, and a huge, open fireplace lit with twinkle lights and tissue paper flames divided the ballroom into two separate areas. To the right was a dance floor, a live string quartet providing the sort of music Mailey had always imagined the rich would dance to. To the left was a space with scattered furniture and well-stocked buffets. The entire room smelled of perfume and spices, and underneath it all, something organic, like good earth.

Mailey went to release her arm from Mr. Thornrake's, but his grip only tightened as he led them toward the tables laden with flowers and fine desserts.

"Miss Ava!" The man who intercepted their path was just as handsome as Mr. Thornrake, his eyes blue, and his cheekbones sharp. "Delighted to see you again. Hello, Remy."

"Hello, Cassian," Mr. Thornrake replied, keeping his hold on Mailey. "Good to see you again."

Mailey had always been tall. She'd endured jokes about basketball, the weather, and beanpoles all her life, as well as warnings that she'd never find a husband. In her low heels, she'd looked over the head of Mr. Thornrake, but Cassian looked her straight in the eye before kissing the back of her hand, with lips that were soft and left a sticky residue on her skin.

"This is my friend, June," Tiffany said. "June, this is Cassian Bathory."

"Hello, Mr. Bathory," Mailey said. She recognized the name immediately. Mr. Bathory owned both of the places she worked at, and she occasionally handled his suits when they were dropped off or picked up by his staff.

"Perhaps I could steal her for a dance?" Mr. Bathory said to Mr. Thornrake, an easy smile showing a line of crisp white teeth.

"I suppose you could," Mr. Thornrake replied, finally releasing his hold on Mailey's arm, just so Mr. Bathory could take her other one and lead her past the marble fireplace and onto the dance floor.

"I'm sorry, I don't know how to…" Mailey had to pause. She only knew one kind of fancy dance and had no idea if this was it or not. "Waltz."

"Just relax," Mr. Bathory replied, cupping her right hand in his and pressing his other hand against her back. "And follow my lead."

The dance seemed simple, but by the time she settled into the rhythm enough to force a smile at her dancing partner, Mailey had already trod on his feet several times.

"I don't recall seeing you here before," Mr. Bathory said, as though it hadn't been several minutes of awkward apologizing between this moment and stepping onto the dance floor.

"This is my first lunar party," Mailey admitted.

Mr. Bathory laughed in delight, a charming sound. "Well, my dear, I hope you enjoy yourself. They say it's always good to have a party virgin at a lunar party."

"A what?" Mailey asked, her cheeks heating.

"It's no judgment on you, just that you've never been before, that's all." He was still smiling, but there was something Mailey didn't like about it. "When did you move to Sarasota?"

"I've been here my entire life," she answered, relaxing slightly as the music brought her back into the simple steps.

"Really? And you've never made one before? Abital should be ashamed."

"Who's Abital?"

"Our lovely host for the evening. The one who sent you the invitation and got you in the door? They're very strict about only letting those with invitations in."

"Yes. Of course, Abital," Mailey said, realizing maybe she should have been less honest about a few details. Determined not to tread on his expensive shoes again, Mailey kept an eye on her feet.

The music ended, and they separated to clap politely. Mailey took the opportunity to excuse herself from the dance floor—and Mr. Bathory— and look for Tiffany. Behind her, Cassian Bathory caught the arm of a woman in a peacock -blue gown, and swept her out onto the dance floor, whispering conspiratorially.

The party had filled in while she'd been occupied. White-suited servers wove in and out of chatting groups, offering glasses of something pink and bubbling. Mailey took one so she'd have something to sip if anyone tried to talk to her as she searched for her friend's red dress and blonde hair.

When she finally spied Tiffany, her friend was sitting in a group with Mr. Thornrake and two of their friends from high school, Kimberly and Erica. Mailey joined them, keeping her glass close to her chest, and nudging Tiffany over to sit on the edge of the chaise lounge.

"How was your dance? Cassian's quite light on his feet." Mr. Thornrake said.

"He was an amazing dancer; I just hope his toes are okay." Mailey forced a self-deprecating smile. To her relief, this earned a polite chuckle around the conversation circle.

"Ava was just telling us how you met at the country club," Mr. Thornrake said, leaning back onto a cushion that probably cost more than Mailey's shoes. "I'd love to hear your side of the story."

"Um." Mailey had never been to the country club. She took a quick sip of her drink. It wasn't the champagne she'd been expecting. Instead, it was a rush of flowers and fruit that filled her mouth with the taste of summer and plenty. She almost lost her first mouthful in a gasp.

"Good, isn't it?" Erica asked. "Go slow; it's stronger than it seems."

"It's *so* good. What is it?"

"We call it Moon Wine. Rumor is Abital makes it in-house," Mr. Thornrake answered. He'd started to say more when someone called to him from across the room and he excused himself.

Together, the woman shared a sigh of relief.

"How the hell did you two get in?" Kimberly asked, a familiar smirk lifting one corner of her mouth.

"I have connections," Tiffany replied, raising her chin. "What about you two?"

"A girl doesn't tell her secrets." Kimberly giggled in a manner she must have meant to sound coy.

"How did *you* get here?" Erica stared Mailey down. "Do the old boys know you're not down for sex?"

"Excuse me." A stunning woman joined their circle, her peacock-blue dress making a striking contrast with her red hair. "Do you mind if I join you? My feet hurt."

Mailey slid closer to Tiffany, and the woman sat next to her.

"I don't think we've met?" Kimberly said, leaning closer. The woman didn't answer. She handed Erica her nearly empty drink and leaned forward to tug off her left shoe. Erica looked at the glass like she wanted to spit in it.

The woman glanced up, an easy smile on her face, her eyes dark wells against pale skin. "I know you two, but not you…" She stared straight at Mailey.

"Her name's June," Tiffany said before Mailey could recover from that intense look. "She's my friend."

"June." The woman took Mailey's hand and stroked her thumb gently along her knuckles. "Delighted. Call me Cadeus."

"That's an interesting name," Kimberly said, sliding closer.

"It's an old family one. Would you dance with me, June?" Cadeus kept her hold, a slight pressure easing Mailey to her feet.

Mailey relented, and Cadeus guided her to the dance floor. The string quartet had switched to a cover of a modern pop song. Cadeus found an open spot and turned to face her, cradling her just as Mr. Bathory had.

"So, June," Cadeus said. "Tiffany brought you tonight?"

"I got an invitation from Abital," Mailey said, remembering her earlier misstep with Bathory.

"Really?" Cadeus's perfect eyebrow rose as she pulled Mailey closer.

No longer confident in her ability to speak, Mailey nodded.

"Well, welcome," Cadeus said, her expression fading into a smile that made Mailey's heart melt. "How long have you known Tiffany, then?"

Something bothered Mailey about the question, and she misplaced her feet, bringing one down on the hem of Cadeus's gown. She stepped back quickly.

"Oh my god, I am so sorry!"

Cadeus flicked her dress back carelessly. "It's fine, June. This dress wasn't really meant for dancing."

The use of her alias made something click in Mailey's head. "Who's Tiffany?" she asked as Cadeus pulled her close once more.

"Your friend, the one you came with. Her name is Tiffany, right?"

Mailey shook her head. "Her name's Ava."

"Of course." She gave a musical laugh. "I must have gotten confused." She moved quickly, pulling her foot out from under Mailey's before it came down again. "Why don't we get a drink?"

Relieved, Mailey let the smaller woman lead her to where floor-to-ceiling glass doors opened onto a stone patio. The moon hung large, its reflection dancing on the surface of a pool that was more water feature than recreational spot. A dark spot had appeared on the bottom of the moon, promising the eclipse was on its way.

Cadeus took two glasses off a passing silver tray and handed one to Mailey. She sipped the other, leaving a lipstick mark along the rim. Her dark eyes caught Mailey staring. Blushing, Mailey looked away.

"Tell me about yourself, June. What did you do that got Abital's attention?"

Mailey shrugged, realizing halfway through it was an inelegant gesture. "I'm not sure. I got the invitation, and Ava persuaded me to come. It sounded like fun, you know?"

Cadeus nodded and took another sip. "And tonight's such a special night, isn't it?"

Mailey covered her confusion with a mouthful of the sweet wine.

"Why is tonight special, June?" Cadeus leaned forward, her voice sensually low, tipping her head to the side.

Mailey froze.

"It was on the invitation, of course," Cadeus added, setting her glass down on the stone wall. "The thing is, none of those whores were on the guest list. Not Kimberly, not Erica, not Tiffany, and definitely not you."

Mailey's heart beat harder against her ribs, the wine in her hands rippling.

"You see, *June*, I am Cadeus Abital. I handwrote every single invitation, so I know that no one who works at the fucking P&C received one."

"We'll go," Mailey promised, stepping back from the fire on Cadeus's face. "I'll grab Tiff and we'll go."

Cadeus bared her teeth. "So. Her name *is* Tiffany."

Mailey turned and ran as quickly as her skirt allowed. She could feel everyone's eyes on her, but when she looked, it seemed no one was paying her any attention.

None of the other women were where Mailey had left them. Steadying herself on one of the thick drapes that hung against the bookshelf at the back of the room, she surveyed the crowd. She spotted Erica at one of the food tables, laughing at something a man had said.

Shoving through the revelers, Mailey grabbed her arm. "Where's Tiffany?"

Erica tried to shake her off. "Geez, Maypole."

Mailey ignored the nickname. "Where is she?"

"I saw her head upstairs with Remy," Erica replied. "Didn't see—"

Mailey hurried toward the sweeping staircases. There were two that curved upward, mirror images leading to the same open hallway upstairs. She stopped before reaching the steps as the butler was closing the front door and watched him use a large key to lock it from the inside. He turned and caught her eye, freezing for a moment. Glancing around, he unlocked the door and opened it again, gesturing sharply for Mailey to exit.

"Have you seen my friend? She's wearing a black dress," Mailey asked.

The butler shook his head. "It's too late for her. Go."

"I have to find her," Mailey replied, turning up the stairs.

"Tiffany?" Mailey whispered, stepping into the hallway at the top. It ran in both directions, but a familiar strappy black shoe lay to the right. She picked it up as she crept forward, trying to listen over the sounds of the party below. The carpet beneath her feet softened her steps. The hall eventually opened into a seating area with a balcony overlooking the dance floor below. Kimberly was seated on one of the overstuffed couches, a woman bending over her, lips on lips. Leaving them alone, Mailey continued, glancing into open bedrooms larger than her and Tiffany's entire apartment. Some were occupied, some were empty.

She found Tiffany's other shoe outside a closed door and paused. Leaning close, she heard moaning.

Needing to know Tiffany was safe, Mailey opened the door as quietly as she could. As the widening gap allowed more sound to drift out into the hall, she realized Tiffany's moans weren't ones of pleasure.

The room was green and gold, dominated by the enormous bed that had more than enough space for the two bodies tangled on it. She couldn't recognize the man by his back, nor the briar-like tattoos covering it, but Tiffany lay under him. She made eye contact and gasped, reaching out.

"Help…me."

Mailey charged, leaping on the bed and aiming the hardest punch she could at the man's kidneys. He fell to the side. Blood gushed from the remains of Tiffany's throat, a liquid-red veil down her chest.

All of Mailey's thoughts of fighting were replaced by cold fear. "Tiffany?" She grabbed her friend's hand, then thought better and instead tried to stop the wound with both hands.

"Behind you," Tiffany rasped.

Instinctively, Mailey ducked, and a blow that would have struck the side of her head instead ripped her hair out of its bun. She screamed and scrambled away.

It was Remy Thornrake, she realized in a cold rush, but his face was wrong. His red-stained teeth were too large and too sharp, the lips that bared them pulled too far back. Mr. Thornrake slid off the bed.

"Come on, Ju-unnne," he purred, drawing her false name out.

"What the hell?" Mailey demanded. She gripped Tiffany's discarded shoe tightly in her hand. It wasn't much of a weapon, but she didn't have time to look for something better.

A scream came from the hallway, and Mr. Thornrake turned. Mailey took advantage of the distraction and drove Tiffany's stiletto into his eye, shoving him back into the door and slamming it closed. She grabbed his short hair and swung again. He caught her wrist and twisted it, sending spikes of pain up her arm. The shoe clattered to the floor as she cried out. Mailey brought her other hand across his face, her cheap manicure jabbing into his other eye.

Mr. Thornrake's shriek was unholy, and he lunged blindly, snapping at Mailey's neck—or where he thought her neck ought to be. But Mailey ducked, struggling to free her numb wrist. The movement brought her down to the open pants, barely hanging on his waist, and she aimed a hard kick.

With a howl of pain, he released her. She crawled back, then got to her feet and kicked again, knocking the sightless and distracted creature onto the floor.

"Tiffany?" she whispered, turning to her friend. The blood had stopped flowing from her throat, and her eyes had gone cold and sightless. Mailey tried to find a pulse, then leaned close to her cheek, searching for breath against her skin. But there was nothing. She swallowed, her vision blurring dangerously. "Tiff?"

The bed shifted. Mr. Thornrake dragged himself upright, sweeping his hand across the rumpled sheets, looking for her. A bloody, gross parody of a mask covered his face from the dripping eye sockets down.

Slamming her good hand over her mouth to muffle any screaming,

Mailey crawled off the opposite side. She crept to the door and slowly opened it. It had a built-in lock, and she shifted it to the locked position. When she looked back, Mr. Thornrake was crouched over Tiffany's body, mouth already finding the wound on her neck again.

Holding back sobs, Mailey exited and closed the door as softly as she could. Something heavy slammed into the other side almost immediately. She yelped, throwing her weight back to keep it shut.

"June?" Mr. Thornrake's voice called. "June, Tiffany needs you." The door rattled again, but thankfully didn't open.

Mailey tried to run, but she was wading through gelatin, and the most she could manage was an unsteady walk. She needed to run, though. How long before Thornrake discovered she'd just locked the door?

The woman in the black dress was still bent over Kimberly. She looked up when Mailey stumbled into view, her bloody teeth sharp and bared.

The music had stopped. All Mailey could hear were pained groans. Giving the woman a wide berth, Mailey made her way over to the edge of the balcony and looked below. The floor was mostly empty, with sprays of red decorating the polished wooden surface. A member of the band lay sprawled across the fireplace, four black tie-wearing guests bent over him.

A wet sucking noise came from the couch where Kimberly lay. Mailey didn't look, didn't turn around, just continued limping toward the sweeping staircases. When the door behind her splintered, a fresh jolt of adrenaline sent her running down the stairs.

Ahead and beneath her was the door, and the heavy lock that held it shut. The butler had tried to tell her to get out. She sat heavily partway down the stairs.

"Where did she go?" a familiar male voice roared above and behind her.

"What happened to you?" an unfamiliar woman replied.

Mailey slid down the stairs, not trying to stand or make excessive noise, heart beating loudly enough that surely someone could hear it. She stopped on the last steps as Erica ran past her, slamming into the front door and clawing for the lock. Her dress was wet. Mr. Bathory strode up, his suit jacket gone and his shirt red-stained. Erica tried to dash around him, but he grabbed her hair and pulled her close.

Mailey left her shoes on the stairs, tiptoeing barefoot around the end of the staircase and putting her back against the wall. The shock of everything gave way to a survivalist calm. She needed to escape. The front door was locked. The doors to the garden were on the other side of the main hall. That was the only exit she knew about.

She slid toward her left, trying to see everything and nothing at the same time. A body blocked her path, pale and still, wrapped in a cheap-looking black suit. Mailey stepped over him.

A huge window covered with floor-to-ceiling drapes offered a hiding spot, but no way to escape. Instead, it showcased the empty driveway leading up to the house, the front garden, and the perfectly sculpted hedges. Beyond all of it, a stone wall blocked the road from view, crushing any hopes of waving down a passing driver.

Taking a deep breath, Mailey opened the curtain enough to peek through it out over the room. A dark eye, surrounded by smokey eyeliner, stared back.

She snapped the fabric closed, stifling a scream with a blood-sticky hand. Long nails slid through the hidden gap in the fabric, and the heavy curtains yanked open. Cadeus wasn't covered in blood, but it was on her lips and finger-painted across her chest.

"June," she said, her voice just as beautiful as it had been before. "Did you find Tiffany?"

The mundanity of the question gave Mailey pause. She nodded slowly.

"Where is she?" Cadeus brought a glass of wine to her lips and took a sip.

"She's dead," Mailey whispered. "He—Mr. Thornrake—killed her."

Cadeus gave a knowing nod, her face shifting into a sympathetic expression. "That must have been disappointing."

Mailey nodded again. The way Cadeus held the curtain, Mailey couldn't see anything but her. She didn't know if the rest of the guests were waiting to attack, or if it was just Cadeus. "He almost killed me."

"How did you get away?"

"I blinded him." As though to prove her point, Mailey held up the finger that was now covered with dried blood.

Cadeus's eyebrows lifted in surprise. "You blinded him? With your fingers?"

"And Tiffany's shoe," Mailey added.

Eyes widening, a slow smile spread across the shorter woman's face, giving way to a brief laugh. "It would appear I've underestimated you, June," she said through a smile that would have, under other circumstances, turned Mailey's knees to Jell-O. "So, what are you going to do now?"

"I've got to get out."

"And then what?" Cadeus finished her drink while Mailey thought. "You understand that I can't allow you to tell the police. What a scandal that would cause."

"Why?" Mailey asked, her voice weak and shaking. "Why are you doing this?"

Cadeus shook her head and clicked her tongue.

"We just…we just wanted to have fun!" Mailey added. "We weren't hurting anyone."

A long, pointed fingernail carefully swept a loose strand of hair off Mailey's face and tucked it behind her ear. Cadeus smiled. Like Mr. Thornrake, the smile was too wide, and the bared teeth were too sharp.

Knowing it was now or never, Mailey lunged, knocking Cadeus backward and dashing across the open floor for the doors to the patio. She slipped on a patch of blood, but managed to keep her feet and making it to the fireplace before something caught her ankle in a vice grip.

"She's mine!" Cadeus's shout reverberated through the room. The hold on her ankle loosened, but it had done its job. Mailey froze, a hand resting on the podium that lifted the fireplace. Now, in the belly of the beast, she couldn't escape the smell of blood and death. Several guests, red dripping from their lips, tracked her every movement as she circled the fireplace. The body with a band lapel pin blocked her from completing a full circle.

Her bare foot caught on something gooey and wet. She slipped again, screaming as she tried to break her fall with her injured hand.

Silence greeted the echoes. Cadeus sauntered around the edge of a pillar, walking with graceful calm, the hem of her gown dragging a red smear behind it. Mailey sent a frantic look around. This was a fireplace, wasn't it? Where was the poker? She didn't find it, but as Cadeus began to bend over her, she found a switch.

The gas lit in a flash, the paper decorations bursting into flames immediately, followed by the body draped over it. As Cadeus' firm hand caught Mailey's chin, forcing it up and back, the flames leaped from the body to a fallen banner, traveling along it to another body, devouring everything in its path. Unfazed, Cadeus seemed focused on getting Mailey's neck in just the right position, her eyes tracing the blue veins hungrily.

"Shh," she whispered, her warm breath sending goosebumps across Mailey's skin. "I'll make it quick."

"Please," Mailey gasped as cool lips brushed the pounding in her throat.

The shriek of the fire alarm startled them both, and Cadeus's grip loosened enough for Mailey to pull free. Inhuman screams came from the other side of the fireplace, and Cadeus stood to see, the fire reflecting oddly in her dark eyes. Mailey made a last, desperate scramble for the doors, only to find they were locked too.

One of the blood-soaked guests ventured too close to the fire, and it hungrily took his pant leg, then his expensive coat. In his panic, he'd fallen against the bookcase. Now the fire climbed upward.

Cadeus had vanished, and the few still-living guests were scattering, trying to rip open the same doors Mailey already knew were a lost cause. The fire crackled. Mailey covered her mouth and nose with her hands and ran down a shadowy hallway. She found herself in a huge kitchen and yet another locked door, the small windows teasing her with a glimpse of the outside world.

"No," Mailey whispered. "Nononononono!" She pounded her fists against it.

"You!" Cadeus's angry voice came from behind her. She appeared from nowhere, grabbing Mailey by the hair and pulling her away. Mailey's despair gave way to a final, gasping panic, a diver realizing there wasn't enough air in their tank, or a rabbit finally seeing the open beaks of the eaglets.

She jabbed for Cadeus's face, but Cadeus caught her hands, and the smaller woman pinned her against her chest, close enough for Mailey to smell the blood on her breath.

"Who *are* you?" Cadeus demanded. She didn't move to bite this time, just stared up at Mailey with an intense heat. "Why are you doing this?"

"I don't want to die." It was the only thought in Mailey's head.

"I don't want to die either, June. I didn't three hundred years ago, and I definitely don't tonight," Cadeus snapped. "But *someone* lit my house on fire."

"Unlock the doors!"

"The butler took the keys when he left, and he won't be back until morning." Cadeus's voice carried an edge of frustration.

Something heavy fell out in the main room. They heard the crash and flinched as a wave of heat and smoke pushed lazily into the kitchen.

"Is there another exit?" Mailey begged.

Cadeus shook her head, her hair falling out of its perfect style. "We didn't want any humans to escape."

"Can we break a window?"

"Shatterproof."

Mailey laughed, her mind fracturing into several different states of rage and other emotions she couldn't name.

Cadeus let her go, and they separated. Mailey slid to the floor and looked around one more time, running her fingers hopelessly along the door edges. A thick, rolling blanket of black smoke formed above them. With sudden inspiration, Mailey dug her nails into the hinge, the pin rising enough that she renewed her effort.

"Help me!" she shouted to Cadeus.

The other woman's fingers were stronger, her claw-like nails scratching the metal as they pulled the pin free. Mailey scrambled to her feet, meeting the sinking smoke as she went for the next hinge. She doubled over, gasping, but fumbling for the second pin. She yelped with contaminated breath as one of her nails broke off. Her hands were brushed aside, and Cadeus used a silvery knife blade as a wedge. After an agonizingly long time, the second hinge gave.

Both women threw their weight against the door handle, and through desperate pushing and pulling, they opened enough of a gap for Cadeus to sink her fingers into it and yank with an animalistic roar. The door gave with a splintering crack, and the women stumbled out into the cool night air, the smoke following them eagerly.

Cadeus, who'd fallen behind Mailey, shrieked as the fire caught the train of her dress. Mailey grabbed her, hauling her further away from the flames while stomping on the smoldering fabric.

They kept moving until they reached the edge of the parking area.

Mailey stumbled to the far side of the blacktop, sitting heavily on the stone wall that separated it from the rest of the grounds. Cool air hit her lungs, and she doubled over coughing.

The mansion burned.

Black smoke boiled up, blocking the bright—no, dimmed—light of the blood-red moon. The eclipse. Of course.

As far as she could tell, Mailey and Cadeus were the only ones who'd escaped.

Cadeus sat next to her, brushing her fingers down her arms as though she was cold. Even sitting on the same surface, Mailey was still a good head taller than her.

"What now?" Mailey asked.

Cadeus looked up through her long lashes.

When she didn't answer, Mailey asked another question. "Are you going to kill me?"

Red lips puckered thoughtfully before Cadeus turned her head toward the driveway, listening. "Sirens," she announced. "Tell them whatever you want. You, my dear June, or July, or whatever your name is, are an extraordinary woman." She pushed herself to her feet, then stroked her fingers down Mailey's jaw one more time. "I don't expect this to be a final goodbye."

She leaned forward and brushed a kiss on Mailey's shocked lips before turning and walking off into the garden.

Now Mailey could hear the sirens. Another fit of coughing doubled her over as the first of the fire vehicles arrived.

The light of another full moon found Mailey hurrying home with the taste of fear in her throat. She hadn't meant to be out after the sun went down—she never was these days—but Mr. Piggly had needed her to cover another shift.

Now the full moon stared down as she hurried from the bus stop to her apartment.

Her key slid into the lock, and she ducked inside.

The door closed, Mailey sighed. She was inside, yes, but their—no, her—apartment was an on the second floor. Above her, the apartment was dark; if she'd known she'd be out so late, she would have left some lights on.

"Come on, Mailey," she whispered, then hefted her bags and walked wearily up the stairs.

Turning on the kitchen light, she opened her box of white wine (she couldn't stomach drinking anything red anymore) and poured it lukewarm into a plastic cup.

"So, this is how you live?"

The dropped cup bounced off the floor, sending wine everywhere. Mailey spun, her feet shifting out from under her, and she landed hard on her hip.

Cadeus stood in the living room shadows. Her face was narrower, but her eyes were still the pools of darkness that had haunted Mailey's nightmares and daydreams.

"Cadeus," Mailey said, not moving to stand.

"Mailey." Cadeus smiled and stepped closer. "That is your name. I know that now." She crouched, setting her soft hands on Mailey's bent knees. The long manicure was gone, and while her nails were still perfectly shaped, there was dirt underneath them.

"Are you here to kill me?" Mailey asked, keeping the "*finally*" to herself.

"I should have drained you the moment we were clear of that fire. I could almost thank you, by the way. As awful as it was, that fire released me from my family." While she spoke, Cadeus stopped caressing Mailey's knees, and despite her fear, Mailey missed her touch.

"So, you owe me."

"Yes," Cadeus admitted, shifting her weight so she was kneeling more than crouching. "Twice over, in fact. So no, I'm not here to kill you."

"Why are you here, then?" She should be screaming for help. The apartment walls were thin. Instead, ignoring her rabbit heart, she leaned closer.

For the first time, Cadeus looked away. "I'm here because you're beautiful, Mailey. Not only are you the most beautiful thing I've seen in the last three hundred years, but," she tipped her head to the side, "ever since we parted ways, I have thought of you every waking hour, and half of my sleeping ones. There is nothing I want more than to spend the next three hundred years discovering why, exactly, you fascinate me so."

Mailey couldn't speak at first, but she needed to know. "Are you offering—"

Cadeus looked straight into her eyes. "I am offering you three hundred years, or more, to find out what vicious delights this world has to offer."

Slowly, intentionally, Mailey tilted her head to the right and brushed her hair off her neck. She wanted this. Cadeus wasn't the only one who'd been haunted since that night.

Cadeus's teeth were sharp, bringing a rush of pain and euphoria that made Mailey gasp.

As Mailey grew too weak to keep her hold, the room began to dim at the edges, and Cadeus sat back. Holding Mailey's narrowing gaze, Cadeus caught her own tongue on her teeth, biting deep enough that blood ran down her chin.

Grabbing Mailey's face, she leaned in for a kiss.

Mailey gagged when the trickle of hot blood hit her own tongue, but she could do nothing but swallow it down. Warmth boiled up, leaving her tingling from her toes to her hair. Her vision cleared, then crisped. On the other side of the wall, her neighbors were watching late night news. On the floor below, a dog snored.

The shorter woman watched, her heartbeat slower than Mailey's, but Mailey's was slowing to match it. Cadeus stood, her clothes rustling, and reached down. "Give me your hand," she ordered, her voice low and soft and full of promise.

Mailey took it, standing in the light of a moon that was brighter than it ever had before.

DADDY'S GIRL

Valerie B. Williams

TED SANDERSON ROLLED his head to the left and watched his daughter sleep. Strapped in and flat on their backs within the capsule, there was little else to do on the week-long journey. The shuttle had been programmed for its destination, and the crew had responsibilities only in an emergency.

Two more crew members lay silently in the rear pods. Ted couldn't tell if they were sleeping or just daydreaming and didn't want to speak for fear of waking Chloe. Assignment to the experimental space outpost had been her goal ever since her mother took command fourteen months ago. With Ted joining the mission as well, the family would be reunited.

Chloe moaned, licking her lips and smiling. That smile hadn't changed since she was six years old—how could she be twenty-six already? She opened her eyes and met his gaze. Dark hair and pale skin made her blue eyes look like they were glowing.

"Dr. Sanderson," she said.

"Lieutenant Sanderson," he replied. "We'll be there in another couple of hours. Can you believe it?"

Chloe reached for his hand and squeezed it. "Thanks, Daddy. I wouldn't be here without you." She gave him a wry smile. "I wouldn't be *anywhere* without you."

Chloe had fallen very ill just before her mother left on the mission. Anita had offered to stay, but Ted could tell her heart wasn't in it. His wife had always been career driven while Ted took on the role of the nurturing parent. Besides, as a medical doctor, he was well-qualified to oversee his daughter's treatment. After the rest of the medical community had given up, he'd researched and formulated a special blend of medicines and organic materials and fed it to her in the form of smoothies. And it worked. A dozen large cartons of the blend traveled in the shuttle with them.

To look at her today, you'd never guess how close to death she'd been.

The airlock hissed open. A dark-haired woman, erect in her uniform, waited in front of a group of crew members. Ted took off his helmet and saluted.

"Captain Sanderson." The beginnings of a smile twitched at his lips.

"Dr. Sanderson." She returned the salute with a full smile.

Chloe echoed Ted's formal greeting. Captain Anita Sanderson stepped forward and placed both hands on her daughter's shoulders.

"Chloe," she said. "You look well. Congratulations on your assignment. I'm proud of you." She gave her an awkward, one-armed hug and moved away to stand with both hands behind her back.

The Sandersons would be the first family to occupy the outpost. There had been one married couple, but never parents and a child.

Chloe stepped aside to allow the other two replacement crew members to enter. Ted suppressed a grin at her serious demeanor. She so desperately wanted to impress her mother.

For the next four days, departing crew members would complete handoff briefings to their replacements. Chloe was replacing the biologist in charge of the rodent population. Ted would be the new Medical Director. With the exception of the captain, crewmembers only served for one year, with a small number of replacements rotating in every quarter. New blood was a good thing in an ongoing project, preventing the complacency that could so easily slip into a monotonous existence.

Ted lay with Anita nestled against his side. The clock showed 5:00 a.m. Along with artificial gravity, the simulation of a twenty-four-hour day gave the illusion of normalcy in a very abnormal environment.

"Don't get uppity just because you're sleeping with the captain," she said, running her fingers lightly through his chest hair.

He gave her a lingering kiss. "Wouldn't dream of it."

"Chloe looks good, really healthy." She propped herself up on her elbow. "Those smoothies you came up with are a miracle. Are you sure you brought enough?"

Ted looked at the ceiling, making mental calculations yet again, then met her gaze. "Yeah, more than enough. She's on a maintenance dose now, just one every other day."

"I still can't believe she risked her career, and her life, for that stupid trip." Anita sat up on the side of the bed, cracking her knuckles in frustration.

Chloe's celebratory postgraduate trip to Bolivia with friends had been a disaster. Lost in the jungle for two weeks before being rescued by missionaries, the three girls returned sick, pale, weak, and listless. Sherry died a week later. Jenn's family whisked her away to a clinic in Switzerland, and she hadn't been heard from since. Chloe pulled through with the constant care and attention of her father and his miraculous formula. Experts had diagnosed her illness as a particularly virulent type of anemia as the result of a spider bite. Chloe still had the scar on her right calf; for a while they thought she might lose the leg.

"She's fine now," Ted said, rubbing his wife's tense back. "And for God's sake, don't mention it to Chloe. She feels guilty enough."

Anita gave Ted a quick kiss, then started for the small washroom. "Enough lazing around. Time to get these newbies in gear. And that includes you."

Ted watched Chloe move down the row of small glass enclosures, making notes on her tablet as she went. The mice and rats were subjects for the effects of long-term space survival. These were the second—and some third—generation of rodents. The first generation had lived surprisingly long lives.

"How do they look?" he asked, coming up behind her.

Chloe spun around with a gasp. "Doctor! I didn't hear you coming."

Ted looked around the otherwise empty lab. "I think it's safe to call me Dad," he said in a stage whisper. He stroked her cool cheek with the back of his hand.

Chloe shook her head. "Don't want to get into the habit. Bad for morale." A frown creased her forehead.

"You're right, sorry. Old habits and all that." They'd become exceptionally close during Chloe's illness, but she was taking this assignment very seriously.

"Anyway," he continued, "come see me when you're done. You're due for your next dose in," he looked at his watch, "twenty minutes."

"I haven't forgotten." Chloe folded her arms and gave a half-smile. "I've really got to finish up before Lieutenant Dietrich gets back. This is my last chance to pick his brain before he leaves." The half-smile spread into a full one. She looked so much like her mother.

He left Chloe muttering to herself over the tablet and headed down the long hallway to the medical bay.

After a week at the outpost, Chloe's energy started to lag. She showed up on schedule for all her smoothies but went to bed earlier, and she'd even overslept one morning. Ted increased her doses to every day instead of every other, and she seemed to perk up again. But two weeks later, she was like a toy in need of fresh batteries.

"Daddy, what's wrong with me?" she whined, sounding like a child. "Mom's gonna notice. She'll send me back!"

"No, she won't. Hop up on the table. We'll figure this out."

Ted took her vitals: pulse, blood pressure, and temperature. All abnormally low since her illness, but consistent. But she looked awful—dark circles under her eyes, her thin face sunken. He peered inside her mouth, and his stomach dropped. Nubs of new growth pushed against her gums behind the cuspids.

"I feel so weird," Chloe said, "like chunks of my day are missing."

"I think you're just coming down with a cold, sweetie," he said, shoving his shaking hands into the pockets of his lab coat while keeping his voice level. "Let's go up to two doses a day for a while. Your immune system can only fight off so much at once. In the meantime, you need a sick day. Get to bed and rest."

"I don't want to end up like Jenn." Chloe's voice quivered.

"You won't. Now go. Shoo."

Ted locked the door of the medical bay and leaned against it, heart racing. Being in space was affecting the key organic ingredient of the formula, red blood cells. Any blood stored here for a long time, which was most of the supply, was degraded as a percentage of the cells died. And without a strong formula, he'd be unable to help her.

Chloe was changing, like Jenn had before being transferred to the Swiss clinic. Her friend had been unable to hold down any food except raw meat. Jenn's doctors thought it was a bizarre iron deficiency. Ted had been convinced he could prevent the change with his formula, but now he was losing the battle. Why had he agreed to the space mission? Why could he never say no to his daughter?

Fresh blood would solve the problem. It had to. Ted unlocked the door and strode down the hallway, making the two sharp turns that would take him to Chloe's lab. Rodent blood wasn't ideal, but it might tide her over.

He pushed open the door to hear a chorus of squeaks from the usually silent rodents. The one in the closest enclosure was racing around and throwing itself at the glass as if trying to escape. A moan from the back of the lab sent him charging down a row of enclosures to find Chloe sitting on the floor, blood staining the front of her lab coat. She clutched a limp rat in her hands, holding it to her mouth and tearing at the furry body, sucking and slurping as she did so. Her eyes were closed in obscene ecstasy.

"Chloe, Chloe!" He shook her, hard.

She snarled, then opened her eyes and recognized her father. She dropped the rat and screamed, spattering blood into Ted's face. He pulled her close, stroking her hair and calming her.

"It's happening, Daddy," she sobbed. "I'm changing!"

The door at the front of the lab opened. Ted reached up, grabbed a screwdriver from the counter, and slammed it through the body of the dead rat. He wiped Chloe's mouth and his face, urgently whispering instructions in her ear, and by the time the other new biologist rounded the corner, she was standing and calm.

"What the hell happened?" asked Lieutenant Mullins as his eyes swept the bloody scene. "Are you okay?"

"My fault," Chloe said. "I got too friendly with number forty-five. I picked him up to give him a kiss and he bit me on the lip. Dad, I mean— Dr. Sanderson, got here in time to get him off and kill him."

They looked at the screwdriver piercing the small corpse.

Chloe gulped and her eyes reddened. "I'm so sorry. I know they're not pets."

"We should get that lip taken care of," Ted said, turning to face Mullins. "Could you clean up?"

Mullins frowned. "Lieutenant Sanderson needs to write an incident report. Number forty-five was one of our oldest rats."

"I will as soon as I get back," promised Chloe. "Can't argue with the doctor."

Ted put his arm around his shaken daughter, and they left the lab.

The incident with the rat drove home just how urgent the need was for fresh blood. The Bolivian tribe who'd taken in Chloe and her friends were all afflicted with this strange condition but had learned to live with it. There were plenty of warm-blooded creatures in the jungle, and the tribesmen were skilled hunters. Human blood was consumed on special occasions and as medical treatment, usually drained in manageable amounts from volunteers.

Occasionally, however, a tribesman developed a taste for human blood and pursued it like an addict. Mowitu, the cook, saw an opportunity when the women arrived. He fed on each of them while they slept, careful not to drain them or to make the marks too obvious. But the chief caught him feeding on Sherry and had him executed. The chief then fed Mowitu's blood, disguised in a native fruit drink, to the women to build up their strength. This drink had given Ted the idea for his formula. Chloe had no idea she'd consumed human blood in Bolivia and had continued to consume it since.

"A blood drive?" Anita looked skeptical. "There'll be a crew change in two more months. Nobody is sick. If we need a fresher supply, I can requisition it and have it delivered with the new crew."

"Self-banking is the preferred protocol for isolated populations in case of emergency. All I need is your sign-off on the formal request." When she didn't look convinced, he added, "This is my recommendation as Medical Director, Captain."

Anita shrugged. "Okay, Doctor. If that's protocol, who am I to argue?" She scribbled her signature and looked up. "On the family front, Chloe looks wonderful. She's so energetic lately."

"Yeah, once I increased her doses, it seemed to help her get over the cold. She's a tough kid."

"Don't let her hear you call her 'kid.'"

"I know, bad dad." He waved the signed form. "Thanks. I'll get this scheduled."

Ted's thoughts raced as he walked the long corridors back to the medical bay. The incident in the lab, he'd reassured Chloe, had been an anomaly. Her body had been crying out for fresh red blood cells, and he'd not seen it. She wouldn't change like Jenn if he came up with a stronger formula. He couldn't let her down.

He passed the glass door to Chloe's lab and peered in to see her talking to Lieutenant Mullins while smiling and gesturing. Mullins touched her on the shoulder, and she stood on tiptoe to kiss his cheek. Romance in the air? Chloe could sure use some distraction. After recovering mentally from the horror of what she'd done, she seemed to have gotten a physical boost from her fresh meal. A week after the incident, she had more energy and was consistently cheerful. Ted had no idea how long this would last, though, so the blood drive was of utmost importance.

Despite the short notice, the blood drive was well attended. Donations were encouraged but not required. Both he and Anita donated to set a good example. Chloe was excused, as were a few other crew members who were unwell.

"That should do it, Doctor." Nurse Evans placed the last bag in the freezer and closed the door. "Twenty-five pints, not a bad haul for such a small crew."

"Especially since we did it all in one day. We have a good group, covering for each other so they all could donate without affecting the mission." Ted beamed. "The captain will be pleased."

"How do you work with your wife like that? If I had to work with my husband, I think one of us would be dead. Not sure which one, though." Evans smiled and touched him on the arm. "Kidding, just kidding."

"When you've been apart as much as we have throughout our careers, some togetherness is a good thing."

"One extreme to the other, huh? Goodnight, Doctor." She pushed the door open and left Ted alone in the medical bay.

He locked the door and retrieved two bags of blood from the fresh supply in the freezer, moving up some older bags to take their place. Then he pulled out Chloe's smoothies. The next couple of hours were spent supplementing the mixture with fresh blood, then adding more frozen fruit and antibiotics to hide the taste and ramp up the desired effect. Flying by the seat of his pants, he prayed this formula would work.

Ted kept a close watch on his daughter over the next week. Daily doses of the reformulated smoothies seemed to have hyper-charged her. She spoke rapidly, slept less, and spent extra time in the exercise facility. He reduced her dosage to every other day, and she returned to a happy medium.

Her work in the lab with Lieutenant Ben Mullins drew the two of them noticeably closer. On more than one occasion, Ted walked in quietly to have the two of them spring apart like repelling magnets. Between her good health and the flush of new love, Chloe was glowing. The fresh supply of blood would get them through the next few months. One more blood drive, and his daughter would complete her dream mission.

Three weeks after starting the new formula, Chloe sought him out in the medical bay.

"Daddy?"

He turned to see her in the doorway, frowning.

"What's wrong? Do you feel okay?"

"I'm fine." She waved a hand. "But we need to talk. About me and Ben."

Relieved it wasn't physical, Ted motioned her to a chair and sat facing her. She took a deep breath.

"You know Ben and I have been seeing each other."

Ted chuckled. "Kind of hard to hide on a station this size. I don't have a problem with it if it doesn't interfere with your duties. And I'm sure your mother would say the same, if she hasn't already."

"She has," Chloe nodded solemnly. "But *she* doesn't hover. Daddy, I'm feeling better, honestly. I'd like to be left alone to do my job. You're always 'dropping by' and it's embarrassing. Ben feels like you're stalking him." She reached for his hands. "Please. Trust me."

"Of course. I'm sorry. I promise to stop hovering." He kissed her on the forehead, then watched his healthy, capable daughter leave.

Three days later, the intercom in the medical bay buzzed insistently.

"Okay, okay," muttered Ted. He pressed the button. "Yes?"

"Daddy, come quick," sobbed Chloe. "It's Ben. He's been hurt."

Ted grabbed his medical kit and raced out. When he reached the lab and found the door locked, he slammed his fist against it. "Chloe!"

The lock clicked, and the door swung open. Ted stepped in and turned to see his daughter pressed to the wall behind the door. Blood covered her mouth and stained the front of her lab coat. Her hands looked like she'd been finger-painting in it. Ted's heart leaped into his throat.

"He smelled so good," she wailed. "We were kissing and the next thing I knew, he was on the ground and bleeding." She buried her face in her hands. "I'm a monster!"

"Where is he?" asked Ted, striding into the lab.

Ben Mullins lay next to a row of empty glass cages, his skin milk-white except for the bloom of bright red blood oozing from a jagged tear in his throat. Ted placed two fingers against the side of the man's neck, reassured to find a pulse. He pressed a gauze pad against the wound and taped it down quickly.

"I need to get him to the sick bay." He pointed at the blood on the floor. "Clean this mess up. Then clean yourself up and meet me there."

"I'm sorry, I'm so sorry," Chloe repeated, staring at her bloodied lover. "I don't know what happened."

"Now!" he shouted. "Before anyone else comes along."

Chloe snapped out of her shock and ran water into a bucket. She helped Ted lift Ben's limp body onto a supply cart, and Ted rolled him back to the medical bay. By some stroke of luck, the corridors were deserted.

By the time she knocked on the door, he'd dressed the wound and Ben was beginning to stir. Chloe sat next to him and took his hand. The injured man opened his eyes, then yanked his hand back and pressed up against the wall, as far away from her as possible.

"What the hell is wrong with you?" he asked in a shaky voice. "You were growling like an animal."

"I'm sorry. I don't know what happened. I didn't mean to hurt you."

His hand went to the dressing on his throat. His gaze shifted to Ted and his eyes hardened. "Dr. Sanderson, Lieutenant Sanderson assaulted me. I want to file a formal complaint."

"Of course, Lieutenant Mullins. I understand."

Chloe's eyes widened. "But…"

"Just let me give you something for the pain first." Ted jabbed a syringe into Ben's arm and pressed the plunger, driving the strong sedative into his body. In a matter of seconds, the man's eyes closed, and he slumped back on the bed.

Ted put his arms around his daughter and held her while she cried. Once she'd calmed, he took her vital signs. Regardless of the emotional trauma she'd just experienced, physically, she was thriving. An examination of her mouth revealed the nubs on her gums had grown into a set of sharp canines, hidden behind her normal ones. The change was well underway. He needed to get her off the station and back home to treat her properly.

The next crew shift wasn't for another three weeks.

He waited until late that night, after sharing a bottle of wine, to make a full confession to his wife. He told her the truth about what'd happened in Bolivia, what he'd done to keep their daughter alive, and what had just gone horribly wrong.

Captain Anita Sanderson paced the small quarters.

"How could you have kept this from me? I'm her mother!" Her eyes flashed with anger. "And how could you have brought her on the mission in her compromised state? You've endangered her and everyone else on the station."

"I realize that now. But this was her dream," he pleaded. "I thought I could manage her condition."

"Well, you didn't!" she snapped. "I agree you both should leave at the next shift change. What will you do until then? The smoothies don't work anymore."

"Yes, they do," he replied. "They work too well. When I went back to the donations that I used in the formula, I realized I'd used Mullins' blood. That's why she lost control. She could smell him. Her body had identified him as food. As long as we keep giving her his blood, no one else is in danger."

"No. Absolutely not." Anita crossed her arms. "I'll not have one of my crew used as a vending machine."

"Hear me out. I'll keep him sedated, and she can feed directly. She won't need as much since his blood won't be diluted. And the sedative that keeps him unconscious will have a mild effect on her, keep her calm." He placed his hands on his wife's shoulders. "It'll be fine for three weeks. She would only need to feed every three or four days. And the rest of the crew will be safe. Once I get her home, I can figure out a new formula." Tears ran silently down his cheeks. "Please, Anita. Help me save our Chloe."

For the first time in her life, Captain Anita Sanderson put family before the mission.

The crew was told Mullins had a contagious virus and was in isolation in the sick bay. The first time Ted led Chloe into the room where Mullins lay unconscious, she pulled away from him.

"I can't do this, Daddy! It's horrible. I'd rather starve." She turned to leave the room, only to have Ted push her back in and lock the door.

He listened to her beat on the door, then watched through the one-way mirror as she paced, then finally settled in a chair next to her lover's bed. She took his hand and brought it to her lips for a gentle kiss. Then lifted it again and inhaled deeply. The next time she raised his hand, she turned it over and bit deeply into his wrist. Her sucking noises and whimpers of pleasure sickened him, but her condition was not her fault. After five minutes, he re-entered the room and pulled her away. Sated and dazed, she obediently followed as he led her to a basin and gently washed her face before sending her back to her room to rest. After that first feeding, she was resigned to what she had to do to survive.

Meanwhile, Anita had requested an adjustment in crew replacements—another medical officer and two more biology lab techs. Her botanists and physicist would have to wait until the next shift change. Ted cared for Mullins and watched his daughter for any signs of her condition worsening. Once fed, she returned to being the same conscientious crew member who'd arrived months ago. The captain even praised her work.

Six days before the scheduled shift change, Ted unlocked the medical bay and went to Mullin's isolation room. The door stood ajar. He rushed in to see his daughter lying on top of Mullins, asleep. Blood covered both of them. Mullins' eyes stared sightlessly at the ceiling, his mouth frozen in a grimace of horror. He pulled Chloe off the dead man and threw her to the floor. She leaped at him, snarling. It was all he could do to hold her wrists and keep her at bay while he talked her down. When realization struck, she shrank away from him, from the remains of the man she had loved, and curled up in a corner with her arms over her head. She began a heart-rending keening, then struck her head against the wall, again and again until Ted stopped her.

"Kill me. Please kill me." She lifted her face. Rivulets of tears ran through the dried blood around her mouth. "If you love me, kill me."

"It was an accident," Ted argued, desperate. "Just hang on until we get home. I can rework the formula; you can live with this."

"But who else will I kill before you get it right?" She had stopped crying, and an eerie calmness overcame her.

"You won't kill anyone else. You won't, because I'll be your food source until we leave. I trust you not to lose control again."

"No," she said, shaking her head violently. "I can't do that."

"You can and you will. Officially, Mullins succumbed to the virus. But not before spreading it to you. You will be in isolation until the shift change."

He led her to a private room, told her to shower and get into bed. By the time he cleaned up Mullins' body and moved it to the freezer, she was sound asleep. He sat next to the bed and stroked the hair from her face, angelic in repose. She looked like the little girl she'd once been, pretending to be an astronaut.

But the snarling creature he'd seen earlier was also his daughter. She'd begged him for death—after her hunger was satisfied. Would she still wish for death when in the throes of her deadly need? He'd barely managed to get through to her after her killing frenzy. He couldn't count on being able to control her as her condition progressed.

After a restless night's sleep, Ted kissed his wife tenderly when she left for the bridge. She would know everything soon enough. He strode to the medical bay, afraid to slow down lest he change his mind.

After checking on Chloe and finding her still asleep, he sat at the desk and set up the video camera. He told Anita of everything that had happened and of Chloe's wish. He then drew pink liquid into a syringe and held it in front of the camera.

"Don't worry, my love. I won't abandon our girl."

He slid the needle into his arm and gasped as the poison entered his body. He staggered from the room, holding onto the wall, and disappeared from view.

The camera remained focused on his empty chair while the audio continued to record.

"Wake up, Chloe. Time for breakfast."

FOREVER

S.R. Bevilacqua

SEVENTY YEARS SHRIVELED away, like the dying wail of a distant train. *The trains don't even come through town anymore*, she thought, unable to recall when they'd stopped. *The weeds through the tracks are so tall.* The company closed the coal mine more than fifty years ago, the factories all shut down in the eighties, and almost every storefront on Main Street was boarded up. Raven Hill was a forgotten corpse lying face down in the mountains of upstate Pennsylvania. Sometimes, in the quiet past midnight, she heard a train, but the sound was far away and she didn't know where those tracks were.

She wondered where the years went, but she never doubted that she was undeniably blessed. Seven decades ago, Martha Durkin met her husband, Mac, on her first day of kindergarten. He was two years older, all the way in second grade.

He was seventy-eight now, Martha almost seventy-six, on the day their house sank into the ground.

Their kids were grown and had moved away. Bill was in Florida, and Alice lived with her girls in Jersey. Alice's husband had left her, but that was good because he was a nasty, abusive drunk. Their youngest, Joey, got mixed up with drugs and a bad crowd and died in a motorcycle crash outside Philadelphia. For a time after Joey's death, the Durkins drowned in sorrow, but ultimately it brought Martha and Mac even closer. They were inseparable, always there for each other, the foundation of each other's lives, and they couldn't bear the thought of ever being apart.

Watching the earth swallow their home shook the Durkins to the core, unleashing dark, inevitable realities they had never been forced to face.

The Durkins were both extremely small and growing frail. Mac stood just under five-foot-two, and Martha wasn't even five feet tall. Last month in the Walmart on Route 61, two women stopped Mac and Martha and told them they were "too cute." The Walmart shoppers gushed that Mac and Martha were the most adorable thing they'd ever seen. The Durkins didn't know how to react, so they simply smiled and nodded uncomfortably until the strangers went away. Afterwards, Mac joked it was one more reason to avoid the Walmart out on the highway, but after the IGA in town closed for good, they didn't have any choice.

During their lifetimes, the Durkins had seen most of the people in Raven Hill move away, but they were still there, and they were sublimely happy as long as they were together. On summer holidays, they had cookouts in their yard on Union Street, usually just the two of them. Mac used the same rusted metal cylinder to start the charcoal fire he'd used since the seventies. Most of Union Street was deserted. Some houses were boarded up, others simply vacated, and all of them were falling apart. Regina Sturgis ran her boardinghouse across the street, but she'd been down to her sole remaining boarder for years, an old army veteran named Billy who hadn't been right in the head since Vietnam and re-lived the worst parts of that war regularly. Regina didn't like most people, but she had a kind heart and had grown very protective of Billy.

The town was crumbling, both above ground and below. Weird sulfuric vapors sometimes wafted from the dirt, giving Mrs. Sturgis her famous headaches, but there was a threat on Union Street that was far more dangerous than the fumes. The mining company had dug tunnels for almost a century, and as the city expanded, nobody paid too much attention to where the houses were being built. The people of Raven Hill bought their houses, but the coal barons still owned the land under their homes, from twenty feet below the surface, all the way to the Earth's core.

Martha remembered the day the mine closed and most of their friends were out of work with no notice. Rumors persisted that the mine would re-open, which kept people hopeful for months, but when the owners cleared out their mansion and moved away, the residents of Raven Hill knew the mine was done for good. The company left miles of abandoned tunnels under the town, and as the decades passed, the old tunnels grew unstable.

Just after three a.m. on a quiet Thursday night, the Durkins' house started to rumble. Martha jolted upright, confused, and grabbed her husband. Their bedroom shook, and the floorboards started creaking loudly enough to wake the dead.

Martha trembled. "What's happening?!"

The house jerked sharply and dropped to one side, making Martha gasp. They heard crashes downstairs, followed by another steep drop. Martha looked across the room and saw her reflection in the mirror on the dresser. She'd never seen herself scared, let alone terrified, and a cold shudder shook deep in her soul. A crack split down the center of her reflection, and for a fleeting second there were two of her staring back in horror until the mirror shattered with a piercing crash.

Mac jumped out of bed while sounds rose from below like the moans of a dying giant. He shouted over the noise, "We have to get out!"

Martha nodded and pulled her housecoat over her nightgown, stumbling as the floor rocked under her feet. They hurried down the stairs, stopping briefly to watch their home spontaneously smashing to pieces. Mac then ran to the front door and threw it open as one hinge snapped off, and the house sank another foot. The front porch rose up before him, its buckling boards cracking. Mac reached for his wife, who'd paused to grab his windbreaker for him. Mac took Martha's wrist and pulled her along, out the front door. They dashed up the bursting boards of the porch and leaped down to the cement path. Martha stopped, but Mac dragged her further away, seconds before the concrete under their feet slid into the pit.

Two hours later, as the cobalt sky grew brighter, the Durkins hadn't moved. The mountain air was intensely alive as they stood at the edge of the sinkhole that'd devoured their home. Mac hugged his wife, whose sobs were drowned out by the creaking and banging of their house collapsing into the earth.

Martha stopped crying. She looked at her husband and said, "You know what we forgot?" She didn't need to add anything further. Mac knew exactly what she meant. They'd left behind Martha's most cherished possession, the thing that'd break her heart to lose.

Without a word, Mac went to work, figuring out how to get into the house.

He took a breath, braced himself, and prepared to jump, but then sat down at the edge of the pit. Martha gasped when Mac pushed off and dropped down on to the roof, now five feet below ground level. He hit the asphalt tiles and tried to steady himself, watching the loose dirt tumble down the sides of the hole. Mac shifted into overdrive, not giving himself time to be scared, crawling to the dormer window that'd shattered. He climbed over the windowsill and fell into the house, out of Martha's sight.

Mac threw himself into a dusty, chaotic nightmare. He slammed to the floor, then forged his way through the lurching attic and kicked down the folding stairs. Tumbling down to the second-floor hallway, he was assaulted by thunderous wooden groans from above and below. The house shrieked in protest from its unwanted plunge as Mac rushed past their bedroom and down to the living room, where he saw the wedding photo in its place on the mantel. The rain of plaster stung his eyes, so he covered them with one arm and grabbed the photo with the other. Part of the ceiling slammed down as he ran back the way he came. His mission was brave, stupid, and genuine, happening without any thought or hesitation, because Mac's mind only had one oversized thought at that moment: Martha wanted that wedding photo with all her heart.

Martha stood at the edge of the pit, frozen in terror at the thought of her husband in the collapsing house. "Aw, hell, not another one," Mrs. Sturgis said as she made her way across the yard. The Pennsylvania Dutch natural thickness of her body had evolved into a heavy frame by the time she'd reached her mid-forties, and walking took some effort. She stood next to Martha, wearing her old quilted bathrobe and slippers that used to have fuzz. Regina Sturgis' face stiffened with shock as she glanced around the yard. "Where's Mac? Didn't he get out?"

"He did," Martha answered.

"Then where is he?"

"He went back."

"What the fuck, Martha?"

Mrs. Sturgis stopped talking when she saw Mac scramble out of the dormer window. A deafening chain reaction of crashes came from inside the house and Mac fell to his knees on the shaking roof, but he kept going. He jumped, reaching for the rim of the pit, his small hands clawing at the dirt. Mac was about to fall back, but Mrs. Sturgis dropped to her knees and grabbed his wrist. "Oh Christ," she grumbled, pulling Mac back to solid ground. "You're worse than a couple of kids."

Mac looked at his wife with a crooked grin. "I got it."

Regina noticed something with sharp corners stuffed inside Mac's windbreaker. He yanked down the zipper and extracted their old wedding photo in the silver frame that Martha's Aunt Josephine had bought for them at Hess's department store in Allentown. It was Martha's most beloved possession, fancy and beautiful, with silver flowers, although their black-and-white wedding photograph had faded to uneven shades of tan.

Her smile flooded his soul, as it always did.

A heart-stopping crack came from the hole, but Martha didn't shift her adoring gaze from her husband. Her eyes flowed with proud tears after his valiant descent to retrieve their wedding photo.

Now that he'd returned, Mac looked down at the pit and his knees went weak. He wobbled on his feet and almost fell but distracted his wife with a smile.

"Mac, stay out of that hole," Mrs. Sturgis said.

Mrs. Durkin smiled sadly at Regina. "I loved our house."

"I know."

Mac and Martha shivered at the same time, because at that moment, with their perfectly synchronized hearts, the Durkins wondered about one thing. The biggest, most important thing in their lives. The idea of a sinking house wasn't new; it occurred with minor regularity around Raven Hill with its miles of derelict tunnels. Martha and Mac, sweethearts since they were five and eight, stared into the chasm and pondered not their sunken house, or where they were going to live, but their future together, and how someday death was going to separate them. They'd kept that thought at bay for years, but at this moment, it was inescapable.

Mrs. Sturgis said to the Durkins, "You two better come to my place. I'll make you some breakfast."

"Do you have Postum?" Martha asked.

"Aw, hell, Martha, nobody's sold that stuff since the eighties," Mrs. Sturgis replied. "I'm not fucking magic."

"I liked Postum," Martha sighed.

The Durkins shared a profound wish that they could live by each other's side forever. They'd never shared as much in actual words, but after six decades of marriage, certain things didn't need to be spoken out loud. They knew. And while there'd never been any genuine possibility of them remaining together in their little house for eternity, the old place sinking into the abandoned coal tunnel brought about that inevitability abruptly, even violently.

The Durkins were gentle people and not skilled to handle this existential threat to their united bliss. Neither one was afraid of dying, nor even minded the idea of dying very much. They had lived long, mostly untroubled lives with each other, and that was all they could ask. Martha and Mac lived blessed with the rare possession of a love so true that it hurt and healed instantaneously, acutely knowing and joyously effortless. What terrified them was the possibility that after they died, they would no longer be together.

Martha and Mac moved into Mrs. Sturgis' boarding house. A few days later, folks from the County showed up and red-tagged the Durkins' home, cordoning off the sinkhole with string held up by three-foot sticks.

"Thank god they put up that string," Mrs. Sturgis chuckled. "Without it, there'd be nothing to protect us."

Mac asked, "What if someone trips over it? They'll fall right into that hole and onto our house."

"Is the string supposed to keep people out?" wondered Martha.

"Ask those nimrods from the County," said Mrs. Sturgis.

According to the County officials, as decreed by the official notice stapled to one stick, no one was allowed to return to the Durkins' house to retrieve any of the "prior occupants' belongings." The Durkins were only permitted to keep the possessions they'd brought with them that morning, so all they had was their wedding photograph in its flowery silver frame.

But Martha and Mac missed certain things. It started with their toothbrushes, which they replaced with new ones, but soon there were other items that'd require too much effort or money to replace, like their clothes and Mac's tools.

Mrs. Sturgis noticed that Martha and Mac began to go missing for long periods of time, and she guessed where they were. The Durkins were climbing down into their old house. Mac pioneered the way, and once down there, he located some of his tools and used them to make an easier path for Martha. He built a makeshift ladder from the roof to the rim of the pit and did his best to camouflage it in case anyone came poking around. He nailed wooden shims onto the shingles, creating a path to help Martha get into the house. Mac had always been good with tools, and the handles he attached to the windowsill were perfectly placed for his wife's frame.

When everything was in place, he rushed to the surface to show Martha the way. She resisted at first, standing at the edge in her faded sundress, but it was just for show. Martha attacked the course like a teenager, climbing down the ladder and stepping across the tilted roof, trembling but without fear. At the window, she radiated that same special smile from their wedding photo. Mac hadn't seen that face in years. He showed her how to grasp the handles and helped her through the window. He was so proud of her.

As they stood in their attic, the Durkins were overcome with a rush of excitement. They laughed, and Mac led the way by the flame of his Zippo lighter, pointing out certain loose boards and crooked steps as they headed down into the house. Despite all the damage, Martha, and Mac thought the old place had held up alright. The people from UGI had come and turned off everything, so there was no power, but Mac dug through the rubble downstairs and found a hurricane lantern. Then he found a flashlight that he held while Martha sifted through the shattered remains of the breakfront in the dining room and retrieved some candles. During the big fall, the hot water heater in the basement had smashed through the dining room floor and now stood at a drunken angle next to their oak dining table and cracked chairs.

The candles and lanterns gave the place a dusty, warm glow. From outside, in the coal tunnel, with the soft yellow light shining through the windows, the Durkins' house looked like a perverted Norman Rockwell painting, homespun and cozy, like the farmhouse in The Wizard of Oz if Dorothy and Toto had been buried alive instead of landing in Munchkinland.

Now that Martha and Mac had made their way back home, the thing they feared most returned. The horrible, unavoidable truth of their eventual separation. There were different possibilities for how the future might play out, but all of them led to the same place: apart. In the house, they could continue trying to ignore the inevitable, but they were certain to fail with their home of forty-five years laying ravaged and decayed in its own grave. The looming prospect of their separation, by fate or by death, was now impossible to ignore.

"It's not safe in that house," Regina Sturgis said the next morning as she dropped pancakes onto their plates. She'd had a long, tumultuous night with Billy, and her round face looked drained.

Mac and Martha stared at her with innocent expressions.

Unfazed, Regina continued, "If you want to get stuff out of there, maybe we can get some people to help. They can go and bring it up for you."

"Where would we put it? Our house is down there," Mac said.

Martha looked at Mrs. Sturgis and said, "Regina, it's fine."

Mrs. Sturgis nodded, knowing that they were done discussing it for now. She simply added, "Be careful. I don't want you to get hurt."

Martha nodded in silent agreement, then Mac did too.

A cry of horror crashed through the ceiling, informing them that Billy was back in the Mekong Delta again. Mrs. Sturgis gave a resigned sigh and left the dining room to go upstairs.

They sat in the living room in the chairs they'd owned for decades. Sometimes they'd go through the things in the house or reminisce with old photo albums. But mostly, they just sat in their subterranean home, holding hands and talking quietly to each other.

Until they heard the noises outside their door. They froze with the realization that there was something in the tunnel. Shouts. Wicked laughter. Mac and Martha sat in their tattered chairs, afraid to move or even breathe.

Then they heard the screams.

"Those are animals lost in the mines," Mac whispered to his wife, but they knew better. Martha and Mac stared at each other, not sure what to do. They could swear they heard a woman sobbing and pleading.

The screams of fear were followed by shrieks of pain. Then came more laughter, with taunting and mocking imitations of the screams. The Durkins' hearts both skipped a beat when they heard the sound of tearing flesh with agonized howls, like animals tearing apart their prey, wolves ripping meat from a deer, but the voices and laughter—although deadened by the dirt walls of the tunnel—were unmistakably human.

Then it was quiet. Mac wanted to comfort Martha—but he didn't dare to whisper. They remained in tense, petrified silence.

There was a knock on the door. Soft at first, and then brutal knuckles slammed against the damaged wood. "Hellooo?" an abrasive voice sang. Burning red eyes peeked through the window, but by then the chairs were empty, because Mac and Martha had made it to the closet under the stairs. Holding their breath in the cramped space, Mac and Martha heard a vicious giggle. "Check out the house..." The voice laughed as it moved away.

When Mac and Martha later climbed back to the surface, the sun had set. They questioned whether it was safe to go down there anymore, but they already knew what their answer would be. Even though it looked like a three-bedroom-one-bath tomb, and despite the horrifying sounds, that house was their home and when they were away, they missed it so fiercely it hurt. Their desire was stronger than their fear, and there was no place else they wanted to be. Martha said quiet prayers that the noises wouldn't return so they could sit in their house, and she was relieved beyond measure when the tunnel remained silent the next day.

The quiet in the tunnel did not last. Two days later, they were asleep in their chairs, holding hands, when a sharp pounding on the front door woke them. Martha gasped and Mac sat up, startled. The banging grew louder.

"I know you're in there," the high-pitched, gravelly voice taunted. "Open the door."

Mac and Martha looked at each other, wondering whether to make a dash for the closet.

A shadow crossed over the living room window, then a face appeared with long stringy hair and beady eyes. It grinned.

They recognized the face. It was Nicky Tillman, the nastiest of all the low-life-thugs in town, who commanded a gang of drugged-out scumbags like the ones that led their Joey astray. Joey had always been a good boy, never any trouble, until he joined the gang and started doing the drugs. Then he became a different person. Those punks as good as killed him, Mac always said. Nicky Tillman was too young to be one of the bikers who'd destroyed Joey, but he was exactly the same kind.

"I won't hurt you, I promise," Nicky snickered. "Open the door."

Mac and Martha remained perfectly still.

"Come ooooon!" Nicky whined impatiently. "I know you guys. I've seen you around my whole life. It's a shame about your house."

Mac stood up from his chair and replied with a sturdy, "You leave us alone."

"I think I can help you." Nicky smiled. "But you've got to talk to me."

Mac thought about it. He looked at Martha.

"Let me in," Nicky repeated, dead serious.

Mac reached for the doorknob, but Martha gasped. Mac raised his hand to assure her and then opened the door. "Hello," he said.

The sinuous smile grew wider across Nicky Tillman's face, showing his gray teeth. He wore crusted jeans with a red flannel shirt so faded and worn that Martha could see the old stained black Metallica t-shirt underneath it.

"Thanks for opening the door."

"We can't let a guest come in through the broken window, can we, Martha?"

A menacing chuckle came from Nicky's mouth. "You guys are so cute," he said. "I'd never dream of hurting you." His grin made Mac and Martha tense up. That evil smirk hadn't changed since the day it appeared on the six-year-old dismembering cats by the train tracks. "Let's talk."

Mac and Martha just stared at him.

"C'mon," Nicky sneered. "I'm not a bad guy." Martha's silent expression won the debate and Nicky shrugged. "Okay, maybe I am. But I like you guys. And if you're gonna hang out down here, there's only so much I can do to protect you."

"We can take care of ourselves," Mac told him.

"Yeah, you think?" Nicky snorted. Mac and Martha grew more nervous, and Nicky continued, "I can help you take care of yourselves."

Mac looked at Martha, and with a quick unspoken conversation, they agreed to give Nicky a chance to explain. Nicky oozed excitement as he began to lay out his plan for Martha and Mac. There were downsides to this scheme that the Durkins didn't care for, but despite the drawbacks, there was one aspect to it they liked enormously because it provided an answer to their biggest problem. Mac told Nicky they'd think about it, because there was no need to rush into something so permanent.

Nicky said he'd give them two days to decide, and if they tried to avoid him, he would find them to get their answer.

Mac said Nicky wouldn't have to look for them. They would make their decision and let him know. Mac suggested they meet at the house at this time in two days, if that was convenient for Nicky.

"Sure," Nicky laughed. Then he looked at Martha and prodded, "Does she ever talk, this one?"

Mac matter-of-factly replied, "Yes," and didn't say anything else.

Martha maintained her owlish stare, which somehow got the upper hand on Nicky, as vile as he was, and he looked uncomfortable.

"Okay then, two days."

That night, in their bed in Regina's boarding house, they discussed Nicky's plan in hushed tones so no one would hear. Mac wondered if they even had a choice, or if Nicky would hurt them if they refused. Mac and Martha were unsophisticated, but they weren't stupid, and they knew what it meant to join Nicky in this new life he'd offered. The only question was whether they could trust Nicky. He was a scumbag, that they knew, but what did he gain by lying to them? Nicky was the type of person who did evil things simply for the malicious joy he felt from doing them, and then they remembered what happened to their Joey when he took up with people like Nicky.

Mac and Martha grew certain about one thing. At heart, this new plan accomplished the goal that mattered to them more than anything else: staying together. So, two days later, the Durkins walked to the pit and climbed down into their house. They were excited and a little nervous. They didn't want to admit it, because they didn't want to seem reckless or bad, but the anticipation made them feel young again. Sitting in their chairs in the living room in the murky light of the hurricane lantern on the propped-up coffee table, they waited for Nicky Tillman to return.

It was hours past their meeting time, and they wondered if Nicky wasn't going to show. They worried they'd missed their chance. The lantern began to flicker, and Mac said he needed to get more batteries for it. He got up from his chair, but then changed his plan. "Let's go find him."

Martha's fearful eyes shifted to the door. "Out there?" she asked, and Mac nodded.

The front door, hanging by one lone hinge, opened slowly. The Durkins stepped through the doorway into the decrepit coal tunnel. Mac carried a flashlight, and Martha tensely clutched his arm as they walked away from their house. Their eyes looked up at the dirt over their heads.

Deeper into the tunnel, they heard sounds. Laughter and talking, then the burst of a violent scuffle, followed by a commanding shout that made all the rest go silent. Nervous but undaunted, the Durkins continued forward. There were lights in the distance, accompanied by nasty bullying laughter. A cluster of five or six people stood in the weird shadows of the tunnel. They appeared young, like Nicky, and Mac just knew they were lowlife punks on drugs.

As they got closer, they saw two of the group were women. One woman was dressed like Nicky in dirty jeans and a threadbare flannel shirt. The other looked like a "lady of the evening," as Martha would say, with skimpy shorts, a revealing top, and high boots. Martha thought she could see bruises on her legs even from that distance and felt bad for her.

Mac and Martha steadily made their way toward the group. One of the men grabbed the streetwalker's crotch, and she slammed a fist into his face. The Durkins grew terrified when they realized Nicky Tillman wasn't among them. They stopped walking. The tunnel dwellers noticed them, surprised and excited to find victims walking toward them down there.

Martha gasped. "He's not here," she whispered to Mac.

The gang rushed at them, surrounding them in a brutal circle. The old couple was shocked at the heavy red scabs on the tunnel dwellers' faces and limbs, pestilent scratch marks covering them like tattoos. Mac and Martha felt extra small as they stood, trapped, and the methed-out ghouls taunted them.

The woman in the flannel shirt poked Mac and cackled. A man

started to grab Martha but was interrupted by a blur and a deafening animal roar. The man was hurled across the tunnel and hit the dirt wall with a sickening thud.

And in the same instant, Nicky was there, grinning in their faces.

They didn't wait for Nicky to speak.

"Yes," Mac told him.

It was fiery and electric, shooting through their hearts, their veins, their skin, their eyes. Soaring through the universe with a dizzying headlong whoosh, the Durkins had never experienced anything like this in their lives. It made them shaky on their feet.

That first night, they were completely overcome and lost their heads. The Durkins threw Regina Sturgis onto her dining room table and slaughtered her in a feral, orgiastic frenzy. Regina's blood splashed across the walls and ceiling. The floor became slippery and then sticky. They drank her blood and ripped out her organs. They ate parts of her. They couldn't stop. They laughed like teenagers and kissed erotically for the first time in decades.

When the rush ended, Mac and Martha looked around the dining room, stunned. They were disoriented, the last hour was a swirling distant memory, and they desperately hoped that someone else had done this. But they knew.

They heard a tortured wail from upstairs. Billy was listening to the slaughter while cowering in the corner of his room, scared shitless and re-living the fall of Saigon. "Maybe the police will think he did this," Mac whispered to Martha. Martha nodded. At least they hadn't killed him too. They looked at each other like guilty children and quietly snuck out of the house. They started walking to the pit, but Martha paused. Mac knew what she was thinking, what they had forgotten. "Stay here," he whispered as he hurried back to the house.

He came back, holding the only thing they'd brought with them, their wedding photo in its fancy silver frame. Mac carried the photo in a burlap tote bag he'd grabbed from Mrs. Sturgis' pantry.

"Oh dear. What happened to your hands?" Martha asked, seeing his burned flesh.

The wedding photo in the silver frame was returned to its old spot. The mantel was cracked and tilted, and part of the fireplace had crumbled, but the faded image of Martha and Mac on their wedding day brightened up their living room like it had for most of their lives.

Martha and Mac sat in their chairs, holding hands in the air thick with dust. They were the happiest people in all of creation.

During the day, they left the house and went deeper into the tunnel. What little sunlight that traveled into the pit was easy to avoid. Even more important was avoiding the mirrors in the house when the sun was out, because reflected sunlight was more caustic than the direct sun. Mac thought they should get rid of the mirrors, but Martha said no, she wanted to keep the house just as it was. Or as close as possible.

The Durkins had gone to church all their lives, but they didn't know what happened when you died. They'd always worried about what would happen if one of them passed away first. They wanted their love to survive and would do anything to make that happen. They refused to risk ruining something that was so much bigger and stronger than either one of them alone. Something so real, and ultimately great, so unassailably perfect that it was almost proof that a higher power did exist.

So how could protecting and preserving it be wrong? This was the only way to ensure they'd stay together and remain themselves. They'd known that immediately when they first heard Nicky's plan. With desperate circumstances and modest resources, the Durkins' love had defeated uncertainty. Their devotion could stay alive for eternity.

They felt terrible about Mrs. Sturgis, but they couldn't help themselves. They'd temporarily lost control as they adjusted to their new selves, and it was a shame. Regina was a lovely person, and hopefully, she was now in a better place.

The Durkins vowed to conduct themselves better in the future, and they knew they'd never do that again.

At least not like that.

At least not to anyone they knew.

They just wouldn't talk about it.

Mac and Martha smiled at each other, because they had so much time to not talk about it.

They had forever.

MAN ON PORCH

Evan Baughfman

The following is a transcript of Chyme™ video doorbell footage recorded from the residence located at ███████████████, Las Vegas, Nevada, 89106, on 07/16/2022

01:47 A.M.

Video shows a shirtless Man standing on the Resident's front porch. Man leans forward to speak into the doorbell camera. Man's eyelids are droopy. His eyes are barely visible. Man appears to be under the influence of drugs and/or alcohol. Resident speaks to Man via the doorbell's intercom system.

Man: Hello, can I get the lunch special? I know it's late, but, um, yeah. Lunch special. That's like five bucks?

Resident: I can't help you.

Man: What was that?

Resident: Sorry, I can't help you.

Man: Can't help? Why [*unintelligible*] Okay.

Resident: This isn't a restaurant. You have to leave.

Man: Hash browns. How much for…for hash browns? Two. Two, please.

Resident: This is a house. Private property. You need to leave.

Man: Just, um, two, ma'am. Only two. Thank you.

Resident: Again, this isn't a restaurant. This is where people live.

Man: And a… One orange juice. Small. No. Guava. Guava juice, yeah. Medium.

Resident: We're closed.

Man: Huh? What's…

Resident: We're closed for the day. Bye.

Man: Shit. My bad. [*unintelligible*] Cool. Night.

Resident: Good night.

Man: Know some place where I can get…get grilled cheese?

Resident: No. Try the Strip.

Man: Oh? If I strip, you'll make me a…?

Man gives a thumbs-up, smiles, and begins to undo the belt on his pants.

Resident: Sir, if you remove your clothing… If you don't leave right now… I will call the police.

Man: The police? Don't… They don't…don't like me. Getting all dramatic 'cause of some goddamn [*unintelligible*]

Man extends both middle fingers to the camera before stepping off the porch. As he steps onto the front lawn, a shadowy figure tackles him, dragging Man down into the grass.

Man: [*unintelligible*] *Man struggles as he is pulled out of frame. The video ends.*

02:13 A.M.

Video shows a shirtless Vampire standing on the Resident's front porch. His fanged mouth and chest are dripping with blood. Vampire leans forward to speak into the doorbell camera. Vampire's eyelids are droopy. His pitch-black eyes are barely visible. Vampire appears to be under the influence of drugs and/or alcohol. Resident speaks to Vampire via the doorbell's intercom system.

Vampire: Hello, can I come inside? Hello?

Resident: You cannot.

Vampire: I'm just…just a little…you know. Thirsty. Hungry.

Resident: Sorry, but no.

Vampire: I'll take some water. Need water. Just killed that…that guy. The one I saw bother…bothering you?

Resident: I didn't ask you to do that.

Vampire: Knew he was drunk or something. But didn't realize how drunk. Soooooo drunk.

Resident: And now you are.

Vampire: And now I am! His blood was so full of…was practically…al-kee-hall. Sorry, I don't…usually don't get like this. So wasted. Usually much more careful. Choose my prey better…more carefully.

Resident: Right. But I can't help you.

Vampire: Sure, you can.

Resident: You have to go.

Vampire: Water. H2O.

Resident: Vampires don't drink water.

Vampire: Every living thing needs water.

Resident: You're a "living" thing?

Vampire: Ha! [*unintelligible*] Got me there!

Resident: Get off my porch, please.

Vampire: Come out and…and make me.

Resident: Don't think so.

Vampire: Boo! Boooooo! No fun! Let's… Let's have fun, yeah?

Resident: Get out of here.

Vampire: Let me in.

Resident: No.

Vampire: Let me in, so I can have fun.

Resident: Leave.

Vampire: Have fun and…and feed on you…on you and your family.

Resident: We've called the police.

Vampire: Police don't scare me. I scare police. They don't know how to…how to handle guys like me.

Resident: The Monster Task Force. We called, and they're on their way.

Vampire: No, they aren't.

Resident: Yes, they are. So, you'd better go.

Vampire: If you called them… If…! Then they told you…told you that it would take a while before anyone got here. Yeah?

Resident: No, they're on their way. Right now.

Vampire: That's just [*unintelligible*] Liar!

Resident: Leave, if you know what's good for you.

Vampire: What's good for me is right here. Right behind this…this door! Inside your house! I can…can smell them. Both of them. Your children!

Resident: MTF says they're getting closer.

Vampire: No. See, what you don't know…don't know is… This weekend, there's a convention… Ghouls and goblins and every nasty thing from around the world, all right there on the Strip. So, no, sorry! MTF isn't getting closer. They're too busy keeping the peace at the hotels and casinos. You and your kids and me… We… We aren't a priority for the police department.

Resident: Just leave!

Vampire: Why do you think I'm out here? Hunting out here? Huh? Because I'm safe! This neighborhood… There's nowhere safer for me to be.

Resident: I'm not opening that door, so you can stand out there all night.

Vampire: Think I might!

Resident: And keep standing there until the sun comes up!

Vampire: [*unintelligible*]

Resident: I'm fine waiting for MTF. For morning. Are you?

Vampire: Shit. Just… I need some water! Some fucking water! Seriously! This guy's blood is all…so goddamn gross! Sticky!

Resident: There's a hose out there.

Vampire: Where?

Resident: Behind you. At the bottom of the porch steps.

Vampire: Yeah?

Resident: Yes. Use it and go. I promise you, MTF's already on their way.

Vampire doesn't immediately respond.

Vampire: O…okay.

Vampire walks off the porch and grabs a water hose. He begins to spray himself clean.

Resident: Forgot to mention, though!

Vampire: What?

Resident: That's holy water! Our pipes were blessed by a priest!

Vampire shrieks, tossing the hose aside. Moments later, he extends a middle finger to the camera.

Vampire: Ha ha. Very funny.

Something large then zips into the frame and grabs Vampire, carrying him, screaming, up into the sky. The video ends.

02:47 A.M.

Video shows a shirtless Monsquito standing on the Resident's front porch. The insectoid's proboscis and chest are dripping with blood. Monsquito leans forward to speak into the doorbell camera. Monsquito's eyelids are droopy. Its compound eyes are barely visible. The insectoid appears to be under the influence of drugs and/or alcohol. Resident speaks to Monsquito via the doorbell's intercom system.

Monsquito: Lost. Am lost.

Resident: You can't stay here.

Monsquito: Feel bad. *[unintelligible]* No good.

Resident: If you're going to throw up, don't do it here.

Monsquito: Eat fast. Too fast.

Resident: Better luck next time.

Monsquito: Food bad. No good.

Monsquito holds Vampire's corpse up to the camera. Vampire's body is shriveled, drained dry.

Monsquito: Food poison? Food yuck.

Resident: Look, you're just drunk. That vamp was pretty sloshed.

Monsquito: No like. Yuck.

Monsquito throws Vampire off the porch.

Resident: If you're feeling sick, I need you to move to the grass.

Monsquito: Dizzy. No more fly.

Resident: Then walk there.

Monsquito: No more fly. Danger.

Resident: Crawl. Stumble. Whatever you need to do!

Monsquito: Lost. [*unintelligible*] Am lost.

Resident: I understand, but I can't help you.

Monsquito: Help? You help?

Resident: No. Look, it's been a long night for me.

Monsquito: This hotel?

Resident: This is not a hotel!

Monsquito: Am tired.

Resident: So am I.

Monsquito: You give room?

Resident: Absolutely not.

Monsquito: Thank you. You nice.

Resident: No room!

Monsquito: Me give money tomorrow. Thank you.

Resident: God's sake…!

Monsquito: Have money. A lot. Tomorrow.

Resident: No hotel! Leave!

Monsquito: No hotel?

Resident: No!

Monsquito: Where hotel?

Resident: Not here!

Monsquito: Am lost.

Resident: I know!

Monsquito: Need friend.

Resident: I'm not your friend.

Monsquito: You no friend?

Resident: No. Sorry.

Monsquito: Am scary? Me?

Resident: Yes!

Monsquito: Am nice.

Resident: Tell that to the vampire.

Monsquito: Eat mean. Mean only. Bad only.

Resident: Only slurp on the bad guys, do you?

Monsquito: You nice. No eat nice.

Resident: Don't think I can believe that. Sorry.

Monsquito: People talk bad. A lot. No like. [*unintelligible*] Am nice. You nice.

Resident: Not as nice as you think.

Sirens approach. Monsquito turns away from the camera.

Monsquito: [*unintelligible*]

Resident: They aren't here for you. They're just late. Bad timing on your part. Sorry.

Monsquito looks to the camera. In the background, Monster Task Force vehicles arrive on scene.

Monsquito: They friends?

Resident: It really depends.

Monsquito: They help?

Resident: Just listen to them, and they'll help you.

Monsquito: You bring friends. Thank you.

Resident: Don't thank me yet.

MTF Officers exit their vehicles and take tactical positions, weapons ready. Lieutenant Unger speaks on the megaphone.

Lt. Unger: You, on the porch! Put your claws on top of your head!

Monsquito: Feel real bad. Real no good.

Resident: Listen to them, okay?

Monsquito: You real nice.

Monsquito does not comply with Lt. Unger's order.

Lt. Unger: Stay where you are! And put your claws on your head!

Monsquito still does not comply.

Monsquito: Am real sick.

Resident: Come on! Do what they say!

Monsquito: Can no sick here. No yuck here.

Resident: Claws on your head!

Monsquito: Yuck in the grass.

Monsquito turns away from the camera, toward Officers.

Resident: Hey! Don't move!

Lt. Unger: For your own safety, stay where you are! Lift those claws slowly!

Monsquito's wings buzz.

Resident: Stop! Don't!

Lt. Unger: Don't move off that porch!

Monsquito raises its claws.

Monsquito: Have to yuck! Sorry!

Monsquito moves toward the Officers.

Resident: No!

Lt. Unger: Neutralize suspect! Neutralize! Neutralize!

Officers open fire. Monsquito falls to the front lawn. Porch furniture is wrecked in the crossfire. Officers stop shooting. The video ends.

After reviewing the transcript of video footage taken on the night of July 16, 2022, it is the opinion of this Committee that decorated Lieutenant Patton Unger and other esteemed Officers of the Las Vegas Metropolitan Monster Task Force acted with sound reason and appropriate restraint and did not use excessive force when responding to the incident at ███ ████████████.

It is therefore also the opinion of this Committee that no members of the Las Vegas Metropolitan Monster Task Force be charged for their involvement in the shooting deaths of the Residents at the aforementioned address. We all recognize that collateral damage is sometimes an unfortunate part of successful police work.

We send our heartfelt thoughts and prayers to the Residents' surviving family members.

CAMERA OBSCURA

Jonah Buck

BEFORE IT WAS a vampire reservation, the section of scrubland was known by the unlikely name of the Guano Creek Wilderness Study Area. The patch of land might've been beautiful once, with a narrow creek running through a shallow canyon, and sage and juniper stretching toward the plateaus that formed a rough bowl around the reservation. But the once untouched landscape now looked like a filthy refugee camp, which was exactly what it was.

Philippa Shimp finished arranging an old sun-grayed sheet of plywood over a spot that'd rusted through on the freight container she shared with twenty other vampires. The shipping container was their only shelter during the day. Part of the container's metal roof had a hole, allowing a narrow sunbeam into the darkness within. All the vampires inside had to move as the sun marched from horizon to horizon, creating a sort of burning sundial inside the cramped, hot space.

Philippa had never been one to sleep in a coffin. Very few vampires did, though there were some eccentrics who swore by the practice. She'd happily accept one now though, stereotypes be damned. What she wouldn't give for some sort of proper dormitory building. Colonel Joseph Locke had denied her every request for permanent structures on the reservation, though.

"Blood truck's coming," Boyd McFall said.

Phillipa squinted. Sure enough, she could see an almighty dust plume rising in the south. Nothing else ever passed through the military checkpoints to visit Guano Creek.

She hopped off the container and grabbed a good-sized rock, one that still burned with warmth from the hateful sun that lingered over Eastern Oregon all day. Several surprised bugs scattered from where the rock had sat.

"Sorry, guys," Phillipa said. She knew the feeling. She'd been undead for the better part of three thousand years when the universe yanked up the rock she'd been quietly living under. As the oldest vampire in the camp, she was nominally in charge. But Philippa knew most of her authority came from her reputation during the war. The press had called her the Butcher of Marquette. She did not wear the moniker with pride, but she found it brought her a certain respect.

Most of her duties consisted of trying to organize enough entertainment to keep everyone here from losing their minds. The little library of battered paperbacks was her doing. As was next month's production of Les Misérables. She'd wanted to put on a stage production of Dracula, since that was sure to leave everyone howling with laughter, but Colonel Locke had torpedoed that plan.

She clambered back on top of the shipping container with the rock, and she immediately knew she'd made a mistake. A quadcopter drone with military markings whined closer with a noise like an overgrown mosquito. A payload of white phosphorus clung to its belly. If the drone operator determined she was getting ready to use the rock as a weapon or about to start trouble, he'd trigger the white phosphorus and incinerate everything within a twenty-yard radius.

Philippa placed the rock so it would weigh down the plywood and then stepped away with her arms raised at her sides. The drone cameras, like all other cameras and mirrors, could only pick the vampires up as blurry, indistinct smears. But she knew there was a human spotter with binoculars looking at her, ready to give the order to burn her to ash.

The drone bobbed in place for a few seconds and then zipped off into the night sky. Had Philippa still needed to breathe, she would have let out a sigh of relief. Drones had killed two vampires since Guano Creek opened its doors. The official explanation was that they'd breached security protocols and become a threat. Most everyone on this side of the fence thought the drone operators had pushed the wrong button by mistake, or else got bored and knew they could get away with it.

Philippa knew the drones and soldiers were mostly for show. Even the perimeter fence was mostly there as a prop. Philippa could leap over the coils of razor wire if she had a good running start. Guano Creek was located in the Oregon Outback, near the border with Nevada. The area had one of the lowest population densities of anywhere in the United States. Maybe Alaska had more barren stretches, but the government didn't want vampires anywhere near those long winter nights that far north. The powers that be had decided the sun-drenched high desert environment was the best way to contain the vampires, and they'd been right.

Even if Philippa escaped—hell, even if every vampire at Guano Creek escaped—where would they go? The sun would get them all before they found shelter. Colonel Locke could tear down the fences and bring the soldiers home, and it wouldn't make one bit of difference. Philippa and all the other vampires were anchored here by the shelter the reservation provided. The only reason to keep soldiers and drones out here was because it helped the public sleep at night.

In the distance, the dust plume grew closer, and Philippa caught the first gleam of the blood truck. She hopped off the container and landed next to Boyd.

"Shall we see what our friends have brought us today?" Boyd asked. He was Philippa's right hand in the camp. He'd once been a minor court poet in Gascony under a different name, but he'd spent the last three hundred years or so quietly raising hogs under a succession of identities in Arkansas. Sometimes Philippa could still envision him as a fussy, prissy courtier, but the centuries had mellowed him.

She and Boyd walked up to the main gate as the blood truck rumbled up. The truck could've been mistaken for a gas transporter. The big silver tank on the back was refrigerated against the desert heat, but it was accompanied by a pair of heavily armed escort vehicles.

Philippa and Boyd stayed behind a line painted on the ground as the gate opened and the vehicles rumbled in. Several more vampires meandered over to see the spectacle, but they stayed further back. Crowds made the guards nervous.

To Philippa's surprise, Colonel Joseph Locke stepped out of the first escort vehicle. Locke oversaw several reservations in the region, but he only rarely visited. It was never a good thing when he came around. He smiled, showing off a set of big, white teeth.

"Howdy-hey, folks. Always a pleasure to see you lot rising and shining your butts off. It is a fine evening for it, I tell you. We're still a couple months away from that summer solstice. The daytime hours will keep getting longer for a while, just the way I like it. A fine evening, I say."

Locke hated vampires. Hated them with a passion. Philippa once heard a rumor that Locke had been an aspiring televangelist when the war started, and he'd enlisted to fight the good fight against the vampiric spawn of Satan. Philippa didn't know if the rumor was true, but she Locke certainly had ambitions. It wasn't hard to picture him selling fire and brimstone to a crowd hungry for salvation. Or maybe hawking used cars with disgusting interest rates.

"Welcome to Guano Creek, Colonel," Philippa said. "Were you planning to run an inspection? No one told us." She hated that she had to roll over and show her belly every time Locke drove through that gate. She also hated that Locke inevitably found something that met with his dissatisfaction whenever he visited. Locke always reminded Philippa of a big sister who had decided to torment her brother by kidnapping his favorite action figures and making him endure tea parties to get them back.

But Locke had a legion of soldiers with stake bayonets and firebomb drones at his back, so Philippa would continue to roll over each time he visited. She took great pleasure in the fact she'd eventually outlive the pipsqueak. She could be patient.

"No inspection today. I can already see this place is a sore on the ass of the world. The specific infractions don't interest me right now. As a matter of fact, I come bearing gifts. And an offer."

"An offer?" Philippa narrowed her eyes, immediately suspicious.

"Gifts first. Let it never be said that I don't spoil you bloodsuckers. First, I'm donating some books to your little community library. For the betterment of your sinister little minds, you understand?"

Locke reached into the escort vehicle and pulled out some books that appeared to have been left out in the rain and then run over by a circus train. He tossed them into the dirt at Philippa and Boyd's feet one-by-one. *Gone With the Wind* in Dutch. A Garfield cartoon-themed thesaurus. The camp's fourth copy of *Twilight*. And an owner's manual for a 1997 Toyota Camry that mostly disintegrated on impact.

"These will be greatly appreciated. Thank you," Philippa said in a cheery tone that she knew would annoy Locke.

Locke gave another big grin, no doubt because he knew it would annoy Philippa right back. "I also have something else. Show me those pearly whites." Locke pulled out a camera, and it flashed, blinding Philippa for a moment.

A second later, a small image began to print from the side of the camera, a bit like the old Kodaks. Locke yanked the image loose and tossed it toward Philippa. It fluttered in the wind and landed facedown a few feet in front of her.

Philippa sighed. Everyone knew vampires didn't show up in mirrors or photographs. They weren't invisible, like some of the old stories. Just incredibly blurry. She picked up the picture, already knowing she'd look like someone took a wet towel to a charcoal etching of Bigfoot. Locke's guards stiffened as she stepped forward and then relaxed as she moved back behind the line.

Flipping the photo over, she blanched. It was a perfect image of her and Boyd. Well, not perfect. The surrounding environment was perfectly crisp, whereas she and Boyd looked like they'd been clipped out of a black and white VHS security camera scene. This was the first time in three thousand years Philippa had seen her own face as anything but a smear.

And she looked like absolute dogshit. Tired. Thin. Sunken-eyed. Was that simply because she'd been dead for three millennia? Was her memory of her face so badly out of date? She didn't think so. She was just beat to hell from a few years of hard living out here.

"But wait, there's more," Locke said like a man advertising a non-stick skillet. He nodded to the crew of the refrigerated truck, and a big hose began to fill several buckets with what Philippa could determine by its scent to be chicken blood. The military contracted with a company that juiced chickens like oranges. Bird blood wasn't as refreshing as mammal blood—that was why Boyd and so many other vampires had been farmers before the war—but chicken blood would keep them alive.

A few matted feathers and cracked beaks clinked into the buckets before the spigot shut off and the hose went dry. A soldier took the bloody buckets and moved them halfway toward the line. Philippa and Boyd would be allowed to grab them and take them to the commissary once Locke left.

"I wouldn't want it said you're abused in some way," Locke said.

"Perish the thought," Boyd said.

Locke's eyes slid over to Boyd and then back to Philippa. "I do treat you right. Or I wouldn't be about to make this offer." He gestured the guards away. They reluctantly moved back.

"You see, there's a woman on my staff, Specialist Emma Crane. She's something of a vampire expert. I'm afraid she has terminal cancer. Now, Emma's a good little soldier, which is why I personally would rather see her dead than turned into a soulless thing like you. But she thinks she might be valuable, since she has a working knowledge of undeath. She's pitched me that she wants to donate her body to science, so to speak. Her soul, too. It's people like her who made the camera that can actually take photos of you. Trying to understand the vampires is important, they say. And some gutless lickspittles in the chain of command agree that it might be helpful to have a vampire expert on the other side. My superiors want you to turn her."

Locke opened the rear door to the escort vehicle, and a young woman stepped out into the moonlight. She was pale and wore a grim expression. Philippa could smell death wafting off her like smoke. The cancer would be quick but not merciful.

"Absolutely not," Philippa said immediately.

"And why, pray tell? I'd think a pair of ghoulies like you would jump at the chance for some warm human blood. Philippa, I know you've personally turned some people. What's wrong? Why the cold feet now?"

Philippa squirmed. She didn't like being reminded of what she'd done during the war. Desperate times. Desperate measures.

"There are laws against that sort of thing. The Vampire Populations Act."

"The VPA? Honey, this is a military matter. You don't need to worry about the VPA."

Philippa looked at the woman. Emma stared pleadingly back at her. Locke's adjutant was clearly afraid, but she also seemed to know the stakes.

But this was all wrong. Locke had fought in the vampire war, fought with tenacity and a grim disregard for anything but victory. Philippa could have used more people like him on her side. He'd no doubt approved of the Marburg plan. He wouldn't want more vampires in the world. It was basically the only thing the two of them agreed on, really.

"We're not going to change her or anybody else just on your say so. We don't make more vampires. That's the rule."

Emma shrank back a little, as if Philippa had just delivered a death sentence. In a way, she had.

Locke scowled. "I let you run your little affairs in there but make no mistake, *I'm* in charge of this operation. My bosses are telling me to do it, and now I'm telling *you* to do it. So do it." Locke gestured like he was talking to a dog that had begged to go outside but then refused to go potty.

"Get it to me in writing," Philippa said.

Locke smiled, but there was no pleasure in it. "I'll do that. I'll just drive back to headquarters and tell General Palma the vampires would like his orders signed and notarized. Anything else?"

"I think we're done here," Philippa said. She watched Locke and Emma climb back into the vehicle and drive back through the night. Locke gave her a tight little smile and dangled his arm out the open window. He looked like a stiff department store mannequin that'd been placed in a "carefree" pose.

"We'll discuss this again later," he said as the vehicle's engine rumbled to life.

She looked down at the photograph still in her hands. An actual photo of her. And now Colonel Locke, of all people, was trying to convince her to turn someone. How the times changed.

And the thing that Philippa had come to fear and dread most in all her long years was change. But inevitably, even all the way out here, change had found her.

Philippa awoke in the darkness of the shipping container. The dream she'd been having clung to her like a spiderweb. She'd heard a lot of people dreamed they were late to college exams they'd just found out about. Philippa had never been to college, in part because she'd lived through a lot of the events any school would've taught, and she knew how much the history books got wrong. When she dreamed, more often than not, she found herself back in Michigan's Upper Peninsula during the closing days of the war.

Widespread testing for a new strain of bat-borne coronavirus had inadvertently revealed the existence of vampires to the world. In the end, her kind had finally been tracked down not by mobs wielding pitchforks and torches but by public health services.

There'd been a panic. Sensationalist news stories pinned every unsolved murder and disappearance in the country on vampires. Real estate owned by vampires was seized by the state under the idea that it had been fraudulently conveyed through generations of owners who'd usually "died" and been replaced with curiously identical looking heirs over and over again. An aging rockstar publicly pledged himself to the forces of darkness, promising to commit any foul deed the Vampire Grand Council desired in exchange for eternal life. There was no Vampire Grand Council, but people assumed there was one after that, and they also assumed it desired a regular supply of foul deeds. Several weirdos and cretins killed people in an attempt to impress the nonexistent vampire hierarchy. And then, several known vampires were killed in retribution attacks.

Philippa had, in fact, killed people before the war. It was actually sort of difficult to go three thousand years without it becoming necessary at least once. The first time happened when several Athenian soldiers landed on the little island in the Aegean, where she'd exiled herself, and tried to steal her sheep. Livestock thieves were the people most likely to die in vampire attacks.

Vampires hadn't regularly preyed on people in nearly eight thousand years. Domesticated animals almost completely obviated the need for human blood. Generally, mammal blood was the tastiest. Pigs, goats, or cows were all vampires really needed for a steady diet.

The rise of agriculture and the fact that people now gathered in settled cities and nations made human beings incredibly difficult prey. Philippa had heard from a few of the old timers, now long dead, that it was easy to snatch the average hunter-gatherer away in the woods. But settled villages? That was a different matter. The handful of aging gourmands who insisted on killing the occasional human being had all been hunted down and destroyed centuries ago. They couldn't change with the times, and their need to kill had given rise to most of the ugly little vampire myths and stories across the world. Everyone else, Philippa included, had been content to live in the shadows, living on secluded home steads as farmers and rancheros.

And then everything went to hell. The viral testing. The news stories. The tit-for-tat raids and attacks. The "war" was never a full-blown conflict between armies of the dead and the living. It was a constant insurgency, with the hunters becoming the hunted each time night turned to day. But the vampires never had the numbers to really mount a coordinated offense. There had been maybe one hundred thousand vampires in North America before the war, and there were about ten thousand now. The so-called war was mostly a slaughter.

Philippa wasn't proud of it, but she'd been one of the hardliners. There'd only been a handful of vampires left in the region at that point, the rest dead or captured. Her justifications to herself seemed sound at the time. If the military wanted to kill vampires, fine. Let them. She turned almost eight hundred people against their will, all of them connected to local militia forces.

Let the military and the vigilantes kill vampires. Let them kill their own mothers. Their brothers and sisters. Their sons and daughters. And they *had* killed her progeny. In droves. Very few of the people Philippa turned in the war's dying days survived.

She'd turned so many people. And in the end, she'd accomplished nothing. Maybe she was a monster, but it had nothing to do with her need for blood. Of course, she wasn't the only self-made monster out in the world. Some of them just got better press than her.

Colonel Joseph Locke hadn't been back since that night two weeks ago. Neither had the blood truck. There'd been no blood available since then. People were getting restless in the camp. They'd all been through lean times before, but they were starting to complain. Philippa had no intention of giving in to Locke's request, though.

She would not turn Emma. Or anyone else, for that matter. She'd done things during the war. Things that seemed like the actions of an entirely different person.

She'd changed a lot of children. Children were her specialty, really. She'd even managed to turn a senator's daughter once, which she'd considered quite the feat at the time.

The military staked the girl. On television. All the news channels covered it, the more tasteful ones blurring some of the footage. Senator Farnsworth turned his daughter over to the military for the staking. It was his idea to televise it, to show the world that the government would not give in to the "terrorist vampire threat."

He was reelected the next year with over eighty percent of the vote. People called his speech before the staking Churchillian and extolled his principled sacrifice and refusal to give an inch to the vampires.

He was currently in his first term as vice president.

And now, the world had come to her doorstep and asked her to do the very thing it once viewed with such horror and disgust. Philippa wondered if lions in zoos felt the same way, once the terror of the savanna, now reduced to a spectacle for tourists. Of course, the lions in the zoo were fed on a regular schedule. People would be outraged if a zoo let their lions starve.

Philippa would make do, as would they all. She'd been forced to explain the situation to the rest of the camp. Some of them accepted her choice, but others grumbled. Philippa had taken a hell of a lot of flak for refusing Locke's request to turn the woman and bringing this famine down on them. In the end, no one would go against her wishes on this. Even among her own kind, there was a strong reluctance to disobey the Butcher of Marquette.

She pulled open the door to the freight container and greeted the night, still shaking the last ephemera of her bad dream away. The war. Marburg. The people handing over their recently changed loved ones to the military for destruction.

Philippa strode across camp to the creek that ran along the edge of the fence. Frogs croaked their songs to the moon. She sat down by the edge of the water and waited, listening. Her hand darted out and came back with a frog grasped in her fingers. She bit into the frog like an apple and sucked at its lifeforce. Its blood tasted like swamp gas and old pennies, but it took some of the edge off her thirst.

"Hey, don't Bogart the frog," Boyd said, appearing out of the night like a specter.

"Sorry." Philippa offered the limp amphibian to him.

He sucked the final dregs of blood out of the animal with a wet slurping noise. Then, he scooped a shallow divot out of the earth and respectfully laid the frog inside, putting a rock over it to create a tiny mausoleum.

"You think we made the right call with Locke?" Boyd asked.

"Not you, too." Philippa groaned. "I'm not changing that woman. Nobody is. Not while I'm around. The world doesn't need more vampires. It doesn't *want* more vampires. The universe tried to teach me that lesson, and it took me a long time to learn it."

Boyd looked at her. "I'm not sure that was the lesson the universe tried to teach you."

Philippa sat for a moment. She could hear another frog nearby. No, a turtle. She could lop the turtle's head off and drink it like a juice box. But no. She needed to leave plenty of small animals for the rest of the camp. There were only so many to go around. No sense in getting greedy. She focused on the sound of the turtle moving along the muddy edge of the creek to hide her annoyance.

"Are you still thirsty? I hear a turtle," she said after a minute.

"I'm good," Boyd said, even though he clearly was not good. His skin was nearly translucent, his veins standing out like worms on a rainy sidewalk.

Finally, Philippa sighed. "I know you want me to ask. What lesson do you *think* the universe was trying to teach me?"

"Well, when you've been around for a few hundred years like I have, you learn some things," Boyd said, cracking his knuckles.

"Youths these days, thinking they know everything," Philippa said, but she smiled.

Boyd smiled too, but it was a sad smile. "The war, I think, was a failure of understanding. Finding out we existed, people reacted the way they do when they find a spider crawling on their arm. They panicked and swatted us off."

"Wise words, oh ancient one."

Boyd ignored the jab. "There was no dialogue. No exchange. If people take the time to get to know us, we're not so bad. Everybody has a few spiders in their home. Mostly, they eat pests and stay out of your way."

"Yeah, and when most people find a spider on the wall, they smack it with a shoe until it stops moving," Philippa said.

"But that's exactly the point I'm trying to make. They shouldn't kill the spiders. People who study spiders mostly either leave them be or put them outside. Live and let live."

"Sure, but do you know how many people study spiders? Probably about three, and I'm guessing they don't get a lot of dates."

"You're missing the point, Philippa," Boyd said, the first hint of frustration entering his voice. "Collectively, we're the biggest, hairiest, skittering-est spider the world has ever seen, and they're pouring resources into studying us. Something like, what, half of the military's budget is vampire research now, right?"

"They're not studying *us*, Boyd. Remember Marburg? They're studying how to kill us."

Boyd waved that away. "One and the same. That camera Locke showed us? Sure, it has military applications. They can track us with their drones better. But you know what? We could also have the first vampire movie star now. People could see us, I mean *really* see us. We're not just something that goes bump in the night now. We look like normal people on camera."

"Let's pretend you're onto something and the world starts to get comfortable with the idea of bloodsuckers roaming around again. I think all that goodwill evaporates the second we turn someone."

"Even if they ask us to? Even if we're ordered to do it? Even if we prevent that person from dying of cancer? This Emma woman is supposed to be some kind of vampire expert. And people like Locke's bosses want us to turn her and then listen to what she has to say? That's our golden ticket, right there. People want to learn about us. They don't want a continuation of the war. Insider vampires are the fast track to a mutual understanding. We *need* inventions like that camera. We need a constructive dialogue. We need to make some vampires who weren't involved in the war so we can have 'safe' vampires people can trust. And once people trust a few vampires, the door opens for the rest of us. Turning that woman could change everything for us."

"It could change everything," Philippa agreed. "And that's what I'm afraid of."

"Come on, Boyd. It's almost sunrise," Philippa said, trying to mask the desperation in her voice. It had been ten days since they split the frog blood together, and she'd watched him grow weaker and weaker since then.

Boyd didn't say anything. He simply lay in the dirt, not moving. His face was drawn and gaunt, and his limbs were stiff with rigor mortis. Healthy vampires did not get rigor mortis after their first night as one of the undead.

Philippa knew perfectly well she didn't look much better. The night was quiet. There was no harumphing of frogs down by the creek. They'd all been drained days ago. Same with the turtles and mice that lived along the banks.

"Dammit, Boyd," Philippa muttered. Half the camp was like this, stiffened up as if turned to stone. Philippa could feel a dull ache in her joints, as if someone had dumped sand in her gears. Every movement came with an unpleasant grinding. A few more nights without blood, and the whole camp would be paralyzed.

The sensation terrified her. She hadn't known the feeling of rigor mortis since the war.

Since Marburg.

The Marburg hemorrhagic fever virus was closely related to Ebola. And like its dear cousin, the bloodborne virus was extraordinarily deadly and caused such lovely symptoms as spontaneous bleeding and psychosis. It killed vampires just as readily, if not more so, than normal people.

Marburg ended the war. The government bombed active vampire areas with viral samples, affecting most of the local population. Like nearly every other vampire, Philippa had been infected. And because the government had a vaccine, the virus had come with an ultimatum.

Surrender and survive. Or continue fighting and perish.

Philippa surrendered, though she knew a handful of vampires who continued the war for about another month before the virus claimed them. Even with the vaccine, a lot of people died.

That was Philippa's first experience with people trying to understand vampires. That was why she didn't believe in Boyd's vision of reaching out and singing Kumbaya. That was why she had refused Locke's request to turn the woman.

Vampires didn't just live in the shadows literally. They lived in darkness metaphorically, too. And conversely, they died in the light, whether from the sun or from the harsh spotlight of scientific understanding.

Philippa pulled at Boyd's arms, trying to uncurl them. It was like trying to straighten out a tire. Boyd groaned. She went to her knees and tried to lift him. Normally, she could've hoisted him over her shoulder like a cheap sack of grain, but she was weak. Weak, weak, weak. She saw the same scene playing out elsewhere around the camp. Those who still had a little fresh blood chugging through their veins tried to care for the others.

A loud whirr made Philippa turn around to see one of the big military quadcopter drones hovering over her head. She held up her hands to demonstrate she wasn't a threat. Instead of annihilating her in fiery glory, a speaker blared to life from the drone.

"Hello, Philippa," Locke's voice said.

"Colonel Locke." She clenched her jaw tight. The drone must have one of the new cameras that could see vampires, because he wouldn't have been able to recognize her from the thermal scanners alone.

"It'd be *General* Locke by now, if you'd just let me help you. You bloodsuckers aren't the only ones affected by how difficult you're being, you know. You're holding up my career here," the drone's speaker said, the words distorted by the sound of the rotors.

"What a crying pity that is," Philippa said.

"Listen, I don't have time to play footsy with you. I'm at a command post nearby. I have Emma with me. She's the one who *really* doesn't have the time for this. It's been weeks. Your little hunger strike has put everyone in a real bind. I could be there in less than twenty minutes with Emma and the blood truck."

"It's not really a hunger strike if your captors intentionally withhold the food," Philippa said.

"What was that? I couldn't hear you over the sound of the anti-personnel chemical flame projector warming up. Listen, toots. I'm going to make this real simple for you. So simple even a bloodthirsty monster can understand. Here's the deal. I don't care if your whole camp dies. Good riddance. There are dozens of other camps. If you lot all stiffen up and die, I'll just tell my commander that you rioted, and I had to burn you out. They won't care enough to investigate past that. But if you change Emma, I'll turn the spigots on again. You all get to keep on slurping down the ol' government-issued red sauce, the cancer doesn't get Emma, and I get a promotion for landing an insider amongst you. Everybody wins. Except Emma, since she's stuck as a vampire, but she swears up and down that's what she wants."

Philippa looked down at Boyd. She thought about what he'd said. The new cameras. The first vampire movie star. An insider who could talk to the military without fear of being burnt to a blackened skeleton just because she got too close to the fences.

She thought about the Marburg virus. She thought about the doctors who injected the vaccine into her as she was taken into captivity. They'd understood something about vampires, and they'd used that knowledge to try to kill her. But in the end, they'd also given her the vaccine and saved her.

Understanding alone wouldn't save them. It took something more. Empathy. Maybe understanding was a start. But she'd understood her enemies in the war. It didn't lead to empathy.

"I'm going to count to three," the voice from the drone said.

"I'll do it," Philippa said, cutting Locke off before he could begin his count.

There was a surprised silence for just a second. "Very good. I'll be there in two shakes of a lamb's tail. Bring your appetite." And with that, the drone flew off.

Philippa knew the next nearest vampire reservation was over fifty miles away, but in the clear night skies of Eastern Oregon, she could still see the distant glow of the fires consuming the camp. Hart Lake. Catlow Valley. Wagontire. All the big vampire camps were ablaze.

In the end, Colonel Locke, now Brigadier General Locke, had been mostly honest with her. The one thing he'd lied about was his superiors authorizing him to offer Emma to the vampires. That was Locke's initiative, and he had his own plans.

Philippa looked down at the newspapers a drone had dropped off at the center of camp. They showed variations of the same picture on the front page. Philippa and the other raggedy, half-starved vampires were sinking their fangs into Emma, who now stood among them. Drones equipped with the newest cameras had captured the images.

VAMPIRE POPULATIONS ACT IN TATTERS

VAMPIRES TARGETING SOLDIERS AT RESERVATIONS

VAMPIRE WAR REIGNITES

All the top stories were the same. And they all contained somewhere in the text the additional detail that newly minted Brigadier General Joseph Locke had a plan to deal with the vampire menace.

The punk had played her like a fiddle. Philippa almost admired the ruthlessness of the plan. She wondered how long Locke had the camera technology before he realized he could use it to get exactly what he wanted: a permanent solution to the vampire problem. The fact that he'd taken the time to have one drone make a special delivery was a nice personal touch. Real Class-A bastard move. The vampires might have won the war, Philippa thought, if they'd had more monsters like Locke on their side.

Philippa heard the whirr in the distance, a wasp-like buzz in the night sky. The drones appeared over the horizon in a swarm, each one laden with white phosphorus and other fiery, anti-personnel munitions. The first rain of projectiles came before the drones even cleared the edge of the valley. The cleansing fire came in a wave, engulfing everything in front of it, sweeping across the camp like a living thing. Vampires screamed, their flesh melting like tallow.

Philippa watched the camp burn around her. The world had changed so much since she'd been turned all those years ago. And all that change had finally caught up with her. She couldn't keep up anymore, and now, after the war, she found she didn't want to.

She closed her eyes, and the fire took her.

DEVOUR

Kelli Etheridge

THE VENTILATOR, WHICH had earlier antagonised Damon with its endless wheezing, comforted him now with its rhythmic, mechanical ebbs, and flows. The many tubes entering and exiting his body, from both his own orifices and those they created, snaked around his hospital bed in a chaotic tangle. Breathing. Pissing. Monitoring. One going in to feed him, another going out to feed *them*. Of all the imagined endings, this wasn't one. Preservation, he'd hoped. Capture, quite possibly. Death, a potential outcome, for sure. After years of mere survival, this powerlessness seemed like an immense disappointment. But when life had become so tenuous that hope had been almost extinguished, he'd had no choice but to try. It'd been the last endeavour to change all their futures.

He had no regrets.

The planning had taken months, and they had contingencies for every scenario, or so they believed. Dawn's glow was a hint on the horizon as Anthony smudged Damon for protection. The white sage and wolfsbane smoke swirled around, grounding him with its pervasive aroma.

As they waited for the base of the sun to break free of the skyline,

Damon contemplated not going at all. He wasn't hero material. He'd been a journalist before this. His stories were light and inconsequential until he'd decided to do an exposé on the Blood Farms. He'd achieved somewhat of a cult following after that. When they created their community, his jovial personality and pertinacious spirit positioned him as a mentor and then, eventually, as their unofficial leader. In truth, he was scared shitless, but it only mattered that their fears overshadowed his own.

In the community, they worried most about contracting the virus. In the beginning, some humans, seduced by immortality, begged the Devourers for a Turning. Those fools were part of the problem, although Damon placed some blame on the media and folklore. Books and movies consistently portrayed the Devourers with a sexy and dangerous allure, but when the myth became reality, all the eroticism had faded away, leaving the humans with only their raw vulnerability. Thirty years later, in 2053, some imbeciles still wished to give up their humanity.

He and Anthony crossed the creek, rushing with steady and continual force, and looked back to see every single community member witnessing his departure. It was too serious a moment for smiles or speech or waves. They supported him as silent spectators, nestled close to one another for comfort, safe behind the flowing waters that the Devourers couldn't cross, not even by boat. Anthony blessed the waters regularly to maintain the purity, like an immense holy-water moat.

"I wouldn't give this up for an eternity of nights." Anthony turned his head to welcome the widening sunbeams. "We've got a pretty good life here, all things considered. I feel more hope than I have in years. Once the virus is no longer a risk, we can really get down to living."

"Yeah. There was a time, right after all that happened with Gemma, that I didn't want to see another tomorrow. Their lure of endless tomorrows just never appealed to me. I'm grateful to you and this community. You saved me, truly."

"And now you'll save us. It's going to be a hell of a long day of waiting. Be safe."

Anthony held Damon in a prolonged embrace, the kind of hug that might be the last. Damon swallowed away the lump in his throat then turned east into the light. He knew he must return by sunset, or he wouldn't make it home at all.

By the time he reached the Devourer's research compound, the sun was soaring with protective radiance. Their facility was austere and utilitarian. Cold, like them. They had no aesthetic aspirations. Their logo, an ankh modified with a dagger at its base and tapered wings extending from its sides, was prominently displayed on the sign perched above the entrance. Half celebration, half warning.

The guard was at his station at the main doorway, standing with his face tilted up to the light streaming down from the sky to savour the warmth, eyes closed.

Damon's boots rustled in the gravel and interrupted the sun-warmed reverie. The guard turned at once and levelled his rifle straight at his head. His eyes, savage with fear, stirred Damon's own panic.

Damon was the prey. He should've been accustomed to that feeling after all this time, but the vestigial belief that humans were still an apex predator persisted within his psyche. He stood frozen, like a rabbit attempting to avoid detection while in the middle of an open field. He held his breath in tight to steady himself as he stared into the gun barrel.

"Lionel, it's me." He glared at the guard, hoping for quick recognition.

"Fuck, Damon, I almost shot you!" Lionel lowered the gun and laughed far too hard. Damon didn't like this guy, and he certainly didn't respect him, but he was the key to the building. Damon had bribed him by offering him a secure place in their group. It only took a few weeks to charm him with the benefits of community living—the fresh food from the garden prepared daily by a talented cooking crew, comfortable lodging, access to alternative medicines and healing practices.

The Devourers had only wanted the doctors and scientists and left the woo-woo types alone—the herbalists, the energy healers, the acupuncturists—which suited their group just fine. They also ignored the artistically inclined—the musicians, the painters, the poets. The community thrived from their collective creativity and connection; they painted murals, hosted musical performances and craft nights, and facilitated sharing circles. It took the edge off being chronically fearful.

He couldn't imagine Lionel there with his stiff black uniform or his inappropriate sense of humour, but if living with Lionel was the only price to pay, he could deal with that.

"Yeah, what the fuck? You knew I was coming. I'm right on schedule."

Lionel gained his composure and motioned him to the door. "Hey, sorry dude. Chill out, though. I didn't shoot you. Let's do this! Are you ready? You need to be sure."

"Absolutely. Are you?"

"I was born ready!" Lionel stood tall, hoisted the rifle over his shoulder, and placed his hands on his hips. His biceps bulged underneath his uniform. His goofy grin made him look like a retro Superman caricature. The only thing missing was his cape. Damon imagined their future life with Lionel; he'd probably talk over others in conversation, never inquiring about others' well-being. He couldn't envision Lionel sitting down to weave a willow basket or help grate carrots in the kitchen. But he'd be perfect as a guard up in the turret, alone. Same thing he was doing now but working with his own kind.

"Thanks so much, Lionel. This will change everything for all of us. I want you to know the entire community is looking forward to welcoming you there."

"Hey, no problem. This is going to be intense!" He acted excited, as if they were going to a rock concert together and not conspiring to pull off a dangerous pharmaceutical heist. It wasn't his youth Damon despised; it was his immaturity.

Lionel pulled back his sleeve and scanned the device around his wrist. A screen lit up beside the door, and he positioned himself as lasers skimmed from chin to forehead. "Facial recognition and retinal scan. They don't take any chances. You know, I had to work here for two years before they would trust me to keep this place safe. I flexed all my good qualities and sucked up a bit to get this job. They believed it all, though. Lucky for you, I've got mad skills."

Damon nodded, resisting the urge to roll his eyes at the guard's overblown swagger. "What about the cameras? All good?"

"Yeah, yeah. Of course. Took care of them first thing. All the security guards are seeing, wherever the hell this gets streamed, is yesterday's feed. Uneventful, typical Wednesday, or in this case, Tuesday. Tested it out last week and no one noticed or said a thing. I streaked through the building fully naked at one point in my shift, just to be sure. If they had seen that, they would've mentioned it. Nothing though. So, we're all good."

"Of course, you streaked. I appreciate you exposing yourself to such risk," Damon quipped. Lionel didn't laugh.

As they entered, Damon's nostrils filled with pungent disinfectants and metallic odours. He swallowed down the urge to vomit. This was the same smell that wafted from the Blood Farm he'd passed by earlier in the day, impeccable and sterile, highly controlled and deep underground to prevent a viral outbreak.

Blood Farms cropped up around five years ago. Donators were bled as often as possible while preserving vitality and longevity. The Devourers also compelled matings to ensure future Donators, performed in much the same unromantic way as people would breed dogs or horses. They would never bleed the offspring until they were sixteen, which was more necessity than kindness. Being immortal meant you could play the long game.

Lionel switched on all the lights, waking the deserted daytime laboratory. This place would be a crowded hub of pale scientists at night. Devourers had turned all the best scientists early on, along with the politicians and the billionaires who could help pave their path to power. And it worked. Too well, in fact.

"Where do they keep it?" He wanted to be expeditious, not hang around for chitchat with this Generation V moron.

Lionel led them to the bowels of the building where all the pharmaceuticals were stored. He scanned his device, lined up for the facial and retinal scan then used a key attached to his belt to unlock the door. A wave of escaping frosty air chilled their faces as they advanced into the cooler. Damon advised Lionel to look for the most recent date on the labels, indicating the freshest and most accurate vaccine.

"Found it!" Lionel yelled despite the fact he was right across from him in the confined space.

The vials were labelled with last week's date. Damon blinked away tears of relief before Lionel could see them and exhaled much of the tension that'd been strangling his lungs. This would change everything. Conditions had grown dire, for the living and the undead, around the time the Blood Farms were created. Reports of unintentional or unexplained Turnings emerged and fears of a viral outbreak proliferated. If transformations were uncontrolled, then the risk was that every human would become a Devourer. At the point of Donator extinction, the Devourers would ensure their own demise. The Devourers initiated the vaccine trials immediately, and Damon's community launched their own strategy in response.

Damon secured the vaccine in the cooler, nested with towels for safety, and they headed outside together. Back in the natural light and fresh air, he felt unfettered and safe again, to a point. It had gone to plan, maybe even easier than he expected. Lionel's assistance proved to be invaluable. Perhaps he would cut him some slack in the future.

"Grab your shit and let's get out of here," Damon commanded.

Lionel lingered, like a child hovering on the edge of a pool, too afraid to jump in. "I... I can't. Your place sounds nice, and I know I'd be welcome after what I did here today, but I have more of a future here."

"Seriously, buddy? Lionel, just come with me, but we have to go now, or we'll lose light."

"I know, but they offered me a Turning one day. Soon, they said. No cap! They were deadass! Come on, who could turn down forever?"

He wants to be one of them!

Lionel was young, but old enough to know what a Turning entailed. All but the children had seen the videos of their transformations that went viral in the early days.

"Lionel, you must remember the Turnings when they first went online, the excruciating dying as the virus overtook their bodies. That greyish pallor of the victims as they writhed in agony, begging for death. Not the animated-insatiable-corpse death that was coming for them, but a true death that would end in nothingness. Think back to before the Devourers controlled the news and social media, before those types of videos disappeared and they sanitised their reputation."

"Of course, but that part's just temporary. Besides, being a Devourer is easier now. I won't have to kill anyone. Live feedings aren't even legal anymore. The Donators guarantee the food supply. I just head the store to buy blood in tidy little bottles," Lionel rationalised.

"Please tell me you understand that Donators aren't volunteers. They're prisoners."

"Well, I don't like to concentrate on that bit. Gotta pick a side at some point. I pick the side that lets me look like this forever. Beats gettin' old and useless."

Damon didn't know which was worse—that Lionel was stupid enough to want to be a Devourer, or that he was naïve enough to believe someone would risk Turning him. In the early years, many Turnings were accidental by novice Devourers, others random and messy with cruelty. Anyone could turn anyone else, and their numbers multiplied as the Turnings became exponential. It took only a single generation in

Homo sapiens' time for them to outnumber humans. The Devourers who held positions of power formed the Council and passed laws to control the Turnings. Devourers needed to fill out an extensive application for each Turning. They abandoned anyone who performed one without permission outside to blister, then vaporise in the sunshine. Who would risk that for Lionel?

"Well, now what? You're just going to stay here?" Damon grew impatient, still hoping for the guard's change-of-heart.

"Yeah, gotta make it look like I put up a fight, though. Here, hit me with my gun, not in the face, please, and I'll pretend I'm passed out until they arrive at dark. I really am glad you got what you came for and all, but I have to think of myself here."

The true Lionel peeked out from beneath all his bravado—more Renfield than Van Helsing. Damon considered, just for a flash of a moment, shooting him with his gun, but that would have made him one step closer to being like *them*. The Devourers could have him. They deserved each other. An extra blow to the head—no, the cheek—with the stock of his gun would suffice. Damon made sure Lionel didn't need to pretend to be unconscious. He'd be back at the community long before Lionel woke up. He laid his gun down on the ground beside the immobile guard, just in case he needed it later.

Damon's hand cramped as he clenched the cooler, racing against the earth before it could rotate back into darkness. This vaccine would save them from the worst fate—a Turning. It couldn't reverse it, just prevent it. It could also never guarantee they wouldn't end up on a Blood Farm, but it ensured they would never become a Devourer. Becoming one of them would be the worst outcome.

The sun was far too low by the time Damon neared home. He picked up the pace for the last stretch. He heard the vials clinking together in the cooler as he scuttled to his destination. The glass-against-glass tinkling stirred the recollection of beach glass wind-chimes his daughter Gemma constructed for him when she was seven. She foraged all the glass during a family vacation to the ocean and proudly presented him with her gift on the next Father's Day.

They were still hanging in his home office window, catching a lovely westerly breeze, when he'd fled from the house with only a small backpack of belongings. Gemma was away at university at the time, finishing up an undergrad degree, preparing for a career as a nurse. She never graduated. She would have been thirty-three now. But she'll be twenty-two forever.

Anthony had almost crossed the moat when Damon reached the shoreline. He climbed in and slumped up against the side, woozy from exertion and remembrances, as Anthony pushed the motor to capacity. It sputtered at full speed to deliver them to the other side before the crepuscular glow abandoned them into the night. He looked forward to Anthony's succession as leader one day, perhaps soon. Anthony had youth and energy on his side as well as a spiritual grounding and innate benevolence. Damon anticipated a relaxed retirement of sorts and then the freedom to die of old age in his own bed, a rare luxury afforded to few anymore.

"Where's dingbat?" Anthony inquired.

"Well, things took an unsuspected turn, pun intended." Damon must have laughed for a solid minute at his own joke, his exhaustion amplifying the humour.

"You're bloody hilarious. Get on with your story. We don't have all day." He giggled as he pointed at the horizon, where only a sliver of sunset remained. That's what he liked about Anthony; he could still find humour in serious situations.

"Our friend, Lionel, decided he'd rather be one of them than one of us. I'm guessing they'll never turn him, though; they can't afford to. I made it look like he wasn't in on it. It'll give him a chance, anyway." It was quite possible he'd end up on a Blood Farm. Damon wondered if he should have shot him. For mercy. A humane killing.

"At least we got what we wanted." Anthony slapped his hand on Damon's back as congratulations.

As they entered the dining hall, everyone gathered. They both wanted to celebrate, but merriment would have to wait until after. Damon held the cooler high above his head, like it was the Stanley Cup from the old hockey days, and the crowd launched into a cheer.

The sounds of rejoicing became an abrupt silence, as if an orchestra conductor closed his fingers to mute them. They lined up as planned along the long banquet table running the length of the hall. Anthony distributed their daily supplements in matching cups. Everyone gulped down the muddy-looking liquid, sweetened heavily with honey to balance and mask its bitterness.

"If you didn't know any better, it'd look like we were at Jonestown drinking the Kool-Aid," he chuckled as he whispered to Damon, handing out the last portion. They often chatted about how the Devourers must have studied Jim Jones' People's Temple handbook. The Devourers charmed a lot of citizens with their cult of forever.

"Hey, don't laugh. It might come to that someday," Damon replied, only half joking.

"Not today, at least, thanks to you." Anthony held his glass up to Damon's. "Cheers!""To our health, my dear friend. Bottom's up!" He guzzled his liquid offering and felt the welcomed tingling on his lips almost immediately.

The line snaked around the end of the table where Damon waited, syringes in hand. Each group member rolled up their sleeves, and he administered the vaccine to everyone. He gave Anthony the penultimate dose, then Anthony plunged the needle into his friend's bicep. They watched together as he pushed the syringe's contents into his flesh with slow and ceremonious intention. They didn't feel any different physically, but a peace settled in with knowing they would never experience a Turning themselves.

Afterwards, they all lost themselves in celebratory joy. They gathered for a meal, accompanied by copious amounts of wine. Glasses clinked as cheers were made and the booze numbed their bodies into a sense of relief.

One layer of fear had dissipated.

It was there, in the hum of happiness, that it started. Emily, one of the youngest in the community, fainted while dancing with her parents. Her eyes peered out in a state of frozen horror as her exanimate body lay strewn across the floorboards. Witnesses gasped and called for help from the healers. Those who didn't see it for themselves rushed over to form a circle of support. One by one, they tumbled like fleshy dominoes.

"They're dead!"

"Get help!"

"Oh my God!"

The gasps widened into shouts until no one was left standing to scream.

Only Anthony and Damon remained upright, and only for a few moments. Long enough for Anthony to say, "Well, if it wasn't the Kool-Aid…" before he slumped down into the mass of warm, staring bodies.

Damon rushed to the vials sitting empty on the table. *Was it a bad batch? We should have tested it somehow first. But we didn't. We were worried about fading potency and a short shelf life. The result of hastiness—I killed everyone in our community.*

He felt a fiery rush of blood in his head and the room spun as if he were inebriated. He clutched the edge of the table to steady himself as his body succumbed to gravity, hitting his head on the table as he descended to the floor. Blood trickled across his forehead as he lost all ability to move his body.

Floral notes of incense against the fruitiness of the after-dinner wine grounded him with hyperawareness. The bodies strewn around the hall seemed to almost move in the swaying of the candles' glow. Damon waited for the purr of the refrigerator, the rustling leaves of the maple trees on the patio, and the songs droning out to the empty dance floor, to fade into silence. It was not death as he anticipated. It was complete paralysis merged with a cruel wakefulness. He couldn't move to check on anyone. No twitching of the fingers. No voice. Pure motionlessness.

Time flowed in a lethargic stream until the candles sputtered into darkness. A thin mechanical spinning in the distance, too far away to identify, startled Damon back into alertness. As it neared, he recognised the noise, and all the fear that had evaporated earlier came flooding back into his cells in a rush of epinephrine.

He didn't know how many helicopters landed in their field; the motors and the wind merged into one deafening sound. The community had equipped themselves for such emergency situations with UV spotlights and wooden-bullet-loaded rifles, but being paralysed hadn't factored into their preparedness plan.

Damon knew they couldn't enter the building without an invitation, which could buy them some time. He hoped they would all wake up from the locked-in state by morning, and the attackers would have to flee in the daylight.

Multiple quick-moving footsteps shuffled around outside, and voices piled onto one another, drowning out any coherent conversations. Then a single set of boots clomped towards Damon.

They were inside the building!

"Over here! Holy shit. I bet this is all of them." His breathing was heavy as he leaned down towards Damon's face. His breath was stale with coffee and cigarettes. "We got ya, fuckers."

More footfalls. Coffee-Breath reached down with warm hands against Damon's skin, grabbed him at the armpits, and tossed him onto a stretcher.

They carried Damon outside and handed him off to others.

An unfamiliar voice ordered, "We'll load them from here. You go get more inside."

The traitors returned indoors to collect more humans.

Cold hands lifted Damon into the awaiting helicopter. They piled bodies beside him; the heavy warmth of others both comforted and terrified him.

"This one is dripping a bit. Can't let it go to waste." The female snickered as her cool tongue licked the blood from Damon's forehead wound. He screamed inside, in his stillness.

The helicopter travelled for quite a distance before landing. He identified their whereabouts by the acrid metal and sharp antiseptic aromas that drifted into the helicopter. The handlers were brutish with indifference as they unloaded them, tossing them like fish at the long-ago Pike Place Market.

"Hey, gentle with the product," a deep and commanding Devourer warned. "You know bruises make the blood taste bitter. Put them in B Ward with Lionel. Get them in quick though; they need to be on ventilators soon. We've only got about twenty minutes until the full effects of the Somnifol kick in."

They laid him down in bed, and a new Devourer wrapped warm blankets around him with some degree of tenderness. Her pointed teeth were diminutive, not fully grown. The deadly canines were not an acute manifestation, as in the movies, but grew over time as they perfected their hunting and feeding, now an unneeded skill.

It was a momentary comfort before the interventions began—the catheter, the feeding tube from his nose to his stomach pumping him full of beige liquid, the intubation hose rammed down his throat, and the bloodline—red liquid flowed out of him through a feeding tube for them. Lastly, they placed surgical tape over his eyes, plunging him into darkness.

His mouth was sour and dry. He craved a chance to swallow, scream, or plead.

"We haven't had this many at once in a long time. Looking forward to a good meal. Maybe they'll bump up quotas for a bit." Her voice was soft and youthful, belying her preternatural blood cravings.

"If we're lucky, but I doubt it. Hey, did you know this other guy well?" Another attendant inquired.

"Lionel? Yeah, a bit. I liked him, for a human. He was a bit cocky, but he was fun. We had some pretty quirky conversations."

"Funny, that's the exact thing I hated about him. Thankfully, we won't have to listen to his self-indulgent stories anymore. Could you imagine hearing them forever? Good riddance, Lionel. Bet he'll taste nice—he was all into healthy food and getting in shape. He wanted to be his best self when he went for the Turning, like that was ever going to happen."

"I know. Poor guy. But give him a little credit. This herd of Donators wouldn't be all laying here if it wasn't for him."

"Yeah, but someone who betrays their own kind can't be trusted."

"I suppose," she agreed with hesitation.

"He made his own bed. Don't feel too sorry for him." His voice drifted off in a yell to the left of Damon's hospital bed. "Lionel, thanks for your contribution to our cause, and we appreciate your personal donation as well. Delicious, I'm sure."

Their laughter continued as they finished with the tube insertions and sewed up Damon's head wound. Damon inhaled the scent of their stench as they worked, rankness with a tinge of rotting fruit.

He drifted off to sleep and woke to a bewildered state, without any sense of the time that had passed, but he soon realised it must be daytime since the hands that touched him next were warm. For a moment, he thought he was being saved, rescued, released. However, the human checked all the connections, pulled the blanket up to Damon's chin, and retreated in silence.

The night shifts and day shifts blurred into an immeasurable passing of time.

Damon heard delicate footsteps approach and felt a numbing shadow as she bent over him. Her hair brushed across his face. Her mouth nuzzled up to his ear. Recently fed, a rusty odour wafted towards him. Void of breath, with an uncanny stillness, she whispered in a sweet voice laced with vitriol, "Hello. It's been a long time."

He knew that voice. It was not the sound of the attendant who'd tended to him since his arrival. This one was familiar from life before these animated corpses outnumbered the living.

"Good try, Dad." She pulled off the surgical tape from across his eyes. Damon blinked in the fluorescent brightness as his daughter's face came into focus just above him. A deluge of tears escaped down his cheek with this unexpected reunion. Joy and solace swirled in his chest, along with heart-wrenching fear.

"Your lot managed to kill twenty-three of us. No one was expecting all your blood to be tainted with *that*. We'll be sure to test for more substances in the future. You've really just helped us fine-tune our processes in the long run."

That plan worked! Damon savoured the transitory joy at their successful poisoning. The whole community had supplemented with garlic, colloidal silver, hawthorn, and vervain. However, those herbs were only in the cocktail as distractions. They knew the Devourers could test for those and filter them from blood. It was the kava kava they'd also consumed that catalysed the true deaths of the undead. Alone, the kava kava would create a mild sedative and hypnotic effect, but combined with Citrate-phosphate-dextrose (CPD), the anticoagulant solution they added to their bottled blood supply, it would induce catastrophic haemorrhaging exsanguination. The Devourers would bleed to death from every orifice.

The Devourers had performed Turnings on who they considered to be the smartest and most useful humans. Immortality bred their overconfidence, and their hubris sealed their fate. They underestimated the remaining humans—the dreamers, the resilient ones, the healers, the holders of ancient herbal knowledge. For two weeks before the vaccine heist, the entire community gulped down glasses of the fatal cocktail, fatal only for Devourers, not humans. It was insurance, in case they got caught. There were worse things than death, many things.

"It's unfortunate, really. I rather admire your effort. Your problem-solving abilities and your tenacity always impressed me. You would have been a great addition to our side. I wish…" She leaned in, meeting his gaze, as her words hovered.

He stared into her delicate hazel eyes, scanning for her humanity, waiting for her to finish her thoughts. Hope that all his years of love and guidance would be enough to overpower this unnatural state repeated in his head like a mantra. Her innate warmth and nurturing could still be there beneath the cold exterior of imperishable flesh.

A sweet, innocuous grin flashed across her face before it retracted back into a hollow expression.

"However…"

She closed his eyelids, her frigid fingers gentle on his skin. He heard the abrupt click of a machine being turned off. *His* machine. Panic and relief whirled in his chest in a strange juxtaposition.

Damon struggled to fix the image of her smile in his mind. One last heaving mechanical drawing of breath wheezed itself into a pervasive silence as darkness devoured him.

SON OF THE DRAGON

Raluca Balasa

1443 A.D. An Ottoman Dungeon

VLAD PRESSED HIS back against the wall until his wounds reopened and the pain blotted everything into a haze. It felt good, drifting away from his senses. Sometimes after a lashing, the ringing in his ears drowned out the others' moans so he could close his eyes and pretend it was just him here, suffering in silence.

The cell door creaked open. A soldier in a rich silk caftan stood before him, pointy helmet tucked under his arm. *"Hadi."*

Vlad remained seated, knees drawn to his chest and body folded away from the sunlight that slanted through his window. It looked like sickness; he'd grown to despise it.

"Hadi," the Ottoman soldier repeated, stooping to grab Vlad's arm. The pressure felt like it would pop Vlad's shoulder. He'd been a tall, strong boy once, but all that remained now were memories, bones, and hanging skin. He let himself be dragged through the dungeon's stone halls, and everywhere he went the screams echoed.

The Turk spoke in his guttural language. Something about the juxtaposition between his harsh accent and his calm, deep voice appealed to Vlad. It was easy, learning to love his captors. They beat him because his father didn't care about him and kept rebelling against the empire. They beat him because, unlike his brother, he made fun of their turbans even now, when it no longer brought him solace. They beat him because watching the executions never made him cry.

"It will be your family one day, boy," the soldier said, stopping before a set of bolted oak double-doors. "You'd best get used to seeing this."

Vlad looked up at the man's sharp-edged features. He'd learned Turkish much faster than his turncoat brother, and knew it unnerved the guards that he understood them. *"Korkmuyorum,"* he said.

I'm not afraid.

The doors swung open, and the stenches of blood, sweat, rot, and human waste greeted him on the dry summer air. Vlad breathed deeply and stepped outside.

1462 A.D. Wallachia

There would be no royal reception for her, Ilona knew. Prince Vlad Dracula of Wallachia was a private man rumoured to hate frivolous attention. It was a good thing, too, because she didn't think she could stomach a celebration today. The two Wallachian soldiers by her side walked wordlessly, perhaps the dullest guides she'd ever had. Who could blame them? The prince had punished men for less than speaking out of turn to his bride.

Ilona cleared her throat. "Surely you know I'm not from here. In Transylvania, things are much…livelier. Where is everybody?"

"At home, Princess," answered the shorter one. "Where it's safe."

The farmer's market echoed with silence. The air hung heavy and stale. Where were the scents she'd grown up with, the basil, dill, and parsley? In Transylvania the markets were jubilant places for socialisation, but here the shoppers seemed jittery, buying only what they needed and exchanging brief nods with those they passed. Old women in headscarves sat on stools, swatting at flies around their produce. Ilona held up her hand to stop her guides. She approached the closest vendor.

"Bună," she greeted with a smile. The old lady grinned toothlessly back. "Where are your customers? Is there a holiday today?"

Sadness creased the woman's eyes. "Not many customers around Poenari Castle, my lady, not with the prince so close by."

"Prince Vlad discourages the buying of fresh produce?" Of all the rumours she'd heard, that was a new one.

"The prince enjoys coming to our markets. That's the problem."

A gust of wind blew Ilona's dark hair around her face. She wrinkled her nose. "What's that smell?"

One of the soldiers drew up behind her.

"Best to keep moving, Princess."

Tossing a coin to the vendor, Ilona followed, eager to be rid of the decaying stench. When she'd insisted upon entering Poenari Castle on foot, she'd hoped to walk through a bustling town, to meet people and ask questions. The people she did meet said little, but their ghost-like demeanour spoke where their lips did not. Just as she'd expected, the prince's reign in Wallachia was a reign of terror.

But I will end it.

"That smell," she said, her eyes fixed on the orange-roofed turrets and whitewashed walls in the distance. "It's coming from Poenari Castle, isn't it?"

"Yes, Princess."

"It's death."

The soldiers said nothing. Hatred washed Ilona's insides, making her tremble. In all these weeks planning the marriage, she hadn't once stopped to consider what she might find in the prince's field of horrors. Could her father's body be there? The memory was still an open wound. Her father, the regent of Hungary and Vlad's ally for years, killed over a minor trading dispute. King Corvinus hadn't been interested in avenging his own uncle. She would do what her cowardly cousin could not, even if it meant selling her freedom. Revenge would be its own reward.

"I hear the prince was previously married," she began with forced calm, lifting the hem of her dress over a puddle. She'd picked a navy blue one to match her eyes, with sheer turquoise sleeves and a velvet cloak. It had seemed like the perfect choice at the time, but now she longed for the embrace of a simple black robe.

"The prince had a wife previously, yes."

"And mistresses?"

"Of course."

"I should like to meet them."

She glanced at him from the corner of her eye as she waited. The soldier seemed to struggle with his words, choking on them. "I'm afraid that won't be possible, Princess."

"Why not?"

"All have committed suicide."

Ilona relaxed. So, the prince killed without restraint, and his wives killed themselves. Good; two rumours confirmed. The faster she weeded out legend from fact, the faster she'd learn Vlad's true weaknesses.

Because despite her sister's claims, the monster had to have some.

1447 A.D. An Ottoman Dungeon

Men screamed outside his cell, no more unusual than the shrieking of the wind or the pale moonlight slanting through his window. But down the corridor, laughter echoed. It was that strange sound that woke Vlad. When was the last time he'd heard laughter? In Wallachia, certainly. He hadn't thought people did that here.

Scrambling to his knees, he listened. Torchlight flickered toward him like a hesitant caress, pulling back when he crawled to his cell's bars. Shadows stirred on the walls down the hall—guards around the corner.

One stood tall while the other two sat cross-legged over drinks on a low table.

"Who would've thought," slurred one man in Turkish. By now Vlad understood it as well as his native Romanian. "I swear, I was starting to believe that bastard was immortal."

"Cowards live longer than most," said another with a snort. "But it was only a matter of time."

"He's been a thorn in the sultan's side for so long. If anyone were to kill him, I was sure it'd be the sultan himself."

Another laugh. "Murdered by an ally. Can you believe it? For all his fierce reputation, The Dragon actually believed he had *friends.*"

Vlad's hands stiffened around the bars. It wasn't true. It couldn't be.

"May he rot in hell!" one man said, and the others lifted their arms and cheered. Clinking glasses sounded.

"Dirty barbarians!" Vlad screamed. The depth of his voice startled him. How long had it been since he'd spoken?

"What's that?" called one of the soldiers. "I think I hear a lizard hissing."

Footsteps and clanking chainmail and more laughter echoed. Vlad struggled to his feet, forcing himself not to lean against the wall as the soldiers approached. His legs—legs that had once mastered horseback riding, fencing, and swordplay—felt like runny cornmeal.

Three men came into view, two of them sagging, their arms slung around each other. The third had a scarf wrapped around his head and walked with his hand atop the hilt at his waist. All wore the long Ottoman caftans with pointed boots.

The sober man's eyes found Vlad's. Vlad stared. They were shockingly bright, clearer than the Danube's waters but darker, redder, as if in the aftermath of a battle. Vlad held that gaze for what might have been three seconds. Even a moment of connection in this prison was enough to extinguish his hate like a candle in the wind. Suddenly, he was a child again.

Don't give them this! Your hate is the only thing they haven't taken.

"Something troubling you, Princeling?" one man asked.

"Your lies offend me. Stop, or I will cut out your tongues and feed them to my dogs."

The drunks roared with laughter. "Your damned dogs are dead, boy, like your father and brother. Buried alive, your brother. Did you hear? It's said they can feel his screams vibrating in the earth all the way to Moldavia."

Blood drained from Vlad's cheeks. Mircea, the only one of The Dragon's sons not taken by the Ottomans. The only one of his sons fit to rule, as The Dragon had often reminded them. Not headstrong and insubordinate like Vlad, but nothing like sensitive little Radu, either.

Vlad's favourite brother.

Before Vlad realised it, a salty drop slid down his cheek. The blue-eyed man inclined his head.

"Would you look here! The little lizard's crying! Your father left you to die, boy, and you weep for him? *Sen gerzeksin.*"

"Want to say goodbye? We can put his head in the cell with you if you'd like."

Vlad rushed at them, bruising himself against the bars. The Ottomans' laughs died in their throats as they took a collective step back.

"Who did it?" Vlad shouted, saliva dribbling down his chin. "Who killed them? *Tell me who killed them!*"

The blue-eyed man's voice echoed in the humid stone dungeon. "The Hungarian general Janos Hunyadi."

1462 A.D. Wallachia

Poenari Castle was both grander and colder than her father's estate in Transylvania. Ilona grew aware of her every footstep, the echo her breaths made as she walked through the halls. Dusty tapestries lined the corridors, portraying the patriarch Vlad Dracul on a hunt, or his eldest son Mircea smiling benignly at the viewer. A handsome family, she had to admit, though handsome in a way she would admire from afar.

Bronze knockers adorned the doors, shaped like female heads or serpents. Every pillar, chair, staircase, and bookshelf was intricately carved from mahogany, making the whitewashed walls look plain by comparison. She saw a few maids scurrying about as if eager not to be seen.

Ilona swallowed. Now she understood the ghost rumours; this place looked old and haunted.

"Up these stairs to the prince's study, Princess," one of her guides said. Both had stopped before a staircase.

She paused with one foot on the bottom step. "You're not coming?"

"The prince would prefer for you to be alone in this most intimate moment."

Intimate. The word brought bile up her throat. A first meeting wasn't intimate, certainly not to that beast.

Her eyes lingered a moment too long on the scabbard at her guard's waist. When he shifted, she remembered herself and started up the steps with her dress's sodden train dragging behind her. No reception, no carriage—he hadn't even gathered his staff to greet her. Of course she couldn't have expected his royal highness to come downstairs.

At the top of the flight, she paused to smooth her hair. It hung frizzy and limp down her back, though she'd put it in rollers last night. What if he found her ugly? He'd send her straight back to Transylvania, maybe even kill her.

She moved down the hall, her breath heavy, the dress weighing her steps. Every door on the landing was shut save one that remained open a sliver. She stopped before it and curled her hand around the bronze door handle. At the last moment, she grasped the knocker instead.

Bang.

The sound burrowed into her bones. Her bladder felt weak; thank God she'd had the sense not to drink this morning.

"Come in."

She did. Light flooded the room in shafts that streamed through the windows, but the prince avoided them all. He stood facing a bookcase with his hands clasped behind his back, his hair flowing long and dark behind him. She'd heard whispers that he'd taken a fall some days ago during a hunt, but from his lordly posture, she could see no evidence of it. He wore knee-high leather boots and a velvet cape like hers.

Ilona felt his presence envelop her like poison. Every breath she took choked her. "Prince Vlad Dracula of Wallachia," she greeted, sweeping into a curtsey as he turned. "It is an honour to meet you."

"Princess Ilona Szilágyi. The pleasure is all mine."

He offered her his hand like some Ottoman sultan. A wild urge to bite him struck her, but instead she forced herself to kiss it. His frigid skin reminded her of her sister's parting words. *No blood runs through his veins, for he is a creature of the night.*

"Come," he said, yanking his hand away. "Let me look at you."

Because she could no longer avoid it, she straightened to face him. She had prepared herself for this moment, had practised the smile she'd offer and the pretty words to go with it. But seeing him in the flesh was another matter entirely. He was here, close enough to touch.

To hit, to strangle, to stab.

The prince was pale as death, with dark soulless eyes and a face of sharp edges. She'd heard his features and aquiline nose were inheritances from his father, a man known throughout Wallachia as "The Dragon." Vlad was said to resemble his father so much that only he of his siblings had earned the nickname *Dracula*—Son of the Dragon.

Having now seen the tapestries, she couldn't deny it. Yet another rumour proven true.

Vlad studied her for what felt like ages, his gaze darting from her face to her chest to her feet. "Who chose your garment?"

"I did, my prince."

Vlad reached for her. She felt her lip curling, but he didn't seem to notice as he took a handful of the fabric and ran it through his fingers. "Such a vibrant turquoise…"

His lips were parted, his thick black moustache quivering when he exhaled. Ilona wanted to tear at his face with her nails. She made herself focus on the movement of his moustache. At least he breathed.

"I am glad it pleases you, my prince." Hopefully the colour of her dress wasn't the only thing about her that did.

A breeze blew from the open window behind Vlad, filling the room with a foetid stench that made her wrinkle her nose.

"Something wrong, Princess?" He chuckled before she could answer, snaking his cold fingers between hers. His touch sent a shiver through her. "Worry not—I know you smell it. Let me show you why my country is the safest in all of Europe, why criminals fear stealing a single plum from the markets, and murderers think twice before attacking their neighbours."

He led her to the window.

Ilona clutched the windowsill with her free hand until her knuckles turned white. Even before she looked, she could smell it, she could *hear* the horror that was the talk of Wallachia. Even before looking, she knew the legend of Vlad Dracula's cruelty was no legend at all.

A stone courtyard lay below her, majestic statues and busts circling its parapets. The Carpathian Mountains glittered like emeralds in the distance, the sky was a perfect blue and the courtyard's lilac trees were in bloom.

Then there were the bodies.

Countless wooden stakes had been drilled into the ground, each thrust through a body as if it were a chicken on a spit. Blood soaked the grass, and the air smelled of iron and moist earth. Men and women impaled for nothing more than petty theft, bleeding to death in the hot afternoon sun while their prince read in his study. Their moans really did sound like the cries of ghosts.

Four servants emerged from the castle carrying a dining table. Ilona stared as they lowered the table in the middle of the carnage and began unfolding the tablecloth. More servants followed with platters of steaming food.

When she finally turned away, she found Vlad looking at her. "Shall we dine?"

1447 A.D. An Ottoman Dungeon

Vlad sat in a puddle of his own urine, humming to the screams.

He studied the open wound on his leg. The infection wasn't spreading fast enough. He rubbed his finger into the mildew in the corner of his cell where he'd thrown his porridge yesterday, then brought it to the wound. The pain was sweet. He dug his finger deeper, relishing the sight of mingling blood and pus.

His vision flashed white.

When he came to, he was staring sideways at a pair of pointed boots like the ones that had kicked a hole into his leg. *"Kalkmak,"* said a voice.

But Vlad didn't have the energy to lift his cheek from the stone. Why should he get up? They had stolen his hate; he had nothing to live for.

Hands turned him onto his back. Vlad found himself blinking up at eyes that looked burgundy in the dim light. Their unnatural colour seemed out of place here, like something from another world.

"You are difficult to kill, Little Dragon."

"I fear I will live forever," Vlad murmured.

"I intend to make sure that you do." The man gripped Vlad's shoulder and pulled him up.

"Who are you?" Nausea threatened, but Vlad swallowed it down. "Did the sultan send you?"

"I am not an Ottoman, and I belong to no man."

"You're a foreigner, then? An enemy soldier? A defector?"

The man chuckled. "I am simply a man—a man with secrets. I come, I see, I learn…" He looked so intently at Vlad that his eyes seemed to emit their own light. "You are strong enough to learn them, too, should you wish to."

Vlad's father had believed in dark magic, and, for some reason, this was what entered Vlad's mind upon hearing this strange man. *Lucifer was beautiful before falling from Heaven,* The Dragon had warned. *Never trust beautiful words and faces. They are the devil's work. They will take your soul.*

But that spark of hate was rekindling, and the devil's work sounded just like what Vlad wanted to do. "These *secrets,*" he said warily. "How will they help me?"

"Do you not yearn to reclaim Wallachia in your father's name? They will give you the power to take back your lands, your titles—your family's legacy." The stranger leaned closer. "I can make you immune to any harm that might befall your body."

What about my soul? "And what do you want in return?" Vlad asked instead.

"That you exact your revenge," the man said. "For it will also be mine."

"What have the Ottomans done to you?"

"Not the Ottomans, Little Dragon. The traitor Hunyadi."

"I will kill him first," Vlad growled.

But the man shook his head and smiled. "Wrong, my friend. You will make sure he lives."

1462 A.D. Wallachia

Keep your eyes on your plate. Breathe through your mouth. Scoop up the cornmeal, chew, swallow.

A red glob landed in the middle of her plate. Ilona tensed, grabbing a handful of the ivory tablecloth. Despite herself, she watched the cornmeal absorb the redness, becoming orange as if the colour were alive and spawning.

"Are you well, my love?"

Ilona's head snapped up. Just like that, everything came back into focus: the moans of men begging to die, the smells of iron and sweat and waste carried on the wind, the blood-slick bodies blistering in the sun, the wooden spikes, crows tearing out eyes, more screams, blood, blood, blood.

Her husband gazing at her from across the table.

"I fear I haven't much of an appetite today, my prince."

Vlad wiped his lips on a linen napkin. "Shall I have the cooks prepare something else? You haven't touched your roast."

The pink, tender beef made her stomach heave. "Please, don't trouble yourself for my sake. I am content simply keeping you company." *Waiting to watch you die.*

The prince smiled at her, his dark eyes crinkling with affection. The man behind him gave a drawn-out moan, but Vlad paid him no notice. He ripped a loaf of bread in two and dunked each half into his saucer as the prisoners around him haemorrhaged.

Ilona bit her tongue to keep from retching. Of all the things she'd seen so far, watching him drink blood was the worst. The way it dripped down his chin and dried on his black beard, how it stained the callouses on his fingertips… She shuddered. How could a man learned in Turkish, German, Italian, and Romanian be so barbaric?

He's not a man! She could still hear her sister yelling that morning. *He drinks his enemies' blood because he doesn't have any of his own. Don't marry that creature; he's not even alive!*

He's a human being like you and me, Ilona had retorted. *And I'm going to prove it.*

"That man behind me," Vlad said, leaning back in his seat. "Do you recognise him?"

She turned unfocused eyes to the swollen lump of flesh propped on a stake; it was still breathing. The one behind *her* had stopped moaning ten minutes ago. "No, my prince."

As Vlad folded his napkin, Ilona slid the dinner knife onto her lap.

"Hard to make much of him now, but this was once the great military leader, Janos Hunyadi. The one who killed my brother, my father…"

He looked up at her with clouded eyes, and her own father's image flashed across her mind. She felt that calm sense of purpose return, coating her insides with ice. "I am glad they have been avenged," she managed.

Are you mad? You can't kill him—he's immortal. His guards saw Janos Hunyadi stab him right through the heart on the battlefield. He didn't even bleed.

Nothing but old wives' tales. Vlad Dracula was a mastermind in the art of psychological warfare, not some undead lord. Attending these meals among his victims and spreading rumours were his ways of ensuring his people's cooperation. Who would challenge the Impaler Lord, the prince who dined on blood and couldn't be killed?

"Is it true that Hunyadi hurt you?" she asked.

Vlad paused with his fork midway to his mouth. His dark hair fell over his shoulders, its tips dipping into the saucer. He smiled, revealing red-smeared teeth. "You worry for me, Ilona?" She lowered her gaze until he said, "Look at me, my love," and she forced herself to. He unlaced the front of his shirt and tugged at the material to show her the lump of gnarled scar tissue over his heart. She saw it clearly even through the curly hair covering his chest. Vlad chuckled at the look on her face. "A simple blade cannot harm me."

"When did this happen?"

"A little over a year ago."

A *year*—and Hunyadi was still alive on that wretched spike?

"It was but a scratch," Vlad finished, returning to his meal.

The blade went straight through his chest and out the other side. His soldiers saw it. He pushed it deeper inside to balance himself, then kept fighting.

Her hands shook in her lap. She clenched them around the knife's hilt to make them stop. What foolishness! That sword had missed his heart, that was all. Tonight, she would stab both sides of his chest and then cut his throat just to be sure.

The prince said no more as he ate. Ilona watched him discard his fork and steady his meat with one hand as he sliced into it with the other. The meat slid on the bloody plate; the knife slipped.

"*La naiba!*" Vlad cursed.

He held up his hand, and Ilona saw a cut between his thumb and forefinger. He was bleeding; he was only a man after all! She almost laughed, but the smell of human suffering sobered her. Fuelled by courage, she stood. Why wait until tonight if she'd spotted her chance? The knife rested safely up her sleeve as she strode to the other end of the table and knelt before the prince.

"Let me clean that for you," she offered, withdrawing a handkerchief from her bosom. Vlad gave her his hand without protest, smiling in a knowing manner that unnerved her. She made herself focus on the cut, pretending not to notice him staring.

Then the wound closed.

Ilona gasped. From the corner of her eye, she saw Janos Hunyadi's hand twitch as if in response to Vlad's healing. She couldn't help turning, realising that she crouched near enough the impaled man to touch him. For the first time, she forced herself to look—to really look at that lump of flesh and blood and dangling bowels.

An open wound festered in Hunyadi's chest over his heart, still fresh. His right leg was mangled and marred by jutting bone. Ilona remembered the fall the prince was supposed to have taken, how his horse was said to have crushed his leg and how she'd marvelled at his strong posture in the castle. Now she watched, open-mouthed, as a cut appeared between Hunyadi's thumb and forefinger.

"Ilona?" She turned back to Vlad, still gripping his hand with both of hers. He reached out with his free palm to cup her cheek. "Didn't I tell you nothing can hurt me?"

She nodded.

But every dragon had its weak spot, and though Vlad had covered his with blood and gore and guts, she had just found it.

The prince didn't stir as Ilona slipped from the bed and pulled on a robe.

She'd practised her defence should Vlad catch her. He hadn't said anything about curfews, secret rooms, or limitations. On the contrary, he'd given her the keys to the castle. Why not stroll the grounds after midnight? He should be glad to see her admiring his art.

Unable to stifle the impulse, she glanced over her shoulder. He was a vague shadow through the canopy, but even from there she saw his chest rising and falling. A shiver coursed through her. She'd felt the unwanted warmth of his skin tonight, had heard the beat of his heart as it pumped with another's life. She now knew that her original plan—stabbing him in his sleep—would have never worked.

The floorboards creaked under her feet. She froze. Vlad was probably a deep sleeper, what with the wind howling up the mountain and the constant moans carrying through the window but being careful never hurt.

Slowly, she hazarded another step, then another, holding her breath until emerging into the hallway. Poenari Castle looked even colder at night, when the colours of the Ottoman rugs were muted and moonlight pooled like ice through the windows. The white walls gave off a palpable chill, making the hairs on her arms rise. She grabbed a torch from its sconce and quickened her pace.

Outside, the wind was warm with rot. Ilona covered her mouth as she walked, red mud oozing wherever she stepped. She fixed her eyes on the figure in the centre of the courtyard—the only one not moaning.

Janos Hunyadi had once been a master of tactics: the greatest general eastern Europe had seen in generations. Now he was a skull with loose skin and poking bones, bowels dangling from open abscesses in his gut.

An odd calm filled Ilona. She lifted the torch. "Can you hear me?"

Hunyadi's eyes flickered open. "My sincerest condolences, child."

"You know of my father?" If she had to hear that her father had been staked beside him in this wretched field, she might go mad.

But Hunyadi answered, "Your marriage."

She flicked her eyes away. "That was my choice."

The general looked like a melting wax figure, lips sagging over a disfigured hole of a mouth when he laughed. Air whistled through openings in his throat where flesh had rotted, the broken skin there flapping grotesquely. "I suppose some women would do anything for power."

"I care nothing for power," she snapped. "I'm here to end your suffering."

"You believe killing me will kill *him*."

Ilona drew her robe tighter around herself and glanced at the castle. Still no light in Vlad's room. She turned back to Hunyadi. "And if I do? I've seen the bond between you. If I destroy the body taking his wounds, he'll be forced to bear them upon his own. Am I not right?"

"You will be punished."

"I will accept my punishment as my father did."

"This is your revenge, then."

"*Our* revenge," she corrected. Wasn't he just as desperate for it as she was?

"Once I knew a man whose only wish was revenge," Hunyadi said, his eyes taking on a glazed quality as if he'd already left this world. "Not for himself, but for his father. He loved him, you see. Everything he did stemmed from this love. It turned him into a monster."

"What are you implying?" Ilona snapped. "I am nothing like that barbarian."

"He took it upon himself to exact justice, as you are doing now."

"Because I'm *right*." She stepped forward, wielding the torch, and Hunyadi cringed in the light. "I don't need your permission to do this. I just thought you should know."

"You are no different from him," Hunyadi whispered. "Your heart is poisoned by hatred. Do not misunderstand me, Princess. It is a good thing, a very good thing."

The ramblings of a madman. What had made her think she could have a logical conversation with a man on a stake?

"Listen to me," Hunyadi said, and suddenly his eyes grew bright and clear. The intensity of his stare made Ilona recoil. "Dracula's poisoned heart is what lets him live forever. Don't you see? It's the price of his magic. If you hate ardently enough, you too could learn it."

"You think that just because I hate someone, I would dabble in dark magic?"

"Not that you *would*, Princess. Only that you could."

Impossible. Even if she could access Vlad's dark magic, she had no desire to live forever. Her only wish was to ensure the Wallachian prince didn't, that he suffered for what he'd done to her father and to countless others.

She wasn't hateful for wishing that. She was just.

Muttering a prayer, she lowered the torch to the stake and stepped back to watch the flames rise. Hunyadi made barely a sound, but she thought she detected a skull's smile on his face before the fire sloughed off what remained of his flesh. She looked away, telling herself it was the smoke making her eyes sting. The scent of burnt hog filled the air.

Soon it was over. Ilona turned away, releasing a breath. Without Hunyadi to hold Vlad's injuries, they would kill him.

She lifted the hem of her sodden nightgown and started back to the castle, feeling lighter than she had in years. Could wounds be blossoming on Vlad's body at this moment? Would he wake with a gasp to find half his blood spilled out in his sheets? Or did she still have to stab him to make sure? She quickened her pace, wishing she'd paid more attention to her grandmother's fairytales of witchcraft and the devil's magic.

Ahead, lights flickered on in Poenari Castle.

Her heart clenched so hard she couldn't breathe. In another moment, three men had emerged onto the grounds with torches. Ilona grew aware of her own torch and knew they'd spotted her. She lowered it, squinting in the darkness.

Prince Vlad Dracula marched in the lead, his long black cloak billowing behind him. No limp, no blood, no wounds.

This can't be! Ilona nearly tripped over her nightgown as she stumbled back, but the guards reached her in no time. She didn't cringe when they grabbed her forearms in a bruising grip; her attention remained focused on the prince. How could this happen? She'd killed Hunyadi!

"You thought that would be enough?" Vlad asked. His palm lashed out; her neck craned as her face whipped sideways from the impact.

"You're mortal now," she spat, needing it, willing it to be true.

"Only until I find a replacement, you fool."

Of course. She hadn't killed Vlad; she'd only opened a window during which he was vulnerable.

On instinct, she struggled against her guards, but their grips remained unyielding.

Vlad laughed. "Do you realise what you've done? You've given yourself the fate my late wife died to avoid. *You* will be Janos's replacement."

Suddenly her legs felt weak, and she was grateful for the guards holding her up. "This is how you think to punish me?"

"It's not a punishment, Ilona. I must." He leaned forward as if sharing a secret, and only years of grooming kept Ilona from spitting in his face. "Did Hunyadi forget to mention this? Poor soul thought only of his release, I'm sure. We mustn't fault him for that."

"Mention what?" she breathed.

Vlad reached to stroke the cut his ring had left on her cheek, then licked the blood from his finger. "I cannot tie my life to just anyone. It must be somebody intimately and deeply connected with my heart. Hunyadi killed my family; I hated him as I have never hated before and will never hate again. But the connection need not be hatred. I fear my first wife took her own life because I fell in love with her. She knew Hunyadi's body would not last forever."

Momentary madness made Ilona laugh. "And you don't have anyone better to love or hate than *me*?"

Vlad's lips tightened. "My traitor brother Radu is a ward of the

Ottoman empire. I'll never have him so long as Sultan Mehmet protects him."

He meant to tell her that Vlad the Impaler found it easier to fall in love again than to make another enemy?

"I am sorry, but this is how it must be," Vlad murmured, turning away.

Ilona's heart raced as her guards began pulling her back toward Poenari Castle, but she didn't struggle. *If you hate ardently enough, you too could learn it.* Well, she already hated this man just as he'd hated Janos Hunyadi. Her heart was ready to use the dark magic, whereas Vlad's still needed time. Perhaps she didn't want to be immortal, but if she had no way of killing the Impaler under his guards' watch, trapping him as he'd trapped Hunyadi was the next best thing. She could rule Wallachia as her father would have seen it done. If she was quick enough, she could beat him at his own game.

A smile curled her lips. Hunyadi had been mistaken; she and Vlad weren't the same.

She was stronger.

BLOODLESS SPIRITS

Marshall J. Moore

I PRETEND I cannot see him.

It is a childish defense, I know. No different from a little girl hiding beneath the covers, clinging to the desperate hope that if she cannot see the monster, then the monster cannot see her. Or at the least that she will not have to see the final, fatal moment.

Once, I would have scorned such hopelessness. Better to meet the end with eyes open, I had thought.

But now I have had a taste of the young girl's helpless terror.

Now I know better.

His eyes, yellow and venomous, trace me as I dance across the ballroom. Crowds of other couples twirl and sway in time to the music, interposing themselves between us, yet his gaze never wavers. Beneath it I feel frail, exposed, like a mouse caught beneath a hawk's shadow.

A whisper in my ear. "Is something wrong?"

I flush guiltily, turning away from the monster watching me. My love peers down, concern etched on his face.

He is not handsome, my love. His mouth is turned slightly down, his nose crooked from having been broken. One of his eyes sits slightly higher than the other. Yet there is a certain appeal in his asymmetry, a comfort in the openness of those mismatched features. Just as there is comfort in his hand upon my back, in the surety of his steps as he leads me waltzing about the room.

"You seem distracted." He glances past me, precisely at the spot where my watcher stands. I wait for recognition to steal across his face, but it does not come. Unlike mine, his blindness to our uninvited guest is genuine.

I want to tell him, but I cannot. My tongue has been tied against uttering any warnings, my hands kept from jotting down the truth. Believe me, I have tried.

"No more than you," I say, forcing a smile. "Don't think I haven't noticed you stealing glances at the strings all night long."

Now it is his turn to flush guiltily. He spins us about, his mouth twisting into a wry grimace as he catches sight of the string quartet mounted on a dais in the ballroom's center.

"The violist is ever so slightly out of tune," he says. "If I could just go over there and have a word—"

"No."

He is a fine violist, my love; the finest. There is nothing in the world he loves so much as the movement of bow over strings, the transmutation of musician and viola into a single instrument.

Nothing, save me.

I cup his cheek in my hand and turn him back to me. "I forbid it, *mi amor*. Tonight, you shall play no instrument but me."

He laughs, delighted and surprised by my unexpected salaciousness. He dips me low in time to the music, plants a kiss upon my lips. I drink him in to the smattering of applause and laughter from those around us. Tonight is the one night such a public display is not only tolerated but encouraged.

Yet even amid light and joy there remain two points of darkness: a pair of yellow eyes burning into my back.

He styles himself Serapis, laying claim to the title of King of the Underworld. I cannot say whether this is a macabre joke, a play on his chosen dwelling, or if he truly was held in reverence by the children of Ptolemy. He claims to be old enough. I can only hope he has no contemporaries to dispute him.

I do not think he is a god, even if he was once worshipped as such. I have read Nodier, Féval, and Nizet. Enough to put a name to the sort of thing he is, though neither my love nor I have ever said the word aloud. Perhaps we thought that to name the thing was to invite its attention, but such superstition was in vain.

We drew his attention regardless.

For the second night in a row, the hiss of cold breath in my ear wakes me.

Now as then I startle awake, open my mouth to scream. But the yellow eyes not an inch from my own catch me and silence me with all the power of an eastern cobra.

"*Bonsoir, mademoiselle.*" Serapis's lips peel from his teeth, unsheathing his fangs. "Or rather, *madame*. Felicitations on your happy union."

Though breath hitches in my throat, my heartbeat is sluggish despite the danger. Beside me my love lies asleep, his chest rising and falling with comforting evenness. I want to shake him awake, but I remain trapped beneath those hypnotic eyes.

Just as those eyes found and trapped me last night.

Serapis came to me then, on the last eve of my maidenhood, and by his mere presence turned my joy to ash. Until then I had thought him destroyed, lost in the fire that had ended the depredations of his vile spawn. The fire my love and I had kindled.

"I hope you will excuse me for arriving unannounced," the monster at my bedside continues, his too-long teeth gleaming in the moonlight. "I never received my invitation, you see. But I could not bear the thought of missing your nuptials, so I came all the same."

He is toying with me, as a cat plays with a mouse. I resolve not to answer, and I shrink away, pressing my back against my love's side.

My husband's side, I correct myself, but the title has become bittersweet. I know even now that our marriage will not be a long one.

Now as then, he does not stir from his slumber. Nor can I wake him. Such is the power of the gaze of Serapis.

"I told you last night I had a special wedding present for you," he says, reaching down to brush my cheek. His touch is cold, the gesture possessive. "Forgive me for forbidding you to speak of it—or of me, for that matter. I did not want you to spoil the surprise."

But it is no surprise. I know already the form his gift shall take.

"Do it then," I say, finding my courage. I return his gaze, hoping he sees the defiance and the hate written there. "If you are to kill me, monsieur, then I suggest you do it now. Before my husband wakes and robs you of the chance."

Serapis's laugh is low in his throat; a death-rattle. "You think I have come to murder you in your wedding bed?"

"Why else?" I spit, sitting upright. His hypnosis permits that much. "An eye for an eye, *oui*? We took your spawn from you, so you have come to deprive us of one another."

His fanged smile does not waver, but something ugly flashes in those yellow eyes. "And you think that an even trade? A single spouse for three children?"

Before I can answer, his hands wrap about my throat, cold and hard as steel. The breath goes out of me, and not even his serpentine gaze can dull the pounding of my heart.

Beside me my love sleeps on, unknowing.

"It is an unfair exchange," Serapis hisses, his lips nearly brushing mine. "The youngest of my children was born when there was still a king at Versailles. The others, older still. Were it not for you and your husband, they might have lived for centuries more."

I would not call Serapis's nocturnal existence living, but neither am I in any position to argue the point. His dead hands squeeze. I close my eyes to quiet the bright spots in my vision and wait breathlessly for the end.

It does not come. Instead, there is another whisper of chill breath against my ear.

"An unfair exchange," Serapis repeats, holding me close. "But one easily redressed."

His lips brush my neck, and I realize with a horrifying lurch what he is about to do. I want to scream, to kick, to beg and plead and curse. But his dead hands are a vice.

"Bid your husband *adieu*," Serapis whispers.

But before I can so much as draw breath, the monster slides his teeth into my throat.

Death is colder than I expected.

Or perhaps that is just the cold within myself. The chill of winter suffuses my every inch, but neither fire nor sunlight shall ever warm me again.

And with the chill comes the thirst.

Mouth, tongue, and throat, all dry. No marooned sailor, no desert exile, ever endured such choking thirst. I feel as if I could drain an ocean, yet no water shall slake me.

Serapis knows this. How could he not? My affliction is his doing.

Arm in arm, he guides me between the winding nighttime streets, the city strangely transfigured by my own metamorphosis. The buildings I once thought grand and elegant now loom like unfriendly strangers. Overhead the serene moonlight shines merciless and cold as we flit between the shadows. We cross the Seine, passing Sainte-Chapelle just as the midnight bells toll. The church rises against the night, its doors barred to me forevermore.

By now my thirst has grown to a consuming fire, my stumbling feet drawing me towards every nighttime reveler and coquette we pass. Only Serapis's sure hand restrains me as he leads me down Saint-Michel, past the observatory and through the Barrière d'Enfer. Beneath those foreboding gates lie the city's famous catacombs: miles upon miles of winding tunnels and unburied bones. What habitation could be more fitting for one who styles himself lord of the underworld?

Serapis takes my hand, almost gently, and leads me down into the night beneath night. Behind me, through the gates of hell, the stars glimmer forlornly.

I do not look back.

How long we traverse the catacombs, I cannot say, for that time is a daze of numbing cold and gasping thirst. Later I recall only an endless sequence of winding passages and sudden turnings, the only sound the echo of our footfalls.

At some point I become aware that, though he is as surefooted a guide as could be wished, Serapis carries no lamp. Even in the utter dark he has no need of one. Nor, to my surprise, do I. My eyes discern their surroundings in every detail, sharp but monochrome. Even through the haze of thirst I feel foolish for not thinking of it sooner. It is only natural for a nocturnal predator's eyes to be adapted to the utter dark—if anything can be said to be natural about a predator like Serapis.

A growl from up ahead, deep and guttural. As we round a corner it deepens into a savage barking, a trio of dogs appearing before us.

I say dogs, but only for want of nearer relation. No mastiff ever rivalled these beasts for size or strength, nor could the fiercest wolfhound hope to match the wicked curve of their yellow teeth. Their eyes burn with an infernal fire. They bound towards us, their barking chorus echoing through the catacombs as they strain against the chains that bind them, corded muscles taut.

Serapis utters a command in a language I do not know. His hellhounds fall obediently still and silent, stiffening like soldiers at attention as we pass them by. Their burning eyes follow me as their master leads me to his lair.

It is an open chamber, its vaulted ceiling like that of an opera house. After the confines of the narrow tunnels, it should be a relief, but I can think only of my thirst, exacerbated by the fragrant, savory scent that fills the air.

I sniff, and realize the smell comes from the figure lying stretched upon the chamber's central dais. A young woman, her hair pillowing out around her, eyes closed. She is dressed like one of the coquettes we passed mere hours earlier, in what now seems a life half-forgotten. I watch in fascination as her chest rises and falls with the steady evenness of sleep.

A high, mewling sound echoes through the chamber. Only once Serapis puts a finger to my lips do I realize that it is coming from me.

"For you, *mon chéri*." Smiling his fanged smile, he releases me from his grip.

Hunger drives me forward, and in the space of a breath my own teeth are at the woman's throat. They slide into her without any resistance, physical or moral.

I drink her in. The taste of her is headier than wine and sweeter than sin. I lose myself in the oblivion of sensation, in the dribbling nectar as it fills me and revitalizes me. The coquette sighs in drowsing contentment, as though consenting to my greedy embrace.

I do not stop until she is cold in my arms.

Only then does my waking mind return, and with it, horror. At the abomination I have committed, the monster I have become. For proof of my sin, I need look no further than the blood still dripping down my chin.

An exhaustion of the soul crashes down around me, driving me to the floor. Grief wars with self-loathing in my heart. The smiling lord of the underworld watches, satisfied in the completion of his vengeance.

A chorus of frenzied barking echoes through the chamber.

And beneath it, the gentle strings of a viola.

Serapis whips towards the sound, his smile vanishing. The viola hums again, and as if in a dream, I recognize the first movement of Mozart's Lacrimosa.

The barking hellhounds quiet, then fall entirely silent.

Anger spasms across Serapis's face. He starts towards the chamber entrance, but suddenly I am beside him, my hands tight about his wrist. He looks down at me, and I smile bitterly at his surprise. I can move as swiftly as he does now.

What other powers I have inherited in exchange for my soul, I am left to wonder. For at that moment my love appears.

His hair hangs about his face, wild and unbound. He is barefoot, still wearing his nightclothes. He must have woken just after Serapis took me from our wedding bed, and I wonder that I did not notice him following us through the Parisian night.

In his hands he holds only the viola and its bow, its notes echoing off the chamber walls. I marvel at this, wondering how he managed to navigate the black catacombs without any light to guide him, save that of faith. But perhaps that alone is sufficient.

My love halts just inside the chamber, feeling the change in air. Or maybe, I think with sudden dread, smelling the metal tang of spilled blood.

"*Mi amor*," he says, in a voice as musical as the instrument in his hands. "I have come for you."

My answer is cut off by Serapis's laugh, a hollow creak piercing the beauty of the viola. "She is not yours any longer, *garçon*. Now she is mine."

"She is my wife."

I no longer need to draw breath, but some noise must have escaped me, for my love's searching eyes turn to me in the dark. "I pledged myself to her, before God and men."

"Until death part you," Serapis says. His serpent's smile has returned. "Just as it has done, more securely than any quiet grave ever could. She is like me now."

I flinch, not wanting to see my husband's face at this terrible revelation.

His playing falters, just for a beat. Serapis tries to move for him, but my hands on his wrist still restrain him.

He cannot bear the song, I think, and I know it is true. The beauty and the tragedy of the Requiem are an anathema to Serapis, to all that he is.

"She is still my wife," my love says, his deft fingers transitioning into Domine Jesu. "I do not believe she has forsaken me."

I would cry, but there are no tears left in my cold body. Instead, I give silent thanks to God Almighty that my husband cannot see the blood on my face. Then I wonder whether He can still receive my prayers. Or if He would want to.

"I haven't." The first words to pass my bloodstained lips since I became what I now am. Serapis turns to me, his brows furrowing with rage. It kindles my own anger, giving me the strength I need.

"I am still yours, my love," I tell my husband, my voice steadier. "As you are mine."

Perhaps God has left me. But he has not.

I release Serapis's wrist. He grabs for me, but in my new state, my strength is equal to his, and I shrug him off with little effort. A handful of steps, and I am returned to my love.

"Keep playing," I tell him. "Do not stop, no matter what happens."

He nods, sweat beading on his brow, but his sure hands do not falter on the viola.

"We are going," I tell Serapis, who remains transfixed by the music. "Do not follow us, or try to find us again."

The monster's yellow eyes bore into mine.

"I will not." His smile is made of venom. "Enjoy the wedding gift."

The words are ice water on my spine, but I do not dignify them with a response. Instead, I turn my husband gently about, so that he faces the chamber entrance.

"I can't see," he whispers to me. "I knew how to reach you, somehow, on the way in. But now it's all black."

"I know." I plant a kiss on the back of his neck. He shivers, and my heart breaks. "But I can."

Gently, I place one hand on his shoulder, the other on his waist. "Let me guide you."

He nods, takes an unsteady step forward. Then another, and another.

Slowly, we begin our climb from that dark underworld, leaving the horror and the monster behind. For a moment, I allow hope to glimmer in my heart.

Then I remember the blood on my lips.

The hellhounds sleep through our return, lulled by the viola's soft strings. The Requiem echoes through the tunnels, a mournful dirge for our return to the world above.

After some time, the song reaches its finale, the last notes fading into the tunnels as my husband finishes the Communio.

"Shall I play something else?" he asks, almost shyly.

I shake my head, then realize he cannot see me, guiding his steps from behind. "No, *mi amor*. Play it again."

And so he does. Over and again, a sad refrain as we climb steadily higher. I wonder if the weight of the Virgin's grief is heavier than my own.

I have killed someone this night. It matters not that I was not myself—I drank that poor girl dry, as hungry and savage as a starving wolf. My remorse will do her no good.

How can I inflict such sorrows upon others, if I am to survive in this cursed state? And how can I reconcile the monster I have become to the life of man and wife? My husband has forgiven me the one murder. I do not know if he has it in him to forgive more. I cannot ask something so terrible of him. I will not ask it.

"Look," my love says suddenly, his playing faltering as he reaches the Lacrimosa. "Light!"

He is right. Surprisingly near, just past a bend in the tunnel, the bright light of morning streams down the flight of steps leading up to the Barrière d'Enfer.

"Come," he says, tucking his bowstring under his arm as he takes my hand. "We're nearly there!"

Excitement hastens his steps as he races towards the light. I follow, pulled along in his wake, knowing what is to come. Welcoming it. Only once he has reached the foot of the stairs does he remember what light means to Serapis and his kind. He hesitates.

Blood still paints my chin. I do not want him to see it.

"Don't look back," I tell him, but he does.

I close my eyes so that I cannot see his horror, and step into the light.

THE BEST MORTICIAN IN TOWN

Christopher Alex Ray

IN THE HEAT of July 1889, Edward Jimenez moved to Carter's Island. He brought his wife and built a house on the main square facing the coast—a two-story home of the usual flat-roofed Spanish design. The top floor contained the apartments that he and his wife lived in. The larger bottom story contained a sizeable sitting room, richly decorated and lovingly maintained. Still, the most striking feature was the floor-to-ceiling windows that faced out toward the street.

The windows showed the rooms in all of their glory, well washed and polished to a gleaming shine every day by local cleaning women. Thick burgundy rugs covered the rich, dark oak floors. A backroom contained the instruments of Edward's trade, the walls lined with glass jars and rubber tubes. A sturdy cooling table in the center of the expanse gave Edward plenty of space to work his craft. Any customers who were fortunate enough to be cared for by Edward Jimenez were given treatment worthy of pharaohs.

It soon became known that if you brought a relative to Jimenez Funerary Services, your loved one would look better dead than they had when they were alive. Edward quickly became respected, beloved, and more than a little wealthy from his business. His fame grew not just around Carter's Island but all over the surrounding counties as well. To help with funeral announcements, Edward would place the bodies of his clients in the full-length windows of his parlor to be displayed for all to see. Rumor and gossip spread faster than obituaries did.

All was well until the accident in 1891. While leaving a ceremony in a large thunderstorm, a wedding carriage carrying the mayor's daughter, her groom, a driver, and the driver's five-year-old son met an untimely end. A rogue bolt of lightning spooked the horses into a dead run. When the terrified beasts rounded a corner, the carriage crashed onto its side and slid for thirty yards before stopping.

All the occupants had been killed, their bodies mangled and smashed by the impact. The driver had been flung free of the wreck. His neck snapped when he collided with a nearby palm. The bride and groom were shattered and beaten by the force of the crash. The driver's son had been thrown under the carriage to be crushed by the mahogany behemoth.

The entire town mourned the tragic loss of young life, and the bodies were brought to the home of Edward Jimenez. The devastated mayor begged Edward to fix them so they might be presentable for the funeral. Edward agreed and worked through the rest of the day and night. He set the bones and sealed the wounds. Their faces and bodies were painted to give the look of life once more, and at dawn the following day, all four stood propped in the windows of Edward's parlor.

They were perfectly restored without a single mark or blemish upon their bodies. The members of the wedding party looked as if they were merely sleeping. The entire town came out and stood before the windows, marveling at Edward's artistry. Edward, however, was not seen as he had fallen ill after exerting himself so hard. The mayor wept with sorrow over his dead daughter and son-in-law but found solace in knowing they had found peaceful respite.

For two days, the bodies remained in the windows to show the world of the genius of Edward Jimenez. Day and night, townsfolk would stroll by the windows and gaze at the bride and groom. Until one night, a passerby saw something that chilled him to the bone. Benjamin Taymour was a known drunkard and louse that frequently passed by Jimenez Funerary Services on his way back from the bar. Late on the second night of the display, Benjamin saw the bride and groom outside of their coffins.

The couple was dancing in the parlor, enjoying their first and final dance together. Edward sat watching them dance to music coming from a phonograph on the table beside him. The couple never looked away from each other's eyes as they languidly swirled and twirled together. The sight of the cadavers dancing drove Benjamin Taymour screaming up the road, and he was later found cowering on the steps of the cathedral. The townspeople and Mayor were so enraged by the story Benjamin told them that he was declared to be insane and was forced into an asylum.

The day of the funeral was a somber affair. The skies wept warm tears as the procession carried the caskets from Edward's home. Edward was finally well enough to appear in public and to accept the kind wishes from the mayor and the rest of the townsfolk. Although pale, he walked through the streets with the procession with his wife on his arm. At the entrance to the cathedral, Edward stopped and claimed to not feel well and decided to wait outside in the fresh air while the benediction was carried out.

The *walk* to the cemetery was long, and Edward grew paler and weaker as he went. By the end of the march, his wife was practically carrying him through the gates. He leaned against a closed sepulcher during the final words at the gravesite of the wedding party. When the priest finished his sermon, the mayor came to Edward and called for a wagon to take him to the hospital. Edward refused and asked only to be taken home so that he might rest.

The mayor watched as the wagon carried Edward and his wife back toward town. The sky thrummed with an oncoming storm, and drops of rain pelted down onto his head. He stayed at the gravesite long after everyone else had filed away. He kneeled by the graves and wept.

Over the sound of the storm, he could swear he heard dance music and the humming of his daughter over the noise of thunder.

Edward remained hidden away from the world for two more weeks. His wife assured everyone her husband was okay, merely drained, and needed rest. Edward's wife, Margarite, was a beloved fixture of the town, like her husband. She was active in multiple women's societies as well as with the public library. The lovely dark-haired Margarite was always there to offer a kind word or an offer of help. She threw lavish parties at her and Edward's home and gave charitably to the church.

Edward loved her more than life itself, and all the town would warm at the sight of Margarite, strolling arm in arm with her husband. Even during the most mundane tasks, they would smile at one another as if they were still newlyweds. People often found them standing on the balcony of their home, dancing together to the music from a nearby phonograph. Their love was beautiful and doomed to be short-lived. Only a year after the disastrous wedding, Margarite fell ill with Yellow Fever and struggled against the disease for weeks.

Eventually, she would succumb. Her once flawless tanned skin turned a horrid yellow, and her eyes sank and were blackened by the disease's ferocity. Edward was lost in a world of suffering and fell into a depression-induced madness. He wailed at the loss of his wife and locked himself away inside his house, forbidding anyone entrance. Throughout the night, the town could hear his moaning cries.

Later, some would claim they could hear laughing that lasted well into the late hours of the night. The following day, nothing was heard from the house, and it remained shuttered and dark except for the light from beneath the door to Edward's laboratory. Everyone assumed Edward had overcome his mania and was preparing Margarite for her burial. He worked throughout the day and night. Attempts to speak to Edward were met by locked doors and silence. The ladies of Carter's Island tried to reach Edward and offer him food and comfort, but all went ignored.

The next day passed with no signs of life from Jimenez Funerary Services. The day passed as usual with only sad glances toward the huge curtained windows of the house. That night, the bar was filled with tired workmen and townsfolk. The room rumbled with quiet gossip until the door opened and Edward strolled in. Everyone was shocked at the sight of him; his skin was ashen gray, and his eyes had sunken into dark pits inside his once tanned face. The light behind those eyes was bright but shined with a madness that was terrifying to behold.

Edward strolled to the bar through the crowd, smiling as he passed each familiar face. He ordered a drink and called out to the musicians to begin playing again. The room remained frozen until the mayor approached. He asked Edward how he was. Edward smiled and clapped him on the shoulder, extolling just how wonderful he was on such a beautiful day. The mayor laid a hand atop Edward's and asked if Margarite had been prepared.

"Prepared? Prepared for what?" Edward asked, genuine confusion laid across his cold, sickly face.

"Why, for burial," the mayor said, shocked. "Surely, you have been getting her ready to bury."

"Why on earth would I do that?" Edward looked horrified. "Margarite isn't dead. She is home safe and sound."

The air seemed to be sucked from the room at this pronouncement. The mayor stumbled over his following words, but Edward quickly cut him off.

"I really must go now. Margarite will be worried about me if I don't return soon." With that, Edward stumbled outside in a shaky, hobbling stride.

The room sat frozen for a long moment before roaring to life. People swarmed the mayor, asking what should be done with the apparent madman that had replaced Edward Jimenez.

The mayor called for silence and agreed that Edward must be looked in on and asked for volunteers from the crowd to escort him to the house. Four strong harbor men jumped into line, and the mayor led them from the bar. They walked through the dim streets toward Jimenez Funerary Services.

When they arrived, the mayor ascended the stairs and knocked, and as his knuckles struck the wood, the unlatched door creaked open. A yawning stygian portal greeted the men and seemed to beckon them inside toward their doom. Hesitantly, the group entered the house, their eyes strained against the gloom. The soft sound of music wafted down the stairs to meet them, and the men followed. Up the stairs, they spied the bedroom open just a crack, and light poured out into the hallway. The mayor crept quietly forward and looked through the opening.

What he beheld in that instant would haunt him until his dying day. Edward, gray and gaunt, was dancing arm in arm with Margarite. The woman looked as young and lively as she had ever been, all but her eyes. Those were flat and glassy, with no soul inside them.

Margarite snuggled her head against Edward's neck, and for a moment, those dead glass eyes met the mayor's just before she opened her mouth and slowly bit into Edward's jugular. She sucked at the skin, and blood ran in crimson rivulets down her chin. Edward never made a sound, only continued their slow waltz. The mayor and the harbor men shrieked at the sight and fled down the stairs into the streets. The front door was left swinging on its hinges.

Jimenez Funerary Services remained dark and lifeless until the next dawn when a crowd formed outside, and the mayor and a group of policemen entered the residence. The house was exactly as it had been the night before, except the bedroom was now quiet and dark. When the men entered, they were greeted by the sight of Edward and Margarite laying together on the bed. Edward's eyes were open and dull with death. The wound on his neck was still slick with blood. His body was covered with bites, and curious markings that had been etched into his flesh.

An investigation of Margarite found her to be just as dead, her heart quiet, her eyes closed, and her lips stained ruby red from blood. Further examination of the house showed that Edward's laboratory, which had once been so clean and orderly, was covered in melted candles, and crude occult markings covered the walls and floor, etched in blood.

Edward and Margarite were taken and buried together in a hasty funeral, and no one ever spoke again of that night.

From then on, all anyone would ever say of Edward Jimenez was that he'd been the best mortician in town.

THE CHURCH OF ST. JANUARIUS

Lawrence Harding

Your Grace,

Please find below certain passages from the diary of Father Alfonso, in the hope they prove instructive in light of our request for a new priest to serve our community.

September 4th, 18—

My journey has been long, but it nears its end. I write from the relative discomfort of my carriage, which rattles along a bumpy road that ascends high into the Carpathian Mountains. This land is far from what I am used to—gone are the rolling vineyards of my youth in Tuscany, gone are the sunlit flagstones of the streets surrounding my seminary in the old town of Salerno. In their place are dark forests and sheer peaks, all barren greys and foreboding blacks, accompanied only by the occasional distant howl of a wolf. If this is to be my home, it will take some time to feel homely.

Soon I will be at St. Januarius'. I still know precious little of it, save that it is a small church serving a small community. I have half an idea that they are penitents—given the harsh landscape, this would not surprise me. This is not what I had hoped for when I first followed this calling of mine. The Lord moves in mysterious ways, however, and moves His servants likewise mysteriously. Bishop Morowski believes I can do good here, and I am obliged to obey.

September 4ᵗʰ, 18—, evening

I arrived at St. Januarius' in the early evening. The coachman did not tarry to help with my luggage. Fortunately, given my vocation, I have few possessions. Despite the bitter wind blowing between the peaks, I was well able to bear my case myself up the short path to my new home.

Father Szymanski met me at the door. He was not as old as I had expected, given I was here as his relief. His hair was not quite grey, his stature almost upright, and the lines on his face were more from hard living than age. His clothes, like his body, appeared careworn and somewhat too large for him; his long and voluminous sleeves, for example, covered his hands almost to the base of his fingers.

My welcome from Father Szymanski was cordial enough, though began inauspiciously, with an apology for the state of the house. He had, he explained, only just risen for the day. This shocked me, though I endeavoured not to show it. A priest, sleeping the day away? No wonder the bishop felt I could do some good here! Nevertheless, I welcomed his invitation to breakfast—or rather supper, for myself—eagerly.

We sat at the rough table in the kitchen and ate rye bread and cheese. It was simple fare but welcome. Father Szymanski made the usual inquiries—how was my journey, how is life in the world below, where was I from, and so forth. I could tell he was trying to be welcoming, but the sense of weariness he gave off was infectious, and I found myself being less friendly than I had intended. I turned the conversation towards him, partly in an attempt to get to know him, but also in the hope that topics familiar to him would make easier conversation. This scheme worked well enough, initially. When I enquired about the community we served, however, a shadow fell over his face.

"Some would see them as terrible," he muttered. "I see them as pitiable. How you will see them remains to be seen." He drained his cup and set it down heavily.

I assured him that I was quite used to penitents, even those of what one might charitably call an excessive temperament. He could have no fears on that account.

Father Szymanski looked at me seriously. "I pray so. You will find that we have our own way of doing things at St. Januarius'." As to what those were, he would answer no further. We finished our meal in silence. I went to unpack my things.

I write now from the small desk in my room. It is the only furniture save for a cot, a chair, and enough shelves to hold my modest collection of books. It will be sufficient. Soon, it will be time for Mass, I am told— at midnight. It is a most unusual time for it, outside the Christmas season, but nonetheless I am grateful. The Blessed Sacrament is just what I need to quieten my distressed spirit.

September 4th or 5th, 18—

I have returned from Mass, and I know not what to think. I am sent here by men of God on God's work, but I cannot help but feel that I dwell among devils and devils alone.

I approached the church with not a little trepidation, given Father Szymanski's allusion to idiosyncrasy. As I walked along the short path through the churchyard, I became aware of other figures approaching from the knot of houses, down what passed for a street. There were six of them in all, wearing cowls that covered their faces. They travelled together as if relying on safety in numbers.

When I reached the church, Father Szymanski was at the door. He greeted me with a nod, and murmured, "Welcome, child. Please enter, *in nomine Iesu Christi.*" No sooner had I crossed the threshold, he turned to those coming in behind me and repeated the same formula. Each pale face smiled thinly and crossed themselves, each with an odd wince, as they entered. They passed by me into the church, and Father Szymanski closed the door. "There will be no others," he replied to my quizzical look, and shrugged.

Once inside, I was struck by how bare the church itself was. Had I not known otherwise, I would have thought I was to worship among Protestants, so empty of ornamentation were the walls. The only adornments were the great cross standing on the altar. As I walked in with my fellow congregants, I noticed that they all kept their heads turned away from it.

As I took my place at a pew near the centre of the church, I could feel the community staring at me. I was something unfamiliar, a new part of my life. Yet, beneath the natural curiosity, I could feel something darker and baser—a hunger. Perhaps, I admit, this is the benefit of hindsight talking, but I cannot deny there was something more than the typical nerves at joining a new parish that bothered me.

My suspicions became positively undeniable as we reached the Blessed Sacrament. As the presence of God flooded the bread, Father Szymanski turned to the chalice of wine. I dread to write of what he did then, but I feel I must.

"This is my blood, poured out for you." So saying, Father Szymanski drew back the sleeve of his alb. I was aghast to see his left arm was covered in scars—some old and knotted, others still raw and fresh. Holding his arm over the chalice, Szymanski took up a knife and drew it across his flesh. Fresh, red blood trickled into the vessel, splashing audibly where it combined with the watered wine which was now, of course, our Saviour's blood.

A shudder ran through the congregants gathered on the pews. There was a new sense in the air, one of *desire*. As we took our places at the altar rail, they all moved with careful, considered motions, as if restraining themselves from some frenzy. I had witnessed the fervour of the zealous before, but this was something else—a physical need for the Sacrament (if it could still be considered such!) I had never before encountered.

When one is about to receive the Blessed Sacrament, one should have his mind on the holy mysteries. Yet I could not, for my dreadful interest in my fellow supplicants was too great. I noted, for example, that Father Szymanski did not give them the host. He offered only the chalice, which each took with trembling hands.

When the young woman next to me took the cup, the sense was most palpable, and I could not tell whether she trembled more with fear or with excitement. She took a careful sip, as if not trusting herself to take more. Tears rolled down her cheeks, and Father Szymanski had to almost drag the cup from her lips. She drew back, crossed herself, and visibly winced. As she did, her lips drew back, revealing teeth too long and pointed for a human mouth.

Father Szymanski then came to me. I was too stunned to do anything but go through the motions of faith. I barely noticed as the host was placed upon my tongue, for I knew that I too had to drink of that cup. God forgive me, I drank, for I feared what might befall me should I fail to do so. The blessed wine was soiled, all bitter gall and copper tang. Even the merest sip coated my mouth with a patina of sin. I spent the rest of the Mass in a daze, going through the long-practised motions, and when we were dismissed, I was the first to flee.

I could see now why Father Szymanski had refused further inquiry. Later that night, he came to my room with what he surely felt was an explanation. "I told you we had our own way of doing things at St. Januarius'," he began.

"They are vampires!" The words were out of my mouth before

I realised. Had I control of myself, I may never had uttered them, so ridiculous they seemed despite the evidence of my own eyes.

"They were mortal men and women once—Christians," countered Father Szymanski. He went on into a tirade—how they were Christian souls, or truly desired to be; how they had not chosen their wretched state. Were they to be cast from God's sight for what they had been made? Was God's mercy not infinite? Was not their worship all the purer for the suffering they underwent to carry it out—the pain of the prayers on their lips, the agony the sight of the cross brought them? Was theirs not a truer example of piety than the righteous who make their obeisance and then thought no more of God until the next feast? His eyes blazed as he spoke, with a fervour that I had found lacking in his preaching.

For my part, I remained quiet. Eventually, Father Szymanski also fell silent. He gave me a heavy look and sighed. "We have the bishop's sanction. Whatever you may think, you will understand in time."

Whether I will remains to be seen.

September 20th, 18–

I have now been at St. Januarius' for two weeks. The kiss given to me by Bishop Morowski in farewell feels more like that of Judas with every passing hour.

For the most part, Father Szymanski has left me to my own devices. I keep daylight hours as far as I am able, in protest at what he calls 'his arrangements.' I read, I eat, and I pray for guidance.

I am only occasionally obliged to interact with those I struggle to think of as my parishioners. When I do, it is in the evening, at what amounts to morning prayer. Wednesdays and Fridays, I am obliged to keep vigil in the confessional, should one of the hellish require absolution (as if there is any question of that!).

Only one of the congregants has joined me in the confessional thus far. Her name is Lucia, who was once—and shall ever remain—a young woman. She is the same woman, in fact, that I watched so closely when she took her bloodied Sacrament that first Mass at St. Januarius'. Our conversations have only cemented my conviction that, though I might grant absolution, there is no guarantee of them securing forgiveness. (*Here I have omitted certain records of their conversation—Your Grace will understand that the confessional is sacrosanct, even if Father Alfonso neglected to.*)

Lucia, however, lives in hope of salvation. Were she not what she is, I should admire that conviction. As it stands, I am conflicted.

That is as much contact with the vampires as I can bear. I have thus far absented myself from Mass, preferring to perform the rite alone. Father Szymanski has indulged me in this, though I suspect it may not last.

September 27th, 18—

Father Szymanski rarely speaks to me. I cannot tell if he considers any argument already won, or is simply waiting for attrition to wear me into acceptance. He does not seem a man minded to conflict. I wonder if it is his charges which keep him so compliant.

The vampire Lucia, however, continues in her efforts to win over my heart to their plight. She is present at every morning prayer (alas that I now admit the evening as morning…!) and engages me in conversation for up to an hour afterwards if I do not escape by some excuse. She also makes her confession with alarming regularity. The devotion she plays at is, to all outward appearances, greater than most priests—truly, it is amazing how the Enemy can wear the guise of holiness so effectively. I wish most fervently that she would leave me alone.

October 7th, 18—

I grow weary of my existence here. Though commanded by the bishop, I have never struggled so with my vows of obedience. I have even begun to put aside some provisions from my meals, in a secret place beneath my cot. I have half a mind that, if I cannot persuade a wagoner to deliver me from this Hell, I may at least chance a journey down the mountain alone.

I may take up the latter course of action. Supplies are delivered but once a month, and are often unloaded before I or Father Szymanski can reach those that deliver them to offer even the barest Christian greeting.

October 16th, 18—

I can scarcely believe what I am writing. I must record it, however, if only to prove to myself in my mind that it is real.

They came for me tonight. My door flew open—four vampires forced their way into my chamber and took me in their cold, inhumanly strong hands.

Father Szymanski must have invited them in. The knowledge of that betrayal, inevitable as it was, still twisted in me like a knife. He stood behind them in the doorway, shamefaced. "I am sorry, my son," he murmured. "It is time for Mass, and I am tired." He held up his scarred and ruined hands. "So tired."

I was dragged, without ceremony or dignity, to St. Januarius'. Lucia was waiting within, kneeling in a pew. She averted her eyes as I was dragged through. Was it shame or reverence? Why should it matter?

They held me fast at the altar, defiling the sanctuary with their presence. Father Szymanski gabbled through the service, tumbling over the prayers and readings until we came to the Blessed Sacrament. Then it was he who took the knife and cup, he who drew the blade through my flesh, he who sullied the wine with my blood.

Between the pain, the shock, and the horror, the moment my captors released me, I fell to my knees. Tears flowed down my cheeks as I watched the hellish congregation pollute the Sacrament while wearing masks of piety. Knowing that it was my blood passing their lips was somehow more terrible than when it had been Father Szymanski's. Worse still was the knowledge they would never be satisfied, not even when my own hands were as latticed as Szymanski's, with dreadful patterns more intricate than those adorning the walls of any cathedral.

I was brought back to my room in a daze. Before allowing me, at last, to return to my bed, Father Szymanski shook his head at me. "I appreciate your misgivings, my son, but they cannot continue. Next time, you must do this yourself, and willingly."

There will be no next time. Whatever is happening here, I refuse to believe it is God's work.

Tonight, I make my escape.

October 19th, 18—

I am back in my cell at St. Januarius'. I know now that I can never leave.

As planned, I tried to flee down the mountain to good Christian folk. I could stand it no longer and would take my chances without waiting to bribe a deliveryman. I set off in the morning, rubbing sleep from my eyes, safe in the knowledge that none but Father Szymanski could follow me. I was satisfied that he was fast asleep, and too infirm to make chase in any case. If I could just make it to the village in the foothills, I would be free.

I had not made it a mile down the hill when the skies blackened. Clouds rolled in from the north, so fast they seemed to be herded by devils themselves. The wind whipped up, sharp with bitter teeth. There had been nary a sign of a storm before I set out, but now thunder growled, lightning flashed, and the snow began to fall so furiously that I could barely see a few feet in front of me.

Still, I pressed on—too eager to escape to consider turning back, too proud to admit defeat, too afraid to do anything but run. Running turned to stumbling, stumbling turned to falling. I hit something in the dark, leg-first. Something cracked, horribly. The pain was so great and the storm so biting that I quickly fell unconscious. By all accounts, I should have died.

Some might call my survival a miracle. It is not. Others might say that I did not survive at all. That, I hope, is also untrue.

I survived, after a fashion, because Lucia found me. How, I do not know. She came upon my half-frozen, unconscious body and dragged me to a lee in the hillside for shelter. It was not enough. My broken leg I could survive, but the cold had sunk deep into me, filling my bones and veins with ice. Lucia felt called to save me. She did so the only way she knew.

As I write this, I trace the marks of her diabolic method with my other hand—twin puncture marks at my jugular.

Yes. I, too, am now a vampire.

When Lucia came to explain—or, rather, to confess—the reason she had laid this curse upon me, she looked me dead in the eye and spoke boldly.

"I could not let you die without confession. I could not condemn you to Hell."

"But I am a priest!" My protest felt empty, even to me. I could not tell whether her answering smile was sad or sardonic. Perhaps it was both.

"Priests can be sinners too, Father. Is that not what you think of our dear Father Szymanski? Besides," she added, "you stole from us," she said. "Stealing is a sin."

"Not a mortal one," I replied.

"Yet you despaired. Why else would you throw your vows aside? Did you not trust God, the way you told us to? Were those words nothing but lies upon your lips? Why else would you abandon the service of God and choose only to serve yourself?"

To that, I could make no satisfying answer. Lucia said nothing more to me. She shook her head sadly and left me to my thoughts. The door was locked behind her.

That was an hour ago. All I have done since then is write. I cannot help but ask: For what purpose? To set my thoughts in order? As an act of prayer? A cry to God for mercy? A confession? I may never know.

It is difficult to continue writing. My thoughts keep turning to a new need inside me, one that sickens me. The desire burns. It is all-consuming. My pen trembles in my hand. I shiver all over, not from cold, but from hunger. I can scarce write what it is I hunger for, but I must. I must face the demon within.

I hunger for blood.

The next Mass is three days away. I pray that I might endure the hunger that long, and that the precious blood will bring me succour.

Domine Iesu Christi—miserere mei.

Your Grace will see from the above that we remain in need of a priest to ease my burden, which has only grown with Father Alfonso's unfortunate succumbing to despair. I beg of you that you respond to our need with all haste, and I pray that his replacement is more understanding of our cause.

Yours in Christ, Father Szymanski

MATCHMAKER, MATCHMAKER

R. J. Howell

"Fine," Ellie said, making a show of looking at her bare wrist. "I was supposed to clock out fifteen minutes ago, but I *guess* I can spare five, so let's see this 'magic corpse' of yours."

At home was a couch, leftover egg foo young, a Guinness, and four episodes of *The Walking Dead* begging for her attention, and if this was another one of Shawn's damn practical jokes…

Shawn threw a scowl her way but didn't break his stride, his heels clicking on the linoleum tile even through the blue disposable booties covering them. "It's not *my* magic corpse. There was a fifty-fifty chance you could've been scheduled to autopsy him."

"Yeah, yeah." She shoved her hands in her coat pockets. Her winter boots squelched and squeaked in her wake.

He was still wearing his autopsy gown and latex gloves, though his face mask hung around his neck. Must've dropped everything to tell her about the magical freaky cadaver in cutting room two. It should have been Kyle walking with him, not her, but the lazy rat was late—as usual—and she'd decided to actually finish writing her reports instead of leaving the task for tomorrow.

This is what I get for being a proactive state employee. Oh, yay.

Shawn held the door open for her, and she entered the cutting room.

The white tiled walls had yellowed with age and the concrete floor was stained brown—the last time anyone had put aside the funds to remodel the Whiling County Morgue was probably in the seventies—but the cutting table in the middle was new.

The naked body of a young Caucasian man was laid out on the table, washed and prepped and ready for the autopsy. It was hard to tell with him horizontal, but he looked short—maybe five foot five, at most—and when he'd been alive, he would've fallen deep in the "drop-dead gorgeous" category. In death, he still had the face of an angel and the body of a Tour de France cyclist, all lithe muscles and ropy tendons. His dark, reddish hair was trimmed to give him a lazy bedhead look, and he had the beginnings of a five o'clock shadow.

But, damn, he was pale, even for a corpse. No purpled extremities or sunken, bruised eyelids or mottled skin; hospital bedsheets had more blood in them than this guy.

"Okay, so what's his story?" Ellie asked, draping her coat across the counter and pulling on a pair of latex gloves as she walked around to the other side of the table. No apparent trauma, no post-mortem bruising—she lifted his arm—or the beginnings of lividity from gravity pulling the blood down under him. He was fresh dead, then. Very, very fresh.

Except, she'd have heard the EMTs delivering him, seeing that the offices were right next door to the entrance. So, when the hell had he gotten here?

Shawn waved his hands at the corpse in a *ta-da!* gesture. "Meet Mr. Jebediah Leeds, dead of an apparent heart attack. We're lucky we got him this quick." The grimace was clear in his tone. "You didn't hear it from me, but I heard from Parson some dispatcher screwed up. There was a burglary reported at 451 Franklin, 'kay, but instead of 451 *West* Franklin, the dispatcher had officers going to 451 *East* Franklin. They knocked, no answer, saw movement inside, heard a crash, and broke the door down. Took 'em awhile, too. Y'know, the guy had three deadbolts, four chain-locks, two sensors for two completely different security systems, and a motion-triggered camera. And that was just what was on the *front* door. Windows, doors, even the chimney—the place was tricked out like Fort Knox."

That's taking "home security" a little far. "I'm guessing there wasn't a burglar."

"Nope, just the fella's cat knocking a cup off the kitchen counter. Anyway, they then found him in bed and called it in—"

"I'm not seeing what's so freaky about this."

"Hold on, hold on, I'm getting there." Shawn paused, doing one of his bullshit *dramatic reveal* moments, hands held out as if to say, *I've got nothing up my sleeve.* Seriously? What did he think she was, five? "He came in almost ten hours ago."

Ellie hesitated in lowering Jebediah Leeds's arm. "You're sure about that? This guy looks like he's been dead maybe ten minutes, not hours." Hell, his arm was still flexible. He should've been rigid and deep into rigor by now.

"At first, I thought so, too, but Parson wrote up his intake papers, and have you ever heard Parson making a mistake like that?"

Her lip twitched in a half-smile, half-grimace. "He'd have a coronary."

"Exactly. I couldn't find any external COD, so I started to open him up—"

Ellie gestured at Leeds's unmarked chest. "With what, X-ray vision?"

But instead of scowling at her or calling her a smart-ass, Shawn leaned forward over the body, the look on his face something between fear and desperation. Ellie leaned back.

"That's what I mean; it's freaky! I swear to god, I finished the Y-incision, turned away for a second, and when I looked back, *nothing!*"

"Nothing, what?"

"Nothing as in, nothing! Except for some blood leakage, there wasn't any sign I'd touched him!"

"But that's impossible."

"That's what I've been trying to tell you! Here—" He fumbled a scalpel off the tools cart. "—just watch."

He shoved the blade into Leeds's shoulder and dragged it diagonally across his chest. The scalpel bumped slightly when it hit Leeds's sternum, but Shawn kept going, slicing the body from shoulder to hip.

Ellie yelped, reaching for the scalpel.

"What the hell, Shawn? What the hell are you doing?!"

"Shhh!" Shawn held the bloody scalpel up like a finger. "I cut him, right?"

"You're damn right, you cut him! No one's going to be able to fix that!" She rubbed her temples with the tips of her fingers. "*Jesus*, that's completely screwed the autopsy."

"Just. Watch."

She opened her mouth to snap a retort, but something in Shawn's expression killed the words in her throat. Instead, she crossed her arms and stared down at Jebediah Leeds's corpse as the blood pooled slightly in the gap sliced into his torso. *That should not be happening with a corpse supposedly this old.*

The clock over the door ticked. The heater kicked in. Her *Walking Dead* marathon walked farther and farther away.

She gritted her teeth. "Damn it, Shawn. Either you're messing with me—"

"I *told* you, I'm not—"

"—or someone else is messing with you. This guy cannot have been dead as long as you think."

"But the report—"

"Shawn! Ten-hour-old cadavers do not seep!"

Shawn flung up the hand with the scalpel and made a *htt-tt-tt-tt* noise with his tongue against his teeth. "Shh! Just a few more seconds!"

Ellie smacked her hands against her legs and rolled her eyes. Fine. You know what? He wanted a few seconds? *Fine!* And to think, she'd actually considered the rude ass kinda cute when she'd first started working here.

He snagged the roll of industrial-brown paper towels off the cart, unwound a length around his hand, then wadded it up and wiped away the thin line of gore over Leeds's heart.

To reveal unmarked, pale white skin.

Ellie leaned closer. "What the fuck?"

Shawn looked too damn pleased with himself as he finished wiping the blood off the corpse. "That's what I'm saying. I've cut him four times now, just to make sure, and every time, it just heals over. I was thinking, maybe I'm seeing things, so I bent this finger backward 'til it dislocated."

She bit back a reprimand about desecrating remains and the living hell that would rain down on them if anyone ever found out.

"Five minutes later, it had just…magically popped back into place."

Ellie shook her head. This was weird. No, this was *too* weird. It belonged on some kind of cable special, like "The Ghosts of Women Serial Killers" or "Unearthed Secrets of Salem." Not on a county morgue table.

"This is some kind of joke, right?" she hazarded. "Like, an early April Fool's prank? Kyle's hiding in the supply cabinet and recording this on his phone?" Wouldn't have been the first time, though the pair's pranks usually never evolved past wrap-yourself-in-a-body-bag or hide-a-remote-controlled-car-in-the-cooler-and-make-it-knock-on-the-wall. *This* would've required forethought and preparation, and maybe a trick scalpel with blood in a reservoir.

Shawn's hopeful expression collapsed. "Damn it, El! It's not a game!" He tossed the scalpel on the cart. Blood spattered in an arc across the steel top. "This is real, I swear."

She looked down at Leeds. She almost—almost—asked to see the scalpel, but Shawn would probably flip out if she did. Well, flip out more. *All right, take it at face value.* And if this was a trick, she'd officially never trust him again. He'd be so far in asshole territory, nothing short of divine intervention could redeem him.

"So, what do we do about it?" she asked after a moment.

Shawn sighed and ran a hand over his chin. Without removing the bloodstained glove first. *Damn, he's really out of it.* "God, I don't know. Tell someone? Record it? Make a report?"

Report it to who? Parson? "Or we could just release the body to the funeral home. No one will look too closely 'til the mortician is working on him, and there isn't a lot they can do about it then, right?"

"You want to just walk away from this?"

"Hell yes! This is messed up!"

"But what if we've stumbled on something important?"

A short burst of laughter wormed its way out from some place deep in her chest. "Like what, an alien? Should I start calling you 'Mulder' now?"

Shawn's lip lifted in a sneer that foretold him throwing back something acerbic, his usual go-to. Then he looked down at the floor.

"Ellie, I'm being serious here. What the hell do we do? It's a self-healing corpse."

"Maybe we should call it a miracle and make a fortune on tourists." She winced. God, that sounded so sarcastic. She swallowed back an apology, took a deep breath instead, and tried again. "Okay, look. My point is, even if we eventually did get someone to take us seriously about this, between then and now, we'd be called crazy and probably lose our jobs, and if we didn't convince anyone, we'd still be called crazy and lose our jobs. And if we smuggle the body out for proof, oh yeah, we are *definitely* getting fired. However you look at it, we lose. Let's just leave it alone, let it become one of those stupid stories we tell the techs to freak 'em out and—Shawn?"

"I heard you," he said, sounding morose.

"Did you leave his eyes open?"

"Eyeballs creep me out; I can barely stand doing vitreous taps. Why would I leave them open?"

Blue eyes. Jebediah Leeds had such pale blue eyes they almost bordered on ice-white, the iris rimmed with a darker line of gray. His pupils were exceedingly clear for a ten-hour-dead corpse and she could've sworn that, for just a second, they seemed to shrink in the glare from the overhead light.

That couldn't be right.

She raised a finger to point at Leeds's face. It felt detached from her, like it was running on automatic while her brain went on vacation.

"He's looking at us, Shawn. Oh—"

Leeds blinked.

"—my—"

Groaned.

"—God."

Leeds sat up as if hinged at the waist. His mouth sagged open, showing off crooked but white teeth, and there was something wrong with his canines. Too long. Too sharp. Too much like fangs.

A ball of manic fear rolled its way up Ellie's throat, starting as a whispered exhalation of breath and morphing into a full-on shriek. Distantly, she heard Shawn scream, but it sounded muffled.

Leeds raised his hand, reaching for her, fingers curled into claws.

He almost looks sad, a weirdly calm part of her brain put in, though the rest of her was still shrieking.

The living corpse breathed out a tiny noise, almost like a, "shh-shhh."

She ran out of breath. Took another, opened her mouth for round two, but Leeds's gaze caught her, held her tight. The world shrunk down to two pinpricks of black in a field of ice, like the surface of a frozen lake in the dead of winter. A feeling—warm, content, safe—pressed against her. Seeped through her skin. Worked its way down through her muscles, her organs, her bones.

Couldn't remember why her throat ached.

"Hear me, you must hear me…"

Ellie let herself fall down into that soft, whispery voice, let it soak through her. Something was not right about it. Something she was forgetting. Might explain why that guy was screaming…screaming something…screaming a name…something about "Ellie" and running…

"Hear me. Listen to my voice, listen and obey…"

Ellie scraped her fingernails over the scabs covering the bite marks along her neck and, one-handed, typed up the last of her report on Ms. Hannah Carmichael. Suicide via acetaminophen overdose. She'd chugged two bottles of Tylenol, gone to bed, and died hours later of liver failure. Sad, but nothing particularly remarkable about it. Not like…

Not like what?

She didn't have an answer.

Stifling a yawn, she hit print just as someone rapped on the open door of her office. She looked up from her computer screen.

Shawn slouched against the doorframe, his hands in his pockets. He was smiling and, damn, it looked good on him. Almost made up for the black eye. She'd asked him about it, and he said he'd walked into a door, but the bruising looked a little too circular, a little too much like a fist for her to believe the excuse. She hadn't challenged him over it, though. Last week, she might have. This week?

This week was entirely different.

"Hey," he said after a moment of studying her. "You ready?"

"Yeah, give me a few minutes."

"Alright, alright." But instead of leaving, he remained in her doorway.

She gathered up the pages of her report, ordered them, slotted them away in the folder, and set the folder in her outbox. "Any reason you're still watching me?"

"You mean besides the fact that you're the hottest woman I've ever had walk into my life?" He shrugged. "Not really. Just…ever get that feeling of déjà vu?"

"Sometimes. Why?" She set her computer to shut down and fished her purse out from under the desk.

"Been having it a lot today, that's all. And I keep feeling like I'm forgetting something important, like I forgot to lock my car or pay my phone bill. You know?"

She paused in pulling on her coat. "Yeah," she said after a moment, though it came out the ghost of a sound. *Yeah, but…* Every time she reached for it, tried to remember what she was forgetting, it slipped away. Left her huffing with frustration and disappointment and a weird sense of not wanting to know. That it was somehow…better?…not to. Ignorance was bliss, after all.

Except, she was pretty sure she hated that adage.

She shook her head, zipped up, and stepped out of the office, looping her arm through Shawn's.

First date. She'd asked him out for drinks that morning with heavy emphasis on *and we can go to my place after.* Couldn't really remember when she'd made the decision to do that; it'd been months since she'd been on a date. And—really, let's be honest—if Shawn hadn't been such a grade-A ass with a side-order of prickly and smug and a prank-slated sense of humor, she probably would've asked him out ages ago. Blame it on the last vestiges of the holiday spirit still clinging on in January.

Yet, for some reason, the words had felt…weird. Right, but weird.

Call me a romantic, but you'd be cute together. You've got repressed urges written all over you. I might be a monster, but I'm still a little bit human.

The words had been knocking around in her head the whole day, said with a man's voice, barely louder than a whisper. Something she'd heard once, maybe a fragment of a catchy song on the radio, but she couldn't remember what came before or after or what the hell the tune was.

Stop thinking about it and let it go.

She glanced up at Shawn, but he wasn't looking her way. Her gaze focused on the pair of raised welts on his neck, and she frowned. "I think we've got some kind of infestation."

"Hm?"

She touched the bites on her neck. "Spiders. We'll have to call in an exterminator or something. They're creeping up and biting us when we're not looking."

But even as she said it, something hollow clawed at her gut, an anxious feeling that she'd forgotten something, forgotten something important…

Eh. Later. She'd work it out later.

BLOOD RED SNOW WHITE

Alice Austin

Life, Death

The apple fit snugly in her hand as if made for her. Its unblemished surface was inviting. Her teeth dug in with a satisfying crunch and juice dribbled down her chin. But something was wrong; the thick red juice kept flowing, filling her mouth with a bitter metallic taste and igniting her every nerve…

Snow opened her eyes. Her mouth was full of iron. Her neck burned. Her belly growled and twisted with a savage hunger. The moonlit sky stretched above her. She'd never seen the stars shining so brightly before, but the luminescence did little to ease the ache.

"You're awake," someone murmured.

She turned toward the voice, confused and feeble. With a shock, she found herself inside a coffin made of glass. The lid lay abandoned on the floor a few feet away. A shiver shot down her back.

"What happened? Who are you?" The apple was all she could remember. It had been a dream, but there must be some truth to it.

"My name is Rowan. I was just passing through when I found you here in this coffin. You were dying."

Snow stared at him, speechless. She didn't want to believe him, but there was a wrongness throughout her entire body that could only be explained by something terrible happening. She pushed herself upright, looking frantically around to try to make sense of the situation. Great firs surrounded them, swaying in the icy breeze. Frost glimmered on the grass of the small clearing they were in. The scene felt familiar, but her memory of it was blurred and distorted beyond recognition.

"I tried to save you, but it was almost too late. This was the only way. I hope you can forgive me."

Snow watched his mouth as he spoke, noticing his sharp, lengthened canines. Bile rose in her throat as the burning in her neck intensified. She ran her fingers along it to discover the two small wounds on her throat. Her hand came back red and wet. The sight triggered a pang of deep, aching hunger.

"Was I dying, or dead?" she asked, although she already knew. She felt empty and hollow. She *felt* dead. Rowan's dark eyes were full of sympathy, answering her question without words. He'd saved her, but he'd cursed her in the process.

"Thank you for saving me." She climbed out of the coffin. She needed some time to process what had happened, some time to mourn her own death. Pulling her cloak tight around her, she began to walk.

"Where will you go?"

The question gave her pause. Where *would* she go? Back to the dwarves, perhaps. But did a dead woman have any right to walk among the living? Her belly twisted with a savage hunger, and as she clenched her teeth, the sharp points of her new fangs scraped against her lower lip. Would she return to them as a friend or as a predator? Would they embrace her as the girl they'd known before, or chase her away like a monster?

"You could come with me," Rowan continued. "It might not be safe for you here any longer."

Snow turned back and eyed him with suspicion, trying to figure out whether she recognized him. He was tall, with a head of short-cropped red hair. His long black cloak was wrapped tightly around him. Nothing about him sparked any recognition.

"How can I trust you? I don't know you."

"That's a fair question, and I don't have a good answer. I won't force you to come with me, but at least let me take you to someone who can help. It wouldn't feel right leaving you to fend for yourself. How much do you know about vampires? It can be dangerous for those who don't fully understand the changes."

Snow's stomach dropped at his words. Of course. All she knew about vampires were the tales about them ripping out peoples' throats while they slept. She had no urge to kill, but what if it was something that developed over time? What if she returned home and murdered everyone she loved? If she couldn't return to the dwarves, she had nowhere else to go.

Besides, she was already dead. What was the worst that could happen if she accompanied this man?

"Maybe I *should* join you." Going with him was the best option until she understood her new life. But first, he needed to know about her stepmother. "I should warn you; I'm being hunted. Queen Sylve has attempted to kill me several times, and she will probably try again. I wouldn't want you getting hurt on my account."

Her thoughts drifted back to the dwarves. What if the queen had harmed them in retaliation for hiding her? Worry grew in her mind, but the glass lip of the coffin reassured her. Such beautiful craftsmanship could only be theirs. If only she could go back and reassure them she was safe, if not alive, but she knew she couldn't. Not yet, anyway.

"But you died. Surely, she has no reason to think you will return."

"She has an artifact. A mirror—"

To Snow's shock, Rowan waved away her concern as if it was nothing.

"You needn't worry about mirrors any longer," he assured her. "Your stepmother will never find you."

Night, Day

Snow hadn't been aware that her rescuer was royalty.

"My father was a vampire king," Rowan explained as they trudged through the leaf litter. "He turned me and my siblings when we came of age. I'd known it was coming, but I still wish I'd had a choice." He glanced at her. "I normally only turn people when they truly want it. I'm sorry I couldn't ask permission."

Snow didn't respond. Thoughts of the queen had poisoned her mind with paranoia, and she wondered if this was all part of the witch's plan. Drug her with an apple, then send Rowan to lead her to her doom while she was still recovering. It was the type of cruel, convoluted plot Sylve would love; tricking her into thinking she'd escaped before springing the final trap.

She'd already paid for her naïvety with her life. She didn't intend to do so again.

Rowan offered her a drink from his flask as they walked through the darkened forest. Her mouth was so dry that she accepted, despite her mistrust. She took a sip and almost spat it out as the metallic taste of blood filled her mouth. Once the revulsion had passed, it tasted good. She had to fight to stop herself from draining the flask.

Melancholy washed over her as they passed through the night. She'd always enjoyed the peace of the woods, broken occasionally by birdsong. The woodland creatures had never been afraid of her, but simply carried on their little lives as if she was not there. There would be none of that now. Surely they would sense her new hunger and flee from her like a wolf. The thought sent a deep ache through her bones.

They stopped for a break, and Snow sat down on a nearby stump. A pale shape in a tree ahead caught her eye, and she grimaced as piercing amber eyes locked with her own. Owls unnerved her. They preyed on her beloved songbirds and snatched their chicks from the nest. She'd never seen one before, only the putrid, bony pellets they left behind. This one had caught something. She felt a stab of sorrow for the limp, furry shape as the owl threw back its head and swallowed it whole.

A moving shadow in the trees ahead of her snatched her attention from the owl. Her senses were sharper than they used to be. The movement had been so swift that she would never normally have noticed. For a few moments there was nothing, then another sleek gray shape. And another. She watched the wolves race past, silent as the grave. Their muzzles glistened from a fresh kill, a sight which both disturbed her and excited her belly.

"I thought it would be quiet here at night," she said to Rowan, listening to the squeals of the bats flying overhead. "But it's not quiet at all." She decided not to finish the sentiment. The night was full of death, the gentle creatures she loved being torn apart by beasts of darkness. She glanced at Rowan, who was staring off into the distance, mesmerized by the ambiance.

"Isn't it beautiful?" he asked. Snow felt a flutter and looked down at her wrist where a moth had landed. It wasn't as pretty as a butterfly, but it made her smile, nonetheless. Despite its muted brown colors, its eyespot pattern was elegant in its own way. Perhaps the dark was not completely devoid of beauty.

Predator, Prey

Rowan's castle was big and cold and silent. Ivy crawled its way up the stone walls, and the cawing of rooks echoed through the empty courtyard. Snow was relieved when Rowan asked a servant to put clean sheets on a bed for her; she'd half-expected to sleep in a coffin.

She slept at night and paced her shuttered room during the day. Rowan delivered flasks of blood each evening and encouraged her to join him. The blood called to her, the coppery scent wafting through her room and sending her belly into a frenzy until she tipped it away or drained the flask dry. Before her death, she had never eaten meat. She couldn't bear the thought of something innocent being hurt for her benefit. This wasn't any different, except now she had no choice.

Weeks passed, every day the same. Her spacious bedroom began to feel like it was closing in around her. She expanded her wandering to the corridors of the castle, a restless corpse, but it wasn't enough. The nocturnal world might be violent and terrifying, but it was better than caging herself away forever.

Rowan was delighted when Snow appeared for breakfast just after sunset.

"I'm worried about you," he said as she sat down. It was only the two of them there, yet the ornate wooden table could have seated twenty. "I've barely seen you. I know it can be hard to adjust, so please let me know if I can help." He eyed her with suspicion. "You're eating, I hope?"

Snow thought back to the time he'd caught her emptying a flask of blood out of the window in a desperate attempt to fight her new instincts.

"I am," she said, pouring herself a glass and taking a sip. Rowan smiled, but Snow barely noticed as the flavor exploded in her mouth. It tasted so *good*. She took another sip, then another, her stomach growling with approval.

The door opened, and one of Rowan's human servants entered with another bottle. All Snow could focus on were the veins in his wrist as he set it down. If she listened closely, she could hear the rush of blood and the faint thumping of his heart. Her mouth watered, iron lingering on her lips. She wanted more. She wanted—

She forced her gaze downward, examining the grain of the wood on the table and the intricate carvings along its edge. Her hands trembled as she clenched them into fists beneath the table. If she didn't control herself, something terrible would happen.

Rowan thanked the servant and waited until he'd left the room to speak. Snow could feel his gaze on her, and knew he'd seen every bit of her internal struggle.

"You did well there," he said. "You're hungry, and the hungrier you are, the harder it is to resist. You need to eat properly. Not just for yourself, but for the people you meet."

"Was that a test?" A sudden fury rushed up inside her, the first strong emotion she'd felt since her death. "You risked that servant's life to scold me about not eating." How could she have been so naïve? Rowan was just another predator, like the queen. Like herself.

"Do you really think—" Rowan began, but Snow was no longer listening.

"I'm going out." Before he could speak, she strode out of the dining hall and pushed open the colossal wooden door to the courtyard. Rowan made no move to stop her. She fled across the moonlit courtyard.

The sounds of the forest were a welcome change from the claustrophobia of her room. It felt peaceful rather than empty. She ran until the foliage thickened and blocked all sight of the castle, then sat on a fallen tree and buried her face in her hands. What now? She didn't want to return to the castle and face Rowan, but she didn't know where else she could go. After the near incident with the servant, she couldn't return to the dwarves.

A faint sound caught her attention, and she watched as a deer raced through the undergrowth. Her stomach turned as three gray shapes sped past it in pursuit. Before she knew it, she was on her feet, chasing after the wolves. They didn't even notice her until she was on them and the taste of blood filled her mouth, fur sticking in her teeth, bone crunching between her jaws.

When she regained her senses, the deer was nowhere to be seen. For the first time since she'd died, she felt fully sated. Awake. Almost *alive*.

The elation faded as she saw the bloody heap of fur before her and realized what she'd done.

"Wolves. An interesting choice. Most new vampires just hunt deer or rabbits."

The voice made her jump. She turned to see Rowan watching her from the shadows.

"Go away," she hissed, doing her best to wipe at the blood. She was still angry, and that he was just standing there watching her with a smirk on his face only enraged her more. He was the last person she wanted to see her like this, her face and hands smeared with gore. She was no better than an animal.

"Snow, I would never put my servants in danger. If I'd known you were coming for breakfast, I would've told them not to disturb us. I was watching you the whole time he was in there and, trust me, I would have stopped you if I had to."

Snow glanced at him, then dropped her gaze. He seemed sincere. As her anger trickled away, despair and shame rushed in to fill the void.

"How am I supposed to live like this?" she asked, gesturing at the wolves. "I can't control myself. I'm no better than my stepmother now. All I can do is cause pain and death. I feel like I'm turning into her."

"That's not true. We may need blood to survive, but that doesn't make us monsters. The monsters I've known have relished in the chaos they caused. You can't even bear to look at it."

Snow didn't answer. Tears pricked at her eyes.

Rowan sighed and sat down next to her.

"My father enjoyed killing and causing pain. He was…ruthless with his raids on the neighboring towns. We need bloodshed to survive, but he took it too far. Your stepmother sounds the same. Why was she so determined to kill you, if I may ask?"

"Jealousy, maybe," Snow said. In truth, she didn't understand why she'd been murdered, but it was the only answer that came to mind. "It was nothing I'd done, just the mere fact that I existed."

"Your stepmother is a different sort of predator. Perhaps it was about survival for her at first, but she began to enjoy it too much. I can't see you ever going down that path, Snow. Please don't worry."

Snow nodded. He was talking sense, but it didn't erase the deep feeling of shame. Despite everything, she was still a killer. Her very existence now depended on the suffering of others.

"I can't stand the thought of harming helpless creatures," she said. "Even if I have to."

"Is that why you hunted the wolves rather than the deer?"

Snow fell silent. Her mind had been too clouded with hunger to make a coherent plan, but she didn't think her target had ever been the deer. Perhaps she didn't have to hurt the innocent. Perhaps she could hunt the predators instead.

"Will you come back to the castle?" Rowan asked, getting to his feet. Snow stood up as well. Perhaps it was because she'd eaten, but her mind felt clearer now. She might have changed, but that didn't mean she had to become a murderous creature of darkness.

"I'll come."

Past, Future

As weeks passed, Snow slowly adapted to her new life. She woke in the evenings and joined Rowan for breakfast, making sure to keep herself well-fed. She often went out to the woods, enjoying the company of the nocturnal creatures as she'd once enjoyed those of the day. There was no birdsong, but the hooting of owls and squeaks of bats made their own kind of music in the still and calm.

Sometimes she hunted, tracking down a wolf or fox in pursuit of prey and draining them dry before they could kill. The more she drank, the better she felt. Starving herself had sent her mood spiraling into darkness, and now that she'd accepted her condition and the constraints that came with it, she felt almost free.

Almost.

At first, she thought this feeling of heaviness inside her was because she missed the dwarves, but as she lay in bed with the faint glow of daylight making its way through the heavy shutters, she realized it was more than that.

Queen Sylve was still out there, and despite Rowan's reassurances, Snow knew she would never be truly safe as long as her stepmother lived. The magic mirror might not be a threat anymore, but all it would take was a rumor whispered in the wrong ear, and her new life would come crashing down around her.

If Sylve discovered Snow was alive, the attack would be insidious, venomous, and she wouldn't realize until it was too late. Just like she had not realized the apple was poison until it had begun corroding her insides. The old Snow would have been helpless to do anything except run and hide, but she had been reborn. She had new options now.

When she went for breakfast, Rowan seemed to know what she was going to say before she even said it. He greeted her with a pleasant smile, but there was something forced about it.

"You seem excited this evening!"

"Rowan, I must leave." Now that it was time, her heart grew heavy. She owed Rowan more than her life. The thought of leaving him alone in this empty castle with nobody but his servants and the rooks made her chest ache. But she had to. She half-expected him to argue, but he nodded slowly, head bowed.

"I knew you wouldn't be here forever, but I hoped you would be here a little longer. I shall miss having you around. You've come such a long way since I first brought you here." He smiled sadly. "What are you planning?"

"I'm going to kill my stepmother." She hadn't figured out the details, but it was the only way she could ever be safe. "I know you'd defend me if it came to it, but I won't ever feel safe until she's gone."

"And after that?"

"I don't know." She hadn't planned that far ahead; she didn't even know if she'd succeed, or if the queen would finally have her way. "I'll decide on the journey. It's a long way."

"It is. I'll make sure you have plenty of blood to take with you. You're capable of feeding yourself, but it's important to always have an emergency supply. And I'll give you a traveling cloak. You can use it to protect yourself from the sun if you have nowhere to go, but stay hidden. All it would take is one curious human to investigate, and you will burn." Rowan swirled his glass. He seemed nervous.

"Are you worried for me?" she asked.

"Of course I am. I've turned a lot of people, and not all of them came back after they left. I would be heartbroken to lose you, but I can't stop you. All I can do is wish you luck and offer you a safe place to stay if you return."

Snow looked down into her drink. She wished Rowan could come with her, but knew he would refuse if she asked. This quest was for her alone.

"Will you be lonely?" she asked. "You're here in this huge castle, all on your own. Where are all the people? What happened to your father and siblings?"

"My family are long dead. The people… some of them fled, some of them died, but there are still a few survivors. Enough to keep us going, at least. I told you about my father's raids on the neighboring kingdoms. Eventually, they banded together to fight back. I was away when it happened, and I came back to find everyone dead. Except *him*." He slammed his glass down so hard Snow was surprised it didn't shatter. "He swore revenge. After losing everyone but me, he still couldn't change. He would've set the whole world alight, and it still wouldn't have been enough for him. I couldn't just let him continue his destruction. So, I killed him myself." He took a moment to compose himself and leaned back in the chair.

"I only turn people when necessary. I refuse to be responsible for releasing another monster into the world, so I always keep a close eye on them afterwards." He gave her a strained smile. "You know you're no monster. But if you're ever in doubt, try to remember that I would never have let you leave if I thought you would become one."

Friends, Enemies

The next evening, Snow bade a teary goodbye to Rowan in the courtyard of the castle. She embraced him tightly, making a silent promise that if she succeeded, she would return. Even if she didn't stay forever.

The sun had barely set as she set off, the deep indigo sky growing darker as the moon rose and tinted the world with silver. The rhythmic thumping of her horse's hooves against the forest floor thudded in her ears. Her heart was still, but the mix of thrill and fear filled her body like a hot rush of blood.

The ride was uneventful, and as the sky started to lighten, she decided to stop. There was no hope of finding shelter nearby, so she gathered fallen branches to build herself a makeshift hut. She passed into a forest clearing and what she saw made her halt in her steps.

It was the glass coffin. She hadn't realized she'd come so far already.

She ran her finger along the ornate rim. Her once distant nightmare now looked like an inviting place to sleep. She lay down in the coffin, pulling the lid on and wrapping herself in the cloak Rowan had given her. Surely nobody would open a coffin and risk exposing a corpse.

She slept undisturbed and woke the next evening, ready to continue her journey. After a few hours, she left the forest behind her, following a path that wound its way through open fields towards the rolling hills ahead. As they drew closer, she came to a familiar split in the road.

One direction led through the fields all the way to the dwarves' cottage; the other led through the hills to the queen's castle. She was eager to finish her task, but traveling alone was beginning to wear on her. She missed Rowan and missed the dwarves even more.

Before she knew it, she'd steered the horse towards the friends who thought she was dead.

The cottage came into view just as the hint of dawn began to lighten the sky. Snow dismounted her horse and drank several mouthfuls of blood from her flask to keep the hunger at bay, then strode forward and knocked on the tiny door. Her dead heart did not stir, but there was a lump in her throat as she heard footsteps. The door opened, and Art stared up at her, mouth wide open.

"Snow? I-I can't believe it!" He took a few steps back, and for a moment, she thought he was going to pass out. Then a smile spread across his face.

"Get up!" he bellowed. "There's somebody here to see us!" He turned back to Snow. "Where have you been?" he asked, as the rest of the dwarves flooded to the front door and stared up at Snow like they'd seen a ghost. Their shouts of surprise and delight brought tears to her eyes and a wide smile to her face.

"I've missed you all so much," she said. But as her grin grew and her fangs pricked her lower lip, the joy drained from their faces.

"Vampire," breathed Trin. The dwarves backed away, except for Art, who stood blocking the door. Snow fondly remembered the time he had stopped Sylve from entering the house whilst she fled from the back door. The memory sent a spike of pain through her chest, now that she was on the other side of the interaction.

"It's me, Art. Please let me in." It was still dark, but the horizon had begun to glow. She would need shelter soon.

"We should let her in," Birn mumbled. "It's Snow! We can't just leave her out there."

"Don't be fooled. That's not Snow anymore. If we let her in, she'll slit our throats and drink us dry."

"I thought you'd be happy to see me," Snow whispered. She'd been so excited; she hadn't thought about how they might react. Her eyes burned, but she couldn't let herself cry in front of them. "I was rescued by a vampire prince, Rowan. I've been staying with him ever since. I know it must be hard for you to trust me—I didn't even trust myself at first. I have missed you so much, but didn't dare come here in case I did something terrible. But now I could never hurt you. Vampire or not, I'm still me. I'm still Snow." The black of the sky had faded to a deep blue. The sun was coming.

"Let her in," said Birn. A few others nodded but said nothing. "We can't let her die out here."

"Don't!" Trin begged, staring at Snow with wide, terrified eyes. "Don't let her in."

"Vote on it. You always settled debates with a vote before. If you decide not to let me in, I'll be on my way," Snow said. The more time they spent arguing, the more danger she would be in if they refused her. The fact they were even considering it made her heart ache.

Art nodded slowly. "A vote." He turned to face the others. "All those who wish to allow her in, to the left. All those who don't, to the right." He strode off to the right. Snow watched with her heart in her throat as Trin followed. But the rest went to the left.

"It's decided," said Birn. "She stays."

Art stepped aside, watching Snow as she ducked to enter the low-ceilinged house. She could feel all their eyes upon her, their fear and mistrust.

"Thank you," she muttered, trying not to let her voice break. "I'll only stay for a day."

She went straight to her old room and pulled the curtains shut, then curled up on the bed and sobbed quietly. She should never have come here. Just because Rowan knew she wasn't a monster didn't mean the dwarves would. She should have stayed away and let their memories of her rest in peace.

The next evening, she wasted no time in gathering her things. Her chest ached as she took one last look at the room she'd spent so long in. She didn't belong here anymore.

Art and Trin stood outside her bedroom as she slipped out. Art's eyes flicked to her bag.

"You're leaving?" he asked. Snow glanced at him and nodded.

"It's night now, so I'll go." She hurried past them, trying not to let them see her stricken face.

"Wait," said Art. "I thought this was one of Sylve's plots and you were here to kill us all. But you could have killed us from the moment you entered the house, and you haven't. I think we've made a horrible mistake."

"I told you I could never hurt you." Snow couldn't look at him. "I know I no longer have a place here, but I was so keen to return, I didn't consider how it might seem. I'm sorry."

"Stay longer if you need to," Trin blurted out. "We were scared at first, but you're clearly still you."

"I wish I could," Snow said. "But there's something I need to do. I can't live in fear of Sylve forever. I'm going to face her. I wanted to come here—" her voice faltered. "I wanted to come here first in case she wins. I never had the chance to say goodbye last time."

Art stepped forward and hugged her, and Trin followed.

"You'll always have a place here, Snow. We'll be here for you when you return."

Death, Life

Snow longed to stay and resume her old life, but she couldn't pretend nothing had happened. Art and Trin weren't afraid of her anymore, but they still weren't entirely comfortable and every wary glance from them hurt. Besides, she couldn't afford to linger. She would never be safe until her stepmother was gone—and she feared her friends wouldn't be, either.

She left that night, memories of her farewell to Rowan echoing in her mind. As she rode away, waving goodbye, she promised herself that if she succeeded, she would come back to them too and prove she was the same person she'd always been.

The fork in the road loomed ever closer, and as she steered the horse down that fateful path, the heaviness in her chest intensified. Her battle with Sylve had been interrupted; not that it'd ever really been a battle when Snow had never stood a chance. Now she was back to finish it, but on a more level playing field.

At long last, she came to the castle gates. A pair of guards stood watch, and she fell back into the shadows of the wall, deliberating on how to get past without harming them. Then she remembered something Rowan had shown her. She hurried out of sight and pressed her hand against the wall. Her body dissipated into mist, seeping through the cracks and the pores of the old stone, trickling through until all of her reached the other side.

She looked down at her hands, now solid once again, before making her way through the silent courtyard. The place felt like a half-forgotten dream. She slipped through the orchard, trees unnaturally heavy with fruit despite the chill in the air. Instead of opening the heavy wooden doors to the castle, she allowed herself to dissolve into mist again and swirled her way underneath. She surged through the passageways, a racing shadow, and took the spiral stairs two at a time. There was not far to go now.

The wooden door at the top of the stairs came into view. She devoured the remaining blood in her flask and threw it aside. This was it. The end of her journey. She walked to the door, twisted the handle, and gently pushed it open.

The room was as she remembered it, the neatly made bed empty and undisturbed. Queen Sylve was not there, but that horrible mirror was. She remembered watching Sylve mutter maniacally to it and the burning look of hatred she'd given Snow when the mirror responded. A shudder ran down her spine.

"Mirror, mirror," she whispered, but it didn't answer. Her reflection wasn't present in its image of the room. She peered into it, wondering if she might be able to view Sylve or if the mirror could no longer acknowledge her. But before she could think of the right words to try, the door opened behind her.

"Who's there?" A glowing orb shot to the ceiling and filled the room with bright light. She couldn't turn around. Her muscles had turned to stone at the sight of her killer's icy eyes boring into her from the mirror.

"Face me," Sylve commanded, and Snow found herself turning without meaning to. Invisible hands wrenched back her hood. Sylve gasped, but composed herself quickly.

"Snow White. You just keep coming back! I thought I'd finally gotten rid of you. How did you survive this time?" Her voice was flat and emotionless, but her pale eyes were full of the frosty rage Snow knew so well. She hadn't aged a day since Snow had last seen her; her skin was still flawlessly smooth, her hair still jet black and perfect.

"I didn't," Snow said, making sure Sylve had a good view of her fangs as she spoke. Now that she was there, her resolve was wavering. It was one thing to slaughter wolves; quite another to kill a person, even her stepmother. Perhaps if Sylve realized Snow could fight back now, she'd reconsider.

Sylve seemed unphased. The corners of her mouth turned up in a smirk.

"Oh. That's surprising. I wouldn't have thought you, of all people, would adjust to living as a vampire. Or is that why you're here? You can't take it, so you've come back to let me finish what I started?"

"I came back to kill you," said Snow, and took great pleasure in seeing that smirk disappear. She stared at her stepmother's face, hoping to see an inkling of fear, but there was only disdain. Her heart sank. There would be no easy end to this confrontation.

"Don't lie. You wouldn't hurt a fly. You're too soft, too weak. Have you been eating enough since you died? Have you hunted any of your own prey, or do you just accept what you're given like a good little girl?"

"I hunt for myself," Snow said coldly, and Sylve burst out laughing.

"You can't expect me to believe that. You don't have it in you. Since the day I was born, I've had to fight my way to get where I am." She pulled her hair to one side. Snow's eyes widened at the sight of her exposed neck, veins visible beneath the skin.

"Maybe you believe you came here to kill me," Sylve said, "but I don't buy that for a moment. If that's truly why you're here, go ahead."

Snow couldn't move, fixated on her neck. All this, and her stepmother was just surrendering?

"I'm not lying," she said. "I'm not the same person anymore." She'd told the dwarves she was still the same, tried to believe it herself, but it wasn't true. Sylve was right. The old Snow would never have chosen to hunt down and kill the woman, no matter how much her stepmother hated her.

"Then show me. One of us is going to die tonight, Snow. You've come back far too many times for me to let you go. Make no mistake, if you don't kill me, I *will* kill you. For good this time."

"And if you're wrong? If I kill you?" Snow took a few more steps forward until she was standing directly beside her stepmother.

"Then maybe I'll hate you a little less in my final moments. You're weak." Sylve's stony expression had devolved to one of pure loathing. "You rely on others to protect you, but you'll never protect yourself. The huntsman saved you, the dwarves saved you, this prince saved you. You've done nothing to earn so many second chances. When are you going to save yourself?"

"Right now," Snow said. She lunged forward and grasped Sylve by the shoulders, nails digging in hard enough to make her cry out in pain. A bead of blood pearled out from the witch's perfect skin. Snow's eyes locked on it and, for the first time, something other than cold indifference crossed Sylve's face.

An invisible force threw the two of them apart. Sylve recovered first and fled to the door, her breathing ragged and irregular. Some part of Snow wanted to let her escape, but she'd come too far now to let her stepmother live.

She leapt to her feet and blocked the exit before Sylve could even touch the handle. The terrified rhythm of Sylve's heart thumped in Snow's ears, making her mouth water and her thoughts turn hungry. Dead though she was, she had never felt so alive.

Before Sylve could cast another spell, Snow lunged.

Flesh tore beneath her teeth, hot waves of blood sprayed from severed arteries. Killing her stepmother wasn't as hard as she'd thought.

It was easy, like biting into an apple.

UNCLE FRANK'S EMPORIUM OF ODDITES

Paul L. Bates

THE CLEAR AFTERNOON sky had turned a decidedly unhealthy yellow. The wind, at first annoyingly curious, died down like a sullen tethered dog, well bored after having sniffed every inch of familiar scrub within the reach of its straining lead. Between the broken straw-covered fields just beyond the eastern edge of town, something barely visible prodded the parched land into a shallow obscuring haze.

At first, it was a mere smear upon the horizon, swelling progressively larger, until one could see what appeared to be a rising fog. After a minute or so, the roiling dust cloud, for by now it had revealed itself at last, resembled a bloated caterpillar, crawling steadily closer to the town with a purpose known only to itself.

At the very spot the topography began its gradual ascent, Rural Route 94 widened abruptly from two to four lanes, sprouted a pair of cracked sidewalks, ancient iron streetlamps with matching signposts at every intersection proudly proclaiming Main Street. Here, the lazy cloud faltered, as if intimidated by the sudden trappings of civilization. A caravan led by an oversized black pickup truck with tinted windows emerged from the hovering dust, creeping higher toward the public green with its granite dais boasting the larger-than-life bronze likeness of one

Cornelius Culpepper, an entrepreneur of dubious reputation who had founded this backwater some three hundred years ago.

Culpepper, his long coat brushing the top of his boots lending him the air of an illustrious outlaw, stood, shoulders squared, disapproving blind eyes fixed upon the encroaching strangers, elbows bent, and open hands thrust before him as if to say *outsiders are not welcome here.* His lips were parted, as if his likeness had been captured sharing these remarkable words of wisdom.

Like waddling ducklings following their mother, six smaller trucks towing squat silver campers, followed by two battered semi-tractor trailers straining and groaning, appeared behind the oversized black pickup truck with its dark tinted windows. The caravan climbed the twelve blocks of Town Hill belching diesel fumes.

From the two diners that faced one another like in-laws across the four lanes of Main Street, and then from the hardware store immediately after them, several panicked customers took to the street to gawk at the odd procession. Even Harold, the barber, popped his bald head from his shop door, turned it slowly following the lead truck with his eyes until the entire parade had passed, then popped back inside to attend the perplexed mayor reclining draped and lathered in Harold's antique mechanical chair.

The caravan wrapped itself about the town green once in a counterclockwise direction, drew to a choreographed stop before the red brick town hall. A turquoise sign painted in the stylized likeness of a circus banner on one of the trailers proclaimed in large dust-covered red letters, "Uncle Frank's Emporium of Oddities."

Two policemen soon scurried down the imposing front steps of the town hall, ceremoniously adjusted their belts to accommodate their girth, then strode purposefully toward the lead vehicle. A tall man, almost painfully thin, as if his sustenance came entirely from something other than solid food, stepped sprightly from the passenger side of the black truck. He wore a black coat with long tails, giving him the air of a rumpled orchestra conductor or perhaps that of a mortician. The policemen waved their arms, pointing at the caravan, the plethora of no parking signs, the reproachful town hall with its dark, brooding windows perched at the very top of the hill. The tall man watched them bemusedly, said nothing until they finished their diatribe. An animated placating gesture not unlike that of Cornelius Culpepper upon his granite dais eventually calmed the stalwart protectors of the peace. The trio marched back into town hall, accompanying the tall man so that he might speak with someone with the authority to grant him the necessary permission to display his oddities for those willing to pay the price of three dollars.

"Don't get many sideshows in these parts," the town clerk drawled. "At least not since everybody's got widescreen TVs, computers, cell phones, iPods and the like. Nowadays folks can see pretty much anything they can imagine without leaving home."

"Yes," the tall man agreed languidly. "We live in an age when a deranged pop star can buy the bones of Joseph Merrick for his own amusement, a television station can fund a search for the mythical Mongolian death worm to while away an hour, and a wealthy grifter can prance and glower to get himself elected President. It is no surprise the common man has grown so jaded at the wonder of it all. There is no passion in his education, no feeling left for what he does, save the dubious satisfaction of sprouting purported facts and figures like an expert, or venting his anger upon any who disagree. But to hear the purveyors of technology tell it, an afternoon on a search engine can be every bit as fruitful as a four-year degree in higher learning. They'd have us believe the world is shrinking before our very eyes simply because so many of us have been overexposed to a constant barrage of electronic fluff."

"Fluff?" the uncomprehending clerk asked.

"My good man, the purpose of education has always been to enlarge the world, not shrink it. And anything that thwarts that purpose is, at the very least, fluff."

"I see," the clerk responded, thinking the tall man did not wish to use profanities. "That'll be five hundred dollars for the permit, another five hundred for the police detail, and you've got until dawn the day after tomorrow to take down your tent. Can't imagine how you'll recoup your money, though, especially without concession stands."

The tall man smiled, peeled ten hundred-dollar bills from the thick roll he withdrew from his pants pocket, signed the waiver, took the cardboard permit that needed to be conspicuously displayed at all times, ambled back to the waiting caravan.

He supped at one of the diners with an equally emaciated woman with strikingly high cheekbones and long copper-colored hair pulled tight and clasped behind her head by an ivory comb, their stoic postures in sharp contrast with the lively throng amiably chatting while devouring plates heaped with baby back ribs and buttered corn on the cob. After a light lunch, he persuaded the owner to display a four-color placard promoting the Emporium in the front window. It depicted a highly stylized and very gaunt man in a top hat beckoning with one hand while pointing at something indistinct behind him in the shadows, something vaguely human in size and shape. Other similar advertisements soon appeared in the other diner across the street, the florist, druggist, dry cleaner, greengrocer, gas stations, and shops up and down Main Street, as the pair paid their respects to all the local businesses. Not one word was said concerning the specifics of the supposed oddities contained within the caravan.

By dusk, a large, frilled pavilion reminiscent of a small circus tent dominated the center of the town green, dwarfing the bronze statue of Cornelius Culpepper who gawked dumbly at it. The esteemed town father looked to have been drafted as a barker for Uncle Frank's Emporium. By the light of the waning sun, his odd gesture resembled an attempt to pacify the unruly.

The harvest moon rose above Rural Route 94, bathing the town in a pale orange light. All night long, four by eight sections of garishly painted partitions vanished beyond the tent flaps to the sounds of hammers and power drills. A small group of vocal onlookers gathered outside the tent to speculate upon what manner of construction went on within, but the sudden presence just beyond the tent flap of a burly bald man whose dark eyes were lost within the deep menacing shadow of his protruding brow dissuaded them from further investigations. Two policemen soon prowled the green like watchdogs, keeping other such impromptu gatherings well back until the last of them went home before midnight.

The tall man breakfasted alone at one diner the next morning, leaving behind a clutch of free tickets, while the woman with the copper-colored hair did the same at the eatery across the street. The tickets were undated, looked to have been used before, were made of heavy white paper, bore the turquoise logo in the stylized likeness of a circus banner with bright red letters proclaiming "Uncle Frank's Emporium of Oddities" and the words in black "admit one" above the slogan and the terse statement "show starts at dusk" beneath it. On the backside, only the curious caption "what do you really know about it?" appeared. Several men attempted to engage the tall woman in conversation by way of inquisition, but she responded to each with a feral smile, her half-closed eyes glinting red by some unnatural light denied the other patrons that both titillated and terrified in equal measure.

The hammering and droning on the town green continued until noon the next day. It was followed by the appearance of a large number of heavily bundled objects that required two and sometimes three nondescript roustabouts, grunting under the load, to carry. These objects disappeared into the pavilion; the tarps that had covered them were removed to the trailers shortly thereafter.

The first oddity noticed by the small crowd of bystanders occurred just as the construction clamor ended. A small child tugged at her mother's skirt, pointing at the frail quivering creeper clinging to the statue of Cornelius Culpepper, one which had seemingly grown over a dozen feet in the space of a few hours. At his bronze shoulder the bright green vine groped and quivered, perhaps three feet away, as if unsure where to proceed from here.

By five o'clock, a significantly larger crowd had gathered in anticipation, comprised entirely of those with free tickets. By then, the statue of Cornelius Culpepper was completely engulfed by a thicket of bright green heart-shaped leaves bearing clusters of tiny blood-colored flowers that left only his thrusting hands visible, the open palms facing the pavilion as if to guide him toward the oddities as he stumbled blindly off his pedestal.

The crowd murmured, gesticulated, avidly discussing this odd phenomenon, when a terrified gray squirrel bolted squealing around the statue's base, an unnaturally bright orange breasted robin perched confidently upon its back like a jockey, the rodent gripped firmly in its claws. An occasional peck to the squirrel's head served as a signal for it to change directions. The odd pair ran in more or less straight lines until the next peck from the robin elicited another heart-wrenching yelp from the squirrel, causing it to alter its course closer to the crowd while always maintaining a discrete distance. The murmuring among the onlookers ceased altogether, save for one woman who tugged repeatedly at the arm of her man, imploring him to take her home, but each time the robin would direct the squirrel back directly across their path as if to block their leaving, or perhaps to simply fascinate them.

At six o'clock, the swollen orange moon broke free of Main Street just as the sun disappeared behind the town hall. The moon began its gradual ascent like a great rheumy eye meant to keep watch over the proceedings. The tall man opened the tent flaps, strode forward, beckoning to the crowd. He was soon taking tickets from any brave enough to venture closer to see what oddities the pavilion contained. He sported a black silk top hat, as well as his long-tailed coat, adding an icy smile to his otherwise morbid demeanor. Behind him, a soft droning, like an unholy chant or an incoming mechanical tide, beckoned the townspeople from within the tent. A thin mist, sweet-smelling and oddly animated, crept from the opening, clinging to the grass, tiny tendrils probing upward, fading, disappearing into the twilight. The robin and the squirrel vanished behind the bright green leaf-tangled statue of Cornelius Culpepper. The squirrel's sporadic shrieking stopped abruptly.

"Trained animals," a young man near the front announced in knowing tones, eliciting a nervous laugh from one of his friends.

"Genetic fertilizer," was the firm reply, with a subtle nod toward the mesh of creepers, not to be outdone.

"Dry ice," the young woman at his side added, poking the crawling mist with her toe.

"What a deliciously lively crowd," the tall man observed, "and so seemingly knowledgeable—absolutely perfect. No more than four at a time with a minute between groups, if you please." He ushered the first four through the open flap.

The bald strongman who'd blocked the pavilion the day before appeared from within carrying a portable ticket stand, which he planted firmly before the vine-covered statue. He flicked a toggle switch beneath the small wooden counter. Tiny white marquis lights surrounding the stand blinked in a hypnotic pattern. Spotlights mounted above the tent flap abruptly bathed the ticket booth in a pale light as the gaunt woman with the copper-colored hair took her place behind it. She wore a bright feathered headdress and an open-weave black shawl, her unnerving smile and glowing red eyes turned upon the crowd as the strongman retreated to the pavilion.

Within the first fifteen minutes, all those who had availed themselves of the free tickets were gawking at the oddities. The ranks of those who waited to purchase tickets were now beyond the capacity of the four policemen sent to maintain order. One of them noted that no one who had entered the pavilion had yet emerged, to which another posited the exit might well be on the opposite side, and the displays might warrant more time.

By eight o'clock the entire green was surrounded by parked cars, the long line before the ticket counter snaking back and forth a dozen times to contain those who waited patiently. The drone of the mechanical tide from within the tent had grown louder by degrees until it reached down every street of the town and into every home, apartment building and rooming house nestled in the narrow lanes eight deep on either side of Main Street. Yet even it could not muffle the odd sound of human voices that rose and fell within the pavilion as if bobbing upon the tide itself; wordless cries, both ecstatic and terrified, as if to experience the *oddities* displayed within was acute beyond description, sensual beyond belief, disquieting beyond imagination.

Four at a time the curious now hurried into the pavilion, traversing the odd brightly colored labyrinth erected within. And still no one admitted emerged without. By 11:30, the crowd had thinned to five groups of four, tickets clutched firmly in sweaty hands, waiting eagerly outside the flap. One of the policemen sauntered to the ticket booth to remind the gaunt woman that the terms of the permit called for the show to close by midnight. Her red eyes blazed even brighter; her feral smile took on an irresistibly seductive leer. She shut off the blinking lights surrounding the stand, gestured the policemen toward the flap as if to say: for them, the price of admission had been waived.

The first officer swallowed like a guilty child caught with chocolate stains upon his face, looked to his superior. The sergeant shrugged, took his place behind the last group as the tall man ushered the next batch into the maze. By now the sounds of that mechanical tide had become almost deafening, the chorus of familiar voices that rose and fell blissfully in synchronization with it swelled like an approaching tsunami, yet not one among the waiting townspeople heard the subtle warning contained therein, only the sounds of rapture.

By midnight, as had been agreed, the pale floodlights dimmed, the strongman hefted the ticket booth back to one of the open trailers, the gaunt man shut the tent flaps, the woman with the blazing eyes and copper-colored hair sauntered back into the pavilion. And for most of the night, the nondescript roustabouts steadily dismantled the tent and the labyrinth it contained, rewrapped the oddities, returning everything to the trailer. Just before dawn, the rumble of large trucks going down Main Street stilled the questioning voices of the owls. The moon, much shrunken and pale, had continued its journey across the clear black sky until the burning stars began to dim, the last of them disappearing behind the red brick town hall.

A cool breeze shattered the spell just as the sun broke free of the night. It rose above Rural Route 94 like a sentry making its appointed rounds. On the town green a baby cried, hungry and disoriented, clinging fearfully to its mother. It was soon answered by other tiny plaintive voices within the transfixed crowd.

The caravan with the turquoise sign painted in the stylized likeness of a circus banner proclaiming in large dust-covered red letters "Uncle Frank's Emporium of Oddities" was long gone, never to be seen in these parts again, as were all the placards in the shop windows, the tickets— anything to suggest it had ever been here.

Everyone in the crowd awoke hunched over, stark naked, their shredded clothes strewn haphazardly about their feet, their wallets emptied. They trembled in the early October dawn, gazing in absolute bewilderment at one another, as if not one of them had ever seen anything as remotely odd as their naked stupefied neighbor, spouse, or children. All of them had aged noticeably. Their faces had taken on a yellow pallor, their eyes swollen and sullen within sunken sockets, as if they had been held captive within the darkness for eons. Many drooled like imbeciles, their skin grown brittle and thin, their vitality inexorably drained away, with no coherent memory of the events of the night before save a vague notion of an endless icy kiss, a lingering embrace as white-hot as an unquenchable passion, yet at the same time colder than any grave, and that musty smell of freshly turned earth that even now lingered unexpectedly upon the morning air.

The maze of creepers clinging to the statue of Cornelius Culpepper had also withered during the night until all that was left were fragile brown leaves, limp brown flower clusters on crumbling crooked stems, drooping and disintegrating before the rising sun, occasionally rattling softly in a passing breeze, although no one present took any notice whatsoever of this final oddity.

Cornelius Culpepper, newly emerged from the thicket of strangling vines, stood mute, mouth agape, his face to the warming dawn, his arms raised before him, hands held open in a horrified gesture of abject banishment, his blind eyes locked in perpetual terror, riveted upon Rural Route 94 and the tiny churning dust cloud clinging to it in the far distance, as the foul thing slithered away like some giant bloated slug, growing smaller and smaller until it disappeared completely between the parched and broken straw-covered fields under that unwholesome yellow sky that stretched out as far as the eye could follow.

ABOUT THE AUTHORS

Alice Austin – Blood Red, Snow White

Alice Austin writes a broad mix of fiction. Her main focus is horror, but she often dips into fantasy, humour, and occasionally sci-fi; anything with a speculative element is fair game. She and her partner live with an adorable menace of a cat.

Raluca Balasa – Son of the Dragon

Raluca Balasa holds an MFA in Creative Writing: Fiction from the University of Nevada, Reno. Currently, she works as an English professor in the Toronto area. Her debut science fiction novel, *Blood State*, was released in 2020 from Renaissance Press.

Paul L. Bates – Uncle Frank's Emporium of Oddities

Paul L. Bates is retired from a career in construction management, has a Bachelor of Architecture from RISD, earned after a 2-year stint at Kenyon College. His publication credits include the novels *Imprint* and *Dreamer*.

Evan Baughfman – Man on Porch

Evan Baughfman is a Southern California author, playwright, and educator. Evan's short horror fiction can be found in various anthologies, including those by No Bad Books Press and Black Hare Press.

Ryan Benson – A Final Request

Ryan Benson (he/him) was a research scientist and lecturer in New England before he packed it up and headed south to the Atlanta, Georgia area where he lives with his wife, children, dog, and fish. Ryan writes across genres, but most enjoys speculative fiction where he can imagine alternative presents and futures.

S.R. Bevilacqua – Forever

S.R. Bevilacqua is a writer in Venice, California.

Hannah Birss – The Piper

Hannah Birss is a writer and aspiring magpie based out of Ontario, Canada. She lives with her partner, children, and multiple animals. She can usually be found in a nest constructed of books, writing journals, and shiny trinkets.

Jonah Buck – Camera Obscura

Jonah Buck wanted to study eldritch knowledge and commune with pale, semi-human creatures that flit across the sunless landscape, so he became an Oregon attorney. His interests include history, exotic poultry, paleontology, monster movies, and professional stage magic. He is the author of *Carrion Safari* and *Substratum* along with numerous short stories.

Kelli Etheridge – Devour

Kelli lives on Vancouver Island, BC. She loves dark beer, dark roast coffee, and dark fiction. While horror is her favourite genre, she is gentle in life. She loves adopting rescued dogs; she doesn't kill mosquitos and will go out of her way to save a fruit fly from a glass of wine. Despite that, she's pretty certain she'd make it to final girl status in a horror movie.

Lawrence Harding – The Church of St. Januarius

Lawrence Harding is a recovering medievalist in Cambridge, England. When not befriending pigeons, she enjoys weaving together the dark, gothic, and fantastic in her writing.

R. J. Howell – Matchmaker, Matchmaker

R. J. Howell is a writer, an artist, and a library nerd. A Chicago native, she earned her MFA in Creative Writing: Popular Fiction from Stonecoast in 2019. Her short fiction has appeared in various anthologies and online publications.

MA Hoyler – The Belly of the Beast

MA Hoyler lives and writes in upstate NY. When she's not writing, she is teaching little humans how to read or watering her twenty-plus houseplants.

B.K. Loomis – Her Own Terms

B.K. Loomis lives with their princess and fellow rodent, Lottie, a rat/squirrel/chihuahua that's scared of paper and is spoiled beyond belief. They paint and draw the monsters inside their head, and have been writing since they could hold a pen.

AJ Martin – Hunters Anonymous

AJ Martin is a speculative fiction writer based in upstate New York, who focuses on themes of gender, disability, and the politics of the American healthcare system. Her previous work can be found in *Aloud*, *Pilcrow & Dagger*, *Wickedly Abled*, and most recently, *AntipodeanSF*.

Marshall J. Moore – Bloodless Spirits

Marshall J. Moore is the award-winning author of the Rites of Resurrection trilogy of high fantasy novels from Shadow Alley Press, the pirate cozy fantasy duology Son of a Sailor and Prisoners of a Pirate Queen, and over thirty short stories appearing in publications such as *CatsCast*, *Mysterion*, *Flame Tree*, and many others.

P. R. O'Leary – Medusa Evermore

P. R. O'Leary writes dark stories tinged with humor, or humorous stories tinged with darkness. Dozens of his pieces have been published all over the world. You can find him at his geodesic dome in central New Jersey.

Rosalie Peng – The Other Woman

Rosalie A. Peng is an Asian-Canadian writer and a graduate of McGill University and Georgetown University Law Center. She now lives in Washington, DC, where she works as a lawyer. When not working on her debut novel, Rosalie daydreams about retiring from the legal profession and becoming a full-time author.

Christopher Alex Ray – The Best Mortician in Town

Christopher Alex Ray is a native-born Georgian. He lives alone with his dog in the misty Appalachian Mountains plotting out new tales to terrify. He has been previously published in *Weirdbook Annual: Zombies!* as well as featured on the No Sleep Podcast.

Michael A. Reed – The Septimus Cure

Michael A. Reed is a speculative fiction writer and dyslexic English teacher. He loves to think about ghosts, disappearing cities, and talking rats.

Deborah Sheldon – Perfect Little Stitches

Deborah Sheldon is a multi-award-winning author and anthology editor from Melbourne, Australia, who writes across the darker spectrum of horror, crime, and noir.

J. Tonzelli – The Halloween Girl of Coldsprings

J. Tonzelli is a writer, film critiquer, and Halloween enthusiast who currently resides in rural South Jersey. He loves autumn, abandoned buildings, the supernatural, and films by John Carpenter.

John Wolf – A Disease of the Blood

John Wolf is a librarian lurking in the Pacific Northwest. He's been writing since eighth grade, and his love for stories stretches back even further. He credits this love of reading and writing to his mom, who never told him what he couldn't watch or read, and the libraries where he grew up.

Valerie B. Williams – Daddy's Girl

Valerie B. Williams' short fiction has been published by Flame Tree Press and Dark Recesses Press, among others. Her most recent story, "Red Lipstick," appeared in the *Dastardly Damsels* anthology from Crystal Lake Publishing in October 2024. Her debut novel, *The Vanishing Twin*, was released by Crossroad Press October 1, 2024.

CONTENT WARNINGS

Please note: because this is a horror anthology, it should be assumed that the basic horror tropes will apply. These include death, gore, and violence.

A Disease of the Blood - elder abuse

A Final Request - assisted suicide, terminal illness

Blood Red, Snow White - animal death

Bloodless Spirits - suicide

Devour - human farming

Her Own Terms - assisted suicide, terminal illness

Hunters Anonymous - death of children (off-page)

Medusa Evermore - attempted suicide

Perfect Little Stitches - death of a child (off-page), terminal illness (off-page), death of a spouse (off-page)

Son of the Dragon - depictions of torture

The Best Mortician in Town - death of a spouse

The Halloween Girl of Coldsprings - death of a child (off-page)

The Other Woman - fetal death, infidelity

The Piper - abuse of a disabled person, death of children

The Septimus Cure - terminal illness, death of a spouse

THANK YOU!